THE GARDEN PLOT

SARA SARTAGNE

Copyright © 2020 by Sara Sartagne

All rights reserved.

No part of this book may be reproduced in any form or by any electronic or mechanical means, including information storage and retrieval systems, without written permission from the author, except for the use of brief quotations in a book review.

This is a work of fiction. Names, characters, places and incidents are the product of the author's imagination. Any resemblance to actual persons living or dead, business establishments or events is entirely coincidental.

Amazon Print edition:

ISBN

If you'd like to keep up with Sara's Sartagne's garden-themed romance series, why not sign up for her *no-spam* newsletter and get early notification about her latest novels and lots more exclusive content, all for free.

Details can be found at the end of The Garden Plot.

❀ Created with Vellum

1

The thin sun only just took the edge off the winter's day. Sam tied the scarf a little more tightly around her neck and settled the bobble hat a little more firmly on her head. She leaned across to the passenger seat to get the white roses and the bag containing the plugs of winter pansies and finally, her trowel.

As she struggled out of the Land Rover, she caught her breath at the freezing wind.

"God, I hope the ground isn't solid," she muttered to herself as she locked the door.

The churchyard was deserted, although she could hear singing floating on the air as she walked up the path. She also saw the pushchairs lined up outside the doors.

Christening, she thought. That would explain the number of cars in the car park. Her feet found the grave without much conscious thought. She was pleased to see the heathers had withstood the worst of the weather which had hit the country just after Christmas. She smiled as she knelt and brushed her hand over the delicate purple bells. Her knees registered the ground was hard, but thankfully not like concrete.

She busied herself emptying the vase at the foot of the grave, the flowers long since past their best. Steeling herself to grip the ancient tap at the side of the church, Sam gasped as icy water sloshed over her hands, and she swore under her breath. Her hands starting to go numb, she walked quickly back to the grave. Once the roses were in the vase, she rubbed her hands together briskly and thankfully pulled on her gardening gloves.

After a few minutes digging, Sam sat back on her heels and looked at the headstone. *Samuel Clarence Winterson, 1960—2017, husband and beloved of Dawn Josephine Winterson, 1963—2004*. And the words, over which there had been such disagreement with Fraser:

...glad to have sat under
Thunder and rain with you,
And grateful too
For sunlight on the garden.

In the end, Sam had given the stonemason the lines from the poem and just ignored Fraser, who had wanted something about 'father, grandfather, sadly missed' to add to her parents' grave.

Shaking off the memories, she swept away some of the leaves and started to dig.

She was just pushing one of the pansies out of its polystyrene container when she heard someone call her name. Charlie and Fraser and her niece Lisbeth were coming out of the church, bundled up in expensive-looking sheepskin.

She waved, and then turned again to the pansies, taking them tenderly from the tray and placing them into the cold earth.

"God, you must be frozen!" Charlie exclaimed. "Do you really need to do this *now*?"

"The grave needed tidying up and I'm really busy over the next few weeks," Sam said, gently patting the earth back into place around the cheery purple and yellow plants.

"White roses," Charlie said softly, looking at the vase. "Mum's favourites."

Sam nodded, remembering the wedding photos of her parents. "Yes, she used to tell us she had them in her bouquet, didn't she? Anyway, I've done now, just need some water."

"It all looks lovely!" Lisbeth enthused, and smiling, Sam rose, brushed the soil from her knees and headed back to the tap. She paused to say hello to the vicar who was busy closing the church after the christening, and it was a couple of minutes before she re-joined them.

Charlie and Fraser stopped talking abruptly as she approached so she assumed she'd been the topic of conversation. Lisbeth just grinned mischievously.

There was some general chat about the state of the graveyard as she watered in the plants and cleared the dead flowers.

"Ok, well I'm done here. Just need to take this back," she waved the watering can.

"I'll walk to the pub," Charlie said, nodding at Fraser and Lisbeth.

"Are you sure? It's damned cold," said Fraser.

"It's ten minutes at the most and they'll have made the tea by the time I arrive."

"Ah yes, you need to go and kiss babies, don't you?" Sam said brightly. Fraser ignored her, but Lisbeth hid a grin.

"Fine, but don't be long." He strode away with Lisbeth in tow. Sam watched his departing back.

"So masterful," she murmured.

"Oh, do stop it," Charlie said wearily. "Honest to God, I don't know why both of you have to behave like such children when you're together. You both get worse with age…"

Sam shrugged.

"Anyway, what's up?" she said as they walked back towards the Land Rover.

"I wanted to ask you whether James had called."

Sam stared at her sister incredulously. What—the bushy-eyebrowed neo-Conservative from that *dreadfully* awkward supper? With the big nose? Sam burst out laughing.

"No! Good God, did you think he would?"

"Why ever not? He thought you were very attractive, he said so after you left on Friday night. I thought you would have heard from him."

"Charlie, it would take a lot more than physical attraction to make *that* relationship work!"

"I'm sure if you really tried, you could find something to talk about," Charlie was defensive.

"*Assuming* I want to talk to him!" A thought struck her. "Anyway—how would he call me? You haven't given him my number, have you?"

Her sister went pink.

"Charlie! After what I said to you on Friday night, you *still* gave him my number? Christ, I don't believe it!"

"He's a nice man, he's well off, he's not bad looking, and he liked you!" Charlie responded hotly to Sam's astounded gaze.

"And for those reasons I should be interested? What about *my* reasons? That we probably have completely different principles? Wildly different politics? Read different newspapers? That I actually didn't *like* him much?"

There was a silence. They had reached the Land Rover.

"I'm sorry. It's been *years* since you and Andrew split up and I thought you might like some decent male company," Charlie said stiffly.

"Good God Charlie, do you think I'm gagging for it or something?" Sam exploded, ignoring the mention of Andrew.

"Don't be crude."

"Oh believe me, if we weren't in earshot of the vicar, I could be one hell of a lot cruder!"

Charlie looked around quickly and saw the vicar was indeed, pinning up a poster on the noticeboard near the entrance to the churchyard.

Sam looked at her helplessly.

"You just don't get it, do you?" Charlie opened her mouth and Sam interrupted. "No, hear me out. I know you mean well, but I'm a big girl now and if I can run Dad's business, I can certainly find myself a bloke if I decide I need one."

"Can you? I despair of you ever finding a decent relationship!"

Sam looked at her sister as though she'd grown two heads.

"A *relationship*? What if all I want is a quick f-"

"Don't say that word!" Charlie cut in.

"What if all I want is a quick roll in the hay?" Sam rephrased, determinedly patient. "I'm pretty busy, what with the business and the village. I don't have time for a *relationship*, and even if I did, the last place I'd look for one is amongst Fraser's constituency cronies."

"And where are you going to find this 'quick roll in the hay'? Some anonymous fumble after a drink in the pub? Or do you save yourself for the Labour Party Conference?" Charlie sneered and Sam thought that for a good-looking woman, her sister could look really ugly.

Sam pulled open the passenger door viciously and flung the canvas bag with her tools on the floor.

"This is none of your business, Charlie, so just butt out please," she said, grimly hanging on to her temper. "If I choose to either shag someone I've just met or live out my days as a spinster of this parish, it's *my* choice and nothing to do with you."

"I'll get you a cat for Christmas," Charlie bit out. "Sounds just perfect for your future life."

Sam watched her stride away on the ancient flagstones and wondered if her elder sister would come a cropper in heels that high. She hoped so and even watched for a few minutes to catch it. Charlie disappeared from sight without so much as a wobble, and shaking her head, Sam huffed and climbed into the Land Rover.

She was still seething ten minutes later when she drew up outside her cottage, and went in, muttering. She shrugged off her coat. Her hand reached for the kettle automatically and clicked it on. Her mobile phone buzzed. A text from Lisbeth.

Has he called yet?

"No he bloody hasn't," muttered Sam, texting the exact same words into her phone. The response was almost immediate.

LOL!

Wryly, Sam typed back.

Hilarious, niece.

Mum just trying 2 help. Lisbeth responded.

"Ha!" Sam took a mug, threw a tea bag into it and waited for the kettle to boil. She reached for her phone, paused and then gave a big sigh.

I know.

There was no response from Lisbeth. Stirring her teabag idly, Sam continued the message.

Trying to fix me up with your dad's bloody Eton friends is NOT the way. A pause, and then a new message flashed up.

What IS right way ?

Sam stared into the garden, lying pale and bare in the weak mid-morning light.

Finally, she reached for her phone again.

Dunno. Perhaps I'm beyond help. Sam remembered something else from that dreadful Friday night and texted—*Have you heard about your friend and her dad?*

No, other than he was in coma. Not looking gd?:(

"No, sweetie, it's not," muttered Sam.

It might be that he's 'stable'—you know, not well, but out of danger she texted instead.

Hope so was the reply.

The room was bright, almost everything white. Magda jerked her head up and refocused. She rubbed her eyes. The soft beep of the machine sounded through her head like a hammer blow.

She kept her eyes on the still, pale face of her father as if her stare alone would bring him round.

Dad, oh dad... she thought. Wake up. Please wake up.

The door cracked open and she turned to see the older, still-beautiful woman and tall, bearded man enter the room. She leaped up and flung herself into her grandfather's arms.

"Opa! Nanna!" Her breath caught, and Friedrich hugged her tightly, murmuring nothings and nonsense into her dark curls.

Niamh, her grandmother, put her arms round both of them, and for a moment, they simply stood there, saying nothing.

Magda saw Niamh's eyes turn towards the figure lying still beneath a pale blue blanket, the only thing of colour in the room, and heard her sharp intake of breath. Friedrich's hand clasped her elbow.

"Calm, my dear," his voice rasped. "He's unconscious, not dead."

Niamh seemed to pull herself together.

"What happened Magda? The message we got wasn't very clear."

Magda sat down again.

"Jane—Dad's secretary—called the school to say he'd collapsed. Miss Trewisham, my housemistress drove me here and I've been here since...well, I suppose since eleven o'clock this morning."

Magda glanced at the clock on the wall. Ten past eight.

"Where is this Miss Trewisham now?" Niamh asked.

"Getting coffee and something to eat." Magda's stomach turned sour at the thought.

Niamh moved to the bed. "Has there been any change since your dad was admitted?"

"I don't know," Magda sighed, and rubbed her eyes. "They won't tell me anything, they think I'm just a kid—they've been waiting for you to arrive."

The door swung open.

"They only had ham and cheese left, so—oh!" The teacher trailed off as she saw Magda wasn't alone. She put the unappetising packs of sandwiches on the side table and wiping her hands down her lumpy winter skirt, held one out to Friedrich. "Sorry, you must be Magda's grandparents—I'm Elaine Trewisham, from Clavedene School."

Even as she watched Niamh and Friedrich introduce themselves, Magda relaxed a little. Her family was with her, she wasn't alone any longer. It would all be fine. Wouldn't it?

Miss Trewisham said she thought the doctor should be coming on his rounds at eight o'clock.

"In which case, he is already late," clipped Friedrich, looking displeased, moving purposefully towards the door and disappearing through it.

"I'm sure Friedrich will find someone to tell us what's going on," Niamh said, returning to the bedside. She absently stroked her son's hair.

Magda was forcing a dry sandwich down her throat when she heard the sound of voices, and the doctor, hustled in by Friedrich, arrived.

"I'll give you some privacy," Miss Trewisham murmured and slipped out of the room.

The doctor was portly, with an untidy shock of auburn hair and introduced himself as Dr Walters. Niamh shook his hand.

"Perhaps we should go into another room...?" Dr Walters suggested delicately, his eyes flicking to Magda.

"I want to hear whatever you're going to say to Opa and Nanna," Magda said firmly, her voice rising a tone. Friedrich smiled and patted her shoulder.

"Natürlich," he agreed calmly, and nodded at the doctor to continue. Dr Walters shrugged.

"Well, we had to resuscitate your son when he came in, he wasn't breathing," he said baldly.

Magda swayed and felt Niamh's hand clasp her arm.

"He's been given something to make him comfortable. We're not completely sure, but we think this is a new, virulent strain of glandular fever," he continued.

"You haven't seen it before?" asked Friedrich.

"No, it's a completely new one on me," Dr Walters responded, a bit too cheerfully for Magda's taste. "We're doing blood tests and we should be a lot clearer in a couple of days."

"Will he be ok?" Magda asked faintly.

"If it follows the normal run of the glandular fever we know, there's no reason he won't make a full recovery, but we're not quite sure *what* it is at the moment. We'll be keeping a close eye on him over the next twenty-four hours, which will be critical, his vitals are rather weak."

"Critical?" Niamh turned pale.

"We're doing all we can, but until the results of the tests come through, we're working a bit blind," Dr Walters said. He looked at Jonas, motionless in the bed. "He might regain consciousness tonight, but again, he might not. You may be in for a long night if you wait."

Magda looked at her grandfather.

"We'll wait," Friedrich said firmly.

Dr Walters pursed his lips for a moment and then inclined his head.

"Right, I'll see what we can do to make you a little more comfortable." He left the room.

Magda clung to Niamh for a moment, struggling with tears. Her head whirled as the impossible thought that her father might die came into focus. She felt Niamh push her gently towards the chair and she sank into it.

"Well," Niamh said, looking at Jonas, still pale, still unmoving.

Five minutes later, Miss Trewisham sidled back into the room.

"I wondered what the news was?" she said hesitantly.

"Dad's got some kind of glandular fever, they think. He might wake up tonight, but they're not sure," Magda said, shaking herself out of her reverie.

The teacher hesitated and Niamh spoke.

"I think you should get back to the school," she smiled. "I'm enormously grateful to you for bringing Magda to the hospital, but we're here now. We'll get a hotel organised as soon as Jonas wakes up."

"If you're sure I can't be of any further use?"

"Quite sure. You've been marvellous, thank you."

Her housemistress looked a little relieved, thought Magda. When she'd struggled into her nondescript beige mac, Miss Trewisham swung round to Magda, and gave her an enthusiastic hug.

"Take care," she said. "Call the office if you need us for anything. And it would be good if you can phone us when you're a bit clearer on what's happening," she added, turning to Niamh, who nodded.

"Of course. We'll let you know as soon as there's news, but I would say Magda won't be back immediately."

With a nod and a last smile at Magda, Miss Trewisham left.

"Thank God," said Magda. Niamh raised her eyebrows in surprise. Magda huffed.

"Oh, anyone with any sense could see that it was serious—she's just been so bloody positive, so upbeat. I wanted someone to treat me like an adult and admit that things were grim..."

"He's not dead yet!" said Niamh with a short laugh. "Stop burying him! The doctors *don't* know what it is, and until they tell us differently, we should expect your dad to recover."

Friedrich came back into the room.

"Well, it's a waiting game," he grumbled. "Wait for Jonas to wake up, wait for the test results, wait to see how strong he feels..."

Magda put her head into her hands. Her grandmother patted her shoulder.

"Now, now, enough drama, Magda. You're dad's strong and fit. I suggest we make ourselves as comfortable as we can and try and be patient. Friedrich, do you think you could find us some coffee? I agree with Dr Walters that it's going to be a long night."

He nodded and with a quick hug to Magda and a lingering glance at his son, Friedrich was gone.

Niamh sat in the chair, Magda perched on the bed, and hand in hand, they waited to see if Jonas would regain consciousness.

2

Sam pushed open the office door, casting a pleased glance at the tub of daffodils and narcissi on the step which were in their full, golden glory, lifting the darkness of February. *Thank God for the daffodils*, she thought, much as she thought every year.

As she expected, Andy was already in the office, checking papers and orders for the week, and so was Steve Johnson, her new apprentice. Sam smiled at him, so much more at ease in jeans and heavy-duty boots than he had been in the hand-me-down jacket and shoes he'd worn at interview. He grinned and wished her good morning.

Andy looked up.

"Sam, glad you're in a bit early," he said, scrabbling for a piece of paper hidden among the pile on his desk. "Mrs Pratchett left a message after you'd gone on Friday about the meeting next week. Something about a developer wanting to build on Jessop's Field."

Sam frowned as she shrugged out of her coat and unwound the thick scarf from around her neck. Dorothy Pratchett was a pain, but someone whose determined nosiness gave her news before most people.

"Jessop's Field? But that's designated green belt." Sam hmmm-ed to herself and pocketed the note with Andy's almost illegible handwriting on it. "I feel a protest coming on…"

She turned to Steve.

"Right then. We'll get you kitted out with our jacket and gloves, and then we'll take you to a garden we're just finishing. You can help us generally clear the site and put some of the finishing touches on it —sound ok?"

Steve nodded.

"Andy, can you find the original brief for the Turner job please? And grab Steve some Winterson's gear. Steve, help yourself to a cuppa while you read the brief. We'll leave after." Sam disappeared into her office to switch on her computer and check her emails.

She bit her lip at the message from the bank. They were sorry, but they couldn't extend her credit facilities. Her face tightened and she thought rude thoughts about her bank manager. She chewed the top of her pencil.

Perhaps we'll be ok. We just need a decent-sized job over the summer and some work lined up for the Autumn… Maybe do some prospecting in nearby counties…

She'd go over the accounts again tonight, see what could be trimmed. She wondered for the umpteenth time if she was cut out for business. Still, Dad had had faith in her. They'd manage somehow.

When she emerged, Steve was standing in the middle of the office, laughing with Andy. Sam looked over the essential brownness of him—brown hair, brown eyes and sallow skin and thought once again that he was a good choice for the business.

The jacket swam on his rather small, wiry form, the sleeves almost down to his fingertips. Sam giggled, pushing the bank email from her mind.

"I'll order one in a medium," Andy sat down and began tapping at his computer. Steve, still grinning, slipped out of the jacket, examining the logo on the back—the letters WGD curled around one another like a growing thing.

"Looks good—sort of says what you do without having to have the words," he said hesitantly. Sam nodded, pleased.

"Good—that's what it's supposed to do. We need to look as professional as possible so we can charge what we're worth."

Steve looked at her questioningly.

"How's that work, then?"

"Well, this is a bit of a hobby-horse for me. The people who buy our services are often wealthy. I took a degree in garden design and Andy has a degree in horticulture. So we charge accordingly—although sometimes I know Andy gets worried about our new business hit rate," she looked over as Andy grimaced.

"I'll say," he said under his breath.

Sam smiled at Steve who was looking a little uncertain. "As far as I'm concerned, designing a garden is as skilled as designing a house, and we do a good job for a fair wage. And as I'm the boss, what I say goes," she added, twinkling.

The door opened, and Paul, their administrator arrived. After brief introductions, Sam hustled Steve towards the van, still clutching the Turner brief.

"If you ever have any questions—ask Paul," she said to Steve as they climbed into the van. "He's been with the firm for about twenty years and knows *everything*. A word of warning, though—never touch his desk. It's a work of controlled art and he'll have your guts for garters if you move anything!"

It took half an hour to reach the Turner house, and by the time they arrived, Steve was asking questions about the design of the garden. Sam hoped his enthusiasm would continue past the first downpour he had to work through.

Today was the final tidy up for the garden before the walk round with the client. Andy handed Steve a big brush, a hose and several large green bin liners.

"We need to clear all the mess from the border planting and get all the mud off the paths. The client is coming back from work at two o'clock for Sam to give them the tour, so it all needs to be sparkling by then."

Sam, heaving a couple of big pots from the van for the patio area, called out to him.

"There are some plants and things at the back which need putting in the beds, so whatever you do, don't chuck them out as rubbish!"

A bright, watery sunshine bathed the garden. Sam breathed in the cold air and felt the damp earth beneath her hands as she planted alliums, imagining their purple globes in the summer. She patted the compost down.

At ten thirty, she called a halt and they drank coffee from a huge flask that Andy produced from the back of the van. As they sipped, Sam walked Steve around the garden, explaining the design.

"We've chosen lots of plants which actually don't need much doing to them as the Turners aren't enthusiastic gardeners." She shook her head, still bemused by this attitude and waved her arm at a choisya, gleaming gold and green in the sunlight. "And I'm going to recommend they get someone to tidy it if they can't be bothered to do it themselves."

Steve nodded. Finishing his coffee, he said: "By the way, I found some onions at the back—what do you want me to do with them?"

Sam wrinkled her nose.

"Onions?"

"I think they're onions..." He went off to get the tray, and when he held it out for inspection, Sam's brow cleared, and she laughed.

"No, you *don't* know much about flowers, do you?" she grinned. "These are daffs!"

Andy chortled. Seeing Steve's embarrassment, Sam quickly added. "It's an easy mistake to make if you're not used to dealing with bulbs."

Steve suddenly laughed. "God, me grandad would be turning in his grave!" He shook his head and walked away, chuckling.

Sam, still grinning, turned back to her pots. *Oh yes*, she thought. *He'll be fine.*

Magda and her grandmother came through the door and looked expectantly at Friedrich, who shook his head. Magda battled a rising tide of panic. They'd left the hospital to buy some new underwear, some teeshirts, toiletries and for Friedrich, a fresh shirt. "If we're not there, *naturally* he'll come around," was Niamh's view. But he hadn't.

Magda saw the blip of her father's pulse, strong and steady at last. There was some desultory conversation around her. Friedrich grinned at the multi-coloured shirt Magda had persuaded her grandmother to buy to cheer him—to cheer them *all*—up a bit.

A nurse came in, checked the drip and disappeared again.

"I'm starting to get rather bored by all this," her grandfather announced. "Tests, more tests, they come, they check his pulse and his drip and then they go away." Niamh clasped his hand and pulled it to her lips.

"They're doing their best," she soothed, and Magda saw a tender look pass between them.

Magda's phone buzzed and puzzled, she hunted it out of her bag. She looked at the phone, thumbing the screen. Text from Lisbeth, she needed to reply to that—and then she saw the new message and groaned.

"Problem?" asked Friedrich.

"It's Geraldine," she said biting her lip. "She must have got my number from Dad's secretary."

"Geraldine? Oh, his girlfriend? Is she still around then?"

"Oh yes, she's still around," Magda said, wrinkling her nose with her finger hovering over the reply button.

"Don't you like her?" Niamh asked, momentarily diverted. "She seemed very...elegant...when we met her."

Magda pulled a face. "It's fine when I'm away at school, but it's a bit grim when I'm home. I get the feeling she'd like to give me money to go to the pictures, or something."

"Ah," said her grandfather, hiding a smile.

"No, it's not like that!" Magda protested. "I get that dad needs company—it's not like he's *old* or anything! I'm just, like..." She tried again. "She always looks like a model and she makes me feel scruffy, and in the way."

She paused, not wanting to call.

"She must be worried, Magda," observed Friedrich gently and feeling the heat spread in her cheeks, Magda punched in the number.

"How's Jonas?" Gerry's voice was sharp down the phone. "I've only just heard—his *idiot* secretary only got in touch ten minutes ago."

Poor Jane, thought Magda.

"He's unconscious."

"*Still?*" The voice was shrill, and Magda saw her grandfather's eyebrows rise as he heard from the other side of the room. "Are you on your own?"

"No, Opa and Nanna are here...my grandfather and grandmother. They've been here since Friday night." There was a pause.

"I'd come to the hospital, but I have a gallery opening tonight, and—well, at least you're not on your own," Gerry's voice faltered and then firmed.

"No, there's no need," Magda agreed, trying to keep the relief out of her voice.

"You'll ring me with any news?" Gerry persisted and reluctantly, Magda agreed and closed the call.

"I could hear she was all concern for you," Niamh observed drily. Magda grinned faintly and shook her head. Her grandparents went to get some of the disgusting hospital coffee. Magda sat down in the chair and watched her father's chest rise and fall, the beep of the machines once again the only noise in the room.

Magda felt the hand on her shoulder and her eyes flew open. She raised her head and sat up—god, her muscles felt concreted into place. The room was dim, and she blinked to make out her father's face.

"Dad?"

"Liebchen," her father's voice, normally velvet and currently like sandpaper, came from chapped lips.

"One sec."

Magda stiffly got to her feet and poured some water. She didn't know what time it was, it felt late. Her eyes felt gritty, and she was longing to change her clothes. Her grandmother was asleep in the armchair, Friedrich was nowhere to be seen.

Jonas struggled to raise himself and Magda tried to support him. He managed a sip of water and then another. He laid back and closed his eyes.

"What happened? The last thing I remember was talking to Neil Laurence ..."

"You collapsed," Magda said, looking at him closely and wondering if she should call the nurse. "Nanna and Opa arrived on Friday night."

"Your Nanna and Opa are here?" Jonas' eyes flew open and he turned his head to see Niamh asleep in the chair.

"Yes, Dad," Magda said, clasping his hand.

He signalled for another sip of water and Magda held the cup to his lips.

"You've been unconscious for nearly two days. We thought you were going to die!" Jonas looked shocked at that and as he lay back, he closed his eyes.

"Dad?" Magda said, suddenly panicking. She pushed the bell for the nurse and clutched her father's hand. To her enormous relief, he squeezed her fingers.

"Nah," he said finally. "You don't get rid of me that easily."

The nurse bustled in and started to check readings and charts. Magda moved reluctantly away from the bed as Niamh stirred at the noise and got stiffly to her feet.

"Jonas is awake then? Thank God for that," she said.

The following day, Jonas swore roundly in German. His mother winced and even Magda's eyes widened. Friedrich translated for the doctor rather more politely. Jonas drew a deep breath.

"*Six months?* You have got to be kidding me!"

"Of course I'm not kidding you," Dr Stephenson said calmly. "When you came in, we had to resuscitate you. We're dealing with a very nasty—potentially lethal—virus. I suspect you won't be recovered for some time. Going back to work will hardly shorten your recovery and may even be dangerous."

"Jonas has a very full job, and he takes his responsibilities seriously," his mother said to the doctor.

"Well, he won't be doing much good for his organisation if he's flat on his back—or worse," was the blunt reply. "Surely his company will understand the seriousness?"

"As he owns the company, it's a little more complicated," said Friedrich heavily.

"Really?" The doctor raised his eyebrows. "I'd have thought taking time off was a lot easier if you owned the company."

Jonas stiffened and Niamh rushed into speech.

"Friedrich just means Jonas has a lot of people relying on him," she said hastily.

Jonas closed his eyes in frustration and dismay.

His mind flew over his work—the new development in Cologne, housing designs being submitted in Berlin, the negotiations in Luxemburg, to say nothing of the joint venture with Anglo Homes. A noise brought him back to the anxious faces of his daughter, his mother and his father.

"Well, you can ignore my advice of course—but I can't take responsibility for the consequences," Dr Stephenson said shortly.

"Dad?" Magda's voice sounded quiet in the silence. He looked at her. "Dad, I really think you should listen to the doctor—it was *horrible* when I got here, and you were unconscious."

Jonas grasped her hand. She looked down at their clasped fingers.

"Surely you can arrange to take things easy for a few months?" Niamh said. Jonas shook his head mutely.

"My advice—and that of Dr Walters, incidentally…is you should take at least three, and probably six months off work, with as much rest and as little stress as can be arranged," repeated Dr

Stephenson, his eyes flicking to the clock on the wall and then back to Jonas. "The blood tests came back showing the virus we expected for glandular fever, but also another type we haven't seen before, so we need to keep an eye on you," he added. "There's no telling how the virus will mutate in the blood stream, but in any case, your immune system has been weakened—so you *do* need to rest."

"But surely six months is overdoing it?" Jonas looked at Frederick in appeal, his deep voice cracking. To his astonishment, his father agreed with the doctor.

"We need to give the antivirals time to work, *ja*?" Jonas heard his father's thickened accent and paused. Looking at his family, Jonas suddenly noticed how pale they were, how worn his parents looked, the deep shadows under Magda's eyes.

The doctor was saying something about the antivirals, but Jonas was no longer listening. He looked at his daughter and saw the glitter of tears in her eyes.

"OK," he said quietly.

Dr Stephenson paused.

"OK what?" said Magda, her eyes darting to his face.

"OK, I'll take time off work."

"How long?" asked his mother immediately. He screwed up his face.

"Three months."

"Six months," insisted Magda.

"Four."

"Five, and we have a deal," she quipped and grinned at him.

Jonas looked at the ceiling, his heart sinking. He felt Niamh's hand cover his and Magda's and knew himself defeated.

"Five," he agreed. He felt Magda sag in relief and Niamh's smile suddenly shone, making him aware of just how tired she had looked. He felt guilty.

"Excellent. We need to keep you in here for another day, I think, but you should be fine to leave tomorrow afternoon. I'll leave you to sort out the details of getting home, but you'll be coming back for further tests. And remember—no work!" Dr Stephenson gave a faint smile and left.

There was a silence after the door closed.

"Well, perhaps your PA can arrange for a car to take us all back to Derbyshire tomorrow?" Niamh said.

"Yes, Magda has the number, will you call sweetheart?"

Magda fairly bounced to the other side of the room to pick up her phone. "On it," she announced, walking out of the door. Niamh followed.

"I know it looks an impossible situation, but it *is* only work, my son."

Jonas nodded, reluctantly.

"I know dad, but you know how it is…"

"But you've been dangerously ill!" Friedrich cut in. "You looked like a corpse when we arrived, *ja?*"

"I'm sorry. It just happened—one minute I was in the office, and the next I was here with Magda asleep next to me."

"It's been a long few days," was all his father responded.

Jonas, to his later chagrin, fell asleep on the way home.

Magda finally pulled herself to full wakefulness and stretched her stiff and aching shoulders.

"I feel like I've been run over by a bus."

"I think we all do," Niamh smiled. Magda eyed her sleeping father.

"I never thought he'd take five months off work."

"It appears he has his priorities in order at last," Niamh said quietly. There was silence as Magda flicked through her phone messages and the car purred its way along the motorway.

"Aha!" Magda said, and Niamh raised her eyebrows. "Connor has sent me a message. Looks like he tried calling Dad at work and couldn't get him." She texted a response to her godfather, saying that they were on the way back to Brook Lodge, and that she'd call him from home.

"Where *is* Connor?" asked her grandfather. "I thought he was in Argentina, doing some hotel commission."

"Mmm. Setting fires alight as he goes, no doubt," murmured Magda, as she thought of her godfather, a tall Irishman with sparkling blue eyes and a wicked sense of humour who was her father's best friend. Niamh laughed softly.

"Aye, that'll be Connor."

Magda's phone rang in her hand and she jumped. Glancing at the screen, she wrinkled her nose and answered.

"Hi Geraldine, I was just about to call you. We've just left the hospital." Magda smiled at her grandmother, who was making faces at her.

"How is Jonas?" Geraldine's voice was smoother this time, less laced with anxiety.

"He's ok, but he's got to take it easy. No excitement."

"So he won't be going back to work immediately?"

"No, he's going to be off work for the next six months. I'm not sure when he'll be in Manchester again," Magda said, suddenly struck that there might be *some* benefit to her father being ill.

"*Six months*? God, he'll die of boredom," said Geraldine, sounding shocked.

"Better than dying of the virus," Magda snapped and felt the eyes of her grandparents on her.

Geraldine was silent for a moment.

"I'll pack a bag and meet you at the house," she announced.

"Um... I think you might need to speak to Nanna...Hang on." Magda put the phone on mute and then turned to Niamh.

"She's talking about packing a bag and coming over!" she hissed. "What do I do?"

"You give the phone to me," Niamh said, holding out her hand. "Hello Geraldine, this is Niamh. Yes, we met in Manchester," Niamh said. "Magda tells me you've very kindly offered to come over to

Derbyshire. That's very sweet, but there's no need—I'll be here for the foreseeable future, and Jonas is under strict instructions to avoid any excitement. Oh, I'm sure the doctors would categorise you as excitement, Geraldine, and frankly, after the couple of days I've been through, *I* couldn't take any more excitement. I do hope you understand?"

There was a pause while Geraldine, Magda imagined, struggled to find something to say.

"And the housekeeper is on holiday at the moment, and I'd be loath to take on guests without her support," Niamh went on. "I'll call you to give you updates, shall I? In a couple of weeks or so when Jonas is back on his feet, you might visit, but not now, I think. Yes, I'll let you know as soon as we think he's strong enough. Of course. Thanks again—bye."

She disconnected the call and tossed the phone back to Magda, who burst out laughing.

"No, more excitement is *not* what we need," Niamh murmured looking back at the still sleeping Jonas.

3

Four weeks later, Jonas was grimly hanging on to his temper.

With the phone clamped to his ear, he got out of the deep leather chair and wandered over to the study window, and stared into the garden, bathing in the pale light of a March sun. A few daffodils remained, but mostly they were over now, and a set of equally straggly tulips were making a half-hearted attempt to greet the coming spring.

Increasing his bad mood was the realisation that the doctors and his daughter—dammit—had been right about his energy levels. He felt sure he would need a nap after the session this morning. He'd suddenly become an invalid, and he hated it.

He tuned back into the discussion. Tyler Fairchild from Anglo Homes was speaking. There wasn't much content, just noise. As Jonas listened, his mind drifted and he looked at the room. It had been right on so many fronts, the move; the house was lovely in a mellow, comfortable way, with beautiful woodwork and large rooms, and Magda loved it.

"So the next series of consultation meetings will be held in the local Library. I'm not expecting any issues with the planning permission," Tyler said.

John Fairchild, who was CEO of Anglo Homes and Tyler's uncle, chimed in. "I'm sure you'd be happy with the drawings, Jonas, they're excellent."

"We've made some modifications to the original spec and approached some different suppliers, but I'm very happy with the way they've turned out," added Tyler. Jonas' ears pricked up at that, but Neil Laurence, his deputy, was in before him.

"Perhaps we can see the changes?"

"Of course, I'll send it to you," Tyler said breezily.

Neil should handle it, Jonas reminded himself with an effort.

"As this is our first foray into the UK market, I'm sure you can understand Neil's interest in the detail," Jonas said calmly.

"Yes, yes, of course I understand," said Tyler with a sigh that Jonas caught on the conference audio.

"You know as well as I do, your reputation is only as good as the last thing you did. And the British public don't appear to have much love for property developers," he pointed out.

"Yes, well—shall we just start the public consultation? People in the area are desperate for the houses, and frankly, we could charge a premium for the view near the site. I'm sure we can handle any local objections—but shall we see what they are before we all start panicking?" There was a slight sneer in Tyler's voice, which Jonas decided to ignore.

"Fine. I'll look forward to the next update. Is that all for the moment?"

"I think so," said Neil. Jonas could imagine him going down his list, ticking things off.

"Your assistant told me you were going to be off for six months—is that right?" John Fairchild asked.

"Five," corrected Jonas, keeping his voice even.

"That's a long time... How will Halcyon cope?" mocked Tyler.

"I've just finished delegating my last project, Neil's handling this one, and I'm keeping in touch with weekly conference calls." Jonas was short. One call, he thought despairingly. A multi-billion-pound company kept in his control with *one* conference call a week.

"Rather a risk in itself, wouldn't you say?" said Tyler. Jonas counted to three before he responded.

"I have complete faith and trust in my team. And *obviously*, this information is confidential. I don't want any rumours in the market about my absence."

There was an awkward pause, and then Neil leapt in to finish the call.

Jonas leaned back in his chair and closed his eyes briefly for a moment. Then he grabbed his phone.

Neil answered on the first ring. "Hi boss. I've started the email to ask for the full *new* spec."

Jonas grinned. Perhaps his team really was capable of running the company without him.

"Great. Get Stephanie to check the financials, will you? I wouldn't put it past that little shit Tyler to try and squeeze some additional profit at the expense of our suppliers, and I don't want him screwing with relationships we've had for years."

He paused, wondering how much to tell Neil.

"Is that all, Jonas?" asked Neil, sensing his hesitation.

"You know the new house we've bought? Brook Lodge?" he said slowly.

"Yes—what about it?"

"It's in Sherton."

"Sherton? You're *on site*?" Neil's voice went up a few tones.

"Just down the road. When I realised last year John was about to hand the project to Tyler, I was worried. All this coincided with Magda going to Clavedene. She needed something more than the Manchester apartment to come home to. So we moved."

Neil whistled. "Fairchild—*both* of the Fairchilds—know nothing about this, do they?"

"No. And obviously, I'd like it to stay that way. The relationship is strained enough as it is, without Tyler *or* John thinking we're checking up on them."

"You'll need to keep your nose well out of it," Neil warned.

"Naturally, but I can read the local papers, and as I'm stuck here for the next four months—"

"Five, wasn't it?"

"—five months, I can talk to the locals about how the whole thing is being handled."

"You should know the MP for Derbyshire—where did I put his name...ah, here it is—Fraser McAllen. He also lives in Sherton."

McAllen. Jonas recalled Magda mentioning that name. "Yes, I knew, and now I think of it, Magda might go to school with someone from the family."

"Does Magda know anything about the development planned for Sherton?"

"No,' said Jonas shortly. "I thought it best not to tell her, but she knows about the discussions with Anglo Homes, and she's not stupid —she may put it together."

There was silence on the line. Jonas could practically hear the cogs in Neil's head whirring.

"OK...Is that everything I should know?"

Jonas paused. "You're doing a great job, Neil," he said seriously. "You've taken a lot off my plate over the past month."

Neil cleared his throat and seemed to struggle for words. Jonas put him out of his misery, smiling down the phone.

"So—speak next week?"

He cut the call and stared out of the window for the next five minutes, wondering what he was going to do next. Apart from take a nap, of course. A run would be out of the question feeling like this, he fretted. Maybe he'd walk to the pub later. Whoopee, what a treat. His phone buzzed in his pocket, and he saw it was Connor.

"Jonas!" boomed his best friend, sounding as though he was in the next room rather than halfway around the world.

"Christ, Connor—what time is it with you? Isn't it the middle of the night?" Jonas glanced at the clock on the mantlepiece.

"Nah, I'm still in Buenos Aires, working on the Luxor Hotel landscape, it's just after lunch here. But enough of that—how are you?

The Garden Plot

Sure, you could have knocked me down with a feather when Magda told me you were ill."

"I'm not ill!" protested Jonas. "Well, not very, anyway. It's just a virus."

"That they don't know anything about?" Connor asked, and Jonas could imagine his eyebrow tweaking. Jonas had teased him about his 'Roger Moore' impression all the way through his teens.

"Well, I'm being watched like a hawk, and not allowed to do anything, so I don't think I'm going to die of anything except boredom! Connor, I'm going to be out of the office for *five* months!"

Connor laughed, his rich chuckle echoing down the line.

"You must have done something very, *very* bad to have deserved this, Jonas! Mind you," his voice suddenly sobered. "Magda was very upset when I finally got to talk to her after you came back from the hospital. What's this about you stopping breathing?"

"I know, I know… But honest to God, although I get tired easily, I feel fine now!"

"*Now*, maybe. Have your folks gone back to Germany?"

"Yes, although my mother is calling every other day to check on me."

"Count yourself lucky I'm off into the mountains next week, otherwise I'd be calling too!"

The two of them talked a little more. Jonas asked about Connor's latest gardening project, and they agreed that when Connor finished it, he'd make his way to Brook Lodge to check on Jonas for himself.

After the call, Jonas found himself smiling. He and Connor had been friends since university, and they were close. They'd cut their teeth together in the city of London in the early days and had been feted as having the luck of the Irish. Well, until Connor had become ill, of course. Jonas blinked away the memories of his friend at his most vulnerable. That was a lesson he ought to heed, it suddenly struck him. Jonas had been there just in time for Connor, but what had pushed Connor to the brink of disaster had been overwork.

A noise made him turn his head and he saw Magda, leaning against the door, watching him.

"What's up?"

She pushed off the door and walked towards him.

"You're really going to do this? Take five months off work?" she asked.

He grinned. "I am."

"You're not going to cheat when I go back to school? Start having them send papers over? Take calls in the middle of the night from Bernard because he forgets the time zone?"

Jonas shook his head, smiling slightly as he thought of his company chairman. Bernard had almost sent his secretary Jane round the bend while Jonas had been in hospital.

"Nope." Magda looked sceptical at his words. "Scouts honour!"

He was rewarded by a huge beam from Magda, her face lighting up.

"Work isn't the only thing in my life, you know," he protested mildly.

She hugged him and chortled. "Yeah, right."

Jonas was taken aback.

"Don't look at me like that!" she grinned, skipping over to the window and peering into the garden. "You work like a slave for the company, you know you do. I reckon you only sent me to Clavedene to get rid of me during the week!"

He frowned, suddenly aware that this was indeed, another benefit of Magda going to private school.

He looked at his daughter curiously. "Do you think I work too hard?"

"I think you work too *much*," Magda agreed. "You don't even play much tennis with me anymore unless we're on holiday."

Guilt lapped over him, particularly in light of his reflections about Connor.

"You need to get out more," she said. "Do more stuff with other people, not just work things."

Jonas stared. "What about Geraldine? I do 'stuff' with her!"

Magda flushed. "Yes, I know. It's just—the women you date don't seem very, like...stimulating. Mentally, I mean," she added hastily, going even redder.

Jonas, who had been thinking of Geraldine and how actually, she was pretty stimulating in many respects, tried not to smile.

Magda turned back to the garden. "I just get the feeling that ever since mum died, you've focused so hard on work that now I'm not sure you ever think about anything else. And the women you go out with seem to be just light relief, a bit, like, *fluffy*."

Although she wasn't looking at him, he could tell she was still red —her ears were pink.

"Are you suggesting I find a nice girl and settle down?" he asked, smiling.

"No, but I think you could do with finding someone who's got something between her ears!" she replied tartly.

"I take it you don't approve of Geraldine?"

Magda shrugged. She couldn't have said 'no' more clearly, Jonas thought, gloomily.

"Well, you're probably going to tell me it's none of my business," she said evenly.

Jonas had been going to do exactly that, and her words made him change tack.

"Gerry and I understand one another, and our relationship is...stimulating...and not too deep. Which is how I want it. I'm not looking for a serious relationship. Neither is she. Understand?"

Magda nodded slowly.

"And you know how I feel about keeping our private life private? Particularly since your mother died," he said. Jonas remembered even now, the photographers' flashes and Magda turning her face into his chest and sobbing. "You know the drill but be particularly careful while I'm recuperating. I don't want our competitors to know I'm not in the office," he continued, moving on swiftly from his love life.

"Of course!" Indignant, Magda tossed her head, her high ponytail bobbing, and he realised how easily she slipped from young girl into young woman and back again. When had that happened?

He pulled her into a hug. "Sweetie, I just wanted to stress—to *both* of us—that we need a certain element of anonymity at the moment. When I'm back at work, we can relax a bit. But we need to be careful, particularly as you're making friends in the village—"

He held up his hand as she opened her mouth to protest. "I'm not asking you to give up your friends, I'd never ask that—just be circumspect, particularly around one of them—I think her Dad's the local MP?"

"Her name is Lisbeth and her Dad is Fraser McAllen and yes, he's the local MP," she mumbled into his chest. "I've just told her—and *everyone*—you're in property and the company's based in Europe. I thought that was vague enough. I've also told her mum drowned on holiday when I was eight."

Jonas nodded and patted her shoulder.

"But will you think about what *I* said?" Magda said, peering up at him.

Jonas smiled. "Getting a little *more* conversation, a little *less* action? I'll bear it in mind," he said.

She glared at him. "It's not a joke, dad! If you're not careful you'll turn into a dinosaur, thinking all women are fit for is a bit of 'light stimulation'!" She made quote marks in the air.

Jonas ducked his head meekly and backed away.

"Oh my god—*really*?" Lisbeth's voice was shocked. Magda, sipping an enormous mug of milky drink masquerading as coffee, nodded disconsolately.

"It's not even as though he's that old, but his attitude to women is nineteenth century! And Geraldine, the bloody woman he's dating now, doesn't do anything except bat her eyelashes and look appealing. She's so plastic, she doesn't even look like she sweats. Her idea of conversation is to giggle and agree with Dad." Magda huffed and slouched into the leather chair, almost as oversized as her mug.

She glared into her coffee. It was all right for Lisbeth, she had a *family* while she had a dinosaur work-mad father and a woman with all the charm of a piranha angling to become her stepmother.

She could just about remember her mother, all glamorous dresses and expensive perfume, but her grandmother had been the central female in her life when she was younger. Magda secretly missed her now they were in England, and she envied Lisbeth her easy relationship with her own mother.

Lisbeth was making sympathetic noises.

"Aren't people weird? Your dad won't look at anyone with a brain, my Aunty Sam won't look at anyone, full stop!"

"Why's that?" asked Magda, staring moodily into her mug.

"Not really sure." Lisbeth considered. "She's a bit different, Aunty Sam. She took over grandad's gardening firm when he died and she's making a really good go of it...Although she's always saying she could do with more business, I think she's good at what she does. She had a boyfriend, like, ages ago, but I can remember her coming to stay with us when they broke up. As far as I know, she's never had another one."

"Really? Is she still smitten?"

Lisbeth laughed. "Oh God, no! I think the bloke she was with comes back to the village occasionally with his wife and baby and they look *so* grim together! I heard her say once to mum that she'd had a lucky escape, so no, I think she's recovered. She's great! She climbed Kilimanjaro a couple of years ago, she goes ski-ing, all kinds of things. And she's so funny, *and* pretty. But I think she might be lonely. I was thinking of sending her details to a dating site without her knowing, but I'm not sure I dare. And it would be like, *impossible* to get her on a date without telling her!"

She rummaged in her bag for her phone. "Look, this is Aunty Sam." She found a photograph and held out the phone to Magda. Magda gazed at the small photo of a pixie blonde smiling out at her. She whistled.

"Wow, she *is* pretty! You're not telling me she's single?"

"For *ages*!" Lisbeth retorted as she took the phone and thumbed through some of the other photos. "My mum's tried to set her up with friends of Daddy, and it's always a disaster. The last time, the chap was soooo dim, and a Tory to boot. Sam's a bit political—she and Dad always used to be rowing about something or other, although I think she says stuff just to get up Dad's nose."

"But she's bright? And interesting?" asked Magda, suddenly intense.

"Yeah, well *I* think so...why?"

"Do you remember my dad?"

Lisbeth rolled her eyes. "Are you kidding me? What a gorgeous..." she trailed off, her gaze meeting Magda's.

"Quite." Magda was dry.

"And you think he needs someone with a brain?" Lisbeth said slowly.

"He does. Someone...stimulating. To give him other interests besides his blasted work," Magda said.

"Is he well enough? He was, like, unconscious for nearly two days and only came out of hospital—what?—three weeks ago!"

Magda waved her hand in dismissal. "Four. But he's doing fine, apart from being a bit tired."

Lisbeth fell silent. She began to look worried. "Do you think it would work?" she asked after a moment.

"No idea," said Magda briskly, "but I think Geraldine fancies herself as my new step-mama, so frankly I'd be willing to give it a go. *Dad* might not want to get married, but I'd bet money Geraldine does!"

"I'm not sure it would be the right thing to do...Aunty Sam is like, well, very independent." Lisbeth sounded dubious.

"Don't be daft!" Magda scoffed. "If they don't like one another, it won't go anywhere."

"But what about Geraldine?"

Magda thought for a moment. "She's in Manchester most of the time, so it might not be *that* difficult. We could throw them together and see what happens...But how can we get them to meet? A blind date would be out of the question."

"And that's even if Sam would go," pointed out Lisbeth.

"What about through work?"

"They do such different things, don't they? Like, your dad builds houses, doesn't he? Aunty Sam designs gardens," said Lisbeth, looking dubious again.

Magda, mindful of her father's last comment about keeping his job quiet, said vaguely, "Dad's off work, on, like, doctor's orders for a couple of months, so it can't be through *his* job." She took a deep swallow of her lukewarm drink and thought hard. "But what about Sam's?" she continued, after a pause.

There was a short silence and then she slammed the mug on the table, slopping milky liquid everywhere.

"That's it! We *do* need some work on the garden! Oh my god, it's totes *perfect*!"

Lisbeth looked alarmed. "What? Magda, you can't be serious! You're going to get Aunty Sam to design your garden? That's mental!"

Magda grinned, at her most persuasive. "Listen, we need our garden re-designing, you just said your Aunty Sam's always on the lookout for business, and this would bring them together *and* earn her some money! What's not to love?"

"But who would pay for it all?" Lisbeth protested.

"I would! I have some Trust money—I can use that!"

Lisbeth hesitated. "I'm not sure—"

"Oh, come on! Where's your sense of adventure? Weren't you trying to fix her up with someone? This way, even if nothing comes of getting them together, I'll have a new garden for the summer!"

In the face of such determined optimism, Lisbeth fell silent. Magda took that as agreement and began to plan.

4

Sam sighed gently as the two middle aged ladies squared up to one another like cross squirrels.

In the red corner was Miss Susan Miles, the corners of her mouth resolutely turned downwards, despite her name.

In the blue corner was Mrs Pratchett, widow of this parish. Since moving into the village five years ago, Dorothy Pratchett had bullied, coaxed and blackmailed everyone in it to participate in village fairs, competitions for best kept village, open gardens' days and to campaign against the Tesco on the high street. The only reason she hadn't resurrected the ancient hunt in the village was that no-one could afford the hounds. She herself was never seen without her bulldog, Bertie, who lumbered around, leaving a trail of slobber behind him. Sam couldn't warm to Bertie and loathed Dorothy's politics, but couldn't help but admire her manipulations.

Susan Miles, with watery light blue eyes and the palest skin Sam had ever seen, exercised power of a less visible sort. Ostensibly the weakling of the pair, she didn't rant or bully or cajole—she was *disappointed* in people if they didn't agree with her. Most capitulated.

Currently, the ladies were arguing over the agenda for the Sherton Environment Protection meeting, which as usual was already late starting. Also as usual, the agenda had too much on it to get through in the two hours allotted.

Strike that—one hour forty minutes, thought Sam as she glanced at her watch.

"Susan, surely you see the main purpose of the meeting is to focus on the clear and present danger which is the proposed new development?" Mrs Pratchett huffed.

"I suggest we spend five minutes sorting out the deadline for the garden competition and then move onto the development near Jessop's Field," said Desmond Black, talking over Miss Miles' response. He was the village's resident painter and decorator, and candidate for most pompous man in Sam's acquaintance.

Mrs Pratchett huffed and bent to fuss over her dog, ignoring the conversation for the next five minutes.

There were about fifteen people at the meeting, all of them known to Sam in varying degrees of intimacy. While Misses Miles and Pratchett and Desmond Black negotiated a fortnight delay to the closure of the garden competition—caused, as Miss Miles explained in exhaustive detail, by a very wet winter and a late spring due to the changes in the Jet Stream and global warming—Sam looked round the room. Her librarian buddy Amanda, and the Vicar Tom and his hippy-ish wife Jenny waited patiently for the main business. There were a couple of other familiar faces, too— teachers, farmers, and bed-and-breakfast owners, who wanted to keep their picture-perfect countryside to entice their punters.

"So now—the development near Jessop's Field," began Desmond Black twenty minutes later.

No-one said anything, so Sam said; "I haven't had chance to look at the plans, has everyone else looked at them?"

Tom and Jenny and the two teachers—who'd come straight from school—had not. As chairs scraped and people wandered over to the displays, Amanda, her hair a new colour of blood oranges and with a nose ring adorning her pretty face, sidled up to Sam and nudged her arm.

"You're not going to like them."

"Mmm. The houses look a bit close to Jessop's Field," said Sam, peering at the plans. She thought the computer-generated visuals looked very attractive—but then again, they were supposed to.

"And look," said Amanda, pointing to another of the boards. "Look where they're linking the development to the main road." Sam looked.

"That's over Green Belt land!"

"Quite. So what with the road's impact on the Green Belt—cutting through a fine chunk of it, no less—and the fact that once these houses are built, there's no reason not to build *more*—"

"A bit of a Trojan Horse, you think?"

"I imagine what they'll say is that any other developments will reduce the distance between us and Stockwell and present that as desirable."

Sam, knowing Stockwell and its history, tried to be loyal to the neighbouring village.

"Not that there's anything wrong with Stockwell, but since the mine closed..." Sam trailed off. "But I thought there were new homes there, I'm not sure why there's a need to build here. I know people need houses, but this will destroy the character of our village."

The rest of the group, having seen the plans, agreed. After hearing those who wanted to say something—mostly, Sam noted, the same thing in slightly different words—the Vicar Tom raised his hand.

"Although the development might seem huge to us, for *this* developer, it's actually very small," he observed in his glorious bass voice, which thrilled the elderly parishioners every Sunday. "Anglo Homes' last development near Nottingham included more than eleven *thousand* houses, as opposed to this, which is just for three hundred and fifty. And although planning permission was refused for the Nottingham site, Anglo Homes appealed the decision and got the OK from the Secretary of State, who overruled the local authority."

There was a burst of protest from the group.

"Damned Government," muttered Mrs Pratchett.

The Garden Plot

"Yes, but the point is, this is not Anglo Homes' normal business," said Tom. "So what are they up to?"

"I think they'll use it as a test case, and if they get planning permission, they'll then build more," Amanda said darkly. There were mutters and protests from the group and then Desmond took charge.

"As we all know, Jessop's Field protects all kinds of wildlife," he began. "Not to mention the impact that the building work and access roads will have on the village. We need to identify where we can object and build our case." He looked up expectantly.

"I'll look at the roads and environment," volunteered Amanda.

"I'll investigate the local plan from the council," said Tom.

"There's legislation to protect wildlife—I'll look at this if no-one else does?" Miss Miles looked around and as people nodded, she scribbled it in her notebook.

"I can go through the plans in detail, and make a list of things we need to put in our objections—but I could do with some help, in case I miss something," Sam said, mentally flicking through her diary and realising it was more or less empty.

Jenny, the vicar's wife smiled at her. "Good idea, I'll do the same."

"We'll need to get a move on—the consultation closes in less than three weeks," Desmond said. Sam, who had noticed whenever something had to be done, Desmond was the last to volunteer, gave him a level look and smiled sweetly.

"I think it would be helpful, Desmond, if you were to talk to your friends on the council—informally of course—about what they know and what their views are?" she suggested mildly.

Desmond—who already spent a good deal of time in the Dog and Duck, 'networking', nodded in agreement.

"What can *I* do?" asked Dorothy Pratchett.

"Well, I think given your skills at rallying support, Mrs Pratchett, you could usefully start one of your wonderful petitions." Tom gave Dorothy a winning smile and she preened.

"Jolly good. Consider it done."

Desmond asked everyone to come to the next meeting with their research, deferred the rest of the agenda and everyone went to the pub.

The Dog and Duck was the same as always—camp mock Tudor décor, a yellowy-golden light which was a bit too dim to read the bar menu, and yet another new landlord. This one had been there for about three months now.

Moving away from the rest of the group, Sam took an order for a gin and tonic from Amanda and looked about. Being a Thursday, the pub was full of people pretending the weekend was already here, and Sam sniffed appreciatively at the steak pie and chips which was heading towards a table in the corner of the bar. Reminded forcibly by her stomach that she hadn't eaten since one o'clock, she took the drinks back to Amanda.

"I'm starving—would you mind if I ordered something to eat?"

"Fill your boots, I'm happy with my G and T."

Sam immediately headed back to the bar and ordered food. Her stomach grumbled again in anticipation, startling a tall stranger next to her at the bar. They both laughed. Sam thought she'd never seen such wonderful green eyes.

When she came back to join Amanda, the redhead was grinning at her.

"What?"

"Now *that's* a nice example of the male sex! He's been giving you the once-over too!"

Surprised, Sam looked back to see the man who had laughed at her noisy digestive system staring at her. He smiled faintly. Going pink, she ducked her head and sat down, taking too large a drink from her glass of wine and starting to cough as it went down the wrong way.

"He's gorgeous," was Amanda's comment.

Sam snatched another glance at the stranger. He was. Tall, dark and with those eyes. He was dressed expensively and looked interestingly gaunt, as if he'd been ill. Her troubles tapped at her and sadly, she refocused.

"Yeah, but I'm not interested." It didn't sound that convincing. In a slightly firmer voice, she continued hunting in her bag for a tissue to wipe her mouth. "I'm too busy."

Amanda looked at her, perplexed. "Too busy? For *that*? You're mad, woman."

Sam's libido echoed the sentiment. Sam shook her head. "If you'd seen our order books for the next few months, you'd know I need to concentrate big time on getting some work, not picking up gorgeous looking men!"

Amanda stopped gawping at the stranger at the bar and focused on her friend's now worried face.

Sam sighed and leaned back against the threadbare upholstery. "It's been going well up to now," she said. "But with actually doing the work, I've not done the marketing for any *new* work. So for the next five months we don't have much on apart from some maintenance contracts. And frankly, I can't keep everyone employed on that income. Or at least, not employed on a living wage," Sam explained gloomily.

"Ah," said Amanda. "Bank loan?"

Sam shook her head. "Already been refused—too many businesses in the area going under." *Thanks in part to the bloody Government.* She took another sip of wine. "I've been wondering if I'm cut out for running a business, despite what Dad thought."

"What, not cut out for being a corporate capitalist?" Amanda grinned as Sam laughed. "Get a grip girl! You just need some luck. I could put some flyers in the library for you, if you like?"

Sam smiled gratefully. "It's really kind, but I think I've exhausted the local market. I need clients from further out, from the Sheffield area, maybe from Stoke on Trent..." Her voice trailed off. "But I don't really know how to get them. I'm not really a marketer, Dad always got his work through word of mouth."

"You've got a website, haven't you? What are you doing with that?"

"Yes, I need to get it updated—we've added some recent projects, but it needs an overhaul, really. I think Dad's photo is still on it, which isn't good." There was a pause.

"What about writing some articles for the local paper?"

Sam hmm'd, thinking.

"Or asking the local radio if you can go on to talk about solving gardening problems?" Amanda went on, warming to her theme. 'If that dreadful woman who flopped all over our TV without a bra can do it, I'm sure you can!"

Sam laughed, but riffled her bag for a notebook and started to write. "If I could afford to employ any more staff, I'd hire you!" she said.

There was a pause as Sam's steak and kidney pie was brought to the table by the new landlord, who presented it with a flourish. He finally left after an appropriate amount of fussing, and Sam tucked into the food.

Amanda continued to make suggestions and Sam made notes with one hand and ate with the other. As she reached the end of her food and indeed, the end of the evening, Sam felt her spirits revive.

As she finished her drink, she caught the eye of the man at the bar, still watching her. He smiled. Ignoring her hands-on-hips libido, she smiled. Amanda was right, he was gorgeous, but something else —powerful? She couldn't put her finger on it, but her stomach dipped slightly when she looked at him.

He raised his glass in courteous salute as she gathered up her jacket and bag and reached for her keys. Amanda, watching the exchange, rolled her eyes and sighed.

"Mad. I think you're mad!" she hissed as they walked out.

And so do I! cried her libido, tossing its head.

Sam laughed ruefully and kept on walking.

"Dad?" Magda said as he walked through the door. "How are you feeling?"

"Knackered, but glad I went out, if only to get some air," Jonas said, shrugging off his coat.

"Did you chat to anyone, or just have a drink?"

"Mmm?" Jonas stretched his shoulders. The little blonde crossed his mind, and he recalled her delicate heart-shaped features and her slight frame covered in the most shapeless of jeans. His mouth tilted slightly. And her grumbling stomach. Yes, she'd been worth the walk to the pub. He remembered Gerry a little guiltily and pushed the stranger out of his mind, sinking with a sigh onto the sofa.

"Just a quiet drink."

"Can I talk to you about something?"

That sounds like trouble, he thought. He patted the sofa and smiled at his hovering daughter. Magda sat beside him, fixing him with her big eyes, so like his. "I want to use some of the money mum left me."

"Oh? What on?"

"Well, as you're going to be here all summer and all the newspapers say we're going to have a brilliant summer—I thought I'd like to get the garden sorted out."

Jonas was silent. And surprised.

He thought of the uninspiring lawn and lacklustre borders. Even the scattering of bulbs that were in bloom looked meagre, as though they could do with some TLC.

"This is a fairly big undertaking, liebchen. Are you sure you want to spend that much money?"

Magda nodded. "This is going to be our home, isn't it? *You* can't do the garden while you're recuperating, even if you wanted to, and I can't do anything while I'm at school, even if I knew where to start! So —time to bring in some professionals."

"Well…It is your money. But it will be a *lot* of money, you know? Have you seen any garden firms you want to invite to tender? Do you want any of my contacts? There's Connor, for example-"

"Connor would just laugh at me and then do what he wants to, not what *I* want! And anyway, I know who I want to design and build the garden," Magda said firmly, dismissing her internationally-recognised godfather.

"Really? Who?"

"The company that did Lisbeth's garden—you know my friend Lisbeth? The garden at her house is awesome—like, really beautiful."

Jonas clamped down on his misgivings but made a mental note to pass by Lisbeth's house at the first opportunity. "Who is this company?"

"Winterson's. They've done a lot of the gardens in the posh bit of the village."

"Do they all look the same?" Jonas asked cynically.

Magda laughed. "God, no! They're all very different—one of them is like, really modern, but Lisbeth's is like something out of A Midsummer Night's Dream. They're both great in their own way."

"Hmmm. Well, it wouldn't do any harm to get them to quote. But I want to have a look at the plans before you agree anything, I want to see the budget, and I want to check out the firm."

"Of course—but really, Dad, do give me credit for checking them out myself! I'm not an idiot, you know."

"No need to get cross," he said, smiling at her. "Of course I trust you, but I don't trust some of the cowboys out there. And I certainly don't want a bunch of amateurs destroying the garden—I know it's not pretty, but it could be a lot worse."

"This is *not* a bunch of amateurs—"

"*Or* some pretentious designer, bringing in weird chunks of sculpture which he couldn't offload on anyone else!" Jonas went on as he warmed to his theme. "I want solid men who know their business and aren't going to leave us with paths sprouting weeds in three months. Neither do I want some female designer who's never got her hands dirty, but simply gardens on paper."

"I think you should have a look at the website, be *completely* reassured, and leave me to liaise with the designer—I want the designs to be a *surprise*, and as you're going to look at them before the work starts, surely that should be ok?"

Jonas stopped himself smiling as he recognised Magda's 'soothing' voice.

"OK, that sounds reasonable." Jonas said after a pause, thinking how grown up she seemed.

"Great. I'll get it organised," Magda said briskly, getting to her feet.

"Magda—"

She stopped, and he smiled warmly at her.

"This is really thoughtful of you."

"I'd like a garden Nanna and Opa would like to visit," she said simply. "Somewhere we can all be together *here*, not just in Germany."

Jonas thought back to German summers in his parents' glorious garden, which never seemed to fade into just green, regardless of the season. Also tumbling into his thoughts was Nicole, Magda's mother. His face tightened.

Magda was looking at him uncertainly and, pulling himself back in to the present, he smiled at her. "I'm sure it will be a wonderful surprise, and it's really sweet of you to think of it."

Magda smiled sunnily at him and left the room.

Lisbeth answered her phone a couple of minutes later.

"What happened?" she said immediately.

"Dad's going to look at the internet site. Is Sam on the website as the owner? Dad muttered something about 'female garden designers' and I don't want him interfering before they even meet. Does it look like she's in charge?"

"Well, Zach normally updates the site, but he hasn't done for a while. Sam's hopeless when it comes to technology. I'm not sure if her dad is still featured on the site. He was called Samuel, and knowing Sam, he's still there...But are you sure we should be doing this?"

"Zach? Is this some boyfriend you've been hiding from me?" Magda ignored Lisbeth's concern.

"Zach? Oh, no! I've known him forever—he was two years above me in infant school!" Lisbeth was diverted for the moment. "He's done bits for Sam's website before."

"So all I need to do now is make an appointment to see her?"

"Well, yes—but honestly, should we be *doing* this, Magda?"

Magda paused. "Look—it can't do any harm, can it? If nothing else, we'll get a fabulous garden and I'm giving your aunt some business. If they don't like one another, neither will be any the wiser, will they?"

"I suppose not," said Lisbeth doubtfully.

"Try not to fret so much—it'll be fine," Magda said soothingly. Lisbeth murmured something unintelligible, and then rang off, sounding unconvinced.

5

Sam put the phone down, feeling pleased with herself. The discussion with the editor of the Northern Chronicle had gone much better than she'd hoped—she had a piece to write about spring planting and a photo to provide. It would go on their website with a credit for Sam and a namecheck for the company.

She rose from her desk, ran her fingers through her short hair and reached for the kettle, to celebrate.

A small piece of work had come in yesterday—a tiny back garden which needed new borders and some serious work on a crumbling pond. She'd stuck to her guns in the initial quote—despite Andy's misgivings. There had been a tense day or so when she thought the quote was too high and they'd lost the job—and then the owner had agreed. Sam was so relieved she could have wept in gratitude.

"I can see you're a proper gardener," the owner had said. "Not just a bunch of labourers doing hard landscaping and traipsing all over my roses."

Andy had grunted, talked about the economy and how they were a luxury commodity. And then hugged her. She'd told him about the bank, and his calm response about cutting back on some basics had steadied her.

"It'll get better," he'd said.

She was stirring her tea and thinking about other ways to bring in business when the phone rang in the main office. She heard Andy answer.

"Winterson's Garden Design, good morning...Yes, I'll just see if she's available. Who's calling?"

Andy put the caller on hold and peered into the tiny kitchenette. "Someone with an enquiry about a garden design. Says her name is Magda Keane."

"One sec," Sam grabbed her tea and retreated to her office, leaving the door open. Andy put the call through and then came in and sat at the table, listening.

"Sam Winterson."

"Hi, my name is Magda Keane. I'm friends with Lisbeth who's told me you're a garden designer. I'd like to talk to you about ours."

Sam wrinkled her nose, recognising the name, but unable to pin it down exactly. "I think I remember Lisbeth talking about you, thanks for calling. How can I help?"

"Our house is Brook Lodge and the garden is a mess," said the voice on the phone. "I'm planning the new design as a surprise for my father."

Brook Lodge? God, that's a huge house.

"That sounds very exciting," she said. "Perhaps we should get together for a chat? It might be better if I came to your house so I can look at the garden."

There was a pause on the end of the line.

"Well, my dad's here at the moment, which would ruin the surprise, so can I come and have a chat with you at your office? We can arrange for you to come to the house when he's out."

"Ok..." Sam said slowly, faint alarm bells starting to ring. "When are you available?" They arranged to meet later that day. Sam put down the phone.

"Sounds promising," said Andy when she said nothing for a moment.

"I'm not sure. She says she's a friend of Lisbeth's—she wants the designs as a surprise for her dad. She lives at Brook Lodge, she says."

"Brook Lodge is an Edwardian mansion. The garden is a big one," Andy said, stroking his beard.

"She sounded very confident, but I imagine she's Lisbeth's age. I've no idea where she'd find the money..."

When Magda walked in three hours later, two things happened. The first was that Sam thought they'd met before. She wondered if she's seen a photo of her with Lisbeth. Something nagged at her but didn't blossom into recognition. The second was that Sam realised just how young Magda was. Her heart sank. This girl wouldn't be able to make the decisions, she would have no idea of the cost of redesigning a large garden, she wouldn't recognise a good design when she saw it, Daddy might not like it...

A thousand objections to us getting any business.

Nevertheless, she smiled, shook her hand and took her into the office, shaking her head when Andy made to follow her. She didn't want to overpower the slender teenager who sauntered in.

"Perhaps you'd like to tell me a bit about the garden?" Sam began with a smile.

Magda reached for her huge handbag—which looked like genuine Prada, Sam noted. *Not that you would have known if it was a fake*, she scoffed at herself.

"The garden is south-west facing, and there's a little stream running down one side where it's a bit boggy. I have the plans here somewhere..." She pulled out some rather crumpled plans and smoothed them onto the table. "The house is Edwardian, I think. I've taken a few photos..." She rifled in the bag again, pulling out some six-by-eight colour photographs, and Sam's eyebrows went up at the teenager's very adult preparation. The garden was big, about a couple of acres.

And Magda was right—the garden *was* a mess, a few ragged bulbs and what looked like apple trees in dire need of pruning, scrubby shrubs, a couple of low walls surrounding the lawn. It would cost a small fortune to put it right, Sam thought a little gloomily.

She took the photographs and looked at them closely, and then back at the plans. Despite thinking it would be too big a job for the teenager in front of her to pay for, her mind started racing with possibilities.

"I think we're quite lucky with the soil which is neutral bordering on acid—or so the housekeeper tells me," Magda said after a pause. Sam looked at her.

"Do you have azaleas? Hang on, I thought I saw one in a photo..." She hunted through the photographs and saw a sad looking specimen on the side of the lawn. "Yes, here we are. I think your soil may be a bit acid, but we'd check..." Sam reined herself in. "You do realise this will cost a lot of money?"

"Oh yeah—I'm not worried about the cost," Magda said blithely. "I have some money of my own and if Dad likes the designs, he'll make up any shortfall."

Sam, used to cost-conscious customers, only just stopped herself from staring.

"What does your father do?" Sam thought Magda withdrew a little.

"He's head of a European company that sells property. He's not been well, and I want to develop the garden so we can use it this summer."

The penny dropped for Sam as she remembered Lisbeth talking about her friend whose father had been so ill. She looked at her, wondering if Magda had been a child of older parents, and what illness her father had.

"Well...depending on the plans, I can't imagine you'll come away with much change out of thirty-five thousand pounds, possibly more than that," Sam said, determined to make sure Magda understood the scope of the project.

Magda nodded her head.

"Yes, that's actually slightly less than I was expecting—I had a budget of around forty."

Sam was silent, her mind reeling. *Slightly less than she'd been expecting?*

The Garden Plot

"Will you take it on?" Magda said, anxiously when Sam hesitated. "I'm good for the money," she added, grinning.

Sam shook her head, remembering details of her conversation with Lisbeth about her 'loaded' friend. Looked like the Prada handbag *was* real, after all.

She said, "How about I come and see the garden when your dad is out? I have a lot of questions about what you want to use the garden for. Then I'll do the design. I'll charge you a set fee for the design and cost the development of the garden separately—ok?"

She paused, and Magda nodded.

"And I'd like payment for the design up front please," she said firmly, but Magda didn't even blink.

"Of course. How much would that be?"

"It depends on what state the garden's in and what you want. The initial consultation would be free."

"Sounds reasonable," Magda said, getting up and starting to gather the photos and plans.

"Can I keep these?" Sam stopped her. "They'll give me something to think about before I see the actual garden."

"Of course." Magda held out her hand and Sam shook it. *Very adult*, she thought, as the teenager—she *was* no more—hoisted her expensive, designer bag onto her shoulder.

To Sam's surprise, Lisbeth was in the office.

"Hello! I wasn't expecting you!" she smiled, hugging Lisbeth.

"I know you're busy," Lisbeth said hesitatingly. "I wondered if you wanted to come for coffee?"

"I can do..." Sam turned suddenly to Magda. "I forgot to ask—have you had a look at our website? That has some of our work on, and you can show that to your dad, if he wants to see it." Andy stood up obligingly and she clicked on his desktop.

"You ought to update the photos," said Andy, pointing at one of Sam, him, and her dad. Sam paused and bit her lip.

"I know," she sighed. She looked at the photos, taken in bright sunlight before her father had died. They looked so happy. "Yes, I know I should. But not quite yet. I might think about changing the text underneath to reflect the fact that dad's gone. I'll do that when I have some time."

There was an awkward silence, and despite herself, Sam found her eyes stinging with tears. She clicked out of the website and looked up to find Lisbeth's sympathetic gaze on her.

"Is coffee on you?" Sam managed to say, brightly.

"Actually, yes!" Lisbeth laughed.

Sam found herself hustled out of the office and into the local coffee shop and gradually, she recovered her equilibrium. She knew she ought to move on from her loss. But taking her father's photo from the website seemed so—final. Maybe at the end of the year...

As the two girls chattered, more around her than to her, Sam sat back and compared them. Lisbeth, while she might look young, seemed very comfortable with her sophisticated, confident friend, and the two had a healthy disagreement about the merits of the latest Tarantino film, which was showing in Ashton. Magda, now Sam looked closely at her, had the polished look of the wealthy, with glossy dark hair, intense green eyes and almost flawless skin. Lisbeth's more delicate colouring—red-gold hair and hazel eyes—was a perfect foil for her. She frowned, trying to place Magda. She couldn't shake the feeling that they'd met before, but eventually decided she must be imagining it.

"Would you like to see it, Aunty Sam?"

Sam was momentarily lost and then realised her niece was asking her about the film. She tweaked a brow. "It's not really about my company, is it? You're just hoping I'll cover for you being underage!" she responded shrewdly.

Lisbeth laughed. "Oh, busted! But I do *like* your company! And you're not shocked by the swearing or the violence and you'll always find something funny when it's getting scary."

Sam agreed and then looked at her watch.

"I must get back. Give me a call about the film—I've nothing on I can think of—oh, apart from the village group on Thursday."

"What are the eco-warriors on about this time?" Lisbeth grinned.

"Some greedy developer wants to build over Green Belt land by Jessop's Field and we're forming our version of the Résistance."

"Who's the developer?" Magda asked, looking up, suddenly intense.

"Some outfit called Anglo Homes, ruining our countryside with their nasty little houses. Have you heard of them?"

"They sound familiar," Magda said vaguely. She glanced at her watch. "Blimey, I ought to be getting home." She swept her phone into her capacious bag, and there was a bit of a scramble as everyone gathered their things.

"So I'll call you about coming around to view the garden, then?" Sam nodded at Magda. "Great. It was nice to meet you, I'll phone as soon as I find out when Dad's out of the house."

As Sam walked back to the office with Lisbeth, she was quiet.

"Are you pleased about the job?" Lisbeth asked after about five minutes' silence.

Sam threw her a quick smile. "Of course! Thanks so much for recommending us. I just wonder…"

"What?"

"I just wonder why it's all so secretive, it makes me a bit nervous. She's not at all thrown about the cost I've quoted her, but her father might think differently. And who knows if they'll have the same views about what the garden should look like? It's hard—if not impossible—to design a garden for someone you've never met."

"Well, your designs *are* brilliant!" Lisbeth said. "If he doesn't like it, he can always say no. And she does have *pots* of money!"

"Yes, you said," Sam said, as she pushed open the door to the office. "Talking about the website, I need to give Zach some new pictures. We've just finished a garden and that needs to go on the site. And I have a new apprentice, too, Steve. Can you let him know to expect something?"

"Send them to me and I'll pass them on," said Lisbeth after a pause.

"Oh, OK. Not to him directly?" Sam said, frowning.

"I think he's changed emails, and I don't have it with me, so probably safest," said Lisbeth. Her colour was heightened, and Sam wondered if there was a teenage love affair in the making. "Have to go!" Lisbeth said, kissing her and then she was gone.

"Rush, rush," tutted Sam, moving into her office and starting to sort through the photos and plans Magda had left. She reached for her sketch pad.

~

Lisbeth jumped as she saw the tall dark figure peering over the wall into the garden. She drew herself up to her full height of five foot three and in a chilly voice, said: "Can I help you?"

Jonas swung round to face her and smiled. Where Lisbeth's heart had jumped, it now melted as the warmth of a powerful half-Irish smile hit her.

"It's Lisbeth, isn't it? I'm Jonas Keane."

Lisbeth's toes curled as the velvet voice floated into her head.

"Oh! Yes, I go to school with Magda."

Jonas glanced back at the garden. "Magda wants our garden redesigned and apparently, the person she has in mind did yours. Could I have a look around?"

Lisbeth gave a silent cheer neither of her parents were in and ushered him through the gates.

Yes, the firm was Winterson's, she said, yes, there had been a few issues with the stream at the bottom, yes, all the work had been done by the firm and yes, it was *completely* beautiful, wasn't it?

Jonas, walking along crunchy gravel paths, admired the budding tulips and primroses mixed in with bushes, and the trees, tender-leafed and starting to bear blossom, and looked captivated.

Lisbeth agreed that indeed, the designer had some fabulous ideas —who'd have thought a modern piece of sculpture would look as good as *that* in a cottage garden? She agreed the planting looked lush and fulsome, and talked enthusiastically about the various roses which twined around the love seat in summer.

He murmured that Magda had not exaggerated—it was very

beautiful, perfectly in keeping with the gracious Georgian house. Lisbeth, by dint of keeping quiet, also learned he'd also been to see the modern garden Magda had mentioned and he was impressed at the range of the designer. Where this garden was like a wonderful, riotous Monet painting, he commented, the garden for the modern house was stylised, sharp, attractive and with a very limited colour palette. It wouldn't do for Brook Lodge, he said, but it was completely in tune with the modern concrete and steel house.

When Jonas thanked her and unleashed what she considered to be a *lethal* smile, Lisbeth felt herself go pink, and told him untruthfully she was sorry her parents were out but was pleased he liked the garden.

As soon as he turned the corner out of her road, Lisbeth pulled out her phone.

"Your dad's been to see our garden and likes it," she said to Magda without preamble. "I can see he thinks you've inherited his business sense and is as pleased as punch."

Magda laughed. "Great—I'll leave the website up on the computer in his study for him to see," she said. "Because Sam hasn't changed the website in ages, it looks like your grandfather is still in charge of the company."

"Make sure he sees it tonight, because when Aunty Sam remembers, she'll send new photos and check that Zach's put them up. I've asked her to send them to me rather than directly to Zach, so I can hold on to them for a bit—but not forever..." Lisbeth chewed her lip, suddenly anxious.

"Will you *stop* fretting, it'll be fine."

God, I hope so, Lisbeth thought as she hung up the phone.

6

Jonas clicked through the website, but if he was honest, he wasn't looking at it properly. He felt he'd seen enough to gauge the skills of Winterson's looking at the gardens in the village. However, he did pause over a photo of a very attractive young woman with long, curly blonde hair next to a grizzled chap and a Viking-looking, strapping young man. He looked hard at her, thinking he'd seen her before. The older man was the owner, Samuel Winterson, he presumed. While he was flicking through the web pages, Magda bounced in.

"Oh, you found it, did you?" she said, looking over his shoulder. "Are you reassured?"

"Yes, you little minx. I had a look at both gardens and even managed to speak with your friend Lisbeth."

"So I can go ahead?"

He nodded.

"Right, I'll get on with it, then," she said and immediately got out her phone and began to tap at the keys.

Jonas grunted, and rose from the desk to get himself a drink, and Magda leaned over and clicked on the website.

"Just checking the email," she said, continuing to tap her phone. Jonas, taking a sip of his whiskey, looked at the bedraggled garden, even more dismal in the drizzle.

The housekeeper, Mrs Gloria Brown, shuffled in. Magda looked up and exchanged a grin with him. Mrs Brown, despite the shuffle, was efficient and an excellent cook. She was never, however, Gloria. She was always Mrs Brown, as Jonas had learned very shortly after meeting her. Jonas, despite his charm, had managed to elicit no more information on Gloria Brown than her name and glowing references.

"Mr Keane, I'll be serving tea at seven," she announced, brooking no arguments. It was always tea, never dinner, Jonas had also learned. She started to turn on her heel, and then stopped.

"Oh aye," she said, in a voice dripping icicles. "A Miss Lord called..."

Jonas looked up. He must have left his mobile off. "On the home phone? Did she leave a message?"

"She informed me she would call back," Mrs Brown said, looking down her nose. "I did understand she would be paying you a visit."

At this, Magda groaned, and Jonas shot her an annoyed glance.

"Thank you, Mrs Brown. Did she say when she would call?"

"No, she did not," Mrs Brown sniffed and continued her shuffling way out of the study.

There was a taut silence, and Jonas downed the last of his whiskey. Putting down the glass with a bit of a snap, he turned to Magda.

"You should know, Magda, that *I* invited Geraldine."

"Why?"

"She offered to go to the hospital with me next Thursday."

"I would have come with you!" protested Magda.

"Gerry is driving me. I didn't ask you as well, because the idea of spending four or five hours with the pair of you spitting at one another like cats is hardly going to be beneficial to my health," he said feelingly. Magda glowered at him but had no answer. "Quite," he said wryly. "She'll stay over on Wednesday evening, travel with me to

Manchester on Thursday and probably stay for a week or two." Magda said nothing. Jonas thought his daughter would find an excuse to stay over with Lisbeth.

"What time's your appointment?"

"Twelve o'clock."

"So what time will you be leaving?"

"About ten, I imagine."

Magda looked sceptical—Geraldine wasn't the fastest off the blocks in the morning, he remembered—and excused herself to wash up before dinner.

He rang Gerry.

"Jonas?" came the breathy tones of Geraldine over the phone. Jonas smiled as the voice warmed parts of his anatomy he had thought comatose.

"Hi Gerry, I'm sorry I missed your call. How are you?"

"Pleased to hear from you. It was so frustrating not to be able to reach you earlier. How are *you* feeling?"

"Perfectly fine," Jonas said. "The hospital appointment will hopefully be a bit of a formality and we'll be in and out quickly. Then I can take you to lunch."

She laughed delightedly, her voice tinkling down the phone and Jonas pushed aside the thought that she sounded, for the first time ever, a bit vacuous.

"Wonderful—I'll do my best to tempt your appetite," she purred. Jonas, strangely at a loss, said nothing and after a pause, Geraldine's tone returned to her normal breathiness. "Seriously, how are you?"

Jonas paused and then decided to come clean. "Actually, I'm feeling knackered. I went for a stroll into the village and I feel I could do with a nap now! I've been to the pub once or twice, but today was my longest time out since I left hospital."

"Poor darling...I daresay it will take some time for you to recover. The doctors said so, didn't they? But why were you walking in the village?"

Jonas paused again, oddly reluctant to share Magda's plans.

"We're having the garden re-designed. I went to look at a garden designed by the company we're thinking of using."

"But why didn't you say? I know a perfectly *marvellous* garden designer who's worked all *over*—I believe he's exhibiting at Tatton Gardens this year. Shall I bring his details? And there's Connor, of course, too!"

"I think this is Magda's call—she's set it all up."

"Magda?" Gerry's voice became a little less breathy. "She didn't strike me as the outdoors-y type. How extraordinary..."

Jonas gave no comment and Gerry chattered on, but Jonas was surprised to find himself wondering when Mrs Brown would call him for dinner.

"...and of course, I simply *had* to have it," Gerry was saying. Jonas said something non-committal, having lost the thread of the conversation.

Mrs Brown appeared and with something traitorously like relief, he rang off, with Gerry's promises of her special kind of 'TLC' floating around his brain. Focusing on that part of the call made him feel more positive. Maybe it wouldn't be so bad, and he would recover his previous enthusasm along with his energy, he thought, making his way towards the spaghetti carbonara.

Sam took one more look at her screen, saved the documents and printed them off for Andy, who seemed to be allergic to any kind of technology with the one exception of his phone. She passed the pages to him.

"I've spent ages on this blasted article, so I hope it reads ok..." Unusually grumpy, Sam went back to her email.

"I like it!" Andy enthused, ten minutes later. "The garden refresh idea looks perfect—enough effort to make gardens look different without costing a fortune, but just enough work to make it profitable. We could do with a new stream of income like this. Particularly as we didn't win the Stockwell job."

"Well, we were *always* up against it there!" protested Sam. "It's hardly an affluent area, is it? I always thought we might lose on price. And the article?"

"Really good," he said. "We need a decent photograph of you to go with it."

"Oh no!" she laughed. "I'm going to give them a copy of our logo and they can use that."

Andy was silent.

"What? *What?*"

"People buy people—they won't buy advice from someone faceless—they'll want it to come from another human being." Andy shrugged.

Sam folded her lips in a firm line.

"Come on Sam—you're gorgeous!" he said.

"No."

Sam folded her arms. Andy tried again.

"How about a caricature instead of a photo? There's this amazing bloke who does them and they're really good—clever too," he said. "That might do it."

Sam stared at him and the corners of her mouth twitched.

"With straw in my hair? That would work." She giggled and he grinned at her encouragingly. "Oh, go *on* then. If I must."

"You must," Andy said firmly, as he picked up the phone and started to dial.

"I'll leave you to it," said Sam, picking up her coat. "I'm off to the cinema with Lisbeth and she's bribed me into buying pizza beforehand, so I need to change."

"The new Tarantino? Buckets of blood everywhere, I hear."

"Yes, I hope I manage to hang on to my quattro Stagioni." Sam pulled a face and left the office.

Lisbeth was always on time, thought Sam as she rounded the corner at speed to see her niece patiently waiting for her outside the busy pizzeria.

"Late at the office *again*?" Lisbeth said, as Sam caught her breath. She straightened Sam's jacket collar and then kissed her cheek.

"I'm going to be famous!" Sam returned, as they walked into the restaurant and were seated by a waiter with the unlikely name of Giuseppe.

"How so?" demanded Lisbeth after they'd settled and had the menus in front of them.

"I'm writing for the *Northern Chronicle*—trying to raise the company's profile. I've just submitted my first column."

"Goodness, the elite of journalism—next stop *Gardener's World?* Or Fleet Street?" laughed Lisbeth. Already unsure about the articles, Sam felt her bubble deflate, and said nothing, looking down at the menu.

"Are you going for pizza?" she said finally.

There was a pause.

"Aunty Sam? What's up?"

"Nothing. I think I'll go for the salad; I've eaten a lot of carbs in the past few days."

Another pause. "No, tell me about the column."

"It's nothing, just a bit of scribbling for the local rag. What are you having?"

"I've pissed you off, haven't I?"

"You'll certainly piss your mother off if she hears you using language like that."

"I *have* pissed you off. Tell me about the column, when will it appear?"

"Next week, I think. But there's probably no need to announce it to everyone." Listening to her own voice, Sam scolded herself. *God, how old are you—twelve?*

"But of *course* there is! Mum and Dad will want to know and *loads* of people!"

Sam gave her contrite niece a level look over the top of her menu. "Look Lisbeth, it's just a short piece about spring planting, I'm not turning into the next gardening whizz-kid. I'm trying to raise the profile of the business because we need some new orders. It was daft of me to announce it like that, when most newspapers will take any old rubbish—God, look at the Daily Mail!"

Lisbeth was silent, and Sam thought she looked a little shocked. *She's so cossetted. She's no clue what working people struggle with. And why should she? She's a schoolgirl.*

She reached over and covered Lisbeth's hand with hers.

"Ignore me—I'm a grumpy old cow. We're not on the breadline—otherwise I'd be tapping up your dad for a loan."

"Would you?" Lisbeth said quizzically, squeezing her aunt's hand.

"Well, certainly if the bank wouldn't help! But really sweetie—don't fret about it, I'm just having a bad day—particularly as bloody Andy wants me to send a photo too!"

"Oh?" Lisbeth looked up sharply.

"You know what I'm like about photos...We eventually compromised on a caricature."

"What, like a cartoon?" Lisbeth said. "Can you tell that it's you?"

"Well, vaguely, I suppose. But as long as no-one comments on my boobs or my bloody hair, I don't much care."

Lisbeth grinned.

"Well, perhaps being *too* recognised might be problematic...It's the Northern Chronicle, you said?" Sam nodded.

"What day?"

"Thursday, I think."

Lisbeth took out a notebook and scribbled in it. Sam looked puzzled. "Just so I can remember to get a copy," explained Lisbeth. "Why didn't you want to send one, anyway?"

Sam smiled wryly. "I just didn't want to send anything which might concentrate attention on what I looked like, rather than what I *said*. I don't want to blow all the work I've done over the last two years getting people to view me as a competent garden designer, rather than her dad's pet who was indulging her."

Lisbeth's frowned.

"*Did* people view you like that?"

Sam's mouth twisted.

"You have no idea. Your grandad, much as I loved him, didn't help. He'd introduce me as 'his little helper'—you can imagine how *that* went down when we were ordering topsoil and granite slabs!"

Her niece giggled.

"I think it's a brilliant thing you're doing, this writing," Lisbeth added warmly. "I'm sure it'll help sales."

I certainly hope so, thought Sam fervently. *Otherwise, Brook Lodge or not, we're screwed.*

Their drinks arrived and Sam took a deep swig of her sparkling water.

"When will you start Magda's garden?" said Lisbeth, between sips of coke.

"I'm meeting her tomorrow for a chat."

"Great. It's a fab house."

Sam caught something in her voice and looked at her niece. "Is she a special friend?"

Lisbeth considered. "Well, yeah, I think she is. We've known one another since September, and we spend a lot of time together. She, like, sees a lot of stuff I see, and we laugh at *loads* of the same things. So, yeah, I suppose she is. I really admire her courage."

"Courage?"

"It can't be easy to lose your mum and then nearly lose your dad—she's so strong, although she can be a pain in the rear when she gets something in her head..." Lisbeth paused and Sam, watching her face, saw a moment of—what? Frustration? Anxiety?

"She's an only child?"

"Yes, I think she's close to her grandparents, as her mum died when she was little—but I get the feeling she's pretty isolated," Lisbeth said thoughtfully.

"You're an only child—do *you* feel isolated?" asked Sam curiously.

"No—but I have both mum and dad, and you and Uncle Jack and

Aunty Sue and cousins, and obviously, there's granny and grandpa McAllen. I have *loads* of family. She doesn't."

Lisbeth grinned suddenly.

"Sometimes I think she might see me as a sister-substitute!"

Sam laughed, thinking of Charlie.

She ought to be careful what she wishes for! she thought.

7

Sam's eyes widened as she drove up the drive, the tyres of the Land Rover crunching on the gravel. A dull overcast day and a brisk wind had given way to warm April sunshine with crystal blue skies overhead. Basking in the pale golden light was Magda's home, and its beauty caught in Sam's throat. Edwardian, elegant, its windows winking in the light—it was glorious.

The garden, however, was definitely *not* glorious. The photos Magda had brought to their meeting had not done its drabness justice. Sam could practically feel her palms itching to get to her tools and start pruning.

Magda, wrapped in a chunky knit cardigan came out to meet her as she climbed out of the Land Rover.

"Morning! Thank God it's not raining—we can have a proper walk round and you can have a good look at everything," she smiled.

Sam hefted her sketch book and note pad, checked her phone was in her jeans pocket, and headed for the wide expanse of lawn.

Garden space all around the house, she thought. She squinted upwards—the back of the house faced south-west, which would make it wonderful in the evening summer sun. She also spied a back gate in the high garden wall, overgrown with ivy and looking as though it had been unused for years.

Magda led the way to a couple of deck chairs outside the patio doors—Sam caught a glimpse of softly shining wood and deep reds and creams inside the house. Leaving her sketchbook on the deck chair, Sam took out her notebook.

"Where shall we start? You mentioned a stream—shall we begin there?"

The stream was tiny but had quite a gush of water. Sam tested the banks with her foot—quite firm, but with a bit of bogginess towards one end. She wondered about a pond.

Magda led the way around the stone walls of the garden, and Sam took photographs and jotted notes. She noticed the apple trees, in dire need of cutting back. *And soon, if they were going to produce any fruit* she thought. She gripped her pen more firmly.

The garden was larger than she'd thought, but although the space was big, there wasn't much to look at. The beds were empty except for a few bulbs one rather ancient rose, and a few scraggy shrubs.

"I wondered if we could put a pergola here, or something?" Magda said hesitantly, waving her hand at a bare patch of wall overshadowed by the branches of a beautiful ash tree.

Sam considered. "Hmmm. Possibly. I need to ask some questions about what you're going to do in the garden, but first, let me take a soil sample."

A middle-aged woman came out of the patio doors with a tray of tea and shuffled with remarkable speed across the lawn. Magda smiled at her.

"Thanks, Mrs Brown!"

Wiping her hand on her jeans, Sam held it out.

"Hello, I'm Sam Winterson. I'm a garden designer."

Mrs Brown shook it with apparent reluctance. "*Samuel* Winterson's girl?"

Sam beamed at her.

"The very same. Did you know him?"

The Garden Plot

"Aye—the whole village knew Sam Winterson," Mrs Brown sniffed. Sam stiffened, hearing the dismissal in the woman's voice.

"I wonder what my dad did to her?" Sam said lightly as Mrs Brown shuffled off. "Mind you, after mum died, he did have a bit of a wild patch with the ladies. Perhaps he missed her out?"

Magda giggled and then grew serious.

"I'm sorry your mum died—mine did too."

"Lisbeth told me. You must have been very young," Sam said.

"I was eight. She drowned on holiday."

"Mine died from breast cancer, back in the time when there were a lot less options for treatment," Sam said easily. "I was about the same age as you were."

"Really? Weird, huh?" Magda said with a smile. Sam nodded and began to walk towards the deck chairs. They sat down in the pale sunshine.

"Right, if it's ok, I'd like to ask you some questions about how you and your dad will be using the garden, and what's important to you. It will guide the design."

"Ok," said Magda, looking a little nervous for the first time. Sam grinned.

"Don't look so worried! I won't ask you to reveal any secrets or dig up any family skeletons!"

She received a wry smile in response.

"So—do you and your dad like to be with lots of people, or are you more likely to be on your own? Or with only a few people?"

"We don't, like, actually do a lot of entertaining, but I know my dad loves it when we go to my grandparents in Zurich and they have all their friends round. We've been living in apartments for ages, so we've never really had the luxury of a garden before."

"And would you use the garden for entertaining?"

"Absolutely! Nanna and Opa—my grandparents—are always having parties in their garden. We have an awesome time when we visit, normally, although we've not been for a while. And when we go to my godfather's place in Ireland, there's just masses of people around which is always a blast!"

"Right." Sam scribbled a note. "I didn't see any signs when I came in, but do you have any pets?"

"No, my mother didn't even want me to have a goldfish!" Magda laughed. "She was allergic to fur, so anything with four legs was never going to happen. It would never have been practical, anyway, I spent all my summers in Zurich when I was younger, so whatever pet I had would have been on its own."

"Ok, what do you like doing? And what does your father like doing?"

Magda paused, as if deciding how much to tell her. "I like all sorts of things—but I do really like playing tennis with my dad. And walking."

"Well, do you want a tennis court or a garden?"

"Oh, a garden, defo! I play at the club."

Of course you do, thought Sam.

"And your father?"

"He works quite a lot, but we used to do, like, entertaining at the weekends in Manchester."

"What's your favourite place in the world?"

"Before we moved here, I would have said Nanna and Opa's house in Zurich...now, it's a toss-up between here," she gestured at the house, "and school. My dad always used to say Florence and Tuscany were his favourite places in the world. We have an apartment in Florence."

How nice. Still, Lisbeth did say they were loaded...

"What do you like about living here?" Sam asked, swallowing the twinge of envy.

"I like the space here, and all the trees, and the fact it's so green. I also like the sense of having people just around the corner. I didn't really get that in Manchester, even though we lived in a block with *loads* of other people," Magda said thoughtfully. "I think my dad also wanted more space. The flat was, like, *huge*, but lots of it was open plan, which made it less private. Does that make sense?"

Sam nodded, writing.

"I think this house suits dad more. He's, like, a bit traditional in outlook, so I think he likes all the wood and stuff."

"And what about your favourite way to pass an evening? Do you like curling up with a book? Going dancing? A nice meal out? Some of these could be designed into the garden, you see."

"I like all those."

"Do either of you like open fires?"

"I *love* open fires!" Magda said eagerly. "We used to go to a ski lodge with a fire pit which was just awesome!"

"Your dad too?"

"Yes, he's quite fit, and he runs—or at least he did before he got ill. We go to the Greek islands more in the summer now rather than hiking—more relaxing stuff than energetic."

Sam shot a glance at Magda. "So, is your dad a barbecue fiend?"

"Oh yeah, Dad really loves a barbecue. He's quite a good cook, actually—he cooks a brilliant Sunday lunch. He hasn't had much time with work over the last few years."

Bit of a workaholic then, thought Sam.

"Do you go for long holidays?"

"Why do you want to know that?" Magda stared at her.

"If you're away for months in the summer, we'd need to put in an irrigation system to make sure the plants survived."

"Oh, I see. Not really—our holidays last about ten days, I suppose. Dad won't be absent from the business longer than that." She stopped and then grinned. "And he's not packed me off to a six-week summer camp yet!"

"Give him a chance?"

"Nah... He wouldn't dare try it. I don't think."

Sam looked down her notes. "Do you think you're looking for a formal, or an informal garden?"

"No idea—is the difference as simple as it sounds?"

Sam laughed.

"Sort of. Let me show you." Sam found a photo of Villandry on her phone from her trip the previous year. Magda screwed up her nose.

"Ugh. Not keen. Looks a bit stiff—all those hedges!"

Sam nodded. "It has its own charm, but it's not for relaxing, I agree. Now this is informal," she thumbed the images to find one of Giverny. "This is where Monet got his inspiration for his water lilies painting."

"Well, I know which one I prefer, but what goes with the house?"

Hmm. Bright young thing, aren't you?

"Great question—your house is Edwardian, so if we were going to simply match it, we'd be looking at the Arts and Crafts movement, which is a mix of both formal and informal..." she thumbed through her photos again. "No, I don't have a photo, but you can Google it to have a look. But do you *like* the style of the house enough to carry it into the garden design?"

"Oh yes, I love it! Dad does too, I think. I used to think Dad liked quite modern stuff—you know, the hotels we stay in—but he seems more relaxed here, you know? Mind you," she added with a giggle, "perhaps that's because I'm at school all week and out of his hair!"

"Is it just the two of you? Does he entertain friends here?"

"It's just the two of us so far," Magda said, her face closing. Sam shifted uncomfortably and grabbed her tea. "Dad normally takes his girlfriends out to dinner. I rarely see them. Except at breakfast."

Girlfriends, plural? Was there a rota? Magda, seeming to read her face, grinned at her.

"I think my dad and your dad sound a bit alike," she said cheekily. Sam stiffened. Her dad had been devoted to her mother. Well, up until she died, obviously.

"I see. Right. Well, if it's a fine evening and it's just the two of you, where might you sit after dinner?"

"Well, we've not done it yet, but I think here, don't you? When the sun goes down, it shines between the trees and I think this part of the patio is quite sheltered. I like this particular spot a lot."

"OK. Just a couple more questions and then I'm done, I think. Favourite colours? Are you looking for a 'scheme' with only a few colours, or would you like lots of different colours and flowers?"

Magda grinned. "Come and have a look at this, and then you'll see."

She led the way into the house and Sam looked with interest at the furniture which had clean lines, but looked comfortable, in soft shades of grey and cream. The rug at her feet was a mix of cherry red, dark turquoise, and dark grey. It looked quietly luxurious. She already knew the answer to her question when she saw the painting.

"Oh, wow!" she breathed.

The painting was big, probably three feet across and two feet high, and it was an abstract starburst of colour, purples flaunted against jade, pink and gold. Flashes of yellow and lime green mixed in, and she stood for a moment, just looking. She loved it.

Sam turned to see Magda watching her reaction. She thought the teenager looked pleased.

"Well, that answers *that* question!" Sam said. She got out her notebook again.

"Do you both like modern art, or are you happier with something more traditional?"

Magda thought about it, her head on one side. Sam absently noted the dark curls brush Magda's cheek, and was struck again by the green of her eyes. Once again, something tugged at her memory.

"Well, yes...I like all the curly bits on the Paris Metro—that's art nouveau, isn't it? I've never thought about it before, to be honest."

"What about sculpture in the garden? Do you think you would like that?"

"That would be awesome! Dad likes...that bloke who does all the stuff outside in Yorkshire." Magda frowned in concentration. Sam's mind went blank for a second and then she grabbed the reference.

"Henry Moore?"

"That's it!"

"I think even your budget won't run to a Henry Moore," Sam said wryly, "but we'll see what we can substitute."

Outside again, Sam looked down her list of questions. "Veg? Will you want to grow your own veg?"

"No, I'm at school during the week normally and Dad won't have time."

"And finally—do you garden at all? Do you or your dad have any interest in it?"

Magda gazed at the garden for a moment before replying. "Me? I don't know much about it—yet. But I *am* interested, and I love fresh flowers in the house. It would be mega cool to be able to pick them from our own garden! Opa and Nanna have a big garden and Dad likes getting his hands dirty when he gets away from the office, but it's more of a holiday thing, you know?"

Sam took a deep breath. She finished writing and closed her notebook.

"Is that enough?"

More than enough, thought Sam. *Quite a lot of food for thought here.*

8

"Can I bring the meeting to order?" Desmond pulled himself to his full five foot seven inches and puffed out his chest. Sam hid a smile. Amanda was right, he really did look like a pigeon.

The vicar, Tom Sanderson, began to report what he'd found about the development. "The planning objectives for the local area have the usual stuff—preserving the local character, sustainable development, etcetera, etcetera, but primarily, the protection of the Green Belt. Sadly, all this is forgotten because the Council needs to meet its five-year housing plans. They're expected to deliver more than two and a half thousand homes between now and the end of the decade—" Tom squinted down at his notes, "—and currently, they're behind by about thirty-five percent. This development would put them back on track for their target."

There were murmurs of concern.

"I couldn't get a straight answer from the chap I know who works in the planning department. Everyone I've spoken to at the Council is tight-lipped, which I think means the Council is for it."

Well, that's very depressing, thought Sam.

Susan Miles, looking even more faded in beige and white this evening, spoke at length, and not terribly clearly about bats. Appropriately, it was Tom, with the patience of a saint, who pulled the information out of her so the rest of the meeting could make sense of her garbled notes. In short, to threaten the habitat of bats was illegal —even if there were none inhabiting the site when development began.

"So if there *are* bats on the site, and the developers don't know and start work, then—they're breaking the law?" asked Amanda.

Susan nodded vigorously.

"Developers can only work on the site if they have obtained a special licence," she explained, beaming.

"And are these licences easy to get?" Sam asked.

"I'm not sure—it depends whether the Secretary of State is involved," Susan said, suddenly gloomy. Thinking of the slug-like creature in the Cabinet whose protestations of protecting the countryside seemed to be accompanied by an increase in the number of homes built on Green Belt land, Sam felt even more depressed.

"The good news," said Susan, brightening, "is that it is *quite* clear —if you carry out work affecting bats or roosts without a license you will be breaking the law. The penalties are harsh."

"Such as?" asked Mrs Pratchett, obviously hoping for something of the 'hung-drawn-and-quartered' level of severity. Sam noted with some surprise Mrs Pratchett didn't look very well, and her dog, normally a constant companion, was nowhere to be seen.

"A fine, up to six months in prison and forfeiture of vehicles, plant and machinery," said Susan promptly. Mrs Pratchett looked disappointed.

"Well, that might put a spoke in Anglo's wheel," muttered Amanda.

"Not for long—I imagine they have deep pockets," responded Sam.

Desmond's piggy eyes watched their conversation and he said loudly, "Ms Devereux, did you find anything about the environmental impact?"

Amanda spoke up at once. "Normally, a development of this size wouldn't need any environmental consideration, *but*, because we're near a 'sensitive' area,"—Amanda mimed quote marks—"it *is* one of the requirements."

Sam frowned.

"That's strange—I didn't see it in the documentation, did you, Jenny?" Jenny shook her head. "But surely they *must* do an impact report?" Sam said hotly. "The plans show the houses on Green Belt land, in an area of outstanding natural beauty, not to mention it's covered with god knows how many protected species—"

"As noted by the Conservation of Habitats and Species Regulations, 2010," put in Susan helpfully.

"—so surely, it *must* be a requirement!" Furious, she scribbled a note.

Jenny and she did a double act in presenting the potential objections to the development.

"The only other schools are in Stockwell, which is already oversubscribed and Ashton, which is ten miles away and you know what the buses are like since the Tory council cut the funding," said Sam.

"Not to mention the difference in the density between houses in the village and those planned for the new development," Jenny said, flipping over the pages in her bright green exercise book. "So yes, I think there's plenty to object to, without even referencing the fact it's on Green Belt land!"

There was some nodding of heads.

"Excellent work, Mrs Sanderson," Desmond said, ignoring Sam. "Would you mind drafting something for me to look at?"

Jenny Sanderson gave him a straight look. "I'll work with Sam and draft something for *all* of us to look at, certainly, Mr Black. I'm sure everyone will want to agree any letter we send." Desmond pursed his lips but said nothing and moved on to Mrs Pratchett.

"Well, I've started the ball rolling and so far, one hundred and thirty-seven people have indicated they'd be glad to support us either through sending a letter or signing our petition—I've offered both. Once we have the letter, we can begin in earnest. I realise this isn't many people at the moment," she glared as Susan sniffed loudly in distain, "but I haven't really had much time because of m 'dog…"

Mrs Pratchett's brown eyes filled with tears and her squat figure seemed to sag. She searched around frantically for a handkerchief and sniffed again. Sam, alarmed, bent her head to Amanda.

"What's happened?"

"Bertie the bulldog is unwell," said Amanda, eyeing the normally redoubtable Mrs Pratchett with sympathy. "On his last legs, apparently. He must be about seventeen which is…" she did some quick calculations in her head "…about a hundred and twenty in human years."

Jenny patted Mrs Pratchett on the shoulder, who nodded and took a deep breath. "So we can begin as soon as we have the letter," she finished in a bit of a rush and blew her nose. Susan rolled her eyes and then subsided as Jenny and the vicar both glared at her.

Desmond, also a little taken aback, was just about to declare the meeting closed, when Sam put her hand up.

"Yes, Ms Winterson?" he said frostily.

"You were going to talk to some of your mates on the council," Sam reminded him. "What came of that?"

Desmond had obviously done a lot of legwork in the Dog and Duck. "Ah. Yes, I have indeed discussed the matter with several of the councillors," he said. "They're split in their opinion, so I might have to work a little harder to bring them round to our way of thinking. But as Mrs Pratchett said, it'll be a more solid conversation when we have the letter."

"Split? Who's for and who's against?" Sam pressed. Desmond looked irritated, glancing again at the clock and his disappearing drinking time just as Tom said firmly, "Yes, we need to know what we're up against, Desmond. Spill the beans, old chap."

In a long-suffering voice which gradually become more self-important, Desmond told the group he'd met five councillors on the planning committee. Two were strongly in favour of the development, two against, and one undecided. All were Conservative councillors except for the undecided, who was independent.

"*Why* do they support it?" asked Amanda.

"Because of the number of houses they need to build," he

responded. "Those against are appalled at the idea of building on Green Belt land and would welcome our comments on the proposal."

"And the independent? What's his position?" asked Sam.

"*Her* position," Desmond corrected with a barely hidden sneer. "She's a proper leftie—wants homes for the masses and is quite prepared to go with the majority if the plans achieve those homes. She's currently undecided and wants to look at the *facts*..."

Sam raised her voice. "If she's left-leaning, perhaps I should have gone to see her, rather than you, Desmond."

"By all means speak to her if you think she is a comrade-in-arms," Desmond, a lifelong Conservative, said loftily as he closed the meeting. Sam took the name of the councillor. She'd have a chat with her previous fling in the Labour group and see what she could learn. He'd been very keen to exchange numbers—he'd surely be happy to give her the information she wanted.

"Coming for a drink?" asked Amanda as she finally locked the library doors.

"Yeah, just the one."

The bar at the Dog and Duck was busy for once. Sam went to get the drinks and was waiting to be served when she became aware of someone staring at her from the end of the bar. Turning her head, she looked straight into a pair of green eyes under frowning brows. She started, resisting the urge to duck her head, and stared back. Ah yes, the mystery man from before. She'd not forget those eyes in a hurry, but she had forgotten how tall he was. He was dressed a bit formally for a Thursday at the local pub, in tan leather jacket and expensive-looking, well-cut trousers. His jaw was strong, clean shaven and she noticed beautiful hands around his pint. His watch probably cost a small fortune.

She waved her hand to catch the eye of the bar girl who finally noticed her.

He was still looking at her when she paid for the drinks and as she turned to face him, she raised her eyebrows, a pleasant smile on her face.

"Hello again," she said, as she picked up the glasses.

"Hello to you too," he said slowly, in a voice which was the vocal equivalent of dark chocolate. Sam's libido swooned and she turned quickly, almost spilling her drink. He frowned. "I feel we've met, but I've no idea where."

Sam stared.

"Well, I've seen you before in this pub…" she said.

"Hmm. No, before that."

"I'm sure I'd have remembered you!" Sam laughed. He smiled.

"I hope that's a compliment!"

Oh no, not going there.

"Nice to keep you wondering," Sam said and turned away from the bar.

She could almost feel his eyes follow her to the table where Amanda was sitting, thankfully occupied with her mobile phone. She felt tingles in places she thought might have been dormant.

The next time she risked a glance to the bar, he was with a beautiful blonde whose simple black dress—also too expensive for the pub—shrieked 'designer'. Sam sighed inwardly, told her libido to shut up, and drank her wine.

"She's great! I think she's going to get on with Dad," Magda enthused. "But thank heavens her column won't carry her photo! That might really mess us up. I'll hide the paper for a few weeks until she's got the contract." The two girls were sprawled over Lisbeth's bed, ostensibly studying French verbs.

"I imagine they'll have very different outlooks, with your Dad being fairly—um—*traditional,* and everything," said Lisbeth doubtfully.

Magda grinned at her.

"You mean he's the CEO of a corporation and she's an avowed socialist?"

"Well, that and the fact Sam dislikes *most* things conservative and

The Garden Plot

corporate. I don't know how she and my dad manage to sit in the same room—they're polar opposites."

"Well you mentioned that, but she owns her own business, doesn't she? Doesn't that actually make her a Tory?"

Lisbeth considered this.

"I never thought about it that way before, but I don't think she's ever voted Conservative in her life. She's even put up banners in her garden for the Green Party, I think."

"Oh, the *Greens*—" Magda waved her hand dismissively. "That's practically like throwing your vote away, isn't it? Especially around here, with your Dad. He's been the MP here for, like, *ever*, hasn't he?"

"Mmm. For the past eight years..."

Lisbeth remembered her father, white-lipped with rage as he saw the banner for another political party adorning Sam's garden wall.

"Even if she won't bloody *vote* for me, she could at least keep her opposition to herself!" he had muttered, slamming around the house.

She pulled herself back to Magda's conversation, who was saying something about her father's girlfriend.

"When they came back from Manchester, she was on about going out to dinner in some fancy place just outside Ashton, but Mrs Brown just said anyone could see Dad was knackered!" Magda said gleefully. "Dad smoothed it over, of course, but he *was* looking tired."

"Is she still here?"

"Yes, but I reckon she'll get bored soon and leave," Magda sounded confident.

"Well, we'll have to see if your dad likes the designs, but I'll be honest, I'm still not sure if they'll get on, even if they *are* both in business," Lisbeth said. "And I don't imagine your dad's girlfriend is going to sit by and just watch your dad fall for someone else, though, is she?"

Magda just grinned.

"I'm sure I'll think of something," she said.

Jonas stared at the screen. It was rare he was rendered speechless, but the design had taken his breath away. The lines of it, the graceful curves, even the sculpture, blended perfectly with the house. The proposed planting—with some vivid oranges and purples and blues—was perfectly in line with his taste, and he loved the planting area by the wall which made the most of the sun trap by the old tree. The lawn area was made a bit smaller, but the way in which Sam Winterson had re-designed the borders made that a blessing, rather than a loss. There were steps down from the patio doors which made the connection between the house and the garden, as though the two had been designed together, not 100-plus years apart.

He sat back in his chair. This Samuel Winterson really did know his stuff. These designs were brilliant, and although he had been expecting something good—Lisbeth's garden had been lovely, as Magda had pointed out—he hadn't expected anything of this calibre. Jonas wondered briefly if Connor knew of this Sam Winterson and if he had a view. He texted him on the spur of the moment. A few minutes later, Connor's text came back.

Never heard of him.

Ah well, thought Jonas, after acknowledging Connor's text. He looked again at the plans and the visuals and thought if Sam had ever designed anything for one of the big competitions. If not, he certainly ought to.

He got to his feet and went to the window to look out. The garden had been long neglected, he thought. He was trying to picture what the design would look like in reality, when the phone rang.

"Keane."

"Hello, Mr Keane, this is Dr Walters. I'm ringing with the results of the tests you had last week."

"Am I going to die?" Jonas said, attempting humour.

"You know you should never ask that question of a doctor, Mr Keane," came Dr Walters' amused voice down the line. "No, you're not going to die—not yet at least—but I bet you're not feeling fully fit, are you?"

Jonas gave a short laugh, lowering himself into an armchair. "No I'm not, and I suppose you're about to tell me why."

"Your white blood cell count is still low and so are the levels of iron in your system. I'll send through another prescription for you, and remember please, you should be taking it very easy—no stress, not too much excitement and most definitely, no work."

Jonas sighed.

"Ok, I hear you."

"Good. How are you sleeping?"

"Like a log."

"Well, that will help. *Are* you managing to keep away from work?"

"I have one conference call a week," grated Jonas.

"Excellent! I know with a blood count like this, you'll be tired—when does it hit you?"

"It depends—when I have the conference call, I can feel like a nap in the afternoon, other than that, I start to flag about four. I'm almost asleep by about ten."

"Hmmm. I'm going to prescribe you some iron tablets and I'd like you to start eating more red meat. In about a fortnight's time, try some gentle—*gentle*—exercise. Swimming is great, otherwise a little walking. No more than twenty minutes a day. Oh, and drink a pint of Guinness a few times a week."

Jonas wondered if the doctor soap opera on TV was missing its physician.

"Any vitamins?" he enquired.

"No, it's all a load of rubbish. No evidence," came the brisk response.

"And how long do I need to keep this up?"

"Why, until you feel able to dispense with my services, Mr Keane," Dr Walters said. "I'll want to see you back here in three weeks' time, please, for more blood tests. I'll send an appointment."

Jonas sat looking at the phone for five minutes after the call had finished, cursing.

Rousing himself, he looked at the clock. Only a quarter to eleven. At this rate, even if his mystery illness didn't kill him, the boredom might. He ought to be grateful Magda was back for half term, otherwise he'd be climbing the walls.

His eyes fell again on the plans on his laptop. At least they were cheering him up. Still, he hadn't looked at the cost yet...he started to search through the email.

And again, he was surprised. Familiar with the costs of hard landscaping, he could recognise at a glance that the materials were appropriate, and the mark-up—if there was one—was modest. Winterson's certainly didn't look to be a firm which took its customers for a ride and he warmed to the proposals anew. He also felt again a glowing pride that *Magda* had searched out the firm and made a good call in choosing them to do the designs. When she got back from whatever nail bar she was at, he would congratulate her.

Rubbing his hands together, he clicked out of his email—after all, Neil wasn't due to report until tomorrow—and went back to his newspaper. He might also go to the local pub at lunchtime with Gerry, if she managed to get out of bed. He needed the exercise, and to see if he could stomach a pint of Guinness. He tried not to think about the blonde.

Magda was speaking excitedly, her hands under the nail lamp at Lola's. "The designs were just brilliant! I can't wait to hear what Dad has to say."

"What about the cost?" asked Lisbeth.

Magda shrugged. "I didn't look closely, but it seemed all right. If dad likes the design, it won't matter much. And anyway," Magda added, "it *is* my money!"

"What are you going to do when they meet? Your dad thinks Aunty Sam is a man."

Magda grinned. "Duh! That's why I've left him alone with the plans. If there's one thing Dad *can't* resist, it's good workmanship! I'm also hoping he'll think it's because I'm *his* daughter that I've found such a brilliant designer. By the time I get back, he'll have fallen in love with the designs just like I did. Sam could be a Martian and he'd still want her to do the work!"

Lisbeth was uneasy. She knew Aunty Sam had taken the death of grandad very hard and anything which dragged up those memories—even something as ridiculous as a mistake over his name—might be hurtful.

She also found it hard to believe Jonas could be *so* old-fashioned that he wouldn't just laugh when he found out Aunty Sam was in fact, female. She found herself feeling anxious. Magda, watching her, saw the change in her face.

"Now don't get all freaked out on me!" she said. "It'll all be fine—they'll meet, there'll be a bit of awkwardness, and I'll tell dad I knew but wanted to play a joke on him. As long as they get thrown together, it doesn't matter, does it?"

"They might not actually *like* one another," warned Lisbeth.

"Maybe—but I know my dad, and I've met Sam, and I think it has distinct possibilities," Magda said. "I'll bet you a fiver there'll be something between them!"

Lisbeth shook her head, unconvinced.

9

Sam was awake hours before she needed to be for the meeting with the Keane family. There was something nagging her about the job, she realised, although she didn't know what. Cradling her hands round a cup of tea at five-thirty in the morning, she replayed the brief conversation she'd had with Magda.

After they'd agreed a date to meet, Magda had said, "About Dad... He can be a bit...old-fashioned about women in companies sometimes."

"Oh? In what way?"

"Um... He hasn't worked with many women and his business is quite male-dominated."

Oh great, thought Sam, reading between the lines. *He probably thinks we shouldn't have been given the vote, either. Bugger. Still, I've handled worse, I daresay.*

"Well, if he likes the designs, hopefully we'll be able to sort it out," she said. She thought she heard Magda sigh with—what? Relief?

She sipped her tea and gazed at her garden, gathering shape and colour as the light came up. No, going back through the conversation wasn't making her feel any better. She rose from the kitchen table, irritated, and looked at the clock. Six. She'd go and check that Dad's grave was tidy, that would calm her down. She could still get into the office for eight. She glanced at the brightening sky.

At least the weather looks okay. I hate arguing in the rain.

～

Jonas wondered if Gerry had woken up yet. Give it another ten minutes, he thought. He looked at Magda, staring into space. He thought she looked on edge.

"Are you ok?" he asked mildly. Magda started, and looked up from the toast she was nibbling. "Me? I'm fine!" she exclaimed.

"You seem a bit...tense."

"No, not at all."

Jonas opened his mouth to speak again and Magda shot up out of her seat. She leant and gave him a brief kiss on the cheek.

"Just off to email Nanna—I want to ask her what she wants for her birthday." She left the kitchen almost at a run.

Jonas stared after her and then, shaking his head, poured a coffee to take to Gerry.

～

"You're very quiet," commented Andy as he climbed into the Land Rover. Sam gave him a faint smile.

"Yes, I am, aren't I? Probably because I'm expecting some ancient old bloke who hates women to be the final decision maker on this job."

Andy laughed. "You'll cope. I can remember how it was with your Dad and you soon got everyone round your thumb."

Sam didn't reply but started the Land Rover.

The journey didn't take long, and Sam was again struck by the beauty of the house as they pulled into the drive. Andy let out a low whistle.

"Bloody hell," he breathed. "Are there bat poles?"

Sam giggled as she parked, suddenly feeling better. After all, the designs were good—some of her best work, in fact—and if Mr Old Fashioned couldn't get over the fact a woman drew them, then that was his problem. She rubbed sweaty hands down her clean jeans and zipped her leather jacket.

Although we could really do with the work came the thought.

"They're here!" Magda swung from the window and ran to the door. "Dad? Are you ready?"

Jonas came out of the study and Magda looked him over critically. First impressions were important. She reached up and smoothed his collar at the back of his neck. Jonas looked at her quizzically.

"Am I presentable?" he asked.

"You could do with a haircut shaggy," Magda said, but really, she thought he looked as handsome as ever. His green eyes twinkled at her and she was relieved he was in a good mood. It might not last too long, she suddenly thought. She drew a breath and Jonas looked at her curiously.

"Shall we?" She took his arm and opened the door.

Sam saw Magda and a tall man at the door as she locked the Land Rover. Looking at him properly, she saw he was *very* tall. He looked familiar, she thought, but from this distance, she couldn't be sure. She glanced at Andy who grinned reassuringly at her and she grasped her portfolio case more firmly and started forwards with a smile on her face.

The tall man came towards them, Magda on his arm. Sam could see his green eyes from where she stood, and she recognised him as the expensively dressed man from the pub. He was as handsome on this view as he had been on the first.

Oh my, was the first thought that went through her head. *Magda is NOT the child of aging parents, then!*

Oh good God, what did I say to him at the pub? Was the second thought. He looked at her, startled recognition dawning in his eyes.

"Hello, I'm Jonas Keane, Magda's father. I think we've met at the pub? And aren't you on the website with long hair?" He smiled and without waiting for a response, he thrust his hand out to Andy. "Could Sam not make the meeting? I wanted to congratulate him on a first-class design job."

Sam's smile, already wobbly when thinking about their exchanges at the pub, faltered even more, and she flicked a glance to Magda.

"Um... I'm Sam—short for Samantha. I designed the garden."

There was an awkward pause as Jonas took in this information and looked at Sam.

"Ah. I was expecting Samuel."

Oh-oh...

Despite the pleasantness of his tone, his voice was now more formal.

"That's my father," said Sam. "He died eighteen months ago, and I took over the company. I'm the garden designer and director of WGD."

Another pause.

"I can see you're under a misapprehension," said Sam as lightly as she could. "I'm Samantha, I developed the plans for the garden, and I'm not my dad. I cut my hair about six months ago. Is there a problem?"

Jonas turned to his daughter, his eyebrows raised.

Magda grinned. "Well dad, you really *did* like the plans, didn't you? You said they were the work of a genius, so I don't think it matters that it's Sam, rather than her father who did them. Does it?"

Jonas shook his head, as if to clear it and gazed at Sam, who looked back at him steadily.

"My daughter is often telling me my attitude is that of a dinosaur," he finally said. "She's possibly quite right, and I owe you an apology, Ms Winterson. The plans *are* fantastic, and I'm delighted to meet the designer who created them. The photo I saw of you on the website might have been old, and it also featured Andy here, hence the confusion. I obviously didn't read the text closely enough. I like your short hair. And I'm very sorry for your loss."

Sam was nonplussed at this sudden change of direction and could feel a blush starting to colour her cheeks. She finally put her hand out and he shook it. His hand felt cool and firm.

"So, shall we start again?" she said, striving for some of his suavity. "My name's Sam Winterson and I own WGD. This is Andy Jackson, my assistant, who's in charge of any hard landscaping we do."

The meeting moved smoothly on after this. Magda skipped about, obviously pleased with herself, Jonas continued to be pleasant, although Sam felt minutely scrutinised. While they walked through the garden in the weak sunshine, she took out the plans, and talked through the decisions and the materials they planned to use.

Andy was calmly supportive, disagreeing on one suggestion Jonas made about the paving, and agreeing with another about the walls surrounding the lawn.

Given the start, she thought after an hour, *it's been ok, despite what he might remember from the pub. I wonder what he'll say about the budget.*

But in the end, it wasn't the budget that caused the tension to flare again.

"When can you start?" Magda asked.

"In about a week, I would say, which will give us time to get the hard landscaping samples to you," Andy replied. "With reasonable weather, I think it will take three and a half months—that's what you had in the project plan, isn't it?" He looked at Sam, who nodded. *Three months and two days, to be precise.*

"How many in the team—four? Five?" asked Jonas.

"Three—Andy, Steve our new apprentice, and me," Sam said, putting her plans back into the portfolio.

"Really? That's it?"

Sam paused.

"Ye-e-e-s," she said carefully. "That's our team."

"I'd quite like the garden finished this year, rather than next," Jonas said, smiling with his teeth, but not his eyes.

The Garden Plot

Sam closed the portfolio with a bit of a snap.

"Mr Keane, we *have* done this before, many times. If I didn't think it was possible to do this in the time on the schedule, I wouldn't have sent *this* schedule, I'd have sent another one. We can certainly deliver with three of us."

"You're going to be on site?"

Andy sucked in a breath. Sam hung on to her temper with an effort. "What did you imagine, Mr Keane?"

"Let's just say you don't look the sort to be carting around bags of manure," Jonas said.

"Dad!" Even Magda looked indignant.

"When my father owned WGD I was expected to do my share of the digging and I'm quite used to it," said Sam.

Jonas looked her up and down and even from here, Sam could see something flare in his eyes.

"Right." Was his only comment. Sam glanced at Andy to see his jaw jut.

Time to be firm before there's a punch-up.

"Just to be clear then, I will be working on the project—in a physical capacity, manure-carting and all—and we should be able to keep to the schedule that I forwarded with the plans," she said.

"*Should* be able to keep to the schedule?" Jonas pounced. Out of the corner of her eye she saw Andy tense again.

"*Will*," Sam said with determined patience. And smiled at him, sunnily.

"Do we have a contract, Mr Keane?"

It took a second for him to answer.

"Yes, I suppose we do."

"Great. If you like we could see if we could bring forward the start date to later this week, rather than next?" she looked at Andy, who nodded.

"That would be great!" said Magda, clearly relieved. "*Wouldn't it Dad?*" She elbowed him discreetly.

Jonas nodded, looking at Sam consideringly. "Yes," he said. "It would be great."

"I'll check the office diary and come back to you formally with a date, then," Sam held out her hand to Jonas. He gripped it, she thought, unnecessarily hard, and kept it for a fraction too long.

Pulling away, she turned to Magda and was surprised to receive a hug and a kiss on both cheeks.

"This is going to be brilliant!" Magda grinned at her, and Sam smiled gently.

"Yes, I'm sure it will," she said. Then they left.

After Sam and Andy had driven off, Magda bit her lip as her father looked at her.

"Why didn't you tell me Sam was a woman? I felt a bit of an idiot and I don't appreciate it, young lady!"

Oh dear, thought Magda. I've turned into a 'young lady'.

"Well, it was probably a good thing I didn't tell you! Sam wouldn't have got a look-in, would she?" she defended herself. "Your views on women are *so* last century, Dad! You thought the designs were *brilliant!* Does it matter what sex the designer is?"

"Gender," corrected Jonas. "You could have told me before they arrived, *after* I'd seen the plans! I told you how wonderful I thought they were! Then they'd have been through the door anyway!"

"But how *hard* a time would you have given her?" shot back Magda. Jonas scowled.

"Well, thanks for the vote of confidence!" he huffed. "That's very unfair—"

"Are you *sure,* Dad?" said Magda. Jonas was silent, and Magda, seeing his face, wondered if she'd gone too far.

"I don't know why you have this, like, *thing* about women. Wasn't mum in business, like you?" she finally said. His gaze snapped to hers.

"Yes, so focused on business she had time for *nothing else*! I don't think a woman's place is in the home, but really—do you think Sam should be humping around bags of compost?"

"If she wants to! And she obviously *does*!" Magda protested. "And I should tell you, Dad, *I'm* interested in the garden—would it be a problem if *I* wanted to hump around bags of manure?"

"Do you?" he asked, looking appalled.

"Surely that's beside the point! But whatever, I *will* want to earn my own living, like Sam does!"

"That's different," he said after a pause. She couldn't see quite *how* it was different. She shook her head.

"But really, Dad, what *did* you think I was going to do after school? Just find a rich bloke and live off them? Or flit around painting my nails and attending gallery openings?" She couldn't resist the dig at Gerry. "Why bother sending me to a private school if afterwards I can't do anything I want to do?"

Jonas looked as though she'd struck him. Uncomfortable seeing him lost for words, she changed the subject.

"Look, Dad, I know it's my money, but you *are* happy with it all, aren't you?"

"Yes, of course!" He seemed to pull himself together and the firmness of his response reassured her. "The finished gardens I've seen are excellent, really well done."

"But?"

"No, there's no but, although I do wonder how a slip of a girl like that will manage the project *and* do the digging, too!"

"There you go again, Dad!" Madga shook her head. "Making assumptions. They'll put you in a museum if you're not careful!"

"Why are they putting you in a museum?" Gerry's languid voice asked from the door.

Magda swung away and watched with irritated as Jonas rose to his feet and kissed Gerry. "I have old fashioned views," he said to her.

"Really? I hadn't noticed," she said, smiling and tossing her hair over her shoulder.

"Thank goodness. Do you want some lunch?"

10

Jonas reined in his frustration. He didn't like the hint of evasiveness that had crept into Tyler Fairchild's voice as they had gone through the meeting.

Tyler had done his best to 'economise' on the specification for the development and invited a couple of suppliers to tender who wouldn't have come within a country mile of the work had Jonas been in sole charge.

He listened to Neil ask some innocuous questions about the public consultation.

"Look, it's all under control," insisted Tyler. "We've had some feedback, sure, but the important thing is that we have some support on the planning committee who are, after all, going to make the final decision."

"What sort of feedback? From whom?" asked Neil.

"Oh, just the normal NIMBY response—residents concerned about the site traffic, the usual stuff."

There was a silence and Jonas waited.

"OK, there seems to be some sort of petition, but it's nothing we can't handle—the PR company is already on it," came the exasperated voice of Tyler down the line.

"And exactly what are the objections in the petition?" Neil's voice was level.

"Just as I said—site traffic, concerns over wildlife, and the access from the main road out of Derbyshire," said Tyler.

"How do we know this?" interjected Jonas.

"We've had word from one of the planning officers," said Tyler.

Jonas frowned. Planning officers should be independent until the recommendation to the planning committee. That one of them was passing information to Tyler's staff didn't bode particularly well for the ethics of the authority—or indeed Anglo Homes.

"But we've briefed the PR agency, as I said and they're working on putting our side of the story to the local press," Tyler insisted.

Phone clamped to his ear, Jonas searched his desk for the as yet unread local paper. As the conversation continued, with Neil getting shorter and more direct in his questioning, Jonas leafed through the pages. There it was. So, it hadn't made the front page—which was something—but there was a large item on page three, with the headline *New Homes to Desecrate Wildlife Haven*.

He closed his eyes in frustration. He opened his mouth to say something about the story and then thought better of it. Neither Tyler nor John knew he was in Sherton and might well ask where he'd seen the local press coverage. So instead, he said casually:

"Has there been any local coverage?"

"We're waiting to hear from the PR agency," said Tyler.

After the meeting, as planned, Neil called back.

"Jonas, I'm starting to get an uncomfortable feeling about this," he said.

"And you'd be right to, I'm looking at the coverage in the local paper right now, and it does not make for happy reading."

He read the headline to Neil.

"Christ, that's all we need," Neil responded with a sigh.

"'A housing development for three hundred-plus new homes in Sherton will threaten a precious wildlife habitat, campaigners have warned,'" read Jonas. "'Campaigners believe property giant Anglo Homes is building too close to Jessop's Field, a protected area of natural beauty. 'This development will place unsustainable demand on local amenities as well as eating into the Green Belt land which characterises the area,' said Mr Desmond Black, chairman of Sherton Environment Protection Group which campaigned successfully against the Stockwell bypass two years ago. 'We've seen the plans and we think we the council should be gravely concerned about the environmental impact of the building work,' he said. Council officers refused to comment, saying the consultation was still underway.'"

"Well, not good, but not yet a disaster," said Neil.

"I think I'll wander down and have a look at the consultation plans," mused Jonas. "It might be the campaigners are just being hysterical."

"Be careful—you don't want to be recognised, particularly looking at plans for a supposedly rival company," warned Neil. "That would be a public relations nightmare, not to mention blowing our silent partner status."

Jonas said nothing. Neil was right.

"I'll go to see the consultation as the Library's closing," he said finally. "There won't be many people about late on a weekday."

"I don't like it Jonas," Neil said. "Apart from anything else, you're supposed to be resting!"

"I know, but I don't have any other ideas—do you?"

"No," said Neil reluctantly. They talked of other projects and then Jonas said, "Neil? Could I ask you something?"

"Sure, what's up?"

"Am I... Have you ever seen me be...damn, I'm not sure how to put this." Jonas raked his hand through his hair. He wasn't used to feeling defensive. He tried again.

"Have you ever noticed me to be prejudiced against women?"

There was such a long pause, Jonas wondered if the line had been cut.

"Well...you have appointed an all-male board," Neil said finally.

"But Stephanie isn't a man," protested Jonas, thinking of his red-haired, temper-to-match finance director.

"Well, yes, but Bernard employed her, not you. I think you wanted an old—*male*—colleague, didn't you?" Neil said. Jonas was uncomfortable.

"Well, erm..."

"And remember the HR director we interviewed last year—she was a woman, and although the rest of the panel wanted to appoint her, you overrode the decision to appoint Mike instead. Ditto our recent legal post."

Jonas sat in silence.

"But what's brought all this up?" asked Neil curiously.

"Magda," sighed Jonas. "I questioned whether the woman designer we're hiring would be able to deliver our garden project with just her and two other workers."

Something suspiciously like a snort came down the phone. "What did Magda say?"

"She suggested I might be a dinosaur."

This time, Neil did laugh and after a second, Jonas joined in.

"So what you're saying is I *am* a dinosaur!"

"We-e-e-l-l..."

"Ok, Ok, I get the picture! Why has no-one said anything before?" demanded Jonas.

"I think you would have just ignored them," said Neil. "Your daughter is a brave girl—I'm not sure *I* would have had the balls to broach it with you!"

Jonas stared out of the window for a long time after he'd put down the phone. Always practical, Jonas tried to organise his memories and think through his recent interactions with women. Geraldine, of course, didn't count—he didn't need to work for a living.

And his mother had been everything Nicole despised—and vice versa, to be fair—but Niamh had never worked, she had been a homemaker for him and his father. He remembered scones, freshly made when he got home from school, pulling vegetables from the garden as she looked on, stories at bedtime—even a stern talking to when she found condoms in his pocket that time. He had always adored her and relished that she was at home. Would he invite her on to his board, knowing her quick intelligence, her magnificent social skills, her wizardry in organising things from scratch, her strength when Nicole died?

No, he wouldn't. But then again, she was his *mother*, for God's sake! She knew nothing about business.

Think of someone else, he thought, irritably. Well, how about Nicole? Looking at her dispassionately, she had possessed relentless drive, and would have seen the weaknesses of any organisation through its balance sheet in minutes. She had been completely unsentimental, even hard. More, in fact, like a man than some of the men currently *on* his board.

He caught sight of himself in the reflection of the patio doors. He looked serious and he shook his head, unbelieving. Whatever Nicole's faults at home, she had been a brilliant business executive.

And yet he still wouldn't have had her on the board. He knew that from the knot in his stomach, feeling sick as he recognised his bias for what it was—unjustified and rather horrifying.

A dinosaur, Magda had called him. That was probably about right. His personal experience had skewed his view and it was difficult to shift it to something more palatable, modern, *human*.

He stifled a groan and he knocked his head gently on the desk. Idiot, he thought. His determination to do better would start with Ms Winterton.

Certainly, it would be good to have The Boss on site throughout the build, he thought. Someone who could take decisions quickly, respond to any changes, speed up the process. Perhaps she would help with the planting when the foundations had been done. He couldn't truly imagine her picking up a shovel.

Only three and a half miles away, Sam was staring rather blindly at her drawing board, her pencil slack in her hand.

"Well, we've got the paving samples coming tomorrow," Andy said from the door and she jumped.

"That was quick," she said. "So you should be able to take them over to Brook Lodge on Friday?"

"Yes, and then we can get cracking. But aren't you coming? You do, normally."

Sam said nothing and drew a line on the paper in front of her. "Yes, but I'm sure you can handle it," she said eventually, not raising her eyes from the drawing board.

Andy came to stand in front of her with folded arms.

"I'm sure too, but why are we changing what we would usually do? Or has something come in I don't know about?"

She shook her head and smiled at him. "I think it would just avoid issues."

"What, prove to him women don't do the big, butch jobs?" he taunted. Sam flushed.

"It's nothing to do with that—"

"Then come."

Sam was silent, and Andy sighed. "Look, he's given us the job. He doesn't think you should be involved in some of it—hard landscaping would probably be one of the areas he doesn't think you either can, or should be, doing. Don't you want to prove him wrong?"

No. I'm scared.

"I didn't want to ram it down his throat."

"Why not simply think of it as an opportunity to show how knowledgeable you are?"

Another pause. "I hadn't thought of it like that," she responded reluctantly.

"So what time shall we suggest? Ten?" Andy grinned at her. She allowed herself to be persuaded.

"Sounds good."

She watched him go to make the call to Jonas and prepared to go to the Sherton Environment Protection group.

Everyone in the meeting was uncomfortable seeing Mrs Pratchett, nobly 'carrying on'—with red-rimmed eyes and an ever-present handkerchief. She was dressed, even in the mild Spring weather, top-to-toe in black. Bertie the bulldog had finally shuffled off his canine coil and Mrs Pratchett was bereft.

The group was discussing the letter of objection to the council, drafted by Sam and Jenny Sanderson. A couple of the teachers in the group had been particularly irritating this evening, Sam thought, as they changed phrases, added semi-colons ("The work of the devil in my opinion," said Jenny *sotto voce* to Sam) and generally made a nuisance of themselves without adding much value. After the fifteenth change, Amanda spoke up.

"Look, as we all agree with the general gist of the letter, shall we leave Jenny and Sam to do the changes, now they've had our input? They can copy it to everyone by email after it's gone."

There was a mass head-nodding, and Jenny patted Sam's hand, and firmly turned the page in her notebook with the amendments, closing the subject.

Mrs Pratchett gingerly rose to her feet, clasping her handkerchief.

"Now then, I can continue with the petition and we can circulate a version of the letter for people to sign and send to their ward councillor," she said, with less volume to her voice than usual. "I shall start tomorrow—it will be good to be occupied," she added, her voice quivering.

"I don't recall you being this affected by anything before," observed Susan Miles acidly. "Not even over your husband's death."

"Now, Susan," intervened Jenny as Dorothy Pratchett glared at Susan, her grief momentarily forgotten. "Dorothy, shall I come around tomorrow and you can tell me how I can be of assistance?"

"I would be most grateful," replied Mrs Pratchett, smiling in a watery way.

"I'll keep an eye on the Council website to see what other comments are made on the application," said Amanda. "And I'll keep a copy of the letter in the Library. We could do with something to tell folk about our objections."

"It so happens..." said Sam, who reached into her portfolio and pulled out several large, brightly coloured posters she'd designed and printed. The posters had the main objections, an exhortation to write to local councillors, and Desmond's email address in bold type.

Amanda grabbed the biggest one and grinning, marched over to the main notice board in the library, where she pinned it up.

"I'm not sure I want to take all the enquiries," said Desmond, seeing he might have to do something.

"Then I'll add my name to it," said Sam promptly. "I'll drop more off tomorrow."

"The consultation period comes to a close next week," said Desmond. "Have you heard from the bat people, Miss Miles?"

"I have approached the Bat Conservation Trust," she corrected, her pale eyes snapping. "They have suggested I write to the local authority to see whether a bat survey has been ordered. I sent a letter last week and will call tomorrow to check what the situation is."

Cowed, Desmond simply nodded and said, "Splendid, splendid."

"We could do with someone in authority on our side," Jenny said thoughtfully.

"We've got some meetings over the next couple of weeks with all of the councillors who sit on the planning committee," said Sam.

"Actually, I was thinking in terms of your brother-in-law," Jenny said, almost apologetically. Sam stiffened and then forced herself to relax.

"I could ask my sister to ask him if he can express an opinion," she said.

"Can't you ask him directly? Or is there a problem?" said Desmond, sniffing gossip. Sam gave him a cold look.

"I think he'll just say he doesn't get involved in local matters and decline to do anything. And that's even if he agrees with us."

Amanda nodded glumly. "Yes, he's not the greenest of MPs, is he?"

"He's a loyal Tory MP," Sam said, hating to have to defend him. "I don't agree with their policies, but his party has other priorities."

"But surely, when his own *neighbourhood* is threatened—" started Desmond.

"Look, I'll ask my sister what she thinks and approach Fraser if it's appropriate!" snapped Sam. The group fell silent and then Desmond rather awkwardly closed the meeting.

"Are you ok?" Amanda asked Sam, as they stacked chairs.

"Fine," said Sam. Amanda's eyebrows disappeared into her red-orange fringe.

"Right..."

Sam stopped, drew a deep breath and turned to face her, smiling apologetically. "I'm sorry, I have a lot on my mind at the moment."

"Fancy a chat over a drink?" Sam opened her mouth to refuse. "Not, of course, that I care about your issues, I'm just desperate for a drink," added Amanda quickly. Sam laughed and her prickliness dropped away.

"Oh, alright. I shouldn't encourage you, you're a bloody lush as it is."

Twenty minutes later in the pub, Amanda plonked a large white wine in front of Sam and sank onto the seat next to her.

"OK, what's up?"

Sam took a tentative sip of the wine. *Mmm,* she thought, *obviously a new bottle.*

"Actually, I'm not sure," she said. "We won a contract this week which is a godsend to the business, and I've started getting tentative enquiries about a new service we're offering, a sort of mini-makeover for your garden. I should be jumping for joy."

"But?"

Sam sighed. "Do you remember that tall, gorgeous bloke we saw in here a few weeks ago? That's my new customer."

"*Really*? And having this gorgeous bloke as a customer is a problem?"

"No—but what *is* a problem is that this bloke still thinks a woman's place is in the home. I can't decide whether to be amused or insulted."

Amanda laughed. "I presume you're going to be amused as there's money involved? And don't forget, he *is* easy on the eye! It'll make going to work *way* more enjoyable!"

Sam grinned. "I suppose so. But we've got a meeting on Friday and frankly, I'm dreading it. His attitude reminds me of the crap I went through when Dad started introducing me around his business contacts..."

Amanda was silent.

"I worked bloody hard to get my qualification and build my contacts out of Dad's business mates. It was only when I started demanding better service, better prices, that anyone began to take me seriously—hell, they only started to take me seriously when I went *elsewhere* for my supplies!" Sam bit out, remembering.

"And hunky client makes you feel like that? But why did he hire you if he doesn't take you seriously?"

"Oh, he loved the design—*even though* I was Samantha, not Sam!" Sam said.

"What?" Amanda listened, her mouth steadily dropping as Sam told her of the mix-up over the name.

Amanda was choking on her drink. "Sounds a pillock," she commented when she'd wiped her mouth. "Shame. He looked like a fashion model. But as you've won the contract even with this auspicious beginning, doesn't that make you feel better?"

Sam thought about it. "He makes me nervous," she said eventually. "I feel like he's going to be watching me, waiting for me to slip up."

"It may not be that bad," Amanda said soothingly. "You may just be building it up in your mind into something it's not."

"I certainly hope so," Sam said, taking a deep drink of her wine. "Otherwise the summer's going to be a nightmare."

When she opened the door to the cottage an hour or so later, she could see the flashing light on the answering machine in the darkness. She cursed as she stumbled through the door and patted her pockets for her mobile. On it, there were two missed calls from Andy's phone.

This feels like bad news, she thought as she flicked lights on, shrugged out of her jacket and toed off her boots.

"Hi Sam, hope you've had a good night." The light tones of Greg echoed round the room. "I tried to get hold of you on your mobile, but you didn't pick up. I'm ringing to say Andy probably won't be in tomorrow as he went down with a migraine this evening, and it's pretty bad. I can't imagine he'll be in any fit state to come in tomorrow—he was throwing up until about an hour ago and you know how these things affect him, poor love. So he's sorry to let you down, but hopes you understand. Anyway, I haven't seen you for *ages* sweetie, so you must come around for dinner soon. When Andy comes back to work, I'll send him with some dates. Toodle-pip!"

Sam sat with a bump on the arm of the sofa and swore viciously.

She took out her phone and sent a text to Greg, saying she'd got the message, and to tell Andy not to worry, she would be fine. She sent love and kisses too, knowing how badly Andy suffered from migraine. Then she shook her head.

It can't be helped, get a grip girl! Time to be a grown up.

11

At five to ten on Friday morning, Sam rang the doorbell at Brook Lodge. She had a number of paving samples and they were (collectively at least) quite heavy. She waited, her tension rising. She hoped Magda would also be included in the discussion which might make things a little less...fraught.

She saw movement behind the stained-glass panel in the door and her prayer that it would be Magda who opened the door went unheard.

"Sam, good to see you," said Jonas, with a faint smile.

Yeah, I bet, she thought while she smiled back brightly. "Good morning! Good to see the rain's held off, isn't it?"

"Yes, isn't it? Come in. Are you all alone?"

"Yes, I'm afraid Andy's unwell, so rather than hold up the process, I thought we could just discuss the samples and we can order the stone and get started."

"Of course," he shut the door, and Sam was struck anew by the beauty of the house, its soft golden wood floors and gentle, but insistent wealth.

*How the other half lives...*she thought with a tiny stab of envy. Then she scolded herself. She had plenty, more than most.

The entrance hall was wide and tall, with a central staircase which rose before splitting to form a balustrade. She gazed upwards and Jonas smiled.

"It's lovely, isn't it?" he said.

"You have a beautiful home," Sam said. "I can imagine this at Christmas, all decorated with ivy and holly..."

"We've not done any wassailing yet," he said, as he led her into what she imagined was his study. "We moved in here in January, so this coming Christmas will be our first."

He sat behind his big old desk. She sat down opposite him, feeling a bit like she was at a job interview. Which she was, in a way, she supposed.

"Is Magda joining us?" she said, putting down the satchel a little hastily—it hit the floor with a bit of a thump, and Jonas' eyebrows raised.

"Yes, I'll call her, but first..."

He paused and then said "I'm sorry about the mix-up about your dad last week. And I was out of order, implying you couldn't do the job in time. You're obviously experienced and organised, and I'm sorry our working relationship got off to such an unfortunate start."

Sam hid her surprise and just smiled. "I should spend more time keeping the website up to date."

He smiled back and she was struck again by how attractive he was. "I'll call Magda," he said, and left the room.

Sam took off her jacket, now feeling a bit hot and bothered, and sat back and blew her cheeks out as she looked at the room. It was as beautiful as the hall, cream carpets, vivid artwork on the walls and impressive looking books in the bookcases. *The odd blockbuster paperback, too* she thought, catching sight of a thriller on the arm of a leather sofa.

Jonas returned with a slender, beautiful blonde who Sam recognised from the pub. This vision looked her up and down and then, thought Sam, completely dismissed her.

"Would you like something to drink?" asked Jonas courteously.

"Strong black coffee, please," replied Sam, needing something to keep her on her mettle. "Hello, I'm Sam."

"Gerry," replied the blonde, nodding regally at her. "I'll make the coffee."

"That's good of you, Gerry," said Jonas, smiling.

Her laugh tinkled, putting Sam's already stretched nerves on edge.

"Don't be silly, I know my way around. You stay and talk to the gardener." She glided out. Magda, bouncing through the door, checked as she saw her.

They were left to talk about the weather for the five or so minutes before Gerry brought the drinks. She kissed Jonas on the top of his head and glided out again, saying something about a call.

Magda, Sam noted, visibly relaxed as Jonas' girlfriend left the room. Sam had some inkling of how Magda felt—Gerry made Sam feel somehow...*dumpy*.

Sam reached for her bag. "We use mostly grey and cream stone," she began, laying the samples carefully on the floor. "We source ours locally. This way we can be sure the stone is quarried ethically."

"There's an ethical issue with stone?" Magda jumped in.

"It depends where it comes from—some suppliers use stone from China and India and there's a potential problem with child labour," said Jonas, before Sam could respond, looking at the samples. "Some of my work includes this kind of issue," he added casually as she stared at him in surprise.

"You're very well informed," she murmured, before pulling herself together and continuing to talk about frost damage, and how slippery stone could be in the wet. Jonas nodded, and she thought she saw a dawning respect in his eyes, as she continued.

"We've brought the stone samples we think will best suit the design and the house, but obviously, you're free to choose others," she finished carefully.

"Should we see them in the garden?" asked Magda and Sam nodded.

"Ideally, yes."

"I'll get some shoes on. See you outside!" Magda said, turning on her heel and dashing off upstairs.

Sam made to put the samples back in her satchel, cursing silently as the flap of her bag frustrated her.

"Let me help," Jonas said, taking the bag from her and holding it open. Sam caught his scent as she placed the slabs in the bag and was uneasily aware of his proximity. Jonas huffed as the last sample went in and he tested its weight.

"Yes, you certainly *are* strong," he commented, and she noticed his arms bracing to take the weight. "I don't think I would have wanted to drag that far!" He grinned at her and she was suddenly a little breathless as his green eyes twinkled. Flushing a little, she held out her hand.

"Oh no, I'm sure you *can* carry it alone, but allow me. Please," he added after a minuscule pause.

"Before I start carting around bags of manure?" she asked sweetly.

He grunted quietly as he hefted the bag on to his shoulder and opened the patio doors onto the garden. "Indeed. After you?"

She stepped down into the garden and seemed to feel his eyes burning into the back of her neck. She smoothed her hair.

Her flat shoes sank into the wet grass and she wished for her boots. *Sensible footwear, Sam*, she thought ruefully.

As she strode across the garden, Jonas kept pace with her easily, his long legs eating up the ground. Glancing sideways at him, Sam was aware of a strength about him. It wasn't just that he was tall, he was *powerful*.

Like he's really used to getting his own way, she thought wryly. *I wonder what his illness is...*

They stopped by the garden wall and she turned to get the samples. A breath of wind swept across her arms and neck and she shivered, wishing she had her jacket. Even under her sweater, she could feel the goose bumps. She took the satchel from him.

"I'll get your coat," said Jonas abruptly and turned on his heel and marched away, to Sam's surprise. After a second staring after him, she placed the samples on the ground and rubbed her arms, peering up at the sky. No rain, at least.

Jonas returned with her coat, with Magda in tow. She zipped it thankfully.

Flicking a glance at Jonas, who seemed entranced by the samples, Sam began to talk about them. Jonas, she noticed, was a little short. She wondered what had changed his mood.

They chose the grey, picking up the tones of the hydrangea she planned to plant, and contrasting with the sunny yellow crocosmia which was also in the plan.

As they walked the rest of the garden, the plan fell into place in her head; Sam's palms itched to get a trowel in her hand and start work.

Magda grinned at her. "You can't wait, can you?" she said.

Sam smiled ruefully while Jonas looked steadily at her. "No," she said. "I like to see changes come quickly."

"As, I imagine, do your clients," said Jonas. "After all, that's what they're paying you for."

Well, that's killed the atmosphere, thought Sam, amused and annoyed in equal measure.

"Yes, I hope our clients get as enthused as I do," she said blithely. "We try and involve them in the various stages of the build as it goes on, and we often take them to the wholesalers so they can choose the plants."

"Mmm, a good idea," he said. They returned to the house in silence.

"Right, well, we'll get these ordered and when I've got a date for delivery, I'll come back to you with a date to actually start work," she said, hefting her bag on to her shoulder and patting her pockets for the keys to the Land Rover.

Magda beamed at her. "Awesome! It's going to be epic!"

Sam laughed. "Perhaps you could let me know when there will be someone in the house? We can reach the garden without disturbing you, but it's always good to know when people are about."

Jonas smiled without much humour. "I'll be around most days, Magda will be going back to school next week."

Oh, goody. That's all I need—misery guts hanging around, thought Sam. "Excellent," she said. "You'll be able to see it all taking shape."

She held out her hand, and he shook it. She thought she saw a slight flush on his cheeks and wondered about it, but then Magda was hugging her.

She climbed into the Land Rover and relaxed properly for the first time that morning.

∽

Back at the house, Jonas viewed his daughter as she stood with her arms folded, glaring at him.

"What?" he said.

"Really dad, I don't know what's got into you!" Magda said. "You're treating Sam like she's some kind of *servant*, not a professional!"

"Don't be ridiculous."

"It's not ridiculous—what was that crack about 'that's what clients pay you for'? How was that called for?"

"Well, how is it untrue?" he shot back. "This isn't a friend, Magda, this is a contractor, and you need to remember that."

Magda stared at him disbelievingly.

"I thought Halcyon always treated its suppliers as 'family'?" she mimicked quote marks. Jonas felt his face grow a little hot.

"That's because we've worked with them for many years," he said.

Magda said nothing and Jonas could see, for the first time, she looked upset. "Dad, I asked you if you were truly OK with this, and you said you were. One second and everything seems fine and the next, you're really snippy with Sam. I don't understand."

Jonas sighed. He could easily explain his attitude towards the young garden designer—but not to his fifteen-year-old daughter.

"I'm sorry, I'm getting very frustrated about being too ill to go to work and I'm taking it out on someone who's getting out, doing her job and getting excited about it," he said finally, ruefully noting his choice of words. "I'm jealous."

Magda's face cleared. "Oh, is that it? Oh Dad, I'm really sorry—I didn't think!" she hugged him, and he hugged her back, feeling a bit of a fraud. After all, some of what he said was true, and he *was* jealous of someone who was obviously in such glowing good health.

But his shortness had been primarily caused by a surge of lust he had not been prepared for. He had practically run back to the house for her coat, cursing himself for his schoolboy reaction to her erect nipples, teased into life by the cool breeze. His response to her had taken him completely by surprise and he'd been both aroused and embarrassed.

Pulling his mind away from the cream sweater and the young woman in it, he finally zoned back into what Magda was saying.

"...but I think it's great they're going to be able to start sooner. Who knows, we might have an Indian summer in the garden!"

He smiled absently. He still thought the timescale was tight and would be thrown if the weather during the build was bad.

Which reminded him, he ought to look at the development drawings in the local library late this afternoon. Gerry came in and sank onto the sofa besides him and Magda, muttering, left the room.

"Shall we go out for lunch?"

Her question caught him by surprise. And then he was pleased.

"Are you trying to fill my days with dissolution?" he grinned.

"Given half a chance," she pouted, running her long nails up his thigh. "I thought it would be nice to go out, just the two of us. I thought we could go to the hotel at Lydcombe."

"Sounds great—do we need to book?"

"I have done," she purred. "I felt sure I could persuade you."

The door of the library was heavy, and Jonas was surprised at the effort it took him to open it. He had been tired after lunch—enjoyable as it had been—but today, he had refused to have a nap. As a result, he thought wryly, he felt knackered.

The library was, as he had thought it would be, almost completely deserted. There were a few staff flitting around, and he caught sight of a woman with orange hair behind one of the counters. As he stared at her outlandish hair, she caught his eye.

"Can I help you?" she said.

"I'm just looking for the consultation exhibition for the property development," he said, smiling his most charming smile. The woman looked at him assessingly.

"It's over there," she pointed, and Jonas noticed the wink of her diamond nose stud. "But you'll have to be quick—we close in ten minutes."

Jonas smiled at her again and walked over to look at the boards. His review was brief, but thorough and his temper rose with every passing minute. These weren't the plans Halcyon had worked on. These took the development onto to the protected area of land. He saw the access road was now splitting Green Belt land—something he certainly hadn't agreed.

"We'll have all kinds of opposition to this," he muttered to himself.

"Do you want more information, Mr...?" said the orange-haired librarian from just behind him, making him jump. Jonas simply smiled at her, not giving his name.

"Who should I contact?" he said instead, just as he caught sight of the brightly coloured poster on the wall. He saw Sam's name and his mouth curled wryly. Of *course* it would be Sam Winterson, he thought.

"Well, I'm Amanda Devreaux and I'm part of the group so you can talk to me," said the librarian. "Or you can talk to either Desmond Black, the chairman, or Sam, who's on the poster there," she gestured to it. "She runs Winterson's Garden Design here in the village."

He smiled, thanked her and walked out of the library. He saw her still watching him from the window as he turned back onto the road.

12

Steve took the mug of tea from Sam with a brief word of thanks. She grinned at him and screwed the top on the thermos.

The garden build at Brook Lodge was going smoothly. Any plants worth saving had been dug up and put in pots. All the hard landscaping was on order and would arrive in a couple of weeks. Today, it was time to dig the pond, and then the firepit.

Sam looked at the plans and pursed her lips. The soil, having lain for some time without anyone coming near it with a garden implement of any kind, was rock hard.

Andy scratched his head. "Well, this pond won't dig itself. Shall we?" He picked up his pick and swung it down. With some effort, it sank into the ground.

Chatter was limited as Sam and Steve joined in, moving the hard, clay-ey soil. In the spring sunshine, Sam felt the beads of perspiration gathering on her brow. After about twenty minutes, she stopped, took out a tissue and wiped her face.

Glancing at the house, she saw the shadows of Jonas and his girlfriend at the study window.

"So—does it look like I'm not doing my share?" she muttered under her breath, as she stuck her spade into the hard earth again.

Andy, catching her words, also looked at the window.

"Don't give yourself a hernia to prove a point, lass," he said.

Four hours later, the pond was dug, and Sam was looking at it with satisfaction. At its deepest, it was up to her thigh. A check with the spirit level, a bit of stamping by Steve and Andy, and Sam was happy. She checked her watch.

"Time for a break, I think," she said. "We'll finish it after lunch."

"Client coming," said Steve, looking past her. Sam turned around, her heart sinking. Jonas was walking over the lawn with a tray with what looked steaming mugs on it.

"I saw you'd paused and thought you might welcome a drink with your lunch," he said. "I brought tea and hope that's ok."

"Thanks, that's kind of you," said Andy. Too surprised to speak, Sam took the hot mug Andy thrust into her hands. Jonas peered over at the pond.

"Is it deep enough? It's a bit shallower than I imagined."

"Nah, it's fine. We planned for a pond, not a lake," said Andy.

"The centre's deep enough so it won't freeze solid in the winter," Sam said, finding her voice again.

Jonas looked at her, his green eyes flicking over her damp forehead and dirty shirt. She managed to keep herself from putting a hand to her hair—it would only spread the dirt anyway.

"And the sloping sides will be better for wildlife," Sam added, wondering if she sounded defensive.

But then again, he might not know about these things she thought, trying to be fair. To better explain, she climbed into the pond to explain about the lining, and how they would cover it with sand to stop the sunlight damaging the membrane which would make it watertight. To her surprise, he jumped beside her into the hole.

"Oh!" she said as his large form arrived alongside her, causing her to lose balance. She grabbed his outstretched arm to save herself from falling onto her backside.

"Ooops! Sorry, that was my fault," he smiled easily, and she was suddenly aware of him—his scent, spicy and warm, and his firm

The Garden Plot

grasp as she found her feet again. She thought she noted a lazy glint in his eyes.

"No problem," she said, and he released her. "So—" she said, turning her back on him and gesturing towards the pile of flat stones nearby, "—we'll place the stones around the edges and these will hide the edges of the liner and help wildlife climb in and out of the water."

"I'm sure it will look great—was there a reason you didn't put it under the tree?" Jonas asked, climbing out of the hole easily with his long legs. Andy and Steve were walking towards the Land Rover.

"Because the tree will lose its leaves in autumn and you won't want to spend all your time fishing them out," she said.

Sam eyed his long legs somewhat crossly, not sure how she was going to get out with any elegance. He held out a hand. After an infinitesimal pause, she took it and he pulled her out. His palm felt smooth and firm.

She nodded her thanks and headed for the Land Rover to get her doubtless squashed sandwiches. To her surprise, he fell in step with her.

"Do you have any other jobs on at the moment?" he asked suddenly.

"We've got a couple of enquiries about a new garden refresh product we've just launched," Sam told him reluctantly. The last thing she wanted to do was have him think the schedule would go to pot. "I'm visiting one potential client this weekend, but please don't worry—as far as the actual labour goes, you're our priority."

Jonas looked at her.

"Good, I'm glad to hear it," he said. "It doesn't sound like you have much of a private life," he added with a smile and Sam's stomach gave a little jump. *I need my lunch*, she thought.

"Well, obviously I do!" she laughed.

"Really?" he replied. "What else do you do outside work?" She looked at him. "Obviously, if you think I'm prying, please tell me to mind my own business," he added smoothly.

Mind your own business.

"Not at all. I love the cinema, I read, I walk, and I judge the village garden competition every year." *Good god, I sound about seventy!* she thought in despair. "I travel whenever I can, and I ski," she added.

He smiled and she rather hated him at that moment.

"Ah. And you're part of the—what is it?—Sherton Protection Group? Is it the one with…what's his name…Daniel Black as its chair?"

"The Sherton Environment Protection Group. And his name is Desmond," she corrected.

"Desmond. Did I see him in the local paper last week?" They were now back at the Land Rover and Sam could see her sandwiches and her flask on the seat, calling to her now grumbling stomach.

"Mmm. He was being interviewed about the housing development we're opposing."

"Ah," he said again. "That's what protest groups do, isn't it? Oppose new building? Are you a local activist?" He said the last word with a slight emphasis.

Sam looked at him, not sure she liked his tone.

"There are plenty of very good reasons to oppose it," she said.

He smiled. "I'm sure you think there are. But I can see I'm keeping you from your lunch—perhaps you could tell me about them another time?" he said. He strode away. She stared after him until her stomach complained again.

"Irritating man!" she muttered under her breath as she reached for her lunch. *"I'm sure you think there are." Patronising git!* she thought as she sought out Andy and Steve, lounging on the grass.

"Big boss happy?" Andy asked, chomping on an apple.

"Yes," Sam said, sinking her teeth into the crusty ham bap she'd brought for lunch. Steve and Andy exchanged glances while she chewed.

"Not sure he wants an *activist* working for him," Sam added, almost spitting out the word. She ran through the conversation as briefly as she could.

Steve grinned. "He's just winding you up," was his view. Andy nodded.

"I agree. Why not tell him about it all? Perhaps he could help—he's in development, isn't he?"

"Only if he agrees with us and I imagine as a businessman he's got profit as his primary concern, rather than the environment." Irritated, Sam took a swig of tea.

"You might be being unfair," insisted Andy. "Didn't you say he knew about ethical sourcing when you talked about the stone?"

Sam was silent.

"True," she said. "However, allow me to suspend judgement until proven otherwise."

Jonas was thoughtful when he returned to the house. Sam was very transparent, visibly irritated by his tone and what she no doubt saw as his nosiness. He thought she'd tell him to go to hell when he asked about her private life—certainly, regardless of what came out of her mouth, she'd been very reluctant to discuss what she did outside work. Politically, of course, they were poles apart.

She was also, he reluctantly admitted, a very lovely woman. He had seen the shirt sticking to her back as she dug the pond, outlining her slim body and small breasts. He sighed, rubbing a hand over the back of his neck.

"Not your type," he muttered.

"What did you say, sweetie?" said Gerry, as she walked in. Jonas said nothing and she peeked over his shoulder. "They've shifted an awful lot of dirt. I wonder if she ever gets it out of her fingernails? Or even if she *has* fingernails?"

Jonas remembered Sam's small hands with their short, neat nails and slender wrists. *Keep quiet*, he thought.

He smiled absently. Mrs Brown bustled into the room.

"What do you think of the progress, Mrs Brown?" Gerry asked the housekeeper, to Jonas' surprise. Mrs Brown also looked taken aback.

"The garden?" she said. "Well, that's a fairly big pond—if the soil at the side is anything to go by. They must be filthy dirty."

Gerry nodded and gave one of her tinkling laughs. "I was just commenting to Jonas that Ms Winterson doesn't seem the feminine type, I was just estimating the amount of soil under her nails..."

Mrs Brown harrumphed. "Regardless, if she's like her father, I imagine she's not without male company."

Gerry looked astounded and then laughed again. "Goodness! A garden seductress! Who would have thought?"

Jonas looked out of the window again, and saw Sam throw her head back and laugh at something. She playfully cuffed the young lad—Steve was it?—on the shoulder and he grinned sheepishly. As they began to work again, however, he caught the look of shy worship Steve gave her.

He was surprised to feel his stomach tighten in protest and put it down to hunger.

~

Charlie sipped her coffee and looked at Sam.

"Well, I can ask him, of course, but I doubt he'll agree," she said.

"No, that's what I told the committee, but they insisted. So here I am." Sam stared into her mug.

"It might be better if *you* asked him, rather than me, anyway," Charlie added.

"Not sure that's such a good idea, Charlie. We don't exactly get on, as you know."

"No kidding."

Sam grinned, unrepentant. "Well, if you *must* go and marry the local Tory MP, you might have known there'd be family tensions!"

"If you argued properly, like you used to when we were first married, it wouldn't be so bad," Charlie protested. "But now you just snipe at one another and frankly, it's unbearable."

Sam bit her tongue. She had enjoyed the banter with Fraser when she was younger. But this had been when he was a candidate and the Lib Dems had held the local seat. When Fraser was elected, he'd...

just changed. As their conversations became louder and more passionate, they also became less forgiving.

When Sam saw Fraser's temper turn on Charlie, she abruptly stopped any conversations which touched politics, and by silent mutual consent, so did Fraser. They'd barely had anything substantial to talk about since.

"OK, I'll talk to him," Sam said. "Is it Friday he gets back from Westminster?"

"Yes, he's running a surgery in Chapel Winston on Saturday. You could go to see him at the surgery...?"

Sam only just repressed a grimace. She couldn't imagine his face if she turned up.

"Perhaps it would be better if I tried to catch him here—I'll pop in around seven, shall I?"

"Do you want to come to supper? Lisbeth's home."

Sam gave her sister a straight look.

"Only if you don't try to fix me up with anyone."

"Cross my heart."

"Hmm. I'll bring dessert, I should have time to whip something up."

"Nothing too rich—Fraser's supposed to be on a diet. All the House of Commons puddings are really piling on the weight."

Sam laughed. "If he fancies taking some time out of Parliament, the job I've got on at the moment would soon slim him down!"

"Dream on, Sam—I'm not sure Fraser knows one end of a spade from the other anymore," Charlie grinned ruefully. "I'm really pleased we're going into recess next week—we don't seem to have seen one another for weeks."

Sam drained the rest of her coffee and stood up, just as the phone rang. Charlie glanced at the display. "It's Fraser, I'd better take it."

Sam waved and left, not looking forward to Friday at all.

How R U? Read the text from Lisbeth the following evening.

Good, thanks. I'm coming to supper on Friday night, it'll be nice to see you. How's the new music teacher? responded Sam, smiling and thinking of Lisbeth's latest crush.

ENGAGED!!!! the whole of my year in mourning...what was he THINKING??

Sam snorted, and put aside the novel she was reading.

OK, so just sombre clothing, then. I'll be respectful, Sam texted.

Quite right. Also—was going 2 ask Magda 2 dinner Friday night—ok? Need 2 check w. Mum, obvs...

"Ah. Don't have much of a choice, do I?" said Sam under her breath. *No problem* she texted. *How were the mocks?*

A pause.

Gruesome. Maths & physics OK, but chemistry set by an alien from another dimension. English OK, French vocab = pants. Will know in a week —then ma and pa will either lock me in my room or buy me driving lessons.

"Good God, really? *Driving lessons?*" Sam muttered, appalled. *Let me know when you've got your results. In no circumstances are you to touch the Land Rover.*

Booooooooo! Ungr8teful! The text had an emoticon sobbing on it. Sam smiled.

What?

Lisbeth's response was swift. *Wot about Magda & this latest job?*

"Bugger," Sam said under her breath. *I offered you cash as a thank you. You refused. You said you did it because you loved me.* She sent back.

If I'd known U were going 2 refuse 2 let me drive Land Rover, wd have taken £!

"Manipulative little cow," Sam said, without heat. She thought a little. *Listen carefully, niece. I will let you drive the Land Rover ONLY in an empty supermarket car park, in good daylight after you've had a couple of lessons. Not before.*

Deal came the response.

Sam shook her head. The clock struck eleven. She texted *Shouldn't you be planning midnight feasts or something?*

Funny—not. Your reading is 40 years out of date! C U Friday!

Take care, pet. Goodnight.

~

Finally in bed, Sam was flicking over the pages of the gardening magazine when an advertisement caught her eye.

Garden Designer of the Year:
£10,000 cash prize, plus the chance to design a show garden for RHS Tatton Park

Rather wistfully, she let her eye drift down the copy, noting the size and specifications required to enter.

Bloody focused on the big firms that get commissions that large... she thought acidly. *I've done nothing big enough...*

She suddenly sat up.

"Oh yes, I have! Or at least I will have!" she muttered, thrusting her legs out of bed and grabbing her wrap.

She ran downstairs to her laptop and tapped her fingers impatiently as it loaded up. Finally able to access her files, she scrolled through her plans and designs. And then she found it.

"Yessss!" She punched the air. The Keane garden was big enough to enter in the competition. She realised she hadn't brought the magazine with her and cursing, raced upstairs again to grab it from the bed.

Breathless, she sat down to read the entry qualifications again, more carefully this time. She was to submit the plans, the brief, photos of the finished garden, and a recommendation from the person who commissioned it.

Tick, tick and tick! she thought almost dizzily. Jonas would surely give them a reference if he was pleased with the garden, he was a businessman and understood the importance of client references. *Surely* he would?

Looking again at the plans, Sam knew Brook Lodge was her best design to date and it deserved—no, damn it, *she* deserved!—a wider audience.

A conversation with her father about another competition floated from her memory.

"Eh lass, are you sure? They'll be a lot of entries from folk with a lot more experience than you, and I wouldn't want you to get your hopes up and be disappointed," he had said.

"Well, you never know, I might actually *win*, Dad!" she had said, trying to laugh it off. Samuel Winterson had shaken his head.

"I dunno Sammy—seems a lot of work."

"But all they want is the plans—and I've drawn those already!"

"And what about the client? Will he want lots of people tramping all over his garden? Or the newspapers coming to take photos?"

"But think of the benefit to the business, Dad! Even if we don't win, it will get us lots of attention! We could probably get some publicity for just entering!" she pressed. "And just think what it would mean if we *did* win! It would be worth thousands!"

"And what if I don't want any more business?"

"What?"

"What if I'm happy with the business just as it is? After all, while you are my daughter and I'm chuffed you're interested in making a career of it, it *is* still my business, or had you forgotten?"

Sam could remember the tide of red creep up her neck and into her face as he fixed her with a stare. She struggled to make her voice work.

"No, Dad, I just—"

"I don't *want* fancy-pants customers with pal-*ettes* and bloody *rooms* to their gardens. I like the kind of customers we have now and they're coming to me because they know me, and they know my reputation. I don't need no competition to help me win business, girl."

He patted her on the shoulder and kissed her forehead. "You do that when I'm dead and gone, pet. When this business is yours."

And that had been that. Sam wiped away a tear that had somehow dripped onto her cheek.

Of course, when the recession struck, even Samuel Winterson's reputation hadn't been enough to keep the business coming in. Sam had looked again at some of the cosy supplier relationships her father had built over the years and re-negotiated some prices. Everyone in the industry was suffering, and she'd made herself mightily unpopular, but the small amounts she shaved off Winterson's supplies had helped to keep them in business.

Her father had seemed to shrink. It was as if he'd looked out into the modern world of business and decided he didn't like it. He grew quieter with the team, although in public he was still as jovial as ever. She'd forced him to get a website, do some small ads in the local press, particularly around the more affluent areas of the county. She'd driven their success and slowly, gradually, the business recovered.

But her father hadn't recovered, not really. Sam shook off the memories and looked again at the magazine.

She ran her finger down the page and stopped at the submission date; 9 September, with judging at the end of October. By then the Keane garden would have started to grow and some of the plants would be looking their best, she thought.

Plenty of time to butter up Jonas Keane to enter Brook Lodge into the competition. Her libido reared its head, pointing out that buttering up Jonas Keane sounded a *lot* of fun.

She tore the page out of the magazine and put it to one side. She'd ask the sceptical, antagonistic owner when the garden was finished and as lovely as she'd planned it to be and he'd have no excuses.

"It's just a matter of timing," she said to herself.

13

The week had gone well, Sam thought, as they loaded up the Land Rover. The threatened downpour of rain hadn't arrived, and they were half a day ahead of schedule. She stretched, feeling her muscles already starting to tighten up.

A long, hot soak she promised herself. She believed herself to be very fit, but really, she was exhausted and aching in places she wasn't even aware of having muscles.

I'll have to take it easier next week or I'll be a wreck before the job's done she thought.

As they emptied the Land Rover of tools and gear, Paul strolled out of the office, with the pay packet for Steve.

"For you, lad," he said. Steve looked a bit nonplussed and Sam smiled.

"We thought you might be a bit short so we've paid you for this week and a week in advance, which won't last long, but it will give you enough to get yourself a drink at the pub," she said.

Steve's face lit up and he mumbled his thanks.

"You've done really well, so thank *you*," said Sam. "Mind you, we're going to work you into the ground next week, so be warned!"

Steve laughed, and calling his farewells, left for home. Andy watched him go.

"I hope *you're* not going to work next week like you did this week, Sam," he said to her. "You've slogged yourself to death, lifting stuff you shouldn't have, and doing more than you should," he added. She felt her face go pink.

"I wanted to get a head start on it," she said.

"More like—you wanted to show the bastard he was wrong. It won't do, Sam—I told you not to try and prove a point, you'll do yourself a mischief."

Sam opened her mouth to deny it and opted mid-breath to be honest.

"Yeah, I know. I'll take it a bit easier next week."

"You will. Or you and me will have words."

Sam twinkled at him.

"Ooh, you're so butch when you go all masterful on me!" she teased. "I can see why Greg loves you."

"Cheeky mare. Got time for a swift one in the Dog and Duck?"

"No," she said, regretfully. "I have to make myself presentable and get around to my brother-in-law so I can ask him on bended knee for his support on Jessop's Field. That's if I can get up from the floor given the state of my muscles."

"I remember. Do you think he *will* help?"

"I doubt it. I'm only talking to him at all because I got ambushed into it at the last meeting. He'll say something bland and—I don't know—*political!*—and we'll probably row. And *then* I'm staying for dinner, joy of joys..."

Andy grinned at her face.

"Well, if it all gets too much with the Right Honourable, you can always pop round to us for a glass of wine."

"Thanks, I might take you up on that!"

As she drove off, Sam was seriously considering making her excuses for supper. She could just get her conversation with Fraser out of the way, and then go to Andy and Greg's snug house.

Still, I haven't seen Lisbeth for a couple of weeks. I can duck Fraser's snide comments, like I always do.

She pulled up into her drive and looked at the late afternoon light glinting invitingly off the windows of her cottage. A deep, hot, long bath called to her.

If I don't fall asleep! she thought.

An hour and a half later, wearing a skirt instead of her normal jeans and carrying a chocolate mousse, she knocked at Charlie and Fraser's door. As she waited for someone to answer, she looked at the garden with a professional eye and noted the delphiniums coming up strongly, although they needed tying up. Charlie opened the door and saw where her gaze was resting.

"And before you say anything, I'm going to be staking those delphiniums tomorrow morning!" said Charlie immediately.

Sam grinned at her sister, who kissed her cheek and took the cut glass bowl of mousse. "Thanks for this. Fraser's in his office. You look nice, incidentally."

Sam thanked her absently, walking swiftly along the passage. She paused, listening at the door, and then tapped. Fraser's light voice asked her to come in.

"Um, hello Fraser," she said.

"Hello, sister-in-law!" Fraser responded a bit *too* heartily. Sam's heart sank, as she sat in the chair Fraser waved her to.

"To what do I owe the honour?"

"Well, I don't know what Charlie—*Charlotte*—has told you—"

"Only that you wanted to see me in—ah—an *official* capacity."

"Oh, no! Not really official. I just wanted to get your opinion as my brother-in-law." She took her file of papers from her bag. "I'm part of the Sherton Environment Protection group and we're objecting to the housing development on Jessop's Field."

"Ah."

Sam looked at him. "You know about it?"

"I've been contacted by Anglo Homes, who explained about the development."

"What did they say?" asked Sam carefully.

Fraser waved his hands airily. "The development is small and contained and will make up a deficit in the council's Local Plan in terms of housing. That homes in this area are badly needed. That it would bring considerable employment to the area." His eyes were cool as they looked at her.

"Did they also 'explain' the access to their development will cut across Green Belt land? That the development itself will encroach on a nationally recognised, wildlife corridor? That there's brownfield land available too?"

She stopped her voice rising with an effort and took a deep breath. "We need the views and beauty spots for our tourism. Building over it will threaten half the B&Bs in the area."

Fraser smiled faintly. She hated that smile.

"But the houses are needed," he pointed out. "For ordinary, working people who want a space of their own to raise families, build their lives."

"We're not anti-housing, of course not," she said patiently. "But we'd like to keep the village beautiful, particularly as there are alternative sites for the development."

"If you build on contaminated land, all it does is delay the build and put the price up. Currently, this is a commercially viable scheme."

"Is it all about the money? Don't you *care* about what happens to the village?" she asked. "Have you *seen* how close the development is to Jessop's Field?" She laid the plans on his desk, over his existing paperwork and stabbed the development with her finger.

He peered at it and Sam thought he really ought to give up his vanity and get some glasses.

"It's about houses for people who need them, Sam. Don't forget if the cost of the build goes up, people in the local area won't be able to afford them and they'll get priced out. So while I recognise your arguments—" he held up a finger as she took a breath to begin another sentence, "—but this is a local matter and will be dealt with by the local authorities. I can't get involved, Sam."

She sat back. "Do you even agree with us?" she asked.

"I have some sympathy with your position," he said.

"That's a politician's answer, Fraser!"

"You're seeing me as a politician, aren't you?" he said.

She shrugged and began putting the plans back in her bag. "I thought I was talking to you as my brother-in-law. Obviously not."

"I'm sorry Sam. I'll watch out to ensure due process is followed, but I can't really express an opinion."

"You can't express an opinion for your local community? Why on *earth* did people vote for you?" Sam rose from her seat, unsurprised at the outcome, but still furious. She walked out hearing Fraser sigh theatrically behind her.

"I can see dinner's going to be a blast," commented Charlie, taking one look at her face.

"A completely pointless exercise! He doesn't care about the Green Belt at all as long as it makes commercial sense to desecrate it!"

Charlie put her spoon down on the counter with a snap and Sam took a deep, deep breath. "I'm not sure I'm going to stop for dinner," she said.

"Then you can explain to Lisbeth," Charlie said shortly, bending down to take a huge rib of beef from the oven. "She's been really looking forward to seeing you, she talked about it all the way back from the station."

"Where is she?"

"Upstairs, getting changed."

Sam could hear the music as she climbed the stairs and Lisbeth's surprisingly rich voice singing along. She knocked at the door.

"Lisbeth?"

"Aunty Sam!" Lisbeth threw the door open, her still wet hair tousled around her delighted face. "Brilliant! You're early!"

Sam's heart sank at the welcome.

"Mmm..."

"What's wrong?"

Sam opened her mouth to tell her niece she wouldn't be staying for dinner and somehow what came out was, "Oh, just a disagreement with your dad."

"Oh? Well, that's hardly news, is it?" Lisbeth grinned at her and then gave her a hug. "I hoped whatever it was wouldn't stop you staying for dinner, but then again, you're a grown-up, aren't you?"

Sam smiled weakly.

"You look *great!*" Lisbeth enthused, looking her aunt up and down. "That lime green looks amazing on you, really makes you look tanned!"

"I thought I'd make an effort as I was speaking to your dad," Sam said, smoothing down her skirt. She rolled her eyes. "Didn't work, though."

Lisbeth made sympathetic noises and then presented two outfits for review and Sam made comments. They exchanged views on the music teacher (sadly now not available), talked about the sitcom they were both addicted to, and at the end of half an hour, Sam felt almost normal again.

Walking back into the kitchen, Sam sniffed and this time, took note of the joint of meat.

"Well? Are you staying?" Charlie demanded. Sam hesitated and then her stomach made the decision for her.

"I couldn't possibly miss out on *that!*" she pointed to the roast. "This is a bit more than normal Friday night supper, isn't it?"

"Well, I thought I'd soften up Fraser before I give him the news he's going on a diet in the summer," said Charlie as she shook a pan of crisp roast potatoes. "And of course we have guests..."

"Oh, of course! I'd forgotten, I hope she's had a chance to look at the garden—although perhaps it would be best if we didn't talk shop," Sam picked at a bowl of raw cauliflower.

"No, I absolutely agree," Charlie said, hoisting a big pan of greens over the sink. "And talking of our guests, it's not just—"

The doorbell rang.

"I'll get it, you've got your hands full," Sam said, walking towards the front door.

"Sam!" called Lisbeth from the top of the stairs.

"Just a sec!" Sam threw open the door, and the words of welcome died on her lips.

Standing on the doorstep was Magda. And her father.

14

She just stood there, looking at Magda and Jonas who loomed over her. Lisbeth slid around her and smiled at Magda.

"Hi both! Come in! Mu-um!" she called. "Magda and her dad are here!"

Sam, who still hadn't said a word, blinked at Jonas as the girls chattered off to the living room.

"Good evening Sam," Jonas said, closing the door. "I take it you weren't expecting us?"

His voice seemed to thrum through her veins. Sam plastered a smile onto her face.

"I was expecting Magda," she managed. "But it would have been pretty mean to leave you at home, I imagine."

"Absolutely," said Charlie, coming up behind her, wiping her hands on a tea towel. "Hello, I'm Charlotte, Lisbeth's mum, and this is my husband, Fraser."

There was a general shaking of hands and Sam slipped away, into the kitchen to grab a glass of wine.

Medicinal, she thought grimly. *You've worked bloody hard this week and you deserve this. Particularly given the evening you're about to have.*

Charlie bustled back into the kitchen.

"And before you say anything at all, Lisbeth sprang this on me about an hour ago, and *she* asked me to include Magda's father as his partner's gone to Manchester!"

Sam took a gulp of her wine, reflecting absently that she'd need to walk home this evening.

"No problem," she said, taking another swig.

Lisbeth came in. "Are you coming into the lounge?" she asked, twisting her hands.

"I'll stay and help your mum," she said. "I'll be there in a minute."

"OK," Lisbeth nodded and staggered out, her arms full of wine glasses.

"What you actually meant was you'll stay and get under my feet," commented Charlie.

"Ah, but I make fabulous gravy!" said Sam, thankfully grabbing an apron.

Jonas sat in the lounge, outwardly relaxed and inwardly on edge. At first, he hadn't been very enthusiastic about coming out, but Lisbeth had asked so sweetly, and Magda had been so keen he couldn't refuse. And anyway, it was good to be out of the house, particularly as Gerry had gone to London to buy the sculpture she wanted.

And now, out of work boots and smelling delicious, the garden designer was here.

The girls were chatting about school and Fraser McAllen was listening, smiling occasionally. Eventually, he turned to Jonas.

"Are you as happy with the school as we are?"

"Clavedene? Oh yes, it seems a great place—Magda loves it."

Fraser nodded in satisfaction.

"We're pleased we managed to get Lisbeth in—much better than the local comp."

Jonas, who'd heard pretty good reports about Ashton's comprehensive, simply looked enquiring. Fraser, needing no more encouragement, launched into what Jonas recognised as his political party's manifesto.

"After all, what else can you do but give your children the best start in life? And let's face it, State schools aren't the best launch pad."

"I thought the Government was ploughing considerable investment into State Schools?" said Jonas.

"Well, yes, obviously, but given the mess the Opposition's made of education, it will take years to recover," Fraser said smoothly. "In the meantime, I have a daughter to educate!"

Jonas stifled an immediate dislike, saying instead, "Magda is certainly enjoying her time there—her grades have gone up."

Magda, catching her name and swiftly zoning into the conversation, gave him a cheeky grin.

"Yeah, but that's because I'm brilliant, it's nothing to do with the school!"

Lisbeth, Jonas noticed, glanced at the door and rather obviously changed the subject, beginning to talk about her planned holiday in France.

"When do you break up, again?" asked Fraser.

"The first Friday in July," responded Magda promptly. "I've started tennis lessons and the next time we play I'm going to wipe the floor with you, Dad! And I hope we can get in a few games too, Lisbeth."

"I'm not quite as good as you are!" Lisbeth said with a laugh.

"Well, I can see about private lessons at the school if you want," Fraser said, and Lisbeth shook her head as Sam came through with a bowl of steaming vegetables.

Jonas found his eyes drawn to Sam as she walked across the open plan lounge and placed the dish on the table. She was wearing some kind of floaty green top under the apron, and an electric blue stretchy skirt which just brushed her knees and tightened over her thighs and bottom as she bent over the table.

Dragging his eyes away from the curve of her rear, he sipped his wine.

"Should we sit at the table, Aunty Sam?"

"Yes please, pet. Fraser, Charlotte wants you to carve the meat." Jonas thought her voice lost some of its warmth.

"Goodness—Charlotte is giving me a knife?"

"To give you a fighting chance, no doubt," Sam said, turning away as Fraser got to his feet.

"Touché!" he murmured as he went to the kitchen.

Lisbeth shepherded them all to the table and there was a momentary lull in the conversation.

Jonas dug up some memories of playing tennis in Zurich and Magda, taking the piss as usual, joined in, making derisory comments about his legs in shorts.

Sam came in again with warm plates and handed them out, went away again and returned with some roast potatoes smelling so delicious, Jonas' stomach rumbled. Sam laughed and he started to apologise.

"Your turn this time!" she said, referring to the first time they'd met in the pub. "But it's good to know you're hungry!" she added, her eyes dancing.

"I didn't realise I was until I smelled your sister's roast potatoes!" he smiled back.

"Just wait until you smell the meat—Charlie's certainly pulled out the stops for her guests tonight."

"That does include you, Sam dear," Charlie swept in, carrying—oh, bliss of bliss, thought Jonas—a pile of Yorkshire puddings.

"Pah! I normally get pasta!" Sam joked, taking her seat opposite him.

"It's nice to welcome new people to the neighbourhood—we should do it more often," said Fraser, entering with the carved beef, switching Jonas' taste buds into overdrive.

"You can increase my housekeeping then," Charlotte said sweetly, and there was general laughter.

15

Best behaviour, Sam thought to herself as she sipped her wine. *With your client across the table and your snarky brother-in-law at the other end, you must be on your best behaviour.*

"Magda was saying she was taking private tennis lessons at Clavedene," said Fraser to Charlie. "I wondered if we should look at getting some for Lisbeth."

Sam glanced across at Lisbeth and saw her bite her lip.

Breathe, Sam, breathe.

She took a huge bite of Yorkshire pudding which kept her mouth occupied for a few minutes. Lisbeth squirmed a bit under the attention but eventually agreed private lessons would be nice. Sam chewed on through the discussion, saying nothing.

Next on the conversation menu was a by-election, introduced this time by Jonas. A Tory MP in a nearby constituency had been caught with his hand in the till of the local constituency office *and* down a prostitute's knickers.

Sam had thought cynically that if it had not been for the syphoning off of funds, the official, Tom Anderson, would probably still be in his seat.

"Yes, unfortunate business," Fraser said airily. "Still, Anderson had a majority of about five thousand, so I imagine the seat will remain Tory."

Sam couldn't help herself.

"You think?" said Sam idly running her finger around the rim of her wineglass. "You don't think his recent voting record on the high-speed rail link might have hacked off the farmers who own the farmland in the county?"

"That was a three-line whip."

"I'm not sure that argument will make too much difference to the farmers I met at the Buxton Agricultural Show last year. They seemed pretty livid about it."

"Not much he can do about the whips, I'm afraid."

"I wonder why people vote for MPs when they don't have the power to represent their views," she said. "You'll have to be careful you don't become just a figurehead, Fraser."

She smiled at him sweetly.

"Sam and I disagree on quite a lot in politics," Fraser said to Jonas, who was looking at Sam intently. "As I'm a Member of Parliament and actually *in* it, I tend to have a different view."

Patronising git thought Sam and then looked around quickly to make sure she hadn't spoken aloud.

"But of course, as *part* of the electorate, I hope you think my view is both important and valid," she said instead.

"And although Sam isn't officially in politics, she's nevertheless involved in local democracy, as far as I can see," Jonas added, to Sam's astonishment.

"Really? Is she making a bid for the local Council?" Charlie asked, looking surprised and slightly appalled.

"No, I think what Jonas is referring to is Sam's involvement with the action group—" the word had the most distasteful of inverted commas around it, "—which is protesting against the development on Jessop's Field," Fraser said, pouring more wine. Sam noticed Magda's eyes swivel to her.

"Jessop's Field? But that would be awful!" Lisbeth exclaimed. Fraser gave his daughter a stern look.

"People need houses, Lisbeth. We're really blessed with our countryside, but we can't put our lovely view in front of places for people to live."

"There's plenty of room elsewhere in the village, Fraser. And don't get me started about the lack of affordable housing in the plan, *or* the fact this is a Tory-controlled council, it has been for ages, and they should have been addressing this *years* ago!" Sam pointed out. "Or, that the developers will walk off with a tidy profit."

"Developers take risk, they need to get a return for it," said Jonas.

"Sam still hasn't forgiven Margaret Thatcher for offering council tenants the right to buy," Fraser put in, smiling conspiratorially at Jonas. "Even though she wasn't born at the time."

Jonas didn't smile back. "Well, neither was I, but certainly, I think the idea amounted to an electoral bribe," he said.

"You do?" Sam said.

"Amazing, isn't it?" he said. "In big business, *and* with a social conscience."

Sam felt her face flush and kept silent.

"So what are *your* views about the development?" Charlie asked Jonas.

"I don't know enough about it," he said. "I think you said you'd talk to me about it?" Jonas looked at Sam.

"I will, certainly."

"But you'd better agree with her, because she flounces off in a huff if you don't," put in Fraser.

"The local authority—in fact, a number of the politicians we've spoken to—either haven't thought about the impact on local tourism or aren't prepared to take a view. Personally, I think that's ducking their democratic responsibilities," Sam said, ignoring Fraser.

"Perhaps you had better speak after dinner," put in Charlie hastily.

Sam, who was about to continue the argument, caught sight of Lisbeth looking anxious, and shut up.

Jonas wrapped his fingers around his wineglass, looking thoughtful. Charlie got up and began to collect the plates. Magda thanked her for the meal, jumping to her feet to help, as did Sam.

"No, you sit down Sam—I'll do it," said Magda, waving her to sit down again.

Foiled again, thought Sam, longing to get away from Fraser. Jonas caught her eye and gave her a small grin. She felt a flash of warmth run through her at the tiny communication and was surprised at it.

There was an awkward silence at the table. Sam examined the table mat with great interest.

"More wine, Jonas?" Fraser said, at length.

Jonas refused with a smile.

"So, what is it you do? Lisbeth said something about development in Europe," Fraser said, topping up his own glass and settling back into his chair. Sam's ears pricked up.

"Well, at the moment I'm on an extended leave of absence. I caught some mystery virus and it knocked the stuffing out of me. I'm on very strict orders not to even *talk* about work in case it stresses me out. The doctor was remarkably explicit, so would you forgive me if I just said—I'm the head of a development company which does most of its work in Europe?"

"Sounds fascinating," encouraged Fraser.

"It is." And Jonas said no more.

So there! thought Sam with an inward grin, seeing Fraser's attempts to get more information fail. *Still... I wonder if Jonas would help us, as it's his area of expertise?*

She looked at him. The warm glow of the lamplight made his hair gleam.

Now, wouldn't that be nice? grinned her libido. *Getting his expertise?*

She looked down quickly into her wine glass, noting with a start that it was empty. So much for her good behaviour. She drank fizzy water through the rest of the meal and asked for strong black coffee afterwards. But there was no question of driving back to the cottage.

"Shall we walk you home?" Magda asked during coffee.

Sam stared at her for a moment.

"Sorry?"

The Garden Plot

"Shall we walk you home, if you're not driving?" Magda repeated. "It's more or less on our way, and we walked over to give Dad a bit of gentle exercise."

"A bit like taking an old dog out," Jonas said. Sam barely heard him.

"That's really kind, but—"

"It's really no problem, is it Dad?"

Sam locked eyes with Jonas and thought she saw an odd gleam in them.

"No problem at all," he said politely. Sam laughed.

"There's no need, I've lived in the village all my life."

"I'd be happier if you let Jonas walk you home," put in Charlie unhelpfully. "The Red Lion's had some trouble the past few Friday nights."

Sam started to feel vaguely panicked. She found Jonas' cool green eyes, watching her. *What is wrong with me, it's a ten-minute walk, for Gods' sake!* She mentally tutted to herself.

"Well, if you're sure—"

"Quite sure. You can talk to me about the development while we walk."

Sam relaxed. That would be a good use of her time, certainly.

"Well, thank you. I'll get my bag."

Magda was chattering as Jonas opened the door to Brook Lodge. He wanted some quiet, a scotch and some thinking time.

His daughter paused.

"Well? What do you think?" his daughter prompted him. He stared at her. "You haven't been listening, have you?"

"Sorry, I've been drifting a bit. I think I'm tired. Could you run that past me again?"

Magda rolled her eyes.

"I *said* perhaps we ought to invite Lisbeth and her family over for a return supper! We should do it to celebrate when the garden's finished!"

Jonas ran his mind over the suggestion and thought it seemed eminently reasonable. So why wasn't he more enthusiastic?

Fraser, that was why. Pompous arse.

"We should invite the whole team—including Sam, and Andy and that young lad who works with them, too!"

Jonas felt his stomach turn over. Of course they'd invite Sam. Perhaps he could cope with Fraser and his pretty, colourless wife if there were other compensations.

"We'll see."

"Did you have a good time tonight Dad? I thought it would be nice to meet a few other families in the village..." Magda seemed to be watching him closely, he thought. He'd better concentrate.

"Mmm, yes, what about you?" He clicked on lamps.

"Oh yeah, but there seems to be a bit of an atmosphere between Sam and Lisbeth's dad, don't you think?"

"They're very different people, I think."

"Yeah... Sam's got a really different view of the world. Lisbeth's dad seems a bit...well, old!"

Jonas laughed.

"He's got a very responsible position as a Member of Parliament; I imagine that ages him a lot!"

"But Sam's got a really responsible attitude too—all this stuff about Jessop's Field, she's really into it!"

He poured himself a drink, sinking into his favourite armchair.

"Can I have a bit?" Magda wheedled.

"A thimbleful—no more. You'll get me arrested for corruption of a minor. Plus, this is my best scotch." Grinning, Magda skipped to the drinks and poured enough to cover the bottom of a glass.

"What do *you* think? About Jessop's Field?" she asked.

"I don't know," Jonas said.

"Will you help her? I think she was telling you about it so you might offer her some advice!"

"Not sure she needs it. They're doing all the right things from what I heard just now. If there's a sensible reason why the development shouldn't go ahead, I think she's got a really good chance of finding what it is."

"But you *know* all about this stuff! Can't you help?" Magda looked at him suspiciously. "It's not one of *your* developments, is it Dad?"

"Anglo Homes is the developer," he said immediately. Not the whole truth, but not a lie either.

Magda was watching him with her head on one side. She was quiet for a second. "Right," she said. Jonas tried to steer the conversation to safer ground.

"I tell you what—if the group looks like they're making a mistake, I'll tell her." Magda gave him what his mother would have called 'an old-fashioned' look.

"Whoopy-doo, Dad."

"It's not up for discussion, Magda. Can you imagine the publicity if I was found to be advising a protest group to interfere with the business of another property developer? It's not that I don't want to help—I can't."

Magda was silent. "I hadn't thought of it like that," she admitted finally. "Sam's really nice, isn't she?"

The question caught him by surprise. "Yes, she's lovely," he said without thinking.

Magda drained the final drops of her drink and jumped up.

"Thanks for coming out tonight Dad—I had a great time. Love you," and she kissed him and then whirled off out of the room.

He smiled as she left and kicked off his shoes, stretching back in the chair. Time for him to go up as well, he felt like he'd been run over by a truck. But he stayed where he was, thinking over the evening.

The prickliness between Sam and her brother-in-law had been impossible to miss, but what he'd been particularly struck by was the way in which Lisbeth had been affected. She'd looked—tense.

And Sam had been fascinating to watch too. He'd known she was feisty simply from their discussions about the garden design. What he hadn't known was how articulate she could be about other things.

He focused with an effort. The plans he'd seen in the library were standard fare, he thought. They didn't have the features which were Halcyon's hallmark and he didn't know why. Sam had been right, too—the position of the site would give plenty of scope for objections. He needed to talk to Neil and sort it out if they were to protect their investment.

He sat in the soft light of the lamps, remembering the conversation at the table tonight. The relationship between the sisters looked complicated, he decided.

Probably because of Fraser... Career politician, he decided with a twist of his lips. Doubtless a very good one, and tipped, according to his lobby team in London, for great things in the Cabinet. Jonas hadn't liked him much. He wondered idly what Charlotte had seen in him, and his thoughts turned back to Sam.

Intelligent, passionate, articulate.

And beautiful, don't forget beautiful, with skin like silk, prompted his brain.

"Bugger," he said softly, before putting down his glass and going to bed. He needed to text Gerry, he reminded himself.

The room was spinning just a bit as Sam flicked on the light.

"Tea," she mumbled to herself. "Tea will sort you out."

She struggled out of her jacket and dropped it carelessly on the kitchen chair, kicked off her heels—*ridiculously high for a dinner with the family*, she thought—and grabbed a *big* mug.

She waited for the kettle to boil. Her mind was a blank. This was probably a good thing—when she started thinking, she felt she might have rather a *lot* to think about.

Minutes later, mug in hand, she walked carefully to the big squishy armchair.

Quite an evening, she thought as she sipped her hot tea.

Fraser—she wrinkled her nose. Well, it was hardly unexpected, but at least she'd tried.

"Tory arse," she muttered.

And then there was Magda. And Magda's father.

She closed her eyes briefly. Dinner, even if you took Fraser and his irritating point-scoring out of it, had hardly been stress-free. Okay, Charlotte had been the perfect hostess, as smooth and vanilla as always, and Magda had been bright and bubbly. But seeing Jonas at the door had been a shock, the first of several during dinner.

The walk home had been tight with tension between them, despite the bright chatter of Magda. Sam had tried to get more information out of Jonas in much the same way as Fraser had done and was met with the same response. He wasn't rude, he was just firm, and remarkably skilled at turning the conversation into other avenues and getting her to talk about herself. Useless.

On Monday she would try again in the hope of squeezing more information and perhaps some advice out of him.

She'd fallen silent as they'd approached her cottage, starting to wonder what the social etiquette was for a situation where a client (with his daughter) had walked you home. A wave from the path? Air kissing? Shaking hands?

A real kiss?

She'd been giving herself such a strong talking-to about even *thinking* about a real kiss, she'd almost walked past her own front gate and stopped abruptly, causing Jonas to bump into her.

"Oh!" she said, as his hands caught her shoulders and steadied her.

"All right?" he said with a lazy smile she could just see in the evening gloom.

"Yes," she said, her breath unsteady. "Sorry, I wasn't looking where I was going."

There was a second's silence and then Magda launched forwards.

"It's been great to spend a bit of time with you! I'm home for the summer in a few weeks so I'll see you then!"

Then Magda planted a kiss firmly on each of her cheeks. Sam turned to Jonas and before he could follow his daughter's example, she thrust out her hand.

"Goodnight—thank you for walking me home."

There was a glint in his eye as Jonas took her hand.

"No problem," he said politely, taking her hand. He pulled her towards him and pressed his lips to one cheek and then the other. She thought he was almost as surprised as she was. "See you on Monday."

Sam stared into her mug and played back in her head the feel of his lips on her face and the slight bristle of his cheek against her skin.

She sat up and shook her head as if to clear it.

No messing with the customers, was one of the cardinal rules of business, she knew.

But now she was simultaneously looking forward to Monday and dreading it.

16

On Monday morning, Jonas had risen at his normal time. So far, he'd nicked his throat shaving, changed his shirt twice and spilt coffee on the kitchen table, soaking one page of the Financial Times.

He was swearing under his breath and mopping up when he saw Andy stroll into the back garden. Then the doorbell rang. Throwing the dishcloth towards the sink, it missed and fell to the floor.

Grumbling, he went to the front door, wiping his hands.

Sam was standing on the doorstep. It was starting to mizzle with rain, and she was peering at the sky.

"Morning!" she said brightly. "Doesn't look all that promising today, does it?"

"No, it doesn't." He held the door open and after a pause, she stepped into the hall.

"I wondered if you were still interested in hearing a bit more about the action group later today?" she smiled hesitantly.

"Yes, of course—but will you really work through this today?" he said, waving at the weather.

"If it's completely throwing it down, it's self-defeating—the soil gets too heavy to work and all you end up doing is making a mess.

This," she indicated out of the now open door, "is just drizzle, and to be honest, it might make the soil a bit softer. And after all, I do have a deadline to meet, don't I?"

She shot him a challenging look and he laughed. She smiled again and then she was gone.

Jonas looked at the closed door for a moment and then went to clear up the mess in the kitchen. Gerry wasn't returning until late afternoon. He needed to hear all about the action group uninterrupted.

Really? said a voice in his head. He cursed under his breath as he wrung out the coffee-soaked dishcloth.

The light rain didn't stop, but it didn't get any worse and as Sam had predicted, it did soften the ground. The air was warm, which was a good job, as although the rain was light, it still soaked Sam's hair. She eventually pulled on a beanie, but the damage was done, she thought, resigned.

She was just pulling out the roots of a dandelion which appeared to be digging to Australia, when Jonas appeared. He was wearing a big waterproof jacket and looked even larger than she remembered. As the previous day, he was carrying a tray, but this time there were only two steaming mugs on it. Sam glanced at her watch—ten forty-five.

"This is kind of you," she said, as the boys downed tools and came over for the drinks. Steve had mud on his face and in his hair, flicked up by the rotavator, but Jonas just nodded as he handed over a plate of chocolate biscuits.

"You're spoiling us!" Sam said. Jonas laughed.

"Yours is inside," he grinned and turned back to the house.

After a brief pause, Sam followed him to the patio doors and carefully toed off her muddy boots before stepping into the room. Her toes scrunched into the luxurious carpet.

"Hello?" she called.

She saw Jonas' dark head pop around the door.

"Come on in. How do you take your coffee?"

"White, one sugar."

"Sugar? I have some here somewhere..." Jonas began to search in a cupboard and Sam forced herself not to apologise for her sweet tooth.

She took off her jacket and hung it over a chair back, pulled off her cap and finger combed her wet hair.

She slid onto a stool at the shiny black granite counter and smiled brightly as he put the mug of coffee, a jug of milk (not the bottle) and after some decanting, a bowl of sugar, in front of her. He smelled wonderful, she realised, as he moved to the other side of the counter.

"Cold?" he asked.

"No, no—I'll soon warm up with the coffee." And she wrapped her hands around the mug, feeling the heat seep into her fingers. She sipped and then coughed as it went down the wrong way.

"Sorry," she croaked. She cleared her throat. "You wanted to know a bit about Jessop's Field?"

He nodded, and she was aware of his eyes fixed on her face. Stumbling at first, and then getting into her stride, she told him about the public response to the development, and its impact on the village.

"What about the local Council?" Jonas asked.

"Completely non-communicative," she replied bluntly. "We've noticed the difference between this planning application and the one we fought against the big supermarket—the officers were really friendly and helpful on that. On this, we can barely get them to take our phone calls."

"And the elected councillors?"

"Mixed views, one undecided. One of our biggest worries is if we fail, and this goes ahead, there'll be little to prevent further developments alongside it. The damage will have been done, the wildlife disturbed, and the Green Belt cut up—so why not build a few more houses next door?"

Jonas looked sharply at her at that, his brows snapping into a frown. Sam wondered what she'd said.

"What's been the response from the developers? Have they come back to you?" Jonas asked carefully.

"Pah!" Sam took a biscuit and snapped the end of it in her teeth. Jonas blinked. "We've asked for meetings and finally, *finally* after three weeks of asking, they're deigning to have a public meeting! It's tonight." She looked at him speculatively. "You could come along, if you want. I'm going."

"Ah...no, I'm sorry, I can't."

"Shame," she said. There was a short silence and Jonas swigged his coffee.

"Anyway, I thought as you worked in development, you might give us some advice," she said smiling. Silence.

Or not.

Jonas took a deep breath.

"Well, as I said at supper, I've been ordered to avoid anything to do with work and giving advice about a development probably falls into the category of work."

Sam tried not to look disappointed.

"Although I think you're doing everything you should," he added hastily. "If you think the development will affect wildlife, make sure the council ask the developers for an environmental impact assessment."

"Yes, we have that on our list."

"And check the proposed number of houses won't put additional stress on existing facilities."

"Yes, we've done that, and it will."

He was silent. Sam swallowed the rest of her coffee and put the mug carefully on the counter.

"Well, if you think of anything we *haven't* done, perhaps you could let me know?" She smiled again but didn't manage to keep the sarcasm out of her voice.

"Of course. I'm sorry I can't be of more help." He sounded formal.

"Well, I don't want to be responsible for you having a relapse. I'm not sure my public liability insurance is up to that."

As a quip, it was weak, but he smiled broadly at her and she felt her stomach dip, as the intimacy she'd felt on Friday returned.

"No, it might not be. But thanks for being so understanding," he said seriously, catching her gaze.

She dragged on her boots and made her way back to Steve and Andy.

∼

The village hall had standing room only, to Sam's amazement. She wasn't the only one surprised, she thought as she saw a young woman in a London-style suit and rather startling dark eyebrows talking urgently into a mobile phone. The woman was gesturing rather wildly at the heaving room.

Amanda squeezed through the crowd and nudged her arm.

"I see the PR girlies have arrived," she said.

"How do you know she's a PR girlie?"

"Ever seen heels like that in the village?"

Sam glanced at the four-inch spikes of shiny leather.

"Fair point." She glanced around. "It's rammed. I never thought it would raise this much interest."

"Sweetie, these are not all supporters of our cause," Amanda said. "I reckon these are folk who've turned out in return for being put at the top of the waiting list for a house."

"You're joking!"

"Sadly not. See that chap by the window with the leather jacket?" Sam's eyes sought him out. "He's from Stockwell, looking forward to moving into a 'posh' part of the district—with his used car and scrap metal business."

"Surely not," Sam said faintly.

"And the lady with the bright blue fingernails? A lobbyist from Manchester, who's worked with a number of developers and she's not choosey—her last developer was looking to introduce fracking in the Lake District."

"How do you know?"

"She was handing a card to the PR woman and she dropped one.

She's from—ELG—Enlist Lobby Group," Amanda explained. "I got the rest from Google," she tapped her phone.

"Our hostess with the mostest," she continued, nodding towards the suit and the heels, "is from a PR firm who'll likely be flooding the village with leaflets, telling us *all* about the new development, the jobs it will bring, how carefully the design has been done—the usual bollocks."

"Good grief, don't we have *anyone* who's really from the village, other than just us?"

"Well, our esteemed chairman Desmond had a game of golf, so he's not coming, but Tom and Jenny, Susan Miles and Dorothy Pratchett, plus a number of the B&B owners are here."

"But there must be about a hundred people here! Surely they can't all be bogus?"

"Oh, they're not," said Jenny Sanders, appearing suddenly behind them. "Quite a lot have been drummed up by Mrs Pratchett while she was collecting signatures for the objection letter."

"Thank God for that!" Sam said.

"Amen," Tom Sanders added, coming alongside his wife. "Have to say, my feelings towards the developers are starting to be decidedly un-Christian. Hang on, is something happening?"

There was a stir at the door and a truly handsome young man strode into the room. The crowds just seemed to part before him and smiling genially, he made his way to the front of the room. The crowd fell quiet.

"The big boss, obviously," Sam murmured.

"He looks about twelve. I'm starting to feel a failure," responded Amanda. A man turned to glare and went 'Ssh!'.

The PR executive introduced him as Tyler Fairchild, Chief Operating Officer of Anglo Homes. She gazed at the young man, who smiled at her with perfect teeth and moved centre stage. Then he began to talk.

Slick, I'll give him that, thought Sam a little while later. The PR company hadn't made the mistake of presenting lots of slides. There were attractive pictures on the walls and in what seemed to be a totally unscripted presentation, Tyler Fairchild waved at them a great deal. Anglo Homes *cared* about the communities in which it built, apparently.

He spoke of houses for the future, homes for Everyday Working People, mentioned some figures about the amount of work the scheme would bring to the area, and generally painted a very rosy picture of the benefits the development of Jessop's Field would bring.

"Blimey, listening to that, I might even buy one of those houses myself," muttered Amanda.

At the end of twenty minutes, Tyler Fairchild finished his presentation 'of the facts' and asked for questions. Both Tom and Sam put up their hands. The PR lady glanced at Sam, who was scowling, and then nodded encouragingly at Tom.

"I'm pleased to see a representative of the developers here," said Tom, standing up. "However, given that objections to the planning permission need to be lodged by the end of the week, I'm really disappointed you couldn't make it earlier."

The PR lady tightened her lips. Tyler Fairchild smiled easily.

"I'm the chief operating officer of a large company—I'm a bit busy."

A gentle snigger went around the room.

"Too busy for *us*, obviously. I'd like to know if this development—which is small for Anglo Homes—is likely to *stay* small, or if you intend to build further phases."

"That will depend on whether we get planning permission for further phases. We haven't got permission for *this* one yet," Fairchild smiled winningly at the room, "but I hope we've managed to convince you this will be very good for the area."

There was a round of applause that surprised Sam. The development had more supporters in the room than she'd realised.

"Actually, no you haven't convinced me," Tom said. "You haven't mentioned the impact of site traffic on local roads, or on wildlife in the area. And while you speak of jobs, you also don't mention how the development will affect our fledgling tourist industry. Which, with the loss of Jessop's Field, may disappear."

"Aye, my bed and breakfast business relies on birdwatchers and photographers a lot of the year," put in someone else.

"We haven't been asked for an environmental impact assessment by the local authority, but obviously, if required, we can do one."

Fairchild pointedly stopped looking at Tom, as if to move on to another question. The PR lady stretched her neck to look for other questions. She avoided Sam's gaze.

"And what would that mean?" pursued Tom. Fairchild flicked his eyes back to Tom and looked a little less genial.

"We'd take all possible precautions to mitigate any impact the development might have on protected species."

Sounds like he's learned that off by heart thought Sam.

"But anyway," said the man in the leather jacket, before Fairchild could say anything. "What's a few birds when what we want are *houses?*"

There was some nodding. The blustery man got into his stride. "It's all very well for you lot. You've *got* somewhere to live—I live in Stockwell and my own son can't live near us because there's nowhere to buy! And because people have to travel so far, I can't get staff to work in my business!"

The PR executive nodded encouragement.

"Then perhaps Anglo Homes should be building in Stockwell, rather than Sherton!" exclaimed Mrs Pratchett, rising majestically to her feet. "Have you any *notion* of the impact three hundred and fifty additional families will have on Sherton's primary school? Or how our GP surgery will cope with an extra thousand patients?"

There was a louder murmur in the room.

"But you don't want to build in Stockton, do you?" Sam challenged Tyler Fairchild. "You'd rather build on pristine Green Belt land, destroying wildlife habitats and as Tom said, ki-boshing the local tourist trade. Rather than impact your profit margin, you'd prefer the local community to bear all the *impacts*, wouldn't you?"

"I'm sure my company will be making reparation to the local authority—"

"There's no reparation for the damage you'll be doing!" Sam burst

The Garden Plot

out. "Once that landscape is gone, it's gone! I played on Jessop's Field as a kid, like loads of people here did! It's a precious resource for the area, let alone the wildlife there, and you want to just bulldoze through it!"

"But people need houses!" The woman with the blue nails spoke calmly and loudly. "They also want them at the lowest possible cost. And how much they pay out in a mortgage determines how much they can spend elsewhere—including in the village. Are you happy for village businesses to close because you want to save where you *played as a kid?*" The last words were said almost as a snarl, and Sam was startled at the aggression in them. But she didn't back down.

"Don't conflate the argument—who's talking about businesses closing? *I* have a business here! I'm saying—and lots of people in the village agree with me—if there are sites other than Green Belt land to build on, shouldn't we do that first? And there *are* other sites available, aren't there, Mr Fairchild?"

Fairchild, who had sat back to let the audience argue it out among themselves, started as Sam addressed him.

"Well..."

"Or have you just gone straight for the easiest option that will get you the biggest return, *regardless* of what it will do to the local environment?"

"I'm in business, I don't work for Greenpeace," Fairchild said. "In order to build houses for Everyday Working People at reasonable cost, we need to make a profit."

"You're not alone in that, you know! But *have* you looked at other sites? For example, Lower Edge Field, which is lying unused at the moment?" Sam demanded.

"I believe it was considered."

Bloody liar! I bet you don't even know where it is!

"And on what grounds did you dismiss it?" asked Amanda. Fairchild looked towards his PR who shook her head in a tiny gesture.

"That information is commercially confidential," Fairchild said.

"Commercially confidential my arse!" shouted Dorothy Pratchett, to the amazement of everyone. "I imagine, sir, that what 'commercially confidential' *actually* means is that you haven't got an answer because you didn't consider it!"

The PR executive stepped forward and appealed for calm. Flushed, Dorothy Pratchett sat down, muttering, and Jenny Sanders went to her, presumably to stop her physically attacking Fairchild.

The arguments went backwards and forwards and everyone got more and more heated. People began to swear at each other and there was lots of noise. It soon became clear that Fairchild, having delivered his pre-arranged messages, was not going to answer any further questions, and the audience began to turn upon itself, with the lobbyist leading what Sam soon categorised as 'the opposition'. After a few more words, Tyler Fairchild and the PR woman melted away.

Sam put a hand on Amanda's arm.

"It's pointless," she said. "They aren't going to listen to us. We'll just end up shouting at one another."

"Maybe, but I'm damned if I'm going to let that blue-nailed cow leave without a word in her shell-like!" Amanda marched over to the Manchester lobbyist and faced her.

"Are you local? Planning to move here? Or are you just a paid troublemaker from Manchester?"

"I don't have to answer to you," she said.

"Yes, you bloody do! Because if you're *not* local, and if you're *not* buying a house on Jessop's Field, what's it got to do with you? I reckon you're here because you're being paid by Anglo Homes!" Amanda pushed her face close to Ms Blue Nails and Sam started to wonder if there would be a fight. Tom obviously thought there would be, and quickly came between the two women before Amanda took a swing.

"Now, let's be civilised," he said firmly.

"It's easy to be civilised when you already *have* a nice cosy property in Sherton!" said leather jacket. "You're just NIMBYs, that's what you are!"

"What's a NIMBY?" Mrs Pratchett asked Jenny.

"It stands for Not In My Back Yard," Jenny said.

Mrs Pratchett swelled with indignation. "It's not *my* back yard, it's *our* heritage!" she snapped. "I want to save Jessop's Field for future generations! Not in my back yard indeed..."

"What bollocks!" Leather jacket sneered and thrust out his jaw towards her. Not to be outdone, Mrs Pratchett squared up to him and for one wild moment, Sam thought the widow would head butt him. Jenny also seemed to think the same, because she took Mrs Pratchett firmly by the arm and led her away.

"Don't waste your breath Dorothy," was all she said, throwing a contemptuous glance at him. "He's an idiot."

Leather Jacket made as if to go after them both, but Tom and Sam both closed ranks, blocking his path. A little startled by the size of the vicar—Tom was over six foot—he slunk off, muttering.

Sam shook her head in disbelief.

"This is unbelievable," she said quietly. "Like a zoo."

"People get pretty het up over places to live, dear," drawled the lobbyist with the blue nails. "Like he said—you're just NIMBYs. I imagine if this represented a chance for *you* to get a home, you'd care a lot less about disturbing the bloody wildlife."

"We're not asking for there to be no development—just not a development *there*," Sam tried for a reasonable tone.

"So it doesn't disturb your view?"

"It's not just *my* view! And it's not just about the bloody view anyway! Did you not hear a thing we said, or are you paid to be deaf?" Sam bit out, finally fed up with her and losing her temper. The woman looked shifty and started to edge away.

"I've a right to my opinion," she said stiffly and flounced off. Sam let out a breath.

"Yo, bruiser," remarked Amanda, grinning at her. She looked round the rapidly emptying room and called to the vicar.

"Hey Tom—I could do with a drink—are you buying?"

Tom, who was with Jenny and trying to keep a flushed Mrs Pratchett from assaulting anyone who disagreed with her, nodded heartily.

They decamped to the pub.

17

Jonas was lying mortified in bed next to Geraldine, who, despite her denial that all was fine, clearly wasn't happy. It was the first time *ever* he'd not been able to perform in bed. His penis flopped against his leg, testament to his failure.

"Of course I understand darling, it's not an issue," Gerry was saying.

"I'm sorry. Perhaps I'm more tired than I thought," he mumbled.

"Don't worry, Jonas! I'm a silly for not remembering how ill you've been," she said, in a husky voice.

Jonas threw off the bedclothes and reached for his robe.

"Although perhaps you ought to talk to the doctor about it the next time you see him?" Jonas looked at the floor.

"Of course."

Geraldine looked about the room. "Mind you, I do wonder if it's something to do with this house," she continued. "It's awfully old-fashioned, nothing like your apartment in Manchester."

He looked at her in amazement.

"The house? Gerry, it's got nothing to do with the house!"

She shrugged her slim shoulders, the covers slipping down to display her tanned body. Jonas looked away.

"No, of course not, it's your illness." There was a pause. "How long did the doctor say your recuperation would take?"

"Don't fancy the wait?" asked Jonas, stung into unreasonableness.

Her mouth dropped open a little, and then she frowned.

"I think that's a little unfair," she said, some of the huskiness leaving her voice. "All I wanted to know was how long you might be —out of action, so to speak—so I didn't pressurise you..."

"Thanks." Jonas raked his hands through his hair, recognising he was being an arse, but strangely unable to stop himself.

She folded her arms over her magnificent breasts.

"Look Jonas, I'm sorry—*really* sorry—about tonight, but unless there's something you're not telling me, it's hardly *my* fault. Don't take it out on me!"

Jonas tried to recall the last time they'd had sex. Lord, had it been before his illness? This virus hadn't just affected his energy levels, it was now affecting his libido.

The thought of Sam Winterson's nipples in that dratted sweater a month ago waved at him over his subconscious. He pushed it away.

He looked at Gerry, with her blonde hair falling over shoulders like a golden waterfall. He'd liked her appetite for lovemaking, she'd been unashamed and adventurous in bed. They'd taken great pleasure in each other's bodies.

But now—nothing.

Geraldine was looking grumpy. Hardly surprising—for someone who had sex regularly, this was a disaster—he'd been out of action for the last two months. It wasn't fair on her, he thought.

"Tell you what," he said. "Why don't I book us a holiday somewhere hot? Mauritius or somewhere? I haven't had a holiday in a while, and it can be just the two of us."

Gerry looked at him and a slow smile spread across her face. She reached and took his face in her hands and kissed him gently and slowly. Jonas knew this was an attempt to arouse him, and also knew that it wasn't working. After a minute, he drew away.

"So—is that a yes?" he said.

She looked at him for a long time before reaching for the glass of champagne which was sitting on the bedside table.

"Sounds fabulous, but don't spring the dates on me. I have some big openings to attend through the summer."

She took a sip and carefully replaced the glass. "I'm sorry you couldn't—you know," she added.

"Mmm. But I am tired, you're right." Jonas lay down on his side of the bed. Now he thought about it, he was completely knackered.

"Well, hopefully you'll soon get better. The holiday is a sweet idea. Thank you."

He could hear her voice from far away.

"Perhaps tomorrow night we could try again? When you're rested?"

"Mmm..."

A couple of hours later, Jonas stirred. The bed beside him was empty and he forced his eyes open to see Geraldine in the armchair, looking at her phone, texting. As he watched, the phone buzzed softly, and she looked at a message. A smile curled her lips.

"Gerry?" he murmured. She looked at him, startled.

"Sorry—message from the States," she said softly, switching off her phone.

"All ok?" Jonas said, barely awake.

"Yes, all fine."

She put the phone into her bag and climbed into bed.

Sam put her drink on the table and looked at Amanda's animated face.

"We have a very rare bat on the site! Protected under UK *and* EU law!" Amanda said excitedly to Sam as they sat in the pub. She peered at her notebook. "Myotis bechsteinii, to be precise. They have the highest level of statutory protection in the UK."

"Wow. Who knew?" Sam grinned over the top of her gin and tonic. "Does this mean they can't build?"

"Sadly not, but it does mean they have to have a licence before they start any work."

Sam looked at her.

"So? What happens next?"

"We ask for an independent ecologist to get involved, one with a bat licence."

Bat licence? thought Sam, smothering a giggle.

"Mrs Pratchett is even now plotting to raise money to pay the ecologist's fees—you should have seen Desmond's face when he thought he might have to put his hand in his pocket!" Amanda laughed. "Apparently the local authority can't agree the development without taking into account whether Nature UK is *likely* to give a licence," she continued.

"Might they not?" Sam looked at Amanda sharply.

"Luke couldn't say, but these bats are on the verge of extinction, so that should stand for something!"

"Luke?"

Amanda flushed lightly.

"Luke Pearson, from Nature UK. He's an expert, you know. In bats. He's one of the foremost authorities in the country."

"Sound like he made quite an impression," Sam said, watching closely as Amanda's eyes went a little unfocused.

"Well, I got his number, obviously. And he took mine."

Sam gaped a little.

"Just like that?"

"Are you kidding? When someone's got a smile like that, you don't hang around."

"How do you know he's single?"

"No wedding ring, and anyway, I get feelings about people and I think he's a good 'un. Plus I'm going to check him out on Facebook later," Amanda added as an afterthought.

Sam rolled her eyes.

"On the basis of a thirty-minute meeting—which wasn't even private!—you've given him your number?"

Amanda gave her a serious look.

"D'you know, Sam, sometimes I wonder about you. Don't you *know* when something's right? When someone looks at you and smiles and your body starts a little jig of celebration?"

Sam took a sip of her drink. "I'm out of practice," she said.

"Time you got back *in* practice, then!"

"You sound like my bloody sister."

"You need to find some blokes who *you* like the look of, not some stuffed Tory! Isn't there *anyone*?"

Oh, no—not going there!

"Stop throwing me off the subject—what did you say to the Lovely Luke? And importantly, what did he say back?"

Amanda looked dreamy.

"Just that I'd enjoyed his talk. He said it was a shame he couldn't become directly involved with us. I just stood there and smiled, and he said perhaps it would be possible for him to be involved, but in an *unofficial* capacity..."

Sam waited as Amanda trailed off.

"So we swapped numbers and he's supposed to be coming to take me to dinner next Friday."

There was a buzz as a text message came into Amanda's phone. She snatched it off the table and grinned widely as she read it.

"And he's saying he's glad he made an exception to come and visit us."

Sam sipped her gin and tonic, feeling suddenly alone and irritated at the same time.

Stop it! You haven't got time, remember? So she smiled at Amanda and listened to her talk of Luke's virtues, potentially all imaginary.

"It could be an ace in our hand, couldn't it? The bats?" Sam said when she considered an appropriate length of time had passed for Luke-love.

"*Bechstein's* bats," corrected Amanda. "Yes indeed. Although I imagine everything can be changed by our esteemed Secretary of State."

"We ought to get a wildlife protection group involved. Something

European. There must be something, they've got laws on everything," Sam said thoughtfully.

"Bear in mind it takes money to go to court."

"Well, that's why I thought aligning us with a big European group might be a good idea. We don't have much cash, but they might. And there's always Mrs Pratchett..."

"Good thinking, batman. Hey—see what I did there?"

They both giggled. Sam made a note on her phone to check out European wildlife action groups and they finished their drinks.

Sam sat by the fire in her cottage and looked through her scribblings.

She'd had a pretty dismal evening, all things considered. First, Amanda's new crush, while deeply satisfying for those involved, simply made her feel more alone.

Then, she'd seen that the European laws protecting wildlife hadn't been fully adopted in the UK. As a result, there would be plenty of wriggle room for the developers—or indeed the current Secretary of State—to ignore any protest they made about disturbing the wildlife on Jessop's Field.

She stared at the flames. This might be a real fight—the Council needing to hit targets, a big, powerful developer, one that could afford lobbyists and PR people. She'd need to have a word with someone from the Labour office to think through possible campaign tactics, at this rate.

Sam thought back to the meeting. Some of the people had been so aggressive, so rough and their comments so biased, with no concern at all for the heritage of the village, or the beauty of the landscape, she'd been dismayed. She doubted any arguments could change them, but the action group should certainly try. She wrote herself a reminder that she should talk to Amanda about a poster with the arguments against the development for the library.

And surely there wasn't that much demand for housing in the area? She must do some research into that...

Three hours later, she was still awake, staring at the ceiling. Finally, she threw off the covers. Hot chocolate was what she needed.

Yeah, right. What you need is NOT hot chocolate! Jeered her libido.

"Oh, be quiet," she muttered as she slammed a pan of milk on the stove to warm.

But she was caught in a persistent loop of sights, sounds and smells in her head, all connected to Jonas. His lips on her cheek, the firm grip of his hand, his spicy scent, that private, co-conspiratorial look at dinner. She thought, unwillingly, of the tension between them, and those green eyes...

She caught the milk before it boiled over and her mouth twisted wryly at the pan.

"You and me both," she breathed as she put the milk into a mug.

The following day was a struggle, not least because of her lack of sleep.

She took several calls about new design jobs, and while she welcomed them, Sam was starting to wonder how they were going do it all. Her phone buzzed again, and it was Paul, back at the office.

"Hi!" she said, squinting across the sunny, hot garden.

"I take it they'd like us to quote?" came Paul's calm, almost somnambulant tones down the phone.

"Yes, I'm due there on Saturday morning, it's good news, isn't it?"

"You're going to be busy on Saturday—a lady called Joan Dunnant also called—this time to ask you to come and see her about a refresh."

Sam screwed up her nose. "Can you get back to her to say I'll be with her just after lunchtime?"

"Will do. Don't go stretching yourself too thinly, will you? I'm not sure how we'll cope with all this new business. We don't want you having a nervous breakdown."

Sam promised Paul she'd take a holiday and rang off.

Sam allowed herself a moment to gaze unseeing into the middle distance and mentally crossed her fingers. The action group had submitted an objection to the development, asking for a wildlife survey, and Mrs Pratchett had thrown herself into the fundraising with a vengeance—at the last meeting, she'd raised nearly ten thousand pounds, which had impressed even Desmond Black. It would certainly pay for an independent ecologist, even if it *wasn't* the lovely Luke.

Reporters from the regional newspaper had contacted Desmond again about the planning application and Sam had persuaded one of the local councillors to issue a blistering attack on the use of Jessop's Field for housing.

All I need now is to increase the number of hours in a day to about thirty-six and all will be well, she thought, heading back to the boys.

Andy stopped his digging as she walked up and wiped the sweat from his forehead.

"More work?"

"Yes. I'm looking on Saturday at a couple of jobs."

"At this rate we'll need to take more people on," commented Steve as he pulled at a deep-rooted weed.

"I think we'll wait to see if we *get* the jobs before we do that," Sam said quickly. "We can't start more work until we finish this, in any case. So put your back into it, Steve!"

Steve huffed, and cursing under his breath, finally pulled the dandelion out of the ground, falling over in the process.

So it was while he was flat on his backside, being laughed at by Sam and Andy, that he first caught sight of Magda.

"Hi there!" Magda called merrily as she strode out of the house. She was wearing skimpy shorts and a practically backless top. She looked gorgeous and Sam, glancing at Steve, couldn't blame him for turning beetroot red while he scrambled to his feet.

"Ah—school's out?" Sam queried, walking over to this vision of teen loveliness.

"Yup, I've just got back." Magda gestured towards the garden. "It looks amazing! What a difference! I *love* it!" Sam looked around at the piles of soil and stacked stone which looked much *less* than amazing and smiled at Magda's excitement.

"Well, yes, it's coming together... I'm glad you like it so far."

"Yes, Dad's just putting the car away, he'll be here any second."

Sam hadn't seen Jonas to talk to all week. She hadn't known whether to be pleased or disappointed, a ridiculous state of affairs. She caught sight of Steve's face, now tightened after his initial slack-jawed response to Magda, and reluctantly, she introduced them. Magda flirted with both men. At the end of ten minutes, she thought Steve would be the teenager's slave for life. Andy looked on, amused.

So when Jonas strolled over to the group, she turned to him with something like relief. What she wasn't expecting was the rush of pleasure she had at seeing him again—as though she had been thirsty, and someone had offered her cool, clear water. Unguarded, she smiled at him and looked straight into his eyes. The sudden blaze in them made her heart jump, and then the look disappeared as quickly as it had come.

"How's it all coming on?" he said, rather abruptly.

"We're on schedule," Andy said promptly, his tongue in his cheek. Jonas grinned and nodded in wry acknowledgement.

"We've finished digging the borders and should be able to start the planting in a couple of weeks," added Sam, looking around, rather than at, Jonas.

"Why don't you give me and Dad a tour?" Magda said.

Sam rubbed her filthy hands down her jeans, suddenly feeling a bit breathless. "Sure. We'll start with the pond, shall we?"

Jonas listened with quiet amusement as Sam led them both around the garden. He'd slowly gathered his composure as they'd walked, and Magda had been a godsend, did she but know it—it was easier to hide his tension around Sam when his daughter was excitedly asking questions about what the gardening team would be doing next. Sam too seemed to be relaxing and soon there was laughter alongside the comments on stone edging and pergolas and pond liners.

He'd noticed over the past weeks, that he'd felt himself strain to hear Sam's laugh floating across the garden. This was even though he stayed inside his study away from the windows and walked to the village for his daily exercise without looking back.

He had followed up with Neil about the inexplicable omission from the plans of all the features the Halcyon team had submitted to the design.

"I've made some objections to some of the suppliers they're using, but the plans look OK," Neil had said, puzzled.

"Well, the ones I saw in the Library didn't look like a development of ours at all—it was bog standard."

Neil rang two days later to say the plans were being re-submitted following the public meeting—now including Halycon's design elements.

Neil had let drop that they'd had a copy of the plans and were disappointed that what was an obvious first draft had gone in through administrative error. Tyler had brushed it off. Nothing was said about the position of the site, currently too close to Jessop's Field, in his view.

But in any case, the current plans might go through because the Council was desperate for new homes, Jonas reasoned. And Tyler was right—they could charge a premium for the view.

He tuned into the discussion again. Sam's passion about the development was infectious, he decided, and strong emotion could be catching—and his life was complicated enough at the moment, particularly with the earlier-than-expected departure of Geraldine after the other night.

"We've got the paving by the wall to do and once that's settled, we can start to make it really pretty with the flowers and shrubs," Sam was explaining.

"So I've come back for the most exciting bit!" exclaimed Magda.

"We've got quite a bit to do yet," Sam warned.

"Oh, but it'll be brilliant to see it all happening! Won't it, Dad?"

"It will."

"What do you think of it so far?" Magda pressed her father.

He felt Sam tense a little and looked at her.

"I think it's really starting to take shape and it will be lovely when it's all completed," he said, smiling.

"Perhaps if you were to go away for a couple of weeks and then come back, you'd see the difference more clearly," said Sam.

"Trying to get rid of me?"

Sam laughed politely.

"Not at all. But you *are* rather on top of me."

Jonas tried to wipe from his mind the images raised by her innocent remark. He took in her brown forearms and the sunshine glints in her short, tousled hair. He could only be grateful she had more clothes on than his daughter.

"Yes, perhaps," he said. He felt, rather than saw Magda hide a smile. Rather awkwardly, Sam showed them the rest of the work.

He listened in with half an ear, trying to keep his eyes off Sam's very neat backside in her khaki jeans.

Eventually he said, "How's the protest going?" Sam turned.

"It's good," she said briefly. "We've got bats in the area and actually," she added casually, "they're very rare. Someone from Nature UK came down and told us."

"Really?"

"Mmm. Do you anything about bats, Mr Keane?"

Jonas knew probably more than the average developer, but he wasn't about to admit it. "Not much, apart from they're a protected species. That will put a spoke in the wheel of your developer, then."

"Let's hope so."

Jonas wanted to ask her more but thought better of it. Instead he asked,

"Have you got an independent assessor?"

"Yes, I think we're sorted, thanks. But we shouldn't be talking about this—it's bad for your health," Sam said.

Ouch thought Jonas. He inclined his head.

Magda was watching closely.

"Is this the development on Jessop's Field?"

"Yes. I'm not sure what our chances are, but we're campaigning hard. We've just got a meeting with the final councillor on the planning committee."

Jonas' ears pricked up. "The independent you told me about?"

Sam looked at him, surprised.

"You've got a good memory. Yes, the independent."

"When is the planning committee?"

"In about four weeks."

As he wished her a rather vague 'good luck', Jonas began to wonder again what could be done to protect his investment. To take some action looked increasingly necessary.

18

Sam perched on the steps, read the postcard and grinned.

"Ooh la, la! French garcons charmante. Henri in particular. Vin rouge trés quaffable. Tan coming along nicely. Stripy tee-shirts de rigeur. Can't think of further clichés, so will sign off. Love, Lisbeth."

Andy peered over her shoulder reading the card and chuckled. "Sounds like she's having a good time."

"Mmm. *Henri* seems to be giving her a good time, certainly. Her first holiday romance..." Sam replied wryly.

"Hmm. We've got enough issues with teenage crushes here at the moment," he grunted, going to help Steve unload the Land Rover.

Sam sighed. Andy was right. Steve had taken one look at Magda and fallen hard.

His behaviour had been impeccable. But he wasn't completely focused when Magda was around, and he was tongue-tied if she spoke to him.

Magda wandered around during the day as teenagers do—at times with more clothes on than at others. She appeared completely unaware of the passion that throbbed in young Steve's breast and treated both him and Andy with open friendliness.

But Sam was worried. Magda was simply being friendly currently, but if she gave any kind of response to Steve—well, it would be like lighting the blue touch-paper and everyone would need to stand well back.

No Lady Chatterley moments, thank you very much she thought, chewing her lip.

"You look deep in thought," came a deep voice from beside her.

She jumped. "Mr Keane! God, you gave me a start!"

"Sorry. Is everything ok? And it's Jonas, please, not Mr Keane," said Jonas, his green eyes scanning her face. Sam hesitated. "Is it your young apprentice mooning after my daughter that's bothering you?" Jonas said.

She stared at him. "You know?"

"I would have to be blind not to know."

Sam felt her face grow hot. "I'm really very sorry."

"Don't apologise. My daughter's looks and his hormones are hardly your fault."

"I don't really know what to do. I do know this can't go on, but he's been very respectful and has said nothing at all to Magda."

"I know he's been respectful, because otherwise I would be pointing out that my daughter is still at school and underage." Sam said nothing. "If *I* speak to Magda of course, and she *hasn't* noticed Steve, this will simply draw her attention to him," he continued. "I don't fancy putting into my daughter's head she's in some Romeo and Juliet equivalent."

There was a meaningful pause. "Mmm. OK, I'll talk to Steve," Sam said reluctantly.

"It may not be that bad," he said gently.

"Maybe not—but I have to work with him afterwards," she said gloomily.

He smiled at her and she felt her stomach clench as its charm swept over her. "Let me know how it goes."

Sam walked back to the Land Rover.

Oh, joy... What I do to design gardens.

Bonjour! Comment la belle France? texted Magda.

Pas mal de tout, merci! How's Sherton? texted back Lisbeth.

Not as pretty as France—saw photos on Facebook—Henri is GORGEOUS♥♥♥

Yup, & no English—so hav 2 find other ways 2 communic8...

Magda's mouth dropped open a little. Lisbeth?

Her phone vibrated with another text from Lisbeth.

What's hap'ning w. Project Romeo?

Magda thought. At the moment, everyone was being tiresomely professional. She hadn't even seen Sam in anything other than the terribly respectable polo shirt she normally wore, despite the heat, and frankly a polo shirt was never going to drive anyone wild. Didn't she possess a vest top, for heavens' sake?

But, she thought, some kind of fizz happened when Sam and her dad met up, however briefly. It was difficult to explain, but something happened to Sam's skin and her Dad seemed to get taller, a bit more tense.

Before Magda could respond, Lisbeth sent a second text.

Not sure Sam likes ur Dad. Called her b4 we went away & tried 2 find out what she thought of ur dad. Either she didn't want 2 tell or she hadn't thght about it!!

Magda shook her head. Maybe she *was* imagining it. It wasn't as though Sam was looking for excuses to touch Dad, like she'd seen Gerry do, and Dad wasn't being more charming—almost the opposite, if his lukewarm comments about how the garden was coming along were an example.

Let's see, she texted back.

Jonas watched Magda run out of the door, wincing as it slammed shut.

"Sorry!" he heard her call through the open window. He sighed. It was probably a vain hope that she wouldn't completely go through her allowance.

Jonas walked slowly back into his study and switched on his computer to browse through his emails. The lack of activity was starting to really get to him.

The phone rang, startling him from his musings.

"Keane."

"Jonas, can't you *ever* answer the phone without sounding like you're in a bad mood?" queried his mother. He smiled.

"Hello, ma. Nice to hear from you."

"*That's* better—much more polite. How are you?"

"What do you think? I'm bored. All I'm doing is watching the landscape gardeners turn our wilderness into something more fitting for the house. Other than that, I'm feeling better, thanks."

"Oh yes, Magda mentioned the garden in her email. How's it coming along?"

"It's taking shape. I think you'll like it—no, actually, I think you'll *love* it when you see it. The designer's really talented."

"When will it be finished?"

"In a month or so, roughly. I've given the designer a strict deadline and her team are working like dogs."

Niamh was silent for a moment.

"*Her* team?" she said, slowly. "I can't wait to see it. The design must have been spectacular for you to give a woman the job."

"The design *was* spectacular," he said evenly. "Magda's planning a grand opening ceremony—you'll get your invitation soon, no doubt." Jonas paused. "Actually ma, I'm glad you rang. Can you come over and spend some time with Magda?"

"Of course! But have you forgotten we're on a cruise in a week?"

Damn, thought Jonas. "Ah. Yes, I had completely forgotten."

"Is there a problem?"

"Not exactly. It's just that she's starting to be a bit more...attractive...to boys and I could do with some female help about how to handle it."

Niamh laughed. "Oh dear—she's getting to that *dangerous* age, is she?"

"Yes, one of the gardening team is completely smitten."

"Oh dear." Niamh sobered slightly.

"He's a nice lad," Jonas said hastily, "and nothing's happened." Yet, he thought. "I've spoken about it to the designer—"

"So she's going to sort it out when they go back to the office?"

"She's part of the team on site," Jonas said, catching sight of Sam through the open patio doors, putting her foot on a spade.

"Goodness. She sounds…energetic."

"I've never seen anyone so slight do so much physical work," Jonas said. His mother was silent on the line for a few seconds.

"Is Magda aware of the boy's feelings?"

"Not a clue. You know what she's like, just goes through life in a bit of a daze…"

"Well, I'm sorry I can't come now, but we can come and visit when we get back. Hopefully things will remain calm until then."

Jonas hoped so.

∼

"Steve? Can you spare me a minute?"

Steve looked up at her. "Course. Is owt—sorry, is anything wrong?"

Sam shook her head.

"I just need a chat with you." She led the way to the far side of the garden and sat down on the grass. Steve joined her, looking wary.

"Before anything else, I'm delighted with your work," she said, watching him. "Everything is going very well. Your tutors tell me you work hard, and your course work is excellent."

"But?" prompted Steve. Sam smiled wryly in acknowledgement and paused.

"I've noticed you're rather sweet on Magda."

Steve coloured immediately. His eyes swept away from her and he looked at his fingers, pulling up the turf.

"It's just that—I'm really sorry, it's unprofessional and I need you to stop," Sam said as gently as she could.

Steve bowed his head. "I haven't done nothing, what is there to stop?" he mumbled.

Sam sighed.

"You *gaze* after her. You stop concentrating when she's around. It's not just me who's noticed. Her father has too." Steve's head came up. "Don't worry, he's leaving me to talk to you. He also knows you've said and done nothing, and he applauds you for it," Sam embroidered.

Steve was silent for a moment and then shrugged disconsolately. "I knew she were too good for me."

Sam frowned. "What are you saying?"

"Well," said Steve, gesturing towards the house, "she'd probably have nowt to do with me anyway. I'm not in her league."

"That's rubbish. If we weren't doing this job, it would be your own business who you asked out!" Sam exclaimed. "But we *are* doing this job and until it's finished, you'll have to put a rein on how you feel."

Steve looked deep in thought. "Right," he said finally.

"While we're on the job, I'd like you to act like she's not there. Do you think you can do that?"

He shrugged. "Dunno. I guess I'll have to, won't I?"

He smiled tightly and slowly made his way back to where Andy was working. Sam could see the droop in his shoulders and cursed hormones, young love and the hot weather. She suddenly felt ancient and glanced at her watch. Nearly two. Thank God, they would finish for the day soon, hopefully before Magda returned from wherever she'd gone.

It was a rather quiet afternoon. They were packing up when she saw Jonas wave at her from the patio. Her heart sinking, she turned to Andy.

"I need to go and talk to Mr Keane. Don't hang around, I think it would be better if Steve was out of here."

"How will you get back?"

"I'll ask Mr Keane to drop me at the office or get a cab. Leave the Land Rover there and I'll pick it up to go home."

Andy nodded and went off without another word.

She strolled over the house, rolling her shoulders to ease their stiffness. He stood, tall and dark, waiting for her and despite the heat of the afternoon, she shivered. Before she got to the patio, he turned and disappeared into the house. She waited, awkward on the patio until he re-appeared with two glasses, ice bobbing in them. He handed one to her.

"Gin and tonic," he said briefly. "You look like you could use it."

He gestured her to one of the garden chairs and she sank into it with a sigh of relief.

"I saw you speak to Steve," he said.

"Yes."

"How'd it go?"

"He asked me what he could stop, seeing as he's done nothing..." she trailed off and took a drink.

"What did you say?"

"We agreed he needed to act like she wasn't there."

Jonas looked at her.

"You don't approve, do you?" he said, watching the ice bob in his glass.

"It doesn't matter what I think. It matters what *you* think. You're the client. I've done as you asked. Steve will stop mooning after your daughter. I hope. He's going to find it hard, I think. He's very smitten."

Jonas was silent at that.

"I wish I could pack her off to her grandparents, but they're off on a cruise," he said finally.

"Well, I've done my best. Hopefully that will be enough."

"I don't envy him," Jonas added unexpectedly. "Some people don't find it easy to hide their feelings."

Sam looked at him from under her lashes. The afternoon sun was hot on her arms and she could hear the bees, drowsily robbing the flowers of pollen. Jonas looked relaxed, elegant and she sensed the power in his long legs.

"Steve is young, so yes, I imagine it'll be a struggle."

"Does it get easier with age, do you think?" he asked, surprising her. She thought a little.

"I think as you get older, you hide things better—get a better mask."

"Do you? Hide things?"

She stared at him, taken aback by the conversation. "I imagine I'm no different from anyone else, although I try to be as honest as I can—otherwise life gets very tiring."

He laughed softly and she was electrified by the sound.

"What about you?" she ventured before she could stop herself.

"I expect I have my own mask," he admitted smiling. "But I agree, it can get very tiring to keep it in place."

"Do you ever let it drop?"

Jonas met her eyes. "Almost never." His smile seemed to slide along her spine.

She took the final gulp of her drink and put it down on the patio rather hurriedly. "Apart from one of my team fancying himself in love with your daughter, are you happy with the work?" she said, desperate to move the conversation to less disturbing ground.

"Of course," he said, leisurely getting to his feet. He put his hand out and before she realised it, he had pulled her upright. "Care to walk me round?"

Her hand tingled from his touch. "Well, we've dug the foundations for the patio by the wall," she said breathlessly.

"Lead on," he said, with a slow smile.

They walked slowly along the garden walls, and Sam outlined the work they'd done and what was next. He listened attentively.

"I think it will be a wonderfully private place to sit in the evening when it's completed," she finished, imagining it in her head. "And this is a lovely tree. The ash is credited with lots of protective qualities according to British folklore, did you know that?"

He shook his head. She smiled ruefully, embarrassed by her own enthusiasm. "Sorry, I get carried away sometimes."

"I like it," he murmured. She stared at him for what seemed like an endless moment.

Sam tore her eyes from his. "I ought to be going."

And how are you going to do that? she suddenly remembered Andy had taken the Land Rover. "I need a cab," she said, changing her mind about asking for a lift.

"I'll take you."

"No, it's fine—"

"Don't be ridiculous, it's less than five minutes. I'll get my keys."

The ride home in his beautiful, leather-smelling car was very quiet.

"It's just right here," she said. Andy had left the Land Rover outside the office as agreed. She hoped the office would be empty, so she could just collect the Land Rover keys and get home. She longed for a bath, and to get the dirt from under her nails.

"Thanks!" she said on a whoosh of breath, as she struggled to undo the seat belt. Their fingers tangled as he reached across to help her, and the tingle shot through her limbs again. At last, she was free.

"I'll see you tomorrow," he said quietly.

She scrambled out of the car and almost ran into the office.

All very well about Steve hiding his feelings! Her libido taunted. *What about you?*

∼

Jonas' phone buzzed.

"I'd better take this," said Jonas. "I haven't spoken to Gerry in a little while…"

Ignoring Magda's scowl, he went into the study.

"Hello Gerry, how are you?" he said warmly.

"Hi Jonas," Geraldine's voice sounded rather crisp, unlike her usual breathy tones. "I'm fine, I hope you're feeling ok?"

Jonas said he was.

"I'm sorry I can't actually be with you, but I thought I needed to tell you as soon as I could…" she paused. "Jonas, you know how fond I am of you, but I think we've grown apart from one another. I think we shouldn't see one another again."

Jonas was speechless for a second. He sat down.

"This is a bit out of the blue," he said finally.

"Is it? I think it's been building up for a while myself," said Geraldine. "I know it's hard, but I do think it's the best for both of us."

The Garden Plot

Jonas' mind went blank. Had he missed the signs? Or had he not cared enough to look? He wasn't sure he wanted to think about that.

"Is there somebody else?"

Gerry's laugh sounded softly down the line. "How *like* you, Jonas. No, there's no-one else. I might ask you the same question."

"Of course not!" Jonas said, pushing aside any doubts.

"Well, I'm sorry, but we're not right together and—well, I don't have time to hang around. I've decided I *do* want a proper relationship, children, even, and I'm not as young as I was. I know you don't feel the same. Not about me, anyway."

Jonas was stunned by her honesty. "I'm not sure what to say... I'm sorry," he said finally. "I know we haven't been able to be together much just lately and obviously, I've been ill."

"Yes, it *has* been difficult, although I'm not sure that it's just your illness. I think since you moved to the village, we've had less and less in common." Her voice cracked. "Which has caused me some pain, if I'm honest. And you know what a coward I am about pain."

"I never meant to hurt you..." Jonas tried again. "Can't we talk about this? Is there anything I can do to get you to change your mind?"

She laughed softly.

"No, I don't think so. It would be dishonest of both of us, and eventually even more embarrassing, I think."

Jonas was silent. He was a little startled at the clarity and directness of her words. He suddenly wondered whether he'd missed a lot about Geraldine Lord in the time they'd been together.

"I don't know what to say. Are you sure?" he asked, knowing she was. There was silence on the line.

He felt he needed to say something more, but he also needed to be truthful. "I have enjoyed your company, Gerry. You've been a delight," he said sincerely.

"Oh, Jonas—don't be nice to me *now*!" She sounded close to tears and it shocked him. He'd never heard Gerry anything but light-hearted, flippant. "I've made up my mind and I think it's better this way. I don't know what's happened—but something has, hasn't it?"

Jonas felt an unexpected pang of loss. She was uncomplicated, sophisticated, urban. He used to be the same. And now—he'd rather not think about what he was now. He'd reneged on the implicit deal they'd had with one another.

"I suppose it has. Would it make it any better if I said how truly sorry I am?"

She laughed with a catch in her voice, a bit like the old Gerry, but not.

"No, Jonas, it would definitely *not* make it better. But it's nice of you to say it, anyway." She drew a deep breath. "Now, being a bit more practical, can you send over anything I left with you? I think there was a silk wrap, and some hideously expensive face cream which I simply can't do without."

"Of course."

"Thanks. I hope to see you around Manchester, but I daresay we won't meet up often. So goodbye, and thanks for a lovely time."

Jonas once again found himself lost for words. And then, while he was thinking what he could say, he heard the phone go dead.

He was still sitting there five minutes later, lost in thought, when Magda came in search of him.

"Dad? Is anything the matter?" she asked anxiously, seeing his face.

"No. No, everything's fine."

"Is Gerry ok? You look a bit—sad."

He sighed.

"She's fine. She's tied up with one thing and another. I probably won't be seeing her again."

Magda stared at him. "You won't?"

"No. She's busy, and I'll be busy too when I get back to the office, so it's probably best." He stood up and she walked over and gave him a hug. There was a silence.

"Mrs Brown has apple pie for pudding," she said into his shoulder.

"Sounds great."

19

Andy peered up at the blue, blue sky.

"Another hot one," he said to no-one in particular. Sam, her glance flicking to Steve's face in the rear-view mirror, stifled a sigh. Another hot day meant Magda and probably Lisbeth walking around wearing not very much, and the tension in the garden, much like the temperature, would rise.

"I heard something about thunderstorms," she muttered. "We could do with a good storm to clear the air."

It was true on so many fronts. For the past two weeks or so, the work had progressed but the working relationship between her and Jonas had disintegrated. There were sharp comments about mud on the paths, observations about the project management (on track, she was grimly satisfied to note) and just general grumpiness.

"If I didn't know better, I'd have said he was in need of a good shag," she'd said to Amanda, noticing that the willowy blonde had disappeared from Brook Lodge.

She'd been working weekends, too—visiting potential new customers on Saturdays, designing and planning on Sundays and during the evenings. Even Andy was starting to comment about the shadows under her eyes.

Some things were going well. Her contacts in the Labour party had given her information about the independent councillor and as she was so stretched, she'd briefed Mrs Pratchett. Mrs Pratchett, taking her new puppy as additional conversation collateral, had cornered the councillor about the development plans, and with all the finesse of a sledgehammer, had secured a promise to seriously consider their objections against the planning application. Calls for a wildlife survey had been made, but as yet, Anglo Homes were taking their time about a response. The council officers still refused to talk to them, which worried Sam, and infuriated Desmond Black.

Steve, true to his word, had changed his attitude to Magda almost overnight. Magda had been puzzled, then curious, and had seemingly set herself a task to draw the unusually taciturn Steve out of his shell. Steve had resolutely ignored her, and finally Magda lost interest.

All of this was almost as painful to watch as it was for Steve to go through, and Sam was desperately sorry.

They drew up outside the house at eight o'clock sharp. They were expecting the paving to arrive at around nine.

Sam itched to get on with it. Once the patio was complete, they could move on to the planting. *Talking of which....* She walked away from the Land Rover and rang Paul while Andy and Steve unloaded.

"Paul? Hi, look, can you check something for me? Can you get on to Johnson's and check the plants," Sam said. "I heard they were having some financial issues and I want to be sure our order is safe. It's due next week."

"Wouldn't surprise me at all, given the state of things, but where did you hear that?" asked Paul sharply.

"Desmond Black," said Sam a little guiltily. She knew how quickly rumours spread and wanted Desmond to be wrong, but she had her own business to run, after all. And for *this* demanding client, she was particularly anxious. "Look, I haven't said anything to anyone else, and I won't, but I'd quite like to double check, please."

With more comments promising dire outcomes, Paul rang off.

The Garden Plot

Sam caught a glimpse of movement from the house and her stomach lurched.

"I wonder if the Lord of the Manor will deign to speak to the plebs today?" she muttered to herself.

She pressed her fingers against her forehead. The temperature was rising rapidly, and she could feel a headache threatening. She reached into the Land Rover and took a swig of water, the bottle already tepid.

Half an hour later, the delivery wagon drew up in the drive with a spray of gravel.

It took only a few minutes watching Andy's body language and gesticulating hands to realise something was wrong. She walked quickly up to the wagon and its sulky driver, who she didn't recognise.

"Hi," she said briefly. "What's up?"

"They've brought the wrong stone," Andy said, crossly. Sam looked, and indeed, the stone slabs were definitely wrong—wrong size, wrong shape, wrong stone.

"Go back with him and sort out the *right* stone. Tell your boss," Sam turned to the driver, "this will put us back a good half day, maybe more. We were very clear about the order, it needed to arrive today because of our schedule. I'm not happy. In fact, don't you bother telling him, *I'll* tell him when I phone." She paused, and the driver simply looked at her. "What are you waiting for? Get going!" she said sharply and then turned away.

"Come on, we've got stuff to sort out," Andy grabbed the driver's arm as he began to bluster and was marching him back to the cab when Sam's phone rang. She looked at it, saw it was Paul and her stomach turned over with a very bad feeling.

"Sam? You were right. They're about to call in the receivers. They suggested you get over there to get as much of the order as you can before the banks arrive," came Paul's lugubrious tones. "It won't be complete, but you'll have something to be getting on with."

Sam closed her eyes. Her lovely schedule, all gone to pot, not to mention the future wrangling over the money...Thank God she'd built in a few days. She called out to Andy.

"Hang on—there are problems with the plant order. Steve, you'll need to head over to Johnson's to get what there is available of our order today, and the rest we'll sort out later. Take the Land Rover, then meet with Andy at the aggregates site to pick him up. Stay in contact by phone." She tossed him the car keys.

"What will you do here?" Andy asked, climbing into the passenger seat of the wagon.

"Given we're going to have a lot of bedding plants which we weren't expecting until next week, I think I'd better prepare some temporary beds and keep the client reassured, don't you?" Andy flinched in surprise and his eyes narrowed.

"Sorry, I didn't mean to growl at you. I'm hot and it's going to be one of those days, isn't it?" She smiled at him ruefully.

"No problem, we'll sort it out. *Won't we* Barry?" Andy said to the driver of the wagon, who muttered something inaudible. He threw the wagon into gear and it lurched off.

"Anything else I should know?" asked Steve, getting behind the wheel of the Land Rover.

"Ask for Tony. He and my dad went back years... Be kind, after all, his business has just gone down the pan, but don't take no for an answer about our order. I've spent fifteen hundred quid with him, and I want at least some of it here before the bastard banks move in."

"Got it." Steve drove off, leaving her standing in the middle of the drive, feeling rather tearful.

Shit. There but for the grace of God...

"Hiya! Fancy a coffee?" came Magda's cheery voice from the patio door. This morning she was wearing tennis whites. Sam fixed a smile onto her face.

"That would be lovely," she managed, starting to walk towards the house.

"All alone today?" Magda asked.

"We've got to sort out a couple of suppliers. Hopefully Andy and

Steve will be back before lunch." Sam undid her boots at the patio door.

"Problems with suppliers?" said the one voice she didn't want to hear.

"Well, a mistake with the stone order—it should be easily sorted, but it's robbed us of the morning, which is irritating."

Sam straightened and looked Jonas in the face. He looked relaxed and casual in blue jeans and a white tee-shirt.

"You look pale. Is everything else ok?" Jonas said, looking closely at her. She forced a smile.

"Just busy," was all she said, walking into the kitchen. "And it's so hot," she added, fleeing to that safest of topics, the weather.

"I know—I'm playing tennis with Lisbeth and I'm beginning to wish we hadn't made the arrangements! I'll be nothing but a grease spot at the end of a couple of games!" Magda put in, spooning coffee into the cafetière.

Conversation was a little strained—Magda wanted to know what they would be working on today, and Sam was evasive. Jonas was quiet, and she felt his eyes on her face as she and Magda talked. It made her skin tingle.

It was with some relief she heard the doorbell ring announcing the arrival of Lisbeth. A brief hello, a hug, and the two girls left for the local courts.

"I must get on too," Sam said, finishing her coffee and easing off the kitchen stool.

Jonas said nothing as she bent to lace up her boots. When she stood up, he was nearer than she realised, and she stepped back hastily, nearly falling over the patio step. His hand shot out and grabbed her wrist, steadying her.

"I didn't realise you were so close," she said, her tension making her a little sharp. His hand dropped immediately.

"Sorry."

She took a deep breath in, and saw his eyes drop to her breasts as they strained the buttons of her shirt. She flushed and almost ran out of the house.

Jonas cursed inwardly, putting the crossword aside impatiently. He couldn't think, the house was too quiet, he was too restless, and it was just too bloody hot.

He glanced at the clock. Nearly twelve. He rose and stretched, feeling the faded blue denim pull against his thighs.

He could see Sam digging in one of the beds, alone. He peered at the sky, which had turned from a rococo blue to a slate grey. The birds seemed to have stopped singing, and the air was heavy, still.

Sam had paused in her digging. From here she suddenly looked exhausted. She must be dehydrating in this heat, he thought, and he walked to the kitchen to get her a cold drink. He was aware they'd barely spoken in the last few weeks, and he'd been like a bear with a sore head. Adding ice to the water, he grimaced.

It wasn't a sore head that was the problem, he admitted wryly.

He heard the rumble of thunder. Seconds later, the heavy thud of raindrops sounded on the skylight in the kitchen. God, it sounded like a real downpour.

Across the patio, he saw Sam gathering her tools and making her way across to the ash tree for some shelter, he guessed. He called to her, but his voice was lost in another roll of thunder.

She dropped the tools under the tree and dragged a tarpaulin over them. She needs to get indoors, thought Jonas.

"Sam! Over here!" he shouted from the patio door. He saw her look over and hesitate. "Come *on!*" he called. "You'll be drenched out there!"

She looked at him for a couple of seconds and then was running over the grass, slipping a little as the rain soaked the ground. Jonas opened both doors and she arrived, panting, fumbling on the doorstep with her bootlaces.

"Don't worry about them, come *in!*"

"You won't thank me for getting mud all over your carpet!" she said sharply, as she kicked them off and left them by the door on the mat.

Face to face without her boots, she was shorter than he remembered. Her hair was plastered to her head, and her tee-shirt to her back. Her khaki shorts slapped against her legs. If he hadn't known better, he would have thought she'd thrown herself into a pool of water.

"I'll get you a towel," he said and turned away. Returning a couple of minutes later, he found her still standing where he'd left her, looking thoroughly miserable and starting to shake with cold.

"Here," he thrust the towel at her.

"Thanks."

"I'll get you a drink—you look frozen."

"Th-thanks."

He glanced sharply at her as he heard the tremor in her voice. She looked upset, he thought.

His mind was a careful blank as he made the coffee. Wet clothes, the two of them alone in the house—it was the worst cliché from a porn movie.

Sam trailed into the kitchen, rubbing her hair. She paused and draped the towel over her shoulders, and hitched her hip onto the tall kitchen stool, cupping her hands around the coffee he placed in front of her. She let out a juddering sigh before taking a drink.

"Are you ok? Not hurt?"

She shook her head.

The rain drummed on the skylight and she looked at it, her mouth twisting. "Looks like we'd have been stuffed getting the paving done today anyway."

"No, you could never lay it in this weather."

There was a silence as she sipped her coffee. She stretched her leg. He saw the damp fabric rubbing against the skin of her thigh. His eyes were riveted to it.

"I'll have to go home to get changed," she said finally.

There was another pause before he said hesitantly, "We have a tumble drier. It would take about thirty minutes to dry your stuff, I imagine. I could lend you a dressing gown."

She flushed. "Erm..." She looked at him and trailed off. The silence stretched on.

"Yes, you're right," he said as she didn't finish her sentence. "It probably wouldn't be a good idea."

She looked at him, a full, honest look, he thought. "No. It probably wouldn't," she said softly.

"No."

Silence.

She gripped her mug so tight he could see her knuckles turn white. He hardly dared to breathe, fearing to disturb the tension in the room swirling around them. And then Sam's phone rang, making them both jump.

"Andy? Hi. What's happened? I see... OK, are you on your way back then? No, it started chucking it down, so I'm sitting in Mr Keane's kitchen, very damp... Yes, I will. OK, see you later." She finished the call.

"I wonder," she said hesitantly. "Could you give me a lift home? The boys won't be back for another hour and I'll catch my death if I don't change soon."

"Of course."

What kind of madness was THAT? Sam wondered during the generally silent drive.

"Just here," she said, indicating her cottage. He pulled smoothly into it and turned off the engine. The rain continued to slash against the windows.

"I'll sit here and wait for you, shall I?"

She paused. "No, of course not. Come and wait in the lounge, I won't be two minutes."

They made a dash for the front door, and naturally, as the wood had swollen in the rain, she had to put her shoulder to it.

"Ooof! I need to get that fixed sometime..." she gasped as she tumbled through into the hall. "Take a seat, I'll be with you in just a sec."

She took the stairs two at a time, pulling off her damp and chilly tee-shirt almost before she was out of sight.

She was listening hard as she rifled in drawers, grabbing fresh clothes. There was silence from her lounge, which was a bit unnerving. As she pushed her khakis down her legs, she called out.

"This is really kind of you, you know. I'd have caught pneumonia without a change of clothes!"

"No problem," his voice floated up the stairs to her. "You have a lovely cottage."

"Thanks. It's late eighteenth century, so it has its peculiarities—uneven floors, low ceilings in some bits—and so much planning red tape you can barely change a tap without getting permission." His low-pitched chuckle licked along her veins.

"God, get a grip, woman!" she muttered to herself as she shoved her tee-shirt into a fresh pair of jeans.

He was scrutinising her bookshelves when she clattered down the stairs.

"You have an interesting selection," he commented, without apologising for looking at them. She looked at him steadily and then sat down on the sofa to pull on her socks.

"How is it interesting?"

"Huxley, Iain Banks, and also Mrs Gaskill—quite mixed." He didn't mention the Labour Party newsletter which blazed red and garish on the coffee table.

"I have wide tastes. And left wing, obviously," she said, her voice muffled as she wrestled with her socks.

"Well, I gathered that at dinner. Do you and your brother-in-law see eye to eye on anything?"

"Not much, no." Sam stood up.

"That must make family life a bit trying."

"We manage. Just."

"Must be stressful, keeping it civil."

"It is. I'm a heart-on-my-sleeve sort of lass, me," she said brightly, and unthinkingly.

His eyebrows tweaked.

She watched warily as he walked towards her. Too close. She could smell him, a faint, spicy scent. She rammed her hands into her pockets to stop her doing anything stupid with them. Like reaching for him.

"Shall we brave the weather?" He was quite still, watching her closely.

"I think we should." Her voice was a little rough, like she'd been shouting.

He strode to the door.

20

Sam couldn't believe her eyes. Her hand clenched in fury around the letter with its Parliamentary logo.

"Thank you for the interest you have shown in my constituency, but I regret I am unable to help. Responsibility for planning applications is entirely the remit of the local planning committee and any involvement from the local MP—no matter how well-intentioned —would be interference.

I am aware of the fledgling tourist industry in the area, and am a strong proponent of its importance to the local economy—last year, for example, figures from the Department of Culture, Media and Sport estimated that visitors to the UK spent more than £21billion. So I am keen to encourage expansion in the area, but to do this requires homes for the hard-working people who service this growth. This development will go some way towards alleviating the housing shortage which exists in my constituency and although it may cause temporary inconvenience to the local population, it will reap benefits in the long term."

It was signed Fraser McAllen, MP.

"Patronising, smug git!" she hissed through clenched teeth.

"*temporary inconvenience*'? *And* what a complete waste of public money to bloody *write* to me! I knew what he thought after I'd seen him!"

Sam crumpled the letter and flung it onto the other side of the room. She paced the floor for a minute or two, muttering. She walked across the room and picked up the ball of paper and noticed it had been copied into the Leader of the Local Council and the Chief Planning Officer.

"Oooh!" she exclaimed and started pacing again. The timing was disastrous, only a fortnight before the local committee met.

After a few minutes, she knew she'd need to get out of the cottage before she broke something and snatching up the letter, her car keys and sunglasses, she strode out.

As it was a Saturday, Fraser would be home. She rang the bell.

"Hi Sam!" said Lisbeth, looking surprised. "Is anything wrong?"

"I just need a word with your Dad—is he in?"

"In the garden with mum. Are you all right? You look knackered."

Sam didn't answer but strode off. She caught sight of them in deckchairs in the shade of the oak tree.

"Sam! To what do we owe the pleasure?" asked Charlie, surprised.

"I need to talk to Fraser," she gritted, feeling even crosser as Fraser looked smug.

"Why so het up, sister dear?"

"This letter." She took the crumpled sheet from her pocket. "Tell me, was it completely necessary to send this to me?"

"You came to me on a constituency matter."

"I came to you to ask for your support as *family*," she said. "I didn't expect a formal response, and I certainly didn't expect a formal response which made your 'unofficial' position so clear to the local authorities!"

"Had I supported your view, you'd want me to act officially, wouldn't you?" Fraser lips tightened.

"Had you indicated you would support us, the *group* would have written to you officially! I thought my visit was a private chat!"

He shrugged.

"And I imagine that in getting all your bloody paperwork in order, you had *no* idea your *unofficial* view would sway the local authorities, did you?" she burst out. "But that's exactly what copying in the leader of the council and the local planning officer will do!"

He took a swig of his drink.

"Sam, I'm sure Fraser didn't mean—"

"Oh, for God's sake, Charlie! Of *course he bloody meant it!* It's what he does, politicking! He's a career politician! Too busy focusing on the next post in the Cabinet to care much about what happens locally, normally!" She drew breath. "Except you made a special exception for the cause I support, didn't you?"

Fraser got up. "Samantha, you always did suffer from too much self-importance," he said. "It's appropriate for me to copy in the relevant parties in cases like this."

"If I'd approached you through your constituency office, maybe, but I didn't! There was no need to send me anything official, but now of course, your paperwork is nice and neat, and you've potentially tipped the balance in the favour of the development. You're a complete *arse,* Fraser."

"Charming."

"Mum? Dad? What's going on?"

Sam spun round to see Lisbeth, her face pale, watching them.

"Sam and your Dad are just having a little disagreement," said Charlie, who was looking between Sam and Fraser anxiously. "It's not important, and anyway, I thought you were off out?"

Sam scowled. "Only you could call my home and the place I grew up and where we both played as kids 'unimportant', Charlie. This may be pretty small beer to you and Fraser, but it's *very* important to me."

"I have other priorities, Samantha," Fraser said, looking into his glass.

"Maybe, but I'm not sticking a knife in your back when we disagree," Sam replied.

"Is this about Jessop's Field then?" asked Lisbeth, looking upset.

"No, it's about how your Dad chose to tell me he wouldn't support me," Sam said, her eyes on Fraser, who frowned.

"This is all a bit over-dramatic, wouldn't you say?" he said.

Sam shook her head in disbelief. "Empathetic as ever, I see." She dropped the letter on the grass and turned to leave.

"Sam...?" Lisbeth's voice followed her.

"I'll see you later sweetie," she said, as Lisbeth caught up.

"But—"

"Look Lisbeth, this is between your dad and I, and it'll blow over eventually, but I'm as mad as hell now, and if we speak now, I'll say something I'll regret. So leave it, ok?"

"But—"

"I said *leave it!*" Sam said, pulling open the gate. Lisbeth stopped dead and Sam left without another word.

It was inevitable she'd head to Jessop's Field. The gentle contours of the landscape and the glint of sunlight through the trees soothed her and would reset her sense of perspective.

She was out of breath when she reached the boundaries, marked by the ancient hedgerows. As she stepped over the stile, she caught the sound of kids playing in the woods and even while still boiling with anger, memories of make-believe dragons and knights, lost treasure and Marmite sandwiches flooded her mind. She marched along the well-worn path, and the trees seemed to shush her frustration and anger. Sam felt the muscles knotted in her shoulders gradually, finally, unwind.

The big pond at the base of the field was deserted and she was grateful as she sank onto the grass.

Her mind ran over the last hour and Sam chewed her lip.

What a complete tosser. How on earth does Charlie put up with him?

She blew out her cheeks and stared at the light reflecting off the water, lost in thought. The minutes ticked by.

"You look fierce."

She jumped. Jonas stood a yard away, his face quizzical.

"Oh! Hi…" The row with Fraser suddenly gone from her mind, Sam made to scramble to her feet. Jonas waved her back down and instead, joined her on the grass.

"Big problem?"

Sam shrugged and smiled wryly. *Oh, if only you knew…*

"No, it's just stuff." She looked sideways at him. "But what are you doing here?"

"Just enjoying the local beauty spots," he said, casually. "This reminds me of somewhere I went as a kid in Germany."

"Really? I thought Germany was supposed to have fairly *spectacular* scenery," Sam said, sceptical. "I love this place, but it's not spectacular."

"But as well as the Bavarian Alps, we also have gentler scenery—quiet hills and still waters. Just like this."

How lyrical, Sam thought, struck by his words and once again by his dark velvet voice. She was brought back to earth as she remembered why she was sitting there. "Well, enjoy it while you can. It may not survive the development," she said dryly.

He was silent.

She recalled the tension during the rainstorm earlier in the week. Since then, she always seemed to be seeking him out, wanting to catch a glimpse of him. And suddenly, instead of never seeing him, she saw him a lot, at the windows, bringing drinks, asking about the garden work. She hadn't really known what to make of it, but she knew she was hungry for more. It was not a comfortable feeling.

Time to go, I think.

Her peace shattered, she brushed imaginary dirt from her thin cotton skirt and got to her feet.

"Well, I must be going—" She broke off as he caught her hand. She stared at his long fingers curled around her own.

"Don't go—I didn't mean to disturb you. Sit a little longer."

Sam looked into his green eyes.

"OK, just a few minutes." She sat down again, careful to put some distance between them.

Jonas looked at the pond, his hand shading his eyes from the sun. "I lived for a while near Cologne and there were woodlands not far from our apartment. I had a tough time with my father at one stage—the usual arrogant teenage rebellion—and after our regular rows I'd escape and calm down looking at trees and water. A lot like this. Looking back, I don't think I knew how much I valued it."

"I can't imagine you as a rebellious teenager," she said. He grinned at her and she changed her mind abruptly. *Or perhaps I can.*

He laughed. "You'd be surprised. When did you start coming here?"

"I can't remember *not* coming here. I spent every day of my summer holidays here when I was at school. We used to bring picnics and stay here all day, Charlie and me. When I visited from college, it was my first port of call after I'd said hello to Dad."

There was a pause.

"You're right. It's a lovely spot," he added in a low voice. Sam's stomach turned over at his tone, soft and intimate.

"It's always brought me some kind of peace."

Well, until about five minutes ago commented her libido.

"I can see why."

Sam could feel the heat from his body beside her, smell the faint tang of his aftershave and she looked at the pond, no longer seeing it, but needing to put her eyes somewhere.

Relax, relax, re—

Then his hand brushed her arm and she gave a quick intake of breath, electrified. She watched his hand trail along her skin.

Sam's mind went blank. Her libido was up and doing a jig, but nothing sensible came to mind to say. So she just looked at him and saw his green eyes gleaming. Slowly, he leaned towards her. *Yes, yes, yes!* shouted her body.

"Is this a good idea?" said her voice and her brain, while all the time looking at his mouth.

"Probably not. But you won't be designing my garden forever," he replied in a thickened voice, his eyes fixed on her face.

"True."

His mouth was a fraction away from hers and closing her eyes and ignoring all rational thoughts about clients and work, and about this *definitely* not being a good idea—she kissed him.

His mouth was just as she'd thought it would be—firm and warm and expert. He touched her lips gently and then, as she shifted closer to him, he deepened the kiss, pushing her back onto the smooth, lush grass.

Oh, my...

Sam felt her body leap to attention—her nipples, her skin, all seemed on high alert, tender, demanding. She felt his weight across her body, his hands capturing her wrists above her head. She arched up, pressing closer, feeling his hardness against her stomach. After a few minutes of being thoroughly kissed, Sam heard him growl in his throat and to her intense disappointment, he rolled away from her. He sat up and stared into the distance. He was breathing hard.

"Wha—" She was bewildered. Sighing heavily, Jonas turned to face her.

"I think if we're going to keep this legal and decent in a public space, we need to stop—*I* need to stop."

Sam grinned and ran her eyes over his back and shoulders. She itched to touch him. Instead she struggled upright and sat on her hands.

There was a pulsing silence. Sam, striving for some sort of normality, and ignoring the blood singing in her veins, said, "You're right. We ought to be sensible. After all, you're my client. So perhaps it's only right that that we complete the garden before..."

He looked at her and his mouth curled when he saw she'd incapacitated her hands.

"I don't mind telling you, I don't *feel* like doing the right thing at the moment."

"But *I* don't feel like being a hypocrite. Remember Steve and Magda?"

"My daughter is under-age—just," he said. "We're consenting adults."

"Nonetheless..."

He nodded, his eyes taking in her face. She felt caressed, and he wasn't even touching her. She pressed her thighs together, feeling the heat rise between them, and swallowed. He sighed.

"You're right of course. It would be supremely hypocritical. How long will the garden take to finish?"

"About three weeks."

"Early August?"

She laughed. "You agreed the schedule! I'm doing my level best to make sure we don't lose any days, I promise you!"

"So if the work goes off course, should I take it you're not interested in continuing our 'discussion'?"

"Jonas, if I've got something to tell you, I'll do it face to face."

He drew closer.

"Mmm. I imagine you would." Despite her best intentions, her eyes flicked to his mouth and she saw it curve. "Hopefully, this will persuade you to *keep* the work on schedule."

He lowered his mouth kissed her again, slowly and languidly. Eventually she drew away, trembling.

"Consider me persuaded."

Magda looked narrowly at her father as he came through the door.

"There you are! Mrs Brown's been asking when you'll be back. She's fretting about the washing machine repairs."

"Mmm? Oh, right. Is she in the kitchen?"

"Yes. Is everything alright, Dad?"

"Yes, fine. Why shouldn't it be?"

"I don't know. You look sort of...different."

His mouth tweaked slightly, and she thought he suddenly looked younger, with a rather devilish air to him. "Do I? Must be the fresh air."

The Garden Plot

"Where have you been?"

"Me? Oh, just down by Jessop's Field. I thought I'd go and have a look at it, given the fuss over the development."

"I've been there with Lisbeth. It's lovely, isn't it?"

"Mmm. Very lovely."

She watched him as he strolled off to the kitchen, whistling.

21

"I don't think it's necessary to be this uptight," Tyler Fairchild said, on the edge of sulkiness.

"I'm sorry if you think this is uptight," said Jonas. "But I'm at a loss to understand why our *shared* expertise—the basis of our original agreement—wasn't reflected in the plans that went in."

"It was just a mistake."

"Then I sincerely hope the rest of the administration is faultless."

John Fairchild cleared his throat. "I'm sure Tyler has a grip on it all now. The new plans are exactly what you would expect."

Jonas kept silent. It was left to Neil to ask about the response from the public meeting.

"Well, there are plenty of eco-warriors in the village, but I'm sure they'll have only limited influence," said Tyler.

"Really? I saw a note on the file which asked for a wildlife survey from Nature UK," Neil said.

"Yes, but we'll just do some slight adjustments and that will be that."

"And the position of the site?"

"That view will enable us to charge premium prices for some of the executive homes and if we're not in breach of the environmental impact assessment, there'd be no need to move it."

"The feelings about Jessop's Field run pretty high," put in Jonas. "I've read the news clippings. Are you planning any changes?"

"If there's no need, why should we?"

"Because," said Jonas, determinedly patient, "Halcyon doesn't do business like this."

"But no-one knows you're involved," Tyler objected.

"That surely is beside the point."

"And news and rumours spread, don't they? We've had our own press office in Brussels ask if Halcyon is involved with any other developers on joint projects," put in Neil.

"Well, that's nothing to do with me!"

Jonas drummed his fingers on the desk, frustrated.

"Look guys, the planning committee meets in less than a fortnight," Tyler said smoothly. "We think we're home and dry and there's certainly no reason to change the plans unless they specifically *ask* for it. The environmental report will be completed by the beginning of next week and if it's just some bats, we'll provide alternative nesting sites for them—simples."

Just some bats? thought Jonas.

He said nothing and the rather bad-tempered call ended. Given he wasn't supposed to be anywhere near the site, let alone thinking of getting a lot closer to a member of the group fighting the development, Jonas knew himself powerless to do anything. Perhaps he should have come clean to John Fairchild about his move to Sherton before this.

"Too late now," he muttered under his breath.

There was nothing to do now but wait for the planning committee meeting.

Jonas forced himself to stay seated at the breakfast bar even though his ears, tuned to the noise of the Land Rover engine, knew the moment it pulled up in the drive. He felt like a teenager. It had been like this for nearly five days now, and he wondered if he was starting to lose his mind. Sam filled his thoughts, awake or asleep and his dreams had begun to turn technicolour and X-rated. They hadn't been helped by Sam changing her work gear—instead of her tee-shirts, she now occasionally wore vest tops which showed off her small breasts and slim shoulders and arms, now golden with the summer sun.

His thoughts were lingering on the previous night's fantasy when the doorbell rang. He almost shot to his feet.

"I'll get it!" called Magda, clattering down the stairs.

He could hear the murmur of voices in the hall and looked at, rather than read the financial columns.

"Morning," came a husky voice. He looked up and saw Sam. He jumped up.

"Morning. How are you?" He held out a chair for her.

"Good, thanks." He could feel her eyes running over him and he tensed. Sam smiled.

"I thought I'd let you know that we're moving on to planting. We've got some of the plants in temporary beds, but we need to get more."

"Ooh! How exciting!" said Magda "You said I could come with you to pick the plants we're going to use—can I still do that?"

Sam's smile faltered. "Of course. It will probably be in a couple of days, and we'll need to go early. Can you be up and ready at six?"

"Really? That early?" Magda looked appalled.

Sam grinned at her. "Sorry, we'll need to get a lot of plants and we need to have time to get them in. So the earlier the better."

Magda grimaced. "If I must, then." Jonas winked at Sam.

"I'll get her up. She may not say much for the first couple of hours."

Sam laughed, waving away the tea Magda offered. "No thank you, I must get on. Got to keep to the schedule," she said, not looking at Jonas. With a cheeky grin, she left.

"Yes indeed," murmured Jonas.

The phone rang just as Jonas was about to leave the house for a walk and escape the distracting sight of Sam working in the sunshine.

"Keane."

"Hello, Mr Keane. This is Dr Walters, I'm ringing with your next appointment."

"*More* tests?"

"Unless you prefer to drop dead unexpectedly."

Jonas hid a smile. "Well, since you put it *that* way..."

They agreed a date.

"How are you feeling?"

"OK, I think. I'm managing to get through the day without a nap and I've increased my exercise."

"Energy levels?"

"Good, I think, although I do get very tired at the end of the day still."

"To be expected, but if you're now getting through the day, that's good progress. Exercise?"

"OK. I miss my runs."

"You'll get back to it eventually. Appetite?"

"Excellent."

"Sex drive?"

Jonas started. "Sorry?"

"How is your sex drive, Mr Keane? Occasionally, ordinary glandular fever has an impact on the sex drive, and as this is the nearest thing we can equate your illness to, your libido may be impacted," Dr Walters said patiently.

"Erm... Well, it *has* been affected..."

But not anymore, he thought, thinking of Sam's smooth tanned skin.

"And is it improving?"

"Yes, I think I can say it is."

The call ended with Jonas smiling wryly at the phone. He glanced out of the window to see Sam stretching to ease an ache in her back.

He could see her flat stomach as the vest top parted from her khaki shorts.

Definitely improving.

∼

Sam saw Jonas stride out of the house. She hadn't thought her agreement with him would be so damned hard to keep. She itched to touch him, to run her hands over that broad back, to feel his lips again. Her calendar now had days crossed from it.

She could feel the beginning of a headache, and she rubbed her temples. Trying to focus, she looked at the paving. It looked even better than she'd hoped, unusual with its chequerboard design. It was ready for some of the plants.

Which raised the sticky problem of Magda, coming to the nursery to make up the plants they'd not received from Johnson's, their now-defunct supplier.

Steve was being very discreet, but Sam, now sharply sensitive because she was in a similar position with Jonas, recognised the signs of someone still very much smitten. Steve glanced at Magda when he thought no-one was looking and listened in to any conversation in which she was involved. His quiet stoicism touched Sam. She wondered how Magda was so blind.

She checked her phone. A text from Amanda, reminding her of an action group meeting, a message from Paul about another new business enquiry. Still no word from Lisbeth.

Charlie had not been in contact either since the row with Fraser a fortnight ago, but Sam was less concerned about that than she was about the radio silence from Lisbeth.

It had taken Sam a while to text her niece to say sorry for snapping at her. The evening of the argument had been spent floating a foot above the ground, remembering Jonas' hands and mouth on her.

She frowned again, feeling her temples throb. *God that hurts...*

"You ok?" asked Andy, from the other side of the patio.

"Bit of a headache," she said. "I need to arrange a visit to the nursery to pick up more plants."

Andy pursed his lips. "Yes—we could plant the borders the day after tomorrow."

"Magda wants to come to the nursery with us."

"Ah."

Sam screwed up her nose. "I know..."

"He'll be fine. Don't worry about it," Andy said calmly.

She sighed and Andy peered at her. "Are you truly ok? You look a bit flushed."

"I'll take some pills."

But the headache got steadily worse and by midday, Sam could barely lift her head.

"This is hopeless. I've got to go home."

Steve tutted at her. "Finally. You should've gone hours ago. I'll run you home." Sam felt too poorly to argue and simply climbed into the passenger seat.

"Tell Jo- Mr Keane I'm not well and that I'll be back tomorrow," she said to Andy. He nodded and then waved her away.

"Get to bed and *stay* there until you're better. Otherwise I'll get Greg on you." She nodded, barely hearing, as Steve drove her away.

Three hours later, she jerked awake. The bedroom spun as she lifted her head and she felt sweat run down her neck. She groaned softly and struggled onto her elbows, waiting for the room to stop moving. It didn't.

She pushed the covers down and crawled out of bed. She winced as she saw herself in the mirror. Her eyes were sunk, her face paper white. Her hair was stuck to her head.

Urgh... Gruesome, she thought and splashed water over her burning face. She fumbled in the medicine cupboard and swallowed some aspirin. She grasped the wash basin and hung on while a wave of dizziness swept over her. Finally, it passed. Everything ached and by the time she reached the bed, she felt as if she'd run a marathon rather than walking twelve feet from the bathroom. She groaned, lay back and shut her eyes.

"Is Ms Winterson around?" Jonas asked, casually.

Andy looked up from the gravel he was raking.

"She went home around lunchtime, she wasn't feeling well. She said she'd see you tomorrow, but I wouldn't bet on it. I think she's been working too hard. Steve said she looked dire when he dropped her off."

Steve nodded. "Awful, she looked. Mam says there's a virus going around—half the people in the store have been off with it."

"Is someone checking on her?"

Andy gave him a shrewd look.

"Yes, Mr Keane. I'll call in later, I have a key."

Oh you do, do you? thought Jonas, irritated. He took a breath. "Right. Let me know when she'll be back, will you? And pass on my best wishes, of course."

"Of course. We're a little ahead of the schedule, so I don't think her absence for a few days will impact it, she prepared quite detailed plans."

"I'm more worried about her health!"

"Actually, she gave me explicit instructions not to let the schedule slip," Andy said, fixing him with a look.

"Yeah, she's been working us like slaves to get it completed early!" piped in Steve. "Anyone would think there's a race on!"

Jonas hid a smile. "Well, please pass on my best wishes for a speedy recovery."

He walked away. Disturbed that Sam was unwell, but smug it wasn't just him longing for the garden to be finished and their professional relationship to end. He glanced at his watch. No, there wasn't time for him to visit the cottage, particularly if Andy was going to call in. He'd think about visiting tomorrow, maybe...

Sam heard the ring of the doorbell through what seemed to be cotton wool.

Go away... She winced as the sharp pain stabbed through her temples and then tensed as she heard someone come through the front door.

"Sam? It's Andy. Are you here?"

"Up here," she croaked, horrified that her voice seemed to have vanished. She tried again. "Up here!"

She heard Andy come up the stairs; they creaked a little with his weight. He pushed open her bedroom door and leaned against the door frame.

"Hiya. How are you feeling? Actually, don't answer that. You look like shit."

"Thanks," she whispered.

He moved into the room, and she vainly tried to straighten the rumpled bedcovers, feeling the sweat prickle on her brow. She made to sit up, but he pressed her back down.

"No, don't move. You look like you might fall over. When was the last time you took pills?"

"No idea, sorry."

"Hmm. Last time you drank something?"

"Hours ago."

"I'll get you some tea and some water. How long have you been in bed?"

"Since I got home."

"Right, stay there."

He disappeared downstairs to appear a short time later with tea and a jug of iced water. She eased up and leaned against the bedhead.

"God, that's marvellous," she whispered as the hot tea hit the back of her throat. He pressed his hand against her forehead and frowned.

"You're quite feverish. I might give Greg a call."

As he talked to Greg, Sam closed her eyes and savoured her tea. She felt wrung out. She caught sight of the alarm clock and eventually, when her groggy brain put it together, realised she'd slept the clock round and it was now morning.

Andy finished his call.

"Greg will be here in about ten minutes to give a second opinion." He eyed the rumpled bed. "I know I told you to stay put, but I think I'll strip the bedclothes. You'll be much more comfortable. Where's your wrap?"

Sam pointed to the back of the door and he took the waffle dressing gown and threw it over her shoulders.

"Can you get up?"

"Think so." Sam put her feet on the floor, swayed, and then Andy caught her.

"Whoa! Nope, not yet, I think. Put your arms around my neck. Here we go."

Sam's head swam as he lifted her up and carried her carefully to the chair by the window. Her phone rang.

"Leave it—oh, it's Lisbeth," he said, catching sight of the screen. "You ought to tell her you're unwell." Sam took the phone.

"Hello?"

"Hi, it's—What's wrong? You sound terrible!"

"It's just a cold."

"Sounds like 'flu to me," muttered Andy as he stripped the bed.

"Who's that?"

"It's Andy. He came around to see how I was."

"I'm coming over," said Lisbeth. "Just stay put, Aunty Sam." And she rang off.

Oh no, thought Sam wearily. *I'm not sure I can stand another ministering angel.* She dropped the phone into her lap.

Andy looked up from plumping a pillow. "Is she coming around? You're going to be overwhelmed with well-wishers. Jonas Keane also sent his regards when you left yesterday."

Sam smiled faintly.

Ten minutes later, Greg was clucking over her.

"I can't believe you didn't call in to see Sam yesterday!" he scolded Andy, who looked suitably contrite. "Now, what have you got in your medicine cupboard...?"

Five minutes after that, Lisbeth arrived.

Sitting in the chair by the window, all Sam wanted them to do was leave, but while Lisbeth was there, she was at least able to take a shower. Her hair felt limp and sticky and she was glad of the chance to freshen up, but by the time she was dry and in fresh pyjamas, she was exhausted.

Lisbeth took control, shoo-ing Andy and Greg out of the door. "It's *fine* Greg, if she gets worse, I'll ring the doctor, I promise. And *no*, Andy—you can't talk about work!"

"But—"

"No, sweetie, she's right. It's doing too much work got her into this state!" Greg agreed. Andy left, protesting.

"Nicely done, bossy boots," croaked Sam as she lay down with a sigh of relief.

"And that's enough from you, too. I saw your temperature and it's only because I know you'll hate the fuss that I'm not calling the doctor. Or mum," she said, pulling the bedroom curtains together more firmly. "I'll be downstairs, call if you need anything."

"Lisbeth?"

"Yes, Aunty Sam?"

"Are we still friends?"

"Don't be daft. Of course we are. I'm sorry I pushed."

Sam's eyes filled with tears. "I'm sorry I snapped."

"Don't worry about it. You can make it up to me in driving lessons."

Sam gave a watery chuckle and drifted off to sleep.

22

Magda looked with intense satisfaction at the mass of plants on the patio. It would be exaggerating to say that they stretched as far as the eye could see, but there were a *lot* of plants.

Jonas came out and stopped dead.

"Good God. No wonder you took a van! Are we setting up a northern version of Kew? Will we actually *need* all of them?"

Andy grinned at him. "You've got a big garden, Mr Keane. Sam has it all planned, I'm pretty sure we'll need all of them."

"How is she?"

Magda's eyes narrowed as she heard the note of urgency in her father's voice.

"I think she's on the mend. She's been doing too much," Andy said.

"Actually, I heard from Lisbeth," added Magda. "She's round there most days and she told me Sam's getting better, but she's still quite weak."

Jonas said nothing, but Magda could see his face tense. Oh, *interesting,* she thought. She turned bright eyes on him. "I'm going to see her later—you should come."

"I'd check she's up to visitors if I were you," Andy intervened. "Now, are you happy with the plants, Magda?"

She nodded happily.

"Then we'll get going." And he moved away with two enormous trays of greenery.

"Did you enjoy the visit to the nursery?" Jonas asked her.

"It was great," she said firmly.

Actually, it had been a decidedly mixed experience, but she wasn't about to tell that to her father.

When she'd climbed into the van, she could sniff the tension, but didn't know what it was about. Sitting between Steve and Andy, she could have sworn she had something infectious—Steve couldn't sit any further away from her without getting out of the van.

While Andy drove, she had sighed inwardly. Although her Dad and Sam hadn't been making eyes at one another exactly, she knew there was *something* there. She felt the tension every time they met—come to think about it, it felt a bit like how it felt *now*. Weird.

She was glad to get back to Brook Lodge.

But looking now at the frothy clematis and velvety roses that were a tiny part of Sam's planting scheme, she realised she *had* enjoyed the morning. She trailed her hands gently over sprouting lavenders, raising their lovely scent, and examined camellias promising glorious creamy white and palest pink blooms next spring.

"You look like you want to help," Jonas observed quietly. She smiled at him.

"Part of me does! But it's probably best to leave it to the professionals!" She turned to him. "I'm going to call Lisbeth. Do you want to come if Sam is well enough?"

For a second he brightened and then she saw his face fall. "I think I'd probably need to check it out with Dr Walters. I don't want to give her anything else while she's unwell."

Magda saw the disappointment in his eyes—and decided to pile it on.

"Oh Dad! I never thought about that! God, no! Perhaps you shouldn't see her until she's *completely* better!"

Jonas gave her a sharp look and she wondered if she'd overdone it.

"I doubt that I'll need to move to another county," he said. "Look, if she's well enough to receive visitors and you go around, you can just say hello from me."

She looked at him, innocently. "Of course. I'll go and call Lisbeth to see what's what."

～

OK 2 call? she texted Lisbeth.

Hang on, moving 2 kitchen.

A few moments later, Lisbeth rang back.

"Hi, how's Sam?" Magda asked.

"She's asleep. When Mum came around yesterday, she took Aunty Sam's temperature and called the doctor. I think it was off the scale and the doctor came straight away."

"Wow! Really? Is she still very ill?"

"She's been sleeping for *days*, it seems, but I think she's getting better. How's things your end?"

"I was wondering if I could visit, and maybe bring Dad?" said Magda, ignoring any danger of contagion.

"Mmm, not sure that's such a hot idea," said Lisbeth. "Aunty Sam looks dreadful—think *Vampire Diaries*. I don't think it would help your cause."

"Oh. Right then. If you think not..."

"Defo. *You* come around and see if I'm not right."

A few hours later, Magda admitted silently that Lisbeth had indeed been right. Sam's face was very pale, with deep shadows around her eyes, framed by limp hair. Her voice was still husky (which was a bonus and probably could be good in a phone call, thought Magda) but she was soon tired from the visit.

"You're as bad as my Dad," Magda teased, as Sam made her excuses after a mere half hour out of bed. Sam turned to her.

"I forgot—your Dad's been ill, hasn't he? Is he getting better?"

Magda thought for a moment. "Well...a bit. He used to need to take a nap during the day but that's stopped now."

"Do they know what it was?"

"No, it was some kind of virus like glandular fever, apparently. It was *awful*. I thought he was going to die..."

"So they still don't know what was wrong?" persisted Sam.

"No. It's frightening, not knowing if it could happen again. He's got another appointment soon, for more blood tests. Perhaps they'll know more after that."

"I'll bring you some water, Aunty Sam," said Lisbeth, firmly shepherding Sam to the stairs.

Five minutes later, with Sam safely back in bed, she flopped next to Magda on the sofa. "Is your Dad really not well, then? Should we be even trying to set him up with Aunty Sam?" she asked.

"Well, we don't know what's wrong with him, but I daresay it's not *quite* as dire as I made it sound," Magda said comfortably. "But if she thinks he's about to die at any time, perhaps she might seize the day, so to speak."

Lisbeth gawped. "You're a nightmare!"

"Well, it might add a little more urgency to things. It's good that Gerry's out of the way now. I think Dad *is* interested in Sam and I think she's interested in him, but so far, nothing's happened! It's really frustrating!"

Lisbeth looked at her over the rim of her coffee cup, shaking her head in disbelief.

"You know, it might just take longer than you think. *Or* we could be wrong."

Magda sighed and bit into a chocolate digestive. "I know. But —*come on!* They're *made* for one another!"

Lisbeth shook her head. "Even when she's better, Aunty Sam will have a lot on her plate, you know. She's got loads of work on. Andy was telling me she's hardly had a day off in the past month or so. She's been seeing people at weekends to try and build up the business and doing some garden designs at the weekend."

"What, and then doing our garden?" Lisbeth nodded. "I didn't know that. But can't she take on more staff?"

"Yeah Andy thinks they should, but Aunty Sam's a bit scared of employing people and then the work drying up. She takes her responsibilities like, really seriously."

"And what's happening with Jessop's Field?"

Lisbeth bit her lip. "I think from what Dad says, they might lose," she said hesitantly. "I haven't told Aunty Sam, but after the row, Mum persuaded Dad to speak to the Leader of the Council about the bats."

"What, trying to stop the development?"

"Doubtful. It was a *huge* row they had, and I think Dad's still sulking."

"Oh dear. So you think Sam's lot will lose?"

"No idea, I only know if they do, Aunty Sam will probably blame Dad, and that will be a nightmare. I think she'll be very stressed, and —I don't want to make it worse," she said in a rush. "I'm not comfortable with what we're doing."

Magda frowned. "It might not make it worse! There's no need to be, like, *quite* so negative, Lisbeth!"

Lisbeth stared at her for a moment.

"I'm not negative, I'm being realistic!" she said.

Magda wrinkled her nose.

"Aren't you *totally* overreacting? Dad could be the best thing to happen to her!"

"So *you* say, but I'm not so sure. And I do know Aunty Sam! But you seem to go deaf every time I say anything!"

Magda stared.

"Why haven't you said anything before?"

"I have! But you're never bloody listening!" Lisbeth said, crossly. "You keep on and on—lying to Sam, lying to your Dad, and all because you don't like his bloody girlfriend!"

Magda stared and her face seemed to harden.

"I *will* start listening, when you start saying something worth listening to! As for 'stopping', I've not *done* anything, other than throw a lifeline to Sam's business, as far as I can tell! So far, your precious

Aunt has had nearly thirty-five grand of *my* money, and if Dad and she don't like each other, she'll *still* have it!"

"But it's not *about* money, Magda!" said Lisbeth, goaded. "Or did you think that your money could *buy* you a family?"

A shattered silence fell as Magda went white. Jerkily, she grabbed her bag and went out of the door without another word.

∽

Two days later Sam woke up and lay there, waiting for the headache to start. It didn't.

Thank God for that.

She got carefully out of bed and her legs didn't feel as rubbery as they had. She took a step. And then another.

"Hallelujah," she muttered and staggered into the bathroom.

Standing under the shower ten minutes later, her head was still clear, and her legs were still holding up. She was cautiously optimistic.

"I wonder what day it is?" she mused, as she towelled herself dry. She heard the ping of a message on her phone and slowly pulled on her robe and went back into the bedroom. Lisbeth was texting her, asking how she was and saying she'd call round later.

She put on some clothes and drew back the covers on the bed, opened windows. She dried her hair and was pleased to see a little shine on it. Her stomach rumbled and she made herself toast and tea and sat at the kitchen table, looking out of the window at the bright sunshine glancing off the leaves of the trees.

Another text arrived, this time from Amanda.

Hi, hope you're feeling better. Did you know the planning decision is on Thursday night? Are you going to attend? Are you well enough? Let me know, lots of love Ax

"Blimey, what's the date?" she muttered, checking the calendar. She'd been ill for more than a week!

And what about the Keane garden?

She dialled Andy.

"Sam! How are you?"

"I'm feeling a lot better, thanks. How are things at Brook Lodge? Have you started the planting? How far behind are we?"

"Sam, relax. It's all under control, and we're still more or less on schedule."

"Really?"

"Really."

She gave a shaky laugh.

"So, I can just go back to bed?"

"If you're not completely better, yes, you bloody well can! You looked like death warmed up when I last saw you. But really Sam, it's all fine. We did the planting just as you designed it, and I think you've done an amazing job."

"How's the client?"

"Jonas? He's been cool with everything. More worried about you than the garden, I think." Sam was silent. "He's got the eye for you, you know—he's been asking after you," Andy said casually.

Sam tried to stop smiling and failed. She pulled herself together. "Well, I hope to be back on Monday. I'll take the rest of this week off to fully recover. Has Paul been taking care of everything else?"

"He's been predicting the end of the business while taking more calls than he's taken for the last six months, but yes, everything's fine."

"Great. I'll call him in a bit and tell him I've not died."

"He won't believe you."

Sam rang off, still smiling and made some more tea before calling Paul. He scolded her for overdoing things—just as he'd told her, mind you—and then spent ten minutes telling her about all the potential clients waiting for her when she returned to work.

She left a message with Amanda to say she hoped to be at the meeting on Thursday and saw the light on the answerphone flashing. Lisbeth had turned off the ringer. She listened to five messages, two from Desmond talking about meetings and voting, one from Amanda asking after her and sending love, one from Charlie clucking that she needed to take care of herself and take on more staff. And one from Jonas.

"Hello Sam, it's Jonas. I presume your sensible niece has turned off the ringer. So I hope you get this...I just wanted to say that I hope you're feeling better and I'm looking forward to you finishing the garden. I'm looking forward to that very much, but if you think it might take longer, please let me know. I hope to see you soon. We need to talk" —he paused— "and get to know one another better."

Sam shivered as she listened to his velvet, slightly gravelly tones over the machine and closed her eyes as the sound swept over her.

Feeling like a teenager, she played it again.

How to respond?

She picked up the phone and paused, weighing the receiver in her hand. Before she could change her mind, she punched the redial button.

"Keane."

"H-hello," she said. "It's Sam."

"How are you? Are you feeling better?" Jonas' voice dropped, sounding soft down the phone.

"Yes, I'm OK. I'll be back on Monday to work, but I thought I might come at the weekend to see what the planting looks like, if that's ok?"

There was a silence on the line.

"That would be wonderful." His voice dropped a tone and she could see her nipples peak under her light shirt.

"When shall I come?" She tried to be business-like.

"Come when you're ready. I'll be in. I might even be alone."

Sam's stomach dropped, even while her libido was cheering.

"Hmm. Not sure that's a good idea. After all, the job isn't finished yet, is it?"

"Not quite. But I'm anxious to see you."

Sam leaned her head back and tried to focus her suddenly wayward thoughts.

"Likewise," she managed.

There was an intake of breath on the line and Sam pressed her suddenly tingling thighs together hard.

"This is all a bit fast, isn't it?" she added with a laugh. "We know nothing about one another. I know you're a convalescent, but apart from that, you're a man of mystery!"

There was a pause.

"I know. But we will talk, I promise. I'll see you whatever time you get to the house on Saturday—I'll be in all day, waiting for you."

Sam put the receiver down very carefully as though it might explode and took a deep breath.

"Well. Roll on the weekend," she murmured to herself.

23

Sam sat down next to Amanda with a gasp of relief.

"Bloody hell, it's a madhouse! Almost as bad as the public meeting."

"Except there we had more space," grumbled Amanda, pointedly shuffling to one side as someone's elbow almost went into her ribs. The Council Chamber wasn't used to hosting this number of people, and in the gallery, there was standing room only. Amanda, blithely ignoring the glares of others looking for a seat, had sprawled with her bag over two seats until Sam arrived.

"Is Luke coming?"

"No, sadly, he's had to confess a conflict of interest," Amanda grinned at her. "I've got to call him when the meeting's finished. His colleague did the investigation for the council instead and she's going to speak. She's sitting down there with someone—I think it's her boss." Amanda pointed out a dumpy young woman at the table with a huge pile of paper in front of her. Behind her was a much older man in a very worn tweed jacket and slightly untidy hair.

Sam grinned at Amanda.

"No Luke, then? *That* serious a conflict of interest?"

"Oh yes." Sam saw her eyes soften and felt a twinge of envy. Still, in a couple of weeks... She shivered.

"But how are you? Are you fully recovered? Should you have come tonight?" said Amanda, looking at her closely.

"No, no, I've been in bed most of today, I'm feeling much better!" Sam said, feeling the warmth on her cheeks.

Looking around, Sam caught sight of other members of the action group. Mrs Pratchett with her new bulldog puppy, Susan Miles seated in the gallery. Down on the Council Chamber floor, Desmond was sitting with the reverend and Jenny, scowling horribly. Sam also saw Tyler Fairchild, looking relaxed and arrogant as well as a lot of people at the back of the hall. Some of them were carrying signs sporting a variety of witty slogans from "Bats over Homes is Batty!" and "Homes for Sherton" to "Rights for Villagers, NOT Wildlife".

"God, there are some real nutters in here tonight, aren't they?" she said.

"If I'd have known it was that kind of meeting, I'd have brought my own banner. I feel a bit underdressed," agreed Amanda.

Finally, the meeting began. The raft of planning applications for lofts and extensions were waved through and then the meeting room seemed to grow tense.

"Us next on the agenda," said Amanda, her eyes fixed on the councillors below.

"Was that the independent councillor Mrs Pratchett talked to?" Sam murmured, nodding at a very tall, well-built woman in a smart suit.

"Yes, Councillor Whitehouse—Dorothy's sitting practically opposite her on the other gallery," replied Amanda. "Very off-putting..."

The Chair of the committee introduced the agenda item.

"Now we come to the application for three hundred and fifty houses close to Jessop's Field. We've taken quite a lot of public feedback for this application. Mr Stanford, would you like to take us through the details?"

The Chief Planning Officer stood up and presented the report. Sam listened as he talked through the implications of the building work—quite fairly, she thought. There were some whistles and heckles from the back of the hall, and the Chair began to look a little nervous.

"The planning department has considered the considerable need for local housing in the area. However, the development has attracted a great deal of correspondence from village residents. I'd like to call forward Mr Desmond Black, the chairman of the Sherton Environment Protection Group. I should remind you, Mr Black, you only have three minutes."

Desmond rose to his feet, to the whistles and jeers of those supporting the development and Sam's heart sank a little as his chest puffed out.

Oh, don't blow it for us, Desmond, she prayed.

But the vicar Tom Sanders had coached him well. Desmond spoke simply and clearly about the history of Jessop's Field, and drew attention to the alternative brownfield site on the other side of the village. He also spoke of the impact of the access road, cutting the Green Belt in half. He didn't speak about the bats, but generally about the impact of the development on wildlife. He sat down bang on three minutes and Sam cheered, just about making her voice heard against the boos of the placard-waving crowd. Desmond's chest puffed out even further.

Mr Stanford stood up again and cleared his throat.

"There is a colony of Bechstein's bats in the woodland and we've taken advice from Nature UK about this. Miss Gordon, would you like to speak?"

"Thank you," said the dumpy Miss Gordon, rising from her seat. Her voice was light and clear. "It is the legal duty of a local planning authority to take note of the Habitats Directive when making decisions about planning applications which may have an impact on European Protected Species," she said. "Before the developer comes to us for a licence, the authority must take into account the three derogation tests which we as Nature UK will consider when deciding whether to issue such a licence. These tests are, as I'm sure you're aware—overriding public interest, no satisfactory alternative to the proposed site, and alternative favourable conservation of the species."

"Blimey," said Amanda under her breath. "Do you think she talks like this at home?"

"In short, the planning authority needs to consider whether Nature UK is likely to issue a licence *before* granting planning permission. The authority can't discharge its duty simply by adding a condition to the application which requires the developer to obtain a licence from us. This is not engaging in the Directive, and as such, any decision can be challenged in the courts."

Sam sat up straighter, listening hard.

"I should like to add that the Bechstein bat has the highest protection in the country and previous conversations with the executives of Anglo Homes don't fill us with confidence as to the provision of proper alternative habitat. I am here to tell councillors that there is no guarantee that we would grant a licence." Miss Gordon sat down, smiling sweetly as Tyler Fairchild scowled at her. Sam approved of Luke's replacement, who had held her own even against the catcalls. The Chair asked for quiet and threatened to have people removed. The noise subsided a little.

Mr Stanford, the Chief Planning Officer, looked a little taken aback at the directness of Miss Gordon's comments and shuffled his papers. "There are provisions made in the plans," he said. "Has Nature UK taken these into account?"

"We've noted the changes made to the plans since the public meeting, certainly," Miss Gordon said acidly. "They have included elements not normally seen in Anglo Homes developments, but even so, the company does not have a stellar record in terms of protecting the environment."

Sam noticed that Tyler Fairchild was muttering to a thin, anaemic-looking man besides him, who nodded slowly. He looked as if he was scribbling a note.

The Chair tried again.

"But your opinion is being sought on this development, not the previous history of the developer, Miss Gordon," he said. She nodded.

"Quite, but our duty is to assess whether the organisation is capable of—in this case—providing a suitable habitat for the bats they will disturb, and I repeat—the developer does not have a stellar record. Or even a mediocre one."

The Chair hmphed and sat back. There were some mutterings in the hall. A clerk passed a note to him and Sam saw his face change. He nodded at Tyler Fairchild, who stood up.

"We've heard a great deal about Anglo Homes' lack of sensitivity to the local wildlife and Ms Gordon has implied that my organisation is incapable of handling the implementation of the wildlife directive. She may be right. As a large builder of many homes for Hard Working People, we tend to value our human customers over the wildlife we find alternative locations for. However, knowing this development was likely to be sensitive, Anglo Homes has teamed up with another developer, and it's some of their work that is reflected in the plans that Ms Gordon—" he nodded at her "doesn't recognise."

Miss Gordon looked at her colleague behind her, who didn't seem to move a muscle.

"Our partner is Halcyon LLP, one of the most sustainable developers in Europe. I presume you've heard of them, Ms Gordon?" Tyler sneered. Miss Gordon's eyebrows almost shot off the top of her round, pleasant face.

"If Halcyon is involved, I presume their credentials would be strong enough to allay your concerns about issuing a licence?" said the Chair. Miss Gordon turned to her colleague and there seemed to be a heated discussion.

"Who?" whispered Amanda. "Who the hell are Halcyon?" She took out her phone and began to tap its face.

Sam looked around and saw a lot of whispering, and from the village action group, some nervous faces. The Councillors, including the independent, were starting to mutter amongst themselves.

"Well, Miss Gordon?" asked the Chair again after a few minutes.

Sam could see the man from Nature UK shaking his head, and some imploring gestures from Miss Gordon. She turned back to the Chair.

"We'd need confirmation that the business proposal is as Mr Fairchild says it is," she said. "But if that is the case, we would be prepared to issue a licence for the development if conditions were laid that an alternative habitat for the Bechstein bats would be arranged."

Tyler smirked and there were cheers and whoops, led by the objectionable man in the leather jacket Sam had seen at the public meeting. Her heart dropped. Amanda was looking grim.

She listened as the councillors said their piece. As Desmond had said, they were split for and against, the only one not declaring her hand was Councillor Whitehouse. She raised her hand and the chair nodded at her to speak.

"The proposals show no evidence that other options for the location of the development have been fully evaluated," she said in a cool, precise voice. "Quite aside from the emotional pull of Jessop's Field, there will be an impact on local tourism, which I understood from figures provided by the Economic Development Unit in Derby," she looked at her papers, "to add more than six million pounds to the area's economy. While we don't have cast-iron evidence that we will lose this if the development takes place, without the green space, the walkers and photographers would surely find our area less attractive. I've heard Mr Stanford's arguments that people here need more housing and I agree. We're faced with a difficult choice. My view is that an amendment is needed so that the site is moved *away* from Jessop's Field." She paused and then sat down.

Tyler raised his hand and the Chair nodded to him.

"I'm sure we can come to some agreement to move the development back a hundred metres or so," he said easily. The Chair nodded.

"I propose we move to a vote," he said. "May I have a motion to approve the application?" A councillor nodded.

"Votes for?" Three hands rose from the group of six, including Councillor Whitehouse and the Chair, who frowned. Sam tensed. "Votes against?" Two hands rose. There was one abstention.

The Garden Plot

"The application for planning permission is approved," the Chair said.

There was roar of approval from some of the crowd, who began to catcall and jeer at Desmond and the Nature UK representatives. Sam was left silent in shock. Tyler Fairchild rose to his feet quickly, gathered his files and swaggered from the hall, followed by his entourage.

Sam looked at Amanda. "We lost. Goddamn it all, we *lost*. Who's this other company?"

"I don't have a strong enough signal," said Amanda in frustration, tapping her phone. "I'll need to move somewhere else." She stood up.

"We'll appeal," declared Mrs Pratchett, bustling towards them as Sam made her way into the main hall. Tom the vicar was sitting with his hands hanging limply between his legs. Jenny was patting him on the back, looking tearful.

"This can't be the end, surely?" Sam said.

The man in the leather jacket swaggered over to them.

"So, common sense won out in the end, eh?"

Sam could see the vicar's hands curl into fists.

"After all, it was a democratic decision and let's face it, that's what this country is all about, innit? A king in his castle and the power of the vote," leather jacket continued.

"When your kids want somewhere to play, you'll be able to show them photos of what used to be around, won't you?" said Amanda through her teeth. He grinned.

"Now, now—no need to be a sore loser. You might have had something there with the bat-lady but after all—what are a few bats when people need homes?" He poked his finger close to Amanda's face. "You lost. Get used to it." Amanda knocked away his hand and headed towards the door, glued to her phone.

Sam turned to follow her when someone tapped her on the shoulder. She turned and faced a pale woman.

"You're Sam Winterson, yes? You fought the development, didn't you?"

Sam nodded warily. The woman threw back her head and cackled.

"I pass your cottage every day when I come into Sherton. You're such a hypocrite, all cosy in your cottage, while trying to stop the rest of us getting a decent home. All you care about is preserving your privilege!"

"It's not just about my *privilege*—it's about preserving part of the village's heritage! For your kids, and *their* kids!" Sam protested, putting her hand on her hips.

"All the time keeping me out of a home of my own!" the woman snapped back at her.

"None of us wanted to stop *anyone* getting a home of their own, we just didn't want the homes *there*."

"And where else would they be?" the woman sneered. "If the development was relocated to somewhere more convenient to *you*, the price would go up because of the work they'll have to do on the land! Which would've scuppered my plans to ever have my own place. So I'm bloody chuffed we won!" And the woman wheeled round and marched in the opposite direction.

Sam stared after her, shaken and then caught sight of the Manchester lobbyist who smiled and put one finger up. Sam looked away and caught sight of Amanda by the door, staring at her phone. She battled her way through the crowds with her head down.

"Have you got a signal yet?" Sam said when she reached Amanda. "I can hardly believe it—it looked as though we'd win and then they brought up this partner company. What were they called? Halston?"

"Halcyon. They're a German company, headquarters in Switzerland, Zurich, I think. I've only just got a signal, this place is like a bunker."

Sam waited as Amanda thumbed through her phone. "Right, let's have a look at you, Halcyon..." Amanda navigated through the pages, commenting as she did. "Sustainable property development... use of recycled materials...solar panels...sympathetic design... I suppose if we *were* to be stuck with development on Jessops Field, they'd be a good company to do it," she said finally. "We could contact them and plead for special consideration, I suppose?"

"Might be a reasonable idea. How do we get hold of them? We

don't want to just write to the company address, we want to write to the boss. Who's the CEO?" Sam peered over her shoulder at the tiny screen.

Amanda navigated to the relevant page. Sam stared at the photo, small but perfectly clear and the noise of the room suddenly faded away.

"He looks familiar..." Amanda said uncertainly, looking at Sam.

"The bastard," Sam said finally, her voice shaking. "The utter bastard. No wonder he wouldn't give us any advice!"

"This is the guy from the pub isn't it?"

"It is, and the bloke whose garden I've designed. The one and only Jonas Keane—CEO of the company ripping up my childhood playground. The *total* bastard."

"Christ," said Amanda. "Are you ok, Sam?"

"No," she said, her voice breaking as she sat down heavily on a chair. "No, I don't think I am."

24

Lisbeth took out her phone and stared at it. She needed to call, but... She hung her head, feeling sick at the memory of her words. Before she could change her mind, she pressed the button. The phone rang for so long, Lisbeth's heart sank. Just as she was about to disconnect, Magda answered.

"Hello?"

"Hi, it's me. Please don't hang up—look, I'm *so* sorry. Can you forgive me?" Lisbeth said in a rush. There was silence on the end of the phone and Lisbeth bit her lip and added in a tight voice, "Magda? Really, I wouldn't blame you for not wanting to see me, but...you're my best friend. How are you?"

There was a deep intake of breath on the phone and Magda said in a small voice, "Miserable. I'm miserable. I hated what you said—but you're right. I thought if I paid for the garden...I feel a complete pillock."

Lisbeth felt her eyes fill with tears. "Do you want to meet up?"

"Yeah, I'd like that. Shall I see you at Jessop's Field? I don't really want to talk at home..." Magda's voice trailed off.

"Of course. Shall I come now? We can go to the lake, there's still ages before sunset."

"I'll be there in twenty minutes. I know you think I'm off base, but I could have *sworn*...But perhaps I was imagining it all?"

"We could just go over it—review the evidence, so to speak?"

"How very sensible of you, Lisbeth!" Magda said with a short laugh which broke in the middle. "I've probably got it all wrong."

"Let's talk it all through. I'll be right there," Lisbeth soothed, shrugging on a jacket with one hand and heading for the door.

∽

"Keane."

"Jonas, we won the planning application for Jessop's Field." Neil's voice came down the line. Jonas felt his stomach lurch.

"How do you know?"

"I've been keeping in touch with one of Tyler's administrative assistants. She texted me about ten minutes ago."

Sam, Jonas thought, bleakly. He shook himself. He should be pleased for the business.

"We'll probably need to make some amendments to the plans to take them back from the protected area." Neil paused. "And..."

"And?"

"Tyler told the meeting Anglo Homes were in partnership with us to swing it with Nature UK—our environmental credentials glow in the dark compared to theirs."

Jonas swore. So much for keeping our heads down, he thought.

"Without clearing it with me? I'll have his bollocks on a plate."

"We'd probably have lost without that."

"Were the press there?"

"Yes—too big a deal in a small village for there not to be," sighed Neil.

As if on cue, the phone in the hall began to ring. Looking at the display, it was the office. "Hang on, Neil." He picked up. "Keane. No, Claudia, of course I didn't agree the announcement beforehand! What do you take me for? Hang on—"

He swapped phones to talk again to Neil. "It's going to be a long evening. I'll call later."

~

Sam was sitting on her sofa, staring into space. She felt close to tears. The silence in the cottage pressed on her head and she tried to focus on what to do next. Write letters to her local MP? Ha, that was a joke. Call the newspapers?

She needed to talk to Amanda, to Tom. God, even to bloody Desmond. She hunted for her phone among the cushions.

"Amanda? It's Sam. I'm sorry, I had to come home."

"Are you ok? You looked as though you'd seen a ghost!"

"Sadly not. He's alive all right. Bastard."

"Let me get this straight—he pumped you for information and then made a pass?"

"More or less. I'm such an idiot..." Sam felt her voice clog with tears.

Amanda sighed.

"Now, sweetie, don't beat yourself up. He's a good-looking man—anyone would be charmed if he put his mind to it! Thank God you didn't sleep with him!"

Yeah, I'm SO grateful for small mercies! Sam thought.

"Anyway, you left just in time, it got quite nasty. Tom took a swing at the bloke in the leather jacket."

"What?"

"Yeah, he just didn't seem to know when to shut up. Christian charity only goes so far, it seems," Amanda sighed. "Tom didn't actually manage to hit him, the bloke ducked. The police let him off with a warning, and Jenny dragged him away."

"Are you at home now?" Sam glanced at the clock—nearly ten o'clock.

"Yes, just got in and I'm about to hit the gin." Sam could hear the ice dropping into a glass and the fizz of tonic.

"What do we do now?" Sam asked after a moment. "I'm feeling a bit floored."

"That's hardly surprising, sweetie. As for what we do next—Mrs Pratchett was all for us meeting tomorrow to develop a plan, but Desmond seems to have accepted the result."

"He has? But that's so—so—*flimsy!*" Sam was diverted for a second from her bruised heart.

"Who knows the workings of Desmond's brain? Perhaps he's realised that in the future they'll be three hundred and fifty more decorating jobs to do." Amanda paused. "But what are you going to do about this Jonas Keane?"

"I'm going to talk to him."

"Is that a wise thing?"

"Probably not, but I won't be able to keep a civil tongue in my head during the remaining garden build unless I do. And I need to know *why* he's doing it. Why team up with that bunch of shysters Anglo Homes? Why bloody come on to me, if I'm fighting the development? Some kind of game?"

"He does sound a bit warped, certainly," said Amanda. "Be careful, won't you?"

"He won't dare touch me after hearing what I've got to say to him."

The following day, Jonas was scowling at Tyler across the boardroom table at Halcyon's offices in Manchester. John Fairchild was looking uncomfortable and was fiddling with his gold pen. Neil sat quietly in the background.

"We had an agreement. Halcyon was not supposed to be in the spotlight at all, let alone announced without any warning. Have you seen our share price this morning?" said Jonas.

"Jonas—" began John.

"It has dropped nearly ten percent, wiping nearly three hundred *million* euro from our value. In addition, I've barely been off the phone all night, fielding calls from my chairman, who's been asking what the fuck is going on, plus more investors than I care to mention. I've had questions about my absence from the company for the last three months—also supposed to be confidential. And you did this to secure a development for *three hundred and fifty houses?*"

Tyler was silent. John took one look at Jonas' face and shut his mouth. After an agonising ten seconds, Tyler said:

"How was I to know the local journo would cover it? Or that they'd pass it to the London business press? It seemed a justifiable risk to take. Otherwise we'd have lost the decision."

"We could have appealed," Neil said. "There was no need for the histrionics."

Silence.

"What do we do now, then?" Tyler said, looking at his fingernails.

"*You* don't do anything. We mop up all this mess with the media and then we'll talk again about the Jessop's Field development. In the meantime, don't talk to the media and don't get involved with the local authority." Jonas' voice was icy. Tyler stared at him, and then left the room.

John sighed. He looked old and tired.

"I'm truly sorry, Jonas. I thought he could handle the project."

"I think we need to sort out the immediate issues and then we'll talk about it some more, John. Can I get back to you when I think things are starting to settle? We're beset with takeover rumours due to the share price, and because the media think I'm at death's door."

"Well, hopefully, that's soon sorted?" John said.

"We're working on it," said Neil, rising to his feet and signalling the meeting was at an end. John stared at him and then rose, gathering his papers.

Jonas was staring out of the window at the unusually sunny Manchester skies when Neil returned.

"We need to get out of the agreement. Get the legal team on it, would you?" he said.

"Will we continue with the development in Sherton?"

"We have to. And at the same time, recover our reputation for sustainability. When we've sorted it with the lawyers, we'll need to talk to the council and redraft the plans, I think." Jonas was grim.

"OK. Are you talking with the press team about the media?"

"Are you kidding? Claudia is practically organising a world tour for me over the next few weeks. I'll be doing nothing *but* talking to bloody journos for the foreseeable future."

"Are you sure you should be doing this? You're not signed off as healthy, yet, are you?" Neil said.

"No. I had a right earful from Magda when I set out this morning. But I don't have a choice, do I? If the media think the company is falling over because I'm dying, only a live appearance will do, right?"

"Does Magda know the whole story?"

"No, although it's only a matter of time. I can only be grateful she doesn't read the newspapers much. I've told her that there's a rumour I'm too unwell to be at the head of the company, so I have to show myself about a bit. She's *really* pissed with me, but she understands, I think."

"But she doesn't know about the deal with Anglo Homes?" Jonas shook his head and Neil took a deep breath. "Right. Take it easy—as far as you can. I'll get other members of the Board working on it too."

"Thanks."

It had been a good game, thought Magda as she and Lisbeth walked back from the tennis courts. They'd talked themselves almost hoarse at Jessop's Field the other night. The rattling tennis game today (Magda had won) had evaporated the last of their argument.

Things weren't all sunny, though. Her father seemed to be back at work, to her tight lipped disapproval. Then Lisbeth had been a bit gloomy about the planning decision on Jessop's Fields. Turning the corner, Magda took one look at the photographer with the long lens hanging around the gates to Brook Lodge and crossed the road swiftly, to Lisbeth's confusion.

"What's happening?"

"Paps," Magda said, swinging her tennis racquet as though she would like to take a shot at him. Lisbeth still looked confused. "Sorry—the paparazzi. We'll go in by the back."

They made their way to the side gate of the garden, now cleared of the choking ivy, and ran across the lawn. Andy and Steve, working on the garden, stared at them.

"A photographer is outside the house," explained Magda.

"Why?" asked Andy, leaning on his hoe.

"Something to do with Dad's work, probably. It normally is," Magda said, pushing Lisbeth through the doors and grabbing the phone. "Dad, there's a photographer camped outside the house. Anything to do with you?"

The swearing could be heard by Lisbeth, who looked slightly shocked.

"I'll be home as soon as I can," Jonas said. "Don't talk to them."

Magda bit her lip as she put down the phone.

"What's up?" asked Lisbeth.

"I'm not sure, but it doesn't sound good news."

Half an hour later, Andy knocked at the door.

"Right, we're finished for the day. You haven't forgotten that Sam's coming tomorrow to have a look at the progress of the work before she comes back on Monday?"

Magda stared.

"Is she? I knew she was coming back to work on Monday but didn't know about tomorrow. Never mind, it'll be good to see her. Will you finish next week?"

"Should do," Andy nodded. Magda beamed at him.

"Fantastic! It's looking amazing, don't you think?"

"It's one of Sam's best designs. I think she's hoping you'll let her enter it into a national competition, but I imagine she'll talk to you about it when she sees you."

"Awesome! Of course we will! Although I'll probably need to talk to Dad," Magda amended. Andy smiled and left, ignoring the photographer as instructed.

A little later, Sam called.

"Hi Sam! I just heard from Andy that you're calling around tomorrow," Magda said.

"Actually, I wanted to know if your Dad was there?"

Magda's ears pricked up.

"I'm expecting him back in a little while. Is anything wrong?"

"I can't make it tomorrow, I'm afraid," Sam's voice was brisk. "If I come now, I'll be able to look at the garden to see what's needed to finish it off and then see him when he gets home. Is that OK? Are you in for a while?"

"Yes, Lisbeth's here too. By the way—there's a photographer hanging around the front of the house, so you might want to come in through the side gate. I'm not quite sure what it's all about, although Dad said that the company's under pressure at the moment."

"Is it indeed?" Sam sounded a bit grim, Magda thought. "OK, thanks for the heads up."

The line went dead and Magda stared at the phone, a sense of unease beginning to nibble at her nerves.

Sam felt as if she'd stumbled into a James Bond film without the script. She drove to Brook Lodge and saw the photographer outside Jonas' gate that Magda had mentioned, and swearing, she drove past.

She turned onto the farm lane, bumping over the rutted ground. She moved quickly to the side gate of the garden, blessing Steve's foresight in repairing the latch on it. Slipping through it, she walked to the patio at the back of the Brook Lodge.

Magda was standing at the window and jumped as Sam suddenly came into sight. Sam quickly waved and Magda visibly sagged with relief, and then opened the patio doors.

"Sam! How are you feeling? You look a bit pale, still."

"Yes, I'm quite recovered thank you," Sam said, ignoring the banging behind her temples.

"Um...good. That's good. Err... Lisbeth's here. Would you like tea?"

Sam forced a smile and nodded, and Magda hurried off to the kitchen. Sam followed and got a friendly hug from Lisbeth.

After some awkward small talk, Sam put down her mug and stood up.

"Right, I'll need to go around the garden."

"Shall we come with you?" Magda asked.

"Probably quicker if I go alone," said Sam. Lisbeth frowned but said nothing. "When will your Dad be home, again?"

"Any time now," Magda said. "Is anything wrong?" she added, hesitating.

Sam paused, and then smiled.

"No, sweetie. All good. Now let me look at what the boys have done. Who knows what they'll have done without me there to crack the whip!"

Walking the garden, Sam's eyes noted work to be done, work she was satisfied with, where plants needed moving. And all the while, half her mind was on what she would say to Jonas. Her eyes felt gritty after little sleep and a lot of tears.

She came to the spot for the pergola and she wrinkled her nose. The pergola needed to be set in and then the climbers added, and it would be complete. Then she could put in the final invoice and say goodbye—relatively unscathed—to Mr Jonas Keane. She took a deep breath and made her way back to the house.

There was an uncomfortable wait of quarter of an hour before Jonas walked through the door. As he opened the door, he checked slightly as he saw Sam. A slow smile spread across his face. Sam stared back.

At the same time, the phone began to ring.

"Excuse me, that's the office. I'll be back as soon as I can," Jonas said, a frown between his brows as he looked at Sam. He disappeared into the study.

"Is everything ok?" Magda asked again. "I heard about Jessop's Field and I'm really sorry—you must be very disappointed."

Sam closed her eyes briefly.

"Yes, we are. We're thinking about an appeal to the CEO, in fact I have a letter here."

Magda looked puzzled. "Are you hoping to get some advice from Dad about it?"

Sam stared. *She doesn't know. He hasn't told her* she thought.

"Yes. Yes, I am."

Lisbeth was looking at her closely. She made to say something, but Sam shook her head slightly and she kept quiet. At last the girls, looking at her curiously, disappeared upstairs.

Sam could hear Jonas' voice on the phone, and he sounded sharp and angry. She stared mindlessly into space and it must have been a few minutes before she registered the silence from the study. She stood up just as Jonas came through the door.

"Could I have a word?" she said.

Jonas motioned her into the study and closed the door. The air in the room smelled of him and Sam felt it wrap round her like a scarf. He looked at her, eyebrows raised in question.

"I wondered if I could give you this letter," Sam said, feeling in her pocket and drawing out the envelope. He looked at his name and title, and his eyes closed briefly.

"Sam, I can explain—"

"Save your breath. Of all the disreputable, sneaky, underhand, *shitty* stunts to pull. When *were* you going to tell me? Or were you hoping to have sex with me before you did?"

Jonas stilled as though she'd slapped him. "Listen, it's complicated, but I was going to tell you who I was when I saw you tomorrow."

"Oh, I *bet* you were! No wonder you wanted to know all about the campaign! And it was hardly surprising you wouldn't give us any advice—after all, why would you help us beat you?"

"It wasn't like that—give me strength..." He grabbed her shoulders and pushed her into a chair. "Now shut up and listen to me. I have five minutes before our press office calls me again to try to repair the damage done by bloody Tyler Fairchild. I'm *sorry* I wasn't upfront about who I was, and I *was* going to tell you. My company was a silent partner in this programme and we weren't happy with the development, either its content or its position—we don't work that way, and if you don't believe me, have another look at our website!" he added quickly, as Sam opened her mouth to speak. "I *have* been ill with a virus and I was ordered to stay off work for six months, so I've not been able to keep an eye on the project as I normally would. I kept my presence here a secret because—as I'm sure you'll see when you watch the financial news tonight—a company without a CEO at the helm is vulnerable to market rumours and takeovers."

He drew a breath as Sam said nothing. "I realise you're disappointed—"

"*Disappointed?*" she cried. "Bloody *betrayed* is a better word! And from the look of Magda when I arrived, you haven't told *her* about the development either, did you?" she added shrewdly. She saw the colour stain his cheeks. "So does she think you're in this house because you wanted to give her more time in the country? Jeez, you're a real piece of work, aren't you?"

"Sam--" Jonas grabbed her arm as she turned to go. "Please, I don't have time for this now, I need to sort the mess with the markets and the press--but surely, you can't think I wanted a relationship with you because of a bloody planning decision? I can barely keep my hands off you!"

She looked at his green eyes and could feel herself swaying towards him. She stiffened and shook off his hand.

"You're about to drive bulldozers through my childhood and you bloody *lied* to me about who you were. You encouraged me to talk and like an idiot, I did. What did you do about that little morsel of information about the bats, I wonder? Or the independent councillor?"

"No-one knew about our conversations!"

"Yeah, I bet. I don't trust you, whoever I thought you were—you're not that person. I don't know you." Her voice broke.

The phone rang and Jonas started towards her. She backed away to the door and opened it.

"You'd better get that. I'll see myself out."

He cursed as the phone continued to ring. He ignored it.

He pinched the bridge of his nose wearily. "Don't leave like this, Sam. We could be good together, I know it."

She shook her head and left, in tears.

25

Sam awoke with a start. She glanced at the clock. It was just past two in the morning. Then she heard the tinkle of glass from somewhere downstairs and froze, catching her breath. Her heartbeat speeded up and she threw back the covers and grabbed her robe. Struggling into it, she walked softly over to her bedroom door and listened. Nothing. Outside, a car roared away and she ran to the window in time to see its rear lights around the corner of the lane. She thought it looked like a Volvo, something chunky. It was too dark to see much more.

She went back to the door and discretion getting the better part of valour, she picked up her phone from the chest of drawers and dialled 999.

"Which service do you require?"

"Police, please," she whispered.

"What? You'll have to speak up, I can't hear you,"

Sam went into the ensuite and closed the door.

"I want the police. I think someone's broken into my house and they're downstairs," she said, as loudly as she dared.

"Where are you now?"

"In the ensuite upstairs."

"Please hold the line."

Sam heard the connection go through with half an ear as she strained to catch any noise from downstairs. It was completely quiet, and all she could hear was the blood pounding in her ears.

A policewoman, calm and steady, came on the line and asked for details. Sam gave her name and address in a shaky whisper.

"You're in the ensuite, yes? Stay there and lock the door. Put your phone onto vibrate, not an audible ring. We'll be with you as soon as we can."

Sam shut off the call and shivered in her dressing gown, despite the warmth of the night. She locked the door, put the seat down on the loo and sat down in the darkness, hoping that whoever was downstairs would stay there. Her mind raced, thinking of how strong the old cottage doors were, whether the lock on the bathroom door would hold if anyone pushed at it. The minutes ticked past.

Her phone vibrated and she answered, her hands shaking.

"Is this Sam Winterson? This is Inspector Williams, we're just drawing up outside now. Stay where you are, and I'll come upstairs. When I do, you ask my name before you open the door, ok?"

Sam nodded, realised he couldn't see that and said "OK".

A few minutes later, there was a knock at the door.

"Who is it?" she said, her voice croaky.

"This is Inspector Williams," a firm voice said. She opened the door and burst into tears at the sight of the young, uniformed man waiting outside. A female police officer came forward and took her arm.

"Now then, it's all right," the woman said soothingly. "You haven't been broken into, someone's chucked a brick through your window. Have you got shoes or slippers? Put something on your feet so they don't get cut, there's glass all over the floor."

Inspector Williams led the way downstairs. Sam blinked at the lights, but also at the mess on her rug.

Broken glass, and a large house brick with something wrapped around it. The brick had also caught a photograph and a vase of roses, so the rug was strewn with rose stems and ruined petals and was soaking. Sam exclaimed and rushed to get a dustpan and brush.

"Hang on, we'll need to get forensics on this," Inspector Williams said, reaching out a hand to stop her.

"On a *brick*?" Sam asked. The policewoman nodded.

"You'd be surprised what information we can get off the weirdest stuff. You just sit down while we wait for the forensics team to arrive. I'll make you some tea, you look like you need it. Kettle over here?" Sam nodded and she sat on a chair, staring at the brick, the glass, greenery and broken crockery.

The inspector spoke into his radio, saying something Sam didn't catch. A thought struck her.

"How did you get in?"

The policeman grimaced.

"Your lock isn't very secure. I got in with my credit card."

"*What?*"

He sighed.

"Let me show you." He demonstrated how easy it was to flick the lock while Sam gaped in horror.

"These old-fashioned locks don't really cut it any more with modern burglars. In some ways, it's a miracle that you haven't been broken into before now!"

Now THAT'S comforting for a single woman at three in the morning, thought Sam.

"I'll send you a leaflet on making your home more secure before we leave, but now I need to ask you some questions." The policewoman thrust a mug of tea into Sam's hand and shakily, she took a sip. It was strong, the usual remedy for shock, and too sweet even for Sam's taste. Sam forced herself to take another drink before putting it down.

Inspector Williams' questions were short and simple. When had she first been woken up? What had she heard? What had she seen? Did she see a number plate on the car? He sighed when Sam couldn't recall much about the car and commented that there wasn't much CCTV to check against on her road. The forensics officer arrived and opening a briefcase, began to dust white powder over the brick and the string. He took photographs of the brick in its position and the smashed window. Then he undid the string around the paper and pulled it open. In large childish handwriting were the words:

BITCH. YOU HAVE ENEMYS IN THIS VILLAGE.

Sam stared at the black, spidery words and tried for lightness.

"I may have enemies, but they can't spell."

"Any reason why you might have enemies in the village?" asked the policewoman.

Sam shook her head and then thought about the planning application.

"I objected to the development on Jessop's Field, and my name is on all the posters. It would be easy to find out where I lived, I've been in the village a long time."

"You run your dad's business, don't you?" asked Inspector Williams. Sam nodded.

"I've read about the development in the paper," commented the policewoman, scribbling notes. "There was a lot of bad feeling against the protests, people need the homes."

"There was also a lot of bad feeling *against* the development running over Green Belt land," snapped Sam. "But surely because I disagree with the decision isn't a good enough reason to lob a brick through my window!"

"No, of course not, we're not saying it is," said Inspector Williams, throwing a glance at his colleague. "And we've had a number of calls about similar incidents over the past couple of evenings."

"You have?"

"Yes, other members of the…action group…seem to have been targeted," said Inspector Williams, looking through his notebook. "Desmond Black, a Miss Susan Miles and a Mrs Dorothy Pratchett. Either unpleasant things through their letterboxes or damage to vehicles."

"Good God! They've done this to Miss Miles? And Mrs Pratchett? That's dreadful! They're elderly women! They must have been terrified!"

"Yes, we're giving the ladies additional protection—we've increased patrols in the area."

"What's happened to Desmond?"

"Someone keyed his car."

Sam put her head in her hands and groaned. Desmond's car was a vintage Jag, his absolute pride and joy.

"Oh my God. Desmond will practically be in mourning," she said. She looked up. "Do you have any idea who this might be? Because I can make some suggestions, if not! There was a lot of threatening behaviour at the planning meeting, and although I don't know the names, I can certainly find out!"

Inspector Williams held up his hand.

"Yes, we have a number of names and we are following several lines of enquiry."

The forensics officer asked if he could take the brick and paper away, and Inspector Williams nodded. He turned to Sam, snapping shut his black notebook.

"Now, Ms Winterson, I suggest you call an emergency glazier to come and sort out your window. We'll be in touch if there are further developments."

"But you don't think you'll be able to find the bastards that did this, do you?" Sam said, all the fight suddenly going out of her.

"We'll be doing our best, but resources are stretched in the county," said the policewoman. The inspector nodded and gave Sam a sympathetic smile.

When they left, it felt suddenly very quiet. She changed into sweats and a tee-shirt, flicked through some names on the internet for emergency glaziers and called one. Gingerly she picked up the roses and cleared up the broken crockery and the largest of the glass shards.

It was nearing dawn two hours later when she finally crawled back into her cold bed, wrung out and sick at heart.

Sam slumped on her sofa. She'd had too much wine, but she didn't care. After the day she'd had…She'd been aghast at the cost of having new locks fitted, the glazier who'd come to repair the window had cost her a small fortune.

And as if the newspapers hadn't covered the planning decision enough, now she was faced with Jonas on the TV. Startled, Sam gazed at the television and watched Jonas's grave face in conversation with an acerbic brunette interviewer. The interviewer was giving him a rough ride, Sam reflected, pummelling him with questions about how a sustainable company with Halcyon's reputation could build on Green Belt land, how they could go into business with a company that had such a poor sustainability record. He was well-drilled, she thought cynically. He looked also tired.

"We're looking at the site again and giving full consideration to the comments of the local people," he said in his deep voice. "Halcyon builds homes that are good for the local community—and this doesn't mean just those who buy our houses. If there is a problem with the site from the perspective of other residents, we'll do our best to address those—"

"So does this mean you'll move the development?" interrupted the interviewer.

"Possibly. We need to talk to the local authority first."

"Won't this have an impact on the price? Surely the residents want houses that are affordable? Your company tends to build houses which are—by UK standards at least—quite expensive."

"We'll need to look at the plans," Jonas repeated.

"And does this U-turn have anything to do with the fact that you *live* in the area and don't want to spoil your own view?"

Jonas' face was like stone.

"If you have a look at other developments we've done, you'll see this is standard practice for my company," he said.

And finally, why had he misled the markets by not informing them of his illness and absence?

"Did we mislead them?" he said, smiling at the interviewer for the first time, who seemed to soften. "No, I took some time away while my extremely efficient staff managed without me for a while. I was in constant contact with my deputy and if you've been watching Halcyon for the last three months, you'll see we've closed a number of property deals and we're on track with the strategy I announced last year."

"But the project with Anglo Homes seems to have gone badly wrong, without your involvement, don't you agree? Was it just *luck* that nothing else went wrong?"

"The relationship between Anglo Homes and Halcyon was very new—there were bound to be a few hiccups—"

"You call a ten percent drop in your share price a *hiccup*, Mr Keane?"

"Actually, the fall in the share price was more to do with the media view that I was at death's door, rather than the development," he responded. He spread his hands and smiled again. "Reports of my demise have been greatly exaggerated."

The interviewer smirked at him.

"So I see. That's all we have time for, thank you Jonas Keane."

Sam switched off the TV and reached for the wine bottle and tipped the dregs into her glass. Her eyes caught the glitter of a shard of glass on her wooden floor and her feet sought her slippers.

The phone rang and she spent a minute locating it in the cushions of the sofa. Amanda burbled at her.

"Sam? How are you? Have you got the window fixed? And have you been watching the telly?"

"I'm fine, yes, the window is fixed and yes, I was just watching the interview."

"How are you feeling?"

"About the window? Mad as hellfire."

Sam took the phone into the kitchen to search out another bottle of wine.

"And what about the interview? Did you hear him say he was going to change the plans?"

Sam focused.

"No, I heard him say he would *think* about posh-*possibly* addressing some of our concerns."

"I think that sounds hopeful! Perhaps he responded to the letter?"

"Maybe. Presumably he'll invite Desmond to any dis-discussions when he gets around to it."

Amanda was silent for a beat.

"Are you a teeny bit pissed, Sam?"

"A teeny *tiny* bit."

Amanda sighed.

"You could be wrong about him, you know. Not all businessmen are bastards. I've been looking at old press coverage—I think he's one of the good guys, he's been involved in all kinds of environmental initiatives, the company is putting loads of money into new engineering processes for sustainable housing—"

"What? He's not canonised, too?"

This time, Amanda was silenced.

"Look Amanda, I'm just glad this all came to light before I made a real idi- idiot of myself. I've finished the garden and frankly, if I never see him again, it will be too soon..."

"Famous last words, sweetie. OK, I'll tell Desmond and Mrs Pratchett they're carrying the can and let you know how it goes. Take care—call me if you need a shoulder to sob on!"

Before Sam could swear at her, Amanda finished the call.

26

Jonas took off the lapel microphone and handed it to Claudia, the press officer, dimly aware that he was pleased with the interview. Only part of him was concentrating. He couldn't seem to wipe the memory of Sam's face, hurt and pale, from his mind.

"...And tomorrow you're on *Financial News* at six-thirty," Claudia was saying, the latest of a long, long list of interviews which seemed to have materialised in the past week. Stephanie, his finance director was also doing the media rounds, Neil was talking to their major suppliers, and Bernard, the Chairman, was briefing selected market analysts. It was an impressive team effort, a part of his brain noted.

Claudia was talking about briefing notes. At this rate it would be the end of next week before he could try to contact Sam.

"Jonas?" his press officer prompted him sharply. Jonas focused.

"Yes, fine—is the presenter Moynihan?" Jonas had been interviewed by Tom Moynihan before and he wasn't relishing the prospect. They didn't call him Mauler Moynihan for nothing.

"Yes. You'll need to be on your game," Claudia said crisply. "I've got a car picking you up at five to take you to the studios. Wear something sombre."

Like a funeral, thought Jonas.

In the car, reading the same page for the third time without understanding it, he threw down the notes. He stared out of the window for a few minutes, watching the streetlights flash past, his mind blank. He reached for his phone and dialled Sam's number.

"Sam, it's me. I wanted to say I'm sorry. Again." he said to the answering machine. "I don't want you to think I deliberately set out to deceive you—I didn't. Circumstances...well, circumstances just overtook me. I hope when you've got over your sense of betrayal, you'll talk to me again and we can sort it out. Because I thought...I thought we might have had something very special."

He disconnected the phone and looked at the brake lights of the cars on the dark road.

He started to read the notes again.

Lisbeth looked rather glumly at the unanswered texts she'd sent to Sam. Without speaking, she passed the phone to Magda.

"She's not talking to me."

"But you're, like, her family! Surely she'll respond to you?"

"Pah. I wouldn't believe everything you see in the Disney films," Lisbeth said, thinking about the rift between her father and Sam, and now it seemed, between Sam and her.

Magda sighed.

"Mind you, I can't blame Sam for being mad at Dad—God, I was *furious* when I found out about Jessops Field!"

"What did your Dad say? Like, how did he explain?"

Magda shrugged.

"He told me he wasn't sure about some guy from Anglo Homes and this coincided with Brook Lodge coming up for sale. It seemed too good an opportunity. He said."

Lisbeth looked up.

"You still mad?"

"Well...yeah, actually. I feel sort of used. I don't know. He *did* want to keep it quiet that he was away from the company."

"Reasonable, I suppose?"

"Suppose…"

"Do you think Aunty Sam and your Dad will get together now?" Lisbeth tried to stay neutral.

"It was such a good idea…"

"But let's face it—Aunty Sam opposed his development, *and* she was asking his advice, but he didn't tell her who he was! I bet Aunty Sam just thinks he's an arse, now."

"He's not an arse! He's a businessman trying to do the best he can for his company!"

"Did you *see* her face last week? I think she'll take some convincing! And *he* might think she's just a trouble-maker now!"

Magda was silent and to Lisbeth's horror, she saw tears in in the green eyes. She retreated rapidly.

"Look, everyone's still mad—Aunty Sam won't take my calls, your Dad's off round Europe doing telly interviews and trying to, like, sort out the company. Why don't we wait a bit until everyone's calmed down?"

Magda looked up.

"I was going to sort of 'launch' the garden but what with everything… yeah, perhaps in a while? And Andy said something about Sam wanting to enter the garden in a competition. That might be one thing to get them talking," she said, her brow furrowed.

"We need to chill," Lisbeth repeated. "And give things time to settle."

"Yeah, Dad'll be worried about the company," Magda said. "Halcyon employs *loads* of people and he'll want to make sure no-one tries to take it over."

"So he's going to be very busy anyway?"

"Mmm. *And* he's gone back to bloody work before the doctors said he should." Magda was gloomy. Then, with effort she added, "It'll blow over. Another company will have a scandal and move ours off the front page…"

"Fingers crossed."

The changes to the development plan were all over the local press. As were photos of Desmond, looking proud, and Jonas, looking enigmatic. Enigmatic but tired, Sam noted with bitter satisfaction

She wrinkled her nose. There *were* changes to the plans—but nothing, in her view, that merited this level of fanfare, given that it was so wrong to build so near to the beauty spot in the first place. The houses which would have encroached on the Green Belt had been moved back and the link road no longer cut across the fields. There were complaints from those who thought the price of the houses would go up. The rest of the site was as it had been, despite Desmond's proclamation of the "triumph of the democratic will of the people".

"Bloody spin!" Sam muttered, throwing aside the paper. She turned to her computer. She looked again at the email from the Labour Party campaign office, gently turning down her suggestion that they support an appeal. When she'd called a few of the local politicians, one of the Labour councillors had even sneered at her and accused her of simply protecting her privilege. She had been flabbergasted. *Privilege?*

"In our view, the homes are badly needed in the area and the development will bring employment which is also below the country average...Halcyon is a developer well-known to us for its sympathetic design..." Her lips twisted at the suggestion that she might care slightly less for the countryside, and slightly *more* for the local economy and jobs, and she wondered if the unemployment figures they quoted were accurate. Hissing between her teeth, she deleted the email and stomped to get tea from the little kitchen at the side of her office. Andy and Paul were discussing invoicing and the conversation faltered when she emerged with her mug.

"Problem?" she asked, aware her voice was sharper than normal.

"No. No problems," Andy said before Paul could draw breath. "How's the design for the Linwoods coming?"

"Getting there," she replied and went back to her desk. She

looked across at the blank paper on her drawing board. She sighed and looked at the photos of the house and again at the brief, which wanted an ultra-modern garden. She waited, but inspiration wasn't playing today.

Sam grabbed her sunglasses and her phone and headed for the door. Paul looked up, startled.

"I'll be back in a bit. I need some air."

She headed to Jessop's Field, aware even as she did so that her usual sense of peace was tangled with the memories of the conversation and the kisses she had shared with Jonas. She gritted her teeth as she looked at the curves of the landscape, wondering if this too, was another thing ruined by bloody Jonas Keane.

She looked at the countryside below her. The developers hadn't appeared yet and there was a cold lump in her throat at the thought that it might soon disappear.

Perhaps it won't come to that.

She sat there for nearly forty minutes, pushing away the thoughts of Jonas' firm lips and warm hands. Finally, she took out her phone to at least complete *one* task today. It was easier, after all, to end a call than storm out of the house.

"Sam?" Charlie said before Sam had said a word.

"Hi, yes it's me."

"I thought you'd never call. How are you?"

"I'm fine. Well, actually, I'm not fine, but I'm ok."

There was a silence and Sam took the plunge. "I'd like to try and mend some fences with you."

"You don't need to mend fences with *me*, Sam," said Charlie, and Sam could hear the grin in her voice. "You're my sister. If I hadn't heard from you this week, I was going to come and break down your door. Are you ok? I read about Desmond's car and I was a bit worried."

Sam told her about the brick and the note, and her bruised and battered feelings were soothed by her exclamations of horror and concern.

"God how awful! God, Sam, why didn't you call me?"

"For what?" asked Sam. "I was ok, the police were there, what would you have done?"

"I'm your bloody sister, Sam! And you must have been scared out of your wits!"

"I certainly was for a while, but I feel a hell of a lot safer with new locks. You could have knocked me down with a feather when the copper unlocked my door with his bloody bank card! And anyway," Sam sighed. "They're just thugs. I can cope with all that as long as *we're* ok."

"And what about Fraser?" Charlie asked. Sam paused.

"Well, I hoped he'd do what he always does—act as if nothing happened," Sam said truthfully. "After all, the development has gone through, which is what he wanted. I thought we'd just return to our usual squabbling."

Charlie laughed, and then sighed. "I think he was hurt by some of the things you said. I'm not sure he'll just forget it."

"Well, I suppose I could come around to see him in person…"

"Well, you will have to see him sometime. Unless you were thinking of getting divorced from the family?"

"No, of course not." Sam thought hard. "I could meet him for a drink in the pub. That might be a good thing. Keep us civil, meeting in public, somewhere neutral. What do you think? You could come too."

There was a pause while Charlie considered.

"How about I join you after an hour, give you chance to say everything to each other you want to?"

"That sounds okay," Sam said, reflecting that it might have been a lot worse. "When?"

"Not sure—I'll send some dates. Now, what's happened up at Brook Lodge?"

"What do you mean?" Sam said warily.

"Don't play games, Sam. You must think I can't see past the end of my nose. And anyway, I saw Amanda."

Thinking of novel ways of torturing Amanda when she saw her,

Sam slowly told the story of her almost-affair. Considering the pain she was feeling, the story didn't seem to take very long.

"Do you fancy him? He *is* gorgeous, even I can see that!" Charlie said, at the end of the tale.

"Yes. Yes, we're very strongly attracted to each other. It's been—difficult—while we were working on the garden."

Charlie laughed. "Oh my god! Meaningful looks, yearning tension, that sort of thing?"

"We were both very professional, Charlie!" Sam said sharply. "It was... It was just..." she trailed off, feeling suddenly, unexpectedly tearful for what might have been.

Charlie sobered immediately. "Oh. It was serious, wasn't it? I haven't heard that tone in your voice since...well, for a long time."

Sam took a deep breath. "Yes. Well, he lied to me, so it's over."

Charlie sucked in her breath.

"But surely, keeping his identity secret isn't all that dreadful? From what I've read in the Telegraph about the share price, there were very good reasons for it. Did he say he was going to tell you?"

"*After* he'd pumped me dry of all the information he could about the bloody development! Frankly, I think if I'd not been involved in the action group, he'd never have given me a second glance!"

Sam heard Charlie sigh gustily. "Believe me, if Keane wanted you, it was certainly not because you opposed one of his developments. Or that he wanted to kibosh your plans. He probably fancied the pants off you! Don't be an idiot, Sam."

Changing the subject, Sam said she'd wait to hear about a date for her drink with Fraser and spent much of the rest of the afternoon staring blankly into space.

27

Sam stared at the stiff cardboard invitation.

"You are invited to the official opening of Brook Lodge Garden
on Sunday 7 August from 2.00pm to 5.00pm.
Ribbon-cutting at 3.00pm.
Donations to go to Ashlow Hospice.
Homemade cakes, tea and fizz available.
RSVP"

There was a note with the invitation, from Magda.

"I thought it would be a good way to raise some money for the local hospice and publicise your wonderful work! I hope you, Andy and Steve can come, and you'll be happy to talk about how you put the garden together. Give me a call to discuss."

"Well, thanks for asking me first!" muttered Sam. Then she laughed. Magda would go far. She'd have to think about it, particularly the invitation to Steve. Yes, she'd have to think about that *very* carefully.

However, when she mentioned it two days later, Andy was keen. So was Paul.

"We're getting in some nice enquiries, but what we could do with is a bit of local publicity which shows people what the finished product might look like!"

"I think we'd need to double-check that Jonas Keane is ok with this—although he might not be there at all..." Sam nibbled her lip.

"All the stuff with the development is over, Sam," said Andy. "Relax. It's not personal, it's just business."

Sam blew out her cheeks.

"OK. I'll accept. But what about Steve?"

"I think you'll find that Steve has a new love interest," Paul grinned. "A new girl started at the supermarket alongside his mum and from his interest in his mobile phone and the look in his eye, I think it's going very well."

"Really? That's a relief!"

"Surprised you didn't notice," Andy said.

Sam left that unanswered and went to make the call to Magda.

It was a stilted conversation, despite Magda's best efforts. Sam was impressed with the scale of the event. More than a hundred and fifty invitations, including the good and great from the local council. Sam twisted her lips thinking about that. The councillors would be keen to butter up the head of a development company, but possibly less enthusiastic about celebrating a key member of the village protest group who gave them so much trouble.

Then there was Fraser and Charlie, Steve's mum, local shopkeepers, the whole of the village action group. Sam was not surprised that members of the local press weren't invited.

"Is your Dad ok with this?" Sam eventually asked.

"Oh yes! He's cool with it."

"And he knows you've invited us?"

"He insisted on it. He's sorry he wasn't here when you finished that day but as you know..."

The Garden Plot

"Yes, he was busy, wasn't he?" Sam made her voice as pleasant and neutral as possible. There was a pause.

"I hope *you're* ok with it all."

Sam felt a twinge of guilt. Magda was trying to help her business, after all.

"Yes, I'm very grateful to you for doing this—it's completely unnecessary, you know. None of my other clients have ever officially launched their gardens with me!"

"Setting a trend, me. I'm mega-excited, it'll be *awesome!*" Magda paused and then said, "By the way, I've also invited my godfather."

Sam was nonplussed.

"Oh? Is he someone special?"

"Well, he's Connor McPherson."

Sam almost dropped the phone.

"What—*the* Connor McPherson? The garden designer?"

"Y-e-e-s," Magda was hesitant. "Is that ok? I did wonder if this was the best thing to do, given that you're both designers. But I thought it might help you—you know, be a useful contact for the future?"

The *enfant terrible* of garden design? The only gardener to have *rejected* an award from the Royal Horticultural Society? *That* Connor McPherson?

"Yes, I imagine he could be useful, thank you," Sam said faintly.

She was smiling as she put down the phone.

Lisbeth was looking anxious again, Magda noted, as she went through the guest list for the umpteenth time.

"Magda, what *exactly* did you say to your dad?"

"Oh, I asked if we could invite a few people to launch the garden and raise some money for the local hospice."

"'A few people'? Were numbers mentioned?"

"Not exactly. I daresay not everyone will arrive at once, will they?" she smiled sunnily. Lisbeth rolled her eyes.

"And how are we going to provide tea and cakes to *more than a hundred people*, Magda?"

"Mrs Brown has agreed to do the baking, if I pay for the ingredients. Apparently, her sister died in the hospice. I've ordered some crockery from the Coffee Cup and they'll deliver it all on Saturday afternoon. I've snaffled some tables and chairs from the library. All in hand, it's all cool."

Lisbeth shook her head. And then she grinned.

"I have to hand it to you, you're properly, like, organised."

"I used to help Nanna plan the Christmas parties in Zurich. It's a real shame she's on a cruise…"

"But won't your dad be mad with like, all these people tramping all over his property?"

"Nah…well, he might be at first. But he *did* say I could do it, *and* he wanted me to invite Sam. I think he's still feeling a bit guilty about the development."

"OK—what can I do?"

"Can you start on the bunting?"

On the day, Sam smoothed her skirt with hands that shook a little. The weather was hot and sunny—even slightly steamy—so she had bare arms and shoulders with a camisole tee-shirt. She wanted to look professional but not too dressed up.

And utterly irresistible. Don't forget that, prodded her libido.

"Oh, for God's sake!" She swung away from the mirror and grabbed her sunhat. She'd arranged to meet Andy and Greg at Brook Lodge. She thought she'd better get there in time for the first visitors —if anyone turned up. As the weeks had passed, she'd become more and more convinced that no-one *would* turn up.

She'd delivered the original garden design plans to Magda at the beginning of the week, pulling out of the drive just as Jonas had driven in. Magda had wanted to put them on a display board so people could see them. As she looked at the taillights of Jonas' car in the rear-view mirror, she didn't examine her feelings. But she'd got home and drunk a lot of wine that night.

She smiled as she saw the bunting and the neon-coloured signs as she got out of the car at Brook Lodge. Magda had certainly gone to town. She heard her name and turned to see Andy and Greg. Greg looked as though he'd stepped out of *Brideshead Revisited* and Andy was wearing a silk striped waistcoat. They made a handsome pair, she thought.

"Glad to see you looking better than the last time I laid eyes on you, darling girl!" said Greg, looking her up and down. "Been on a diet?"

"Ready for this?" asked Andy, saving Sam from answering.

"I think it might be fun. Well, hopefully. And if anyone comes, of course."

"I'm looking forward to meeting the man of the house! He looks a dish from the photos in the papers!" said Greg, while Andy nudged him, exasperated.

"I'm sure you'll be thrilled with him, Greg," murmured Sam, looking at her feet.

Magda was flying down the path towards them and Sam turned to her in relief. Magda hugged her.

"I'm so glad you're here! Come and have a look at where we've put the plans. Lisbeth talked with Paul and got some flyers too. Would you like some tea? Or a glass of champagne? Or we have coffee? And there's *lots* of cake, Mrs Brown seems to have been working all night!"

Sam blinked.

"Um—it all looks brilliant. I'd like some tea, please. This is Greg, Andy's partner."

Now it was Magda's turn to blink, but she put out her hand unhesitatingly and Greg shook it solemnly.

"Great Oxford bags," she said. "Are they original?"

"Clever girl," twinkled Greg. "They are indeed."

She grinned and then skipped away to find tea. Sam looked around and unable to stand still, decided to walk around the garden.

It is glorious, she thought as she walked slowly around. The pergola and the chequerboard patio were Sam's favourite part of the garden. They'd planted different kinds of thyme and Corsican mint around the stones to soften them, and although they'd grow much more over time, the effect was now visible, and the scent was glorious. She breathed it in.

"It's heavenly, isn't it?" said a deep voice behind her. She turned sharply and there was Jonas, looking cool and relaxed in chinos and a white polo shirt. She swallowed.

"I'm glad you like it, Mr Keane."

His lips tightened.

"So formal, Ms Winterson. I take it we're still not friends?"

Sam didn't know how to respond to the direct question.

"I was hoping as you'd come, you'd decided to forgive me. Perhaps not," he added, his green eyes locked on her face.

"There's nothing to forgive. You did what was best for your company, I'm doing what I think is best for mine."

"Just business?"

Sam's chin went up.

"Hi, I brought you tea!" said Magda cheerily. "Dad, Connor wants a word, he's in the house. Sam, your sister is here with Lisbeth and the vicar and his wife."

Sam took the mug and swigged from it gratefully. She didn't feel she was up to meeting the designer just yet. Jonas gave her a cool look and made to turn away.

"Jonas!" Sam blurted. "Mr Keane—I'm sorry, I sound very ungracious. I'm very grateful for the opportunity to show off the garden like this. And I also need to say that I know people have been really pleased about some of the changes to the plans for Jessop's Field."

"Try to keep your gratitude in check, Ms Winterson," said Jonas. "My company is in business to try to protect the environment as well as build houses, the plans you saw were not what I wanted. As I told you. As for today, it's good that your family and a few friends will have the opportunity to admire your work." He walked away.

Sam stared. *Family and a few friends? Oh my god, Magda hasn't told him about the guest list!*

The Garden Plot

She made to walk after him and then checked. Let Magda handle it. She giggled. Perhaps this afternoon would be more fun that she'd anticipated.

God, how many more people would arrive? thought Jonas forty-five minutes later. He'd lost count of the people he'd shaken hands with. To his secret relief, Sam had taken charge of introducing him to the people coming in, and he had been thanked time and time again for the changes to the development. The Vicar had practically pumped his hand while talking in detail of the birds that inhabited Jessop's Field.

Extricating himself from a conversation about the price of land with a local councillor, he found Magda with flushed cheeks, serving tea at a trestle table. Now he looked, there did seem to be a lot of cups and saucers about, not to mention a mountain of home-made cake.

"Magda? Can I have a word?"

"Lisbeth? Are you ok for a minute?" Lisbeth nodded, and Magda came towards him.

"It's going really well, Dad, isn't it?"

"Exactly how many invitations did you send out?" Jonas said, coming straight to the point.

Magda's smile dropped.

"Um...about two hundred, although not everyone could make it."

"*What?*"

"Well, I wanted to raise as much money as possible for the hospice," she said. "*And* I wanted to promote Sam's company! It's a brilliant garden!"

Jonas stared.

"You're not mad, are you? Look, everyone's being lovely, they're not in the house or anything and they think the garden is *awesome!*" Magda pleaded, holding out her hands.

Jonas caught Lisbeth's eye. She looked anxious as usual. His gaze swept the garden. About ninety villagers were milling around, laughing, drinking tea and stuffing themselves with Mrs Brown's delicious cake. Sam was at the flower beds, pointing out the details to keen horticulturalists. It was an idyllic scene, he thought. Exactly right to introduce the Keane family to the village, and enable him to rebuild some of Halcyon's tarnished reputation.

He should be thanking Magda, not telling her off.

"No, pet. I'm not mad." Magda relaxed. "It would have been nice to be told, though. I might have been able to get you a deal on the champagne."

Magda hugged him.

"Thanks Dad, I did get a reasonable deal from the off-licence, but you'd probably have done better!"

Privately, Jonas wondered if he would have. Magda looked at her watch.

"I'll set up the ribbon cutting. I thought we'd do it by the pergola?" she said.

"Yes, great. I'll get Sam, shall I?"

Sam saw Jonas out of the corner of her eye. A veteran bore from the local horticultural society was scoffing gently at her choice of rambling rose while blue-eyed Connor McPherson looked on with a mixture of mischief and sympathy.

"Of course the choice of roses and pastel colours do tend to make the garden a little—*girly*—don't you think?"

"Ah but sure, roses are a mainstay of traditional gardens, and fit beautifully here," Connor put in smoothly. "Some people have some outmoded views about colours. And the bright orange of the daliahs add just the right touch of modernity."

Horticultural man went red at the implication that he was outmoded, and Sam smiled brightly.

"Did you know everyone talks about the rose as a flower of love, but to the Arabs, originally it was a flower associated with masculinity," she said hastily. She could do without Connor McPherson's input, but he was here as a guest of her client.

"Really?" said Steve's new girlfriend, a robust-looking creature with jet black hair and a nose ring.

Sam nodded, opened her mouth to say more and then closed it.

"And?" prompted Jonas, joining the group.

She was embarrassed. "I can run on a bit... I didn't want to bore you."

Steve hit her gently on the arm.

"Don't be daft! You're never boring!"

"No," said Jonas, his eyes on her face. "You're never boring."

Sam felt Connor's blue gaze snap to Jonas and a speculative glint enter his eye. She rushed into speech.

"Do you know the term 'sub rosa'?" she asked. Steve's girlfriend looked puzzled and shook her head. "It means under the rose, or in confidence. In the Middle Ages, diplomats used to hang a garland of roses over the door of the meeting room as a sign of confidentiality."

"Wow," Steve's girlfriend said, looking awed, and sniffing the rose. The horticulturalist slunk away. Connor grinned at her.

"Well played," he said.

"Magda is asking for you to come and cut the ribbon," Jonas said.

"I'll get a glass to toast it all," said Connor and he strolled off, his long legs eating the ground.

Sam and Jonas walked in silence to the pergola. Magda had found a handbell from somewhere and was ringing it. People obligingly gathered by the pergola.

Magda thanked people for coming and welcomed them to the newly-renovated gardens. She then asked Sam to say a few words. It was an astonishingly assured address from the teenager, thought Sam, suddenly nervous at the last moment. She fumbled with her notes.

"Thank you Magda—"

"Can't hear you, duck! Can you speak up?" came a shout from the back.

There was a ripple of laughter and Sam straightened her back and raised her voice. It was a bit stilted, but after a moment, she got into her stride.

She talked about the importance of gardens to people and their well-being. She talked about the skills she wanted to help keep alive and mentioned Steve, who went red and whose girlfriend giggled. And finally, she talked about Brook Lodge.

"Magda had a clear vision for the garden here," she said. "In an age when most new houses have envelope-sized gardens, this is a luxury--" Sam glanced at Jonas, who looked steadily back at her, "--and she wanted it to be a part of, rather just bolted onto, the house. She wanted it to be part of her life and her family's life, to be something to be loved and lived in, not simply looked at. I love what we've developed together and I hope that everyone coming today—well, I hope that you will too." She raised her glass. "To Brook Lodge."

The audience responded, drank, and there was applause. The Vicar and Jenny came to congratulate her on her speech and the garden, Connor raised his glass to her from a distance. Sam kept a wary eye on Jonas, who was mingling and smiling.

"Brilliant!" Lisbeth said, hugging her. "I think you'll get loads of new business out of this!"

Sam smiled.

"We'll see. They've been interested in this garden, certainly."

Magda bounced up, Jonas following her more slowly. Sam tensed.

"Before I forget, ages ago, Andy mentioned something about a garden design competition," said Magda. Sam's eyes flew to Jonas' face.

Hell, I'd forgotten all about that...

"It had gone out of my mind," she said. "I'm not sure in the circumstances that it's appropriate."

Magda stared.

"What do you mean? What circumstances? Oh—" she waved her hand. "The development? I thought that was being sorted out now?"

There was an awkward silence. Jonas smiled bitterly.

"I'm not sure that Sam has forgiven me for trying to hang on to my privacy or for being a developer in the first place."

You bloody toe-rag. As if that was all it was! Sam fumed. She shook her head and kept quiet.

"So for once at least, we are in agreement," said Jonas. "It's not appropriate. We have enough problems with the press as it is, I don't want to add to those, *particularly* given where we live. And if Sam doesn't want the garden to be entered, then there's nothing more to be said, is there?"

Sam felt her heart was being ripped in two. No, of course it wasn't appropriate, but *God!* How she wanted recognition for this glorious garden.

"And you wouldn't want to be accused of siding with the enemy, would you?" Jonas added. "Bribed into accepting the development through a competition entry?"

Sam's head went up and she felt the flood of red pour over her cheeks.

"No, as you said—completely inappropriate," she gritted.

Magda was looking between the pair of them in disbelief, Sam thought. She turned away to find Andy and Greg looking at her in concern.

"Let's get some champagne, sweetie," said Greg, linked her hand through his arm. "You look like you could do with a drink."

28

"It's all so *idiotic!*" Magda wailed to Lisbeth the following week. Lisbeth was thoughtful.

"I'm not quite sure why it happened like that," she said, settling a cushion behind her on the bed. "It was a golden opportunity for Sam and Wintersons, your Dad seemed OK with the idea, and the development *has* changed. I talked to my Dad about it last night. I know Aunty Sam was unhappy at *any* houses being built, but it's so much better than it was, and that's down to your Dad! So what she said doesn't make any sense!"

"And then Dad got the hump--"

"Well, I *do* think they're both being a bit irrational. I looked online and the winner isn't announced until October, so everyone will have forgotten about the development by then."

"Oh, I could scream! He's like, *impossible* to live with at the moment, even Connor said so! I'll be glad to get back to school at this rate! I nearly asked to go back to Ireland with Connor, I was so fed up. Did you see Sam afterwards with Andy? She looked, like, sick to her stomach," Magda said glumly. She punched one of the cushions strewn over Lisbeth's bed in frustration.

"It's such a waste, and sooooo stupid! And *I'm* disappointed too! After all my planning! I even bloody paid for the garden!"

Lisbeth looked struck. "Yes, you *did*, didn't you?" she said slowly. Magda looked at her.

"What?"

"The contract was with you, wasn't it? Not your dad?"

Magda looked blank for a second and then an unholy grin spread across her face. "Yes, it was. Technically, I'm the client, aren't I?"

Lisbeth watched her. "Do you dare?" she asked finally.

"Yes, I bloody *do* dare! I have the plans Sam drew, and everything! What does the entry form look like?"

They scrambled to the computer.

"Well, that doesn't look too difficult. Although we could do with some Winterson's headed paper," said Madga, scanning it.

"Zach designed the logo—I'll get the template from him," Lisbeth reached for her phone and started to text.

"We'll need to get photos," Magda said, her previous grumpiness completely forgotten. "I'll take those tomorrow. We've only got a week or so, *but--*" Lisbeth looked up as she paused. "Are you ok with this?" Madga said seriously.

"Are you *kidding* me?" Lisbeth exclaimed. "Sam's a *brilliant* designer and frankly, I think she'd stand a good chance of winning! It'll be good for her—just like the garden launch."

Magda grinned and bumped shoulders with her and then began tapping on the keys.

Charlie, coming in to announce lunch an hour later, said to Lisbeth, "Well, I'm pleased to see a bit more colour in Magda's cheeks. We can do without all this drama…"

"Mum!" Lisbeth protested. Charlie went on. "She needs a calming influence in her life and I'm glad she's got you, Lisbeth. It's a shame you don't have as much influence over Sam. Or your father…"

"So—what'll you have?"

Sam winced slightly at Fraser's fake bonhomie, asked for a gin and tonic and then changed her mind to a white wine spritzer.

Great start. Dithering is not what's needed here.

"I'm sorry about the planning application," Fraser said when they'd sat down. Sam took a sip of her drink to give her time to think of a response.

"Well, at least the developers are listening to local opinion now. And it was a democratic decision, we have to live with it," she said finally, smiling.

"Who knew we had a property magnate to dinner?" Fraser took a sip of his drink. Sam clenched her teeth together. "And I daresay it'll hit the press next week, so keep it quiet—but Halcyon has put in a bid to develop the brown field site on Lower Edge Field."

Sam stared.

"Didn't you know? I'd have thought your *client*—" Fraser stressed the word "—would have told you."

Sam let that slide, concentrating on the other information.

"They're developing Lower Edge Field? But that's marvellous! Are they withdrawing from Jessop's Field?"

"Well, no. But there may be *fewer* houses on Jessop's Field, as a result. So everybody wins—the local authority gets its housing, local people have places to buy, the wildlife is protected."

"But the wildlife is *moved*."

"You can't have everything. Compromise is the adult thing to do, Sam."

Sam ignored the snipe and tried to remain focused. The news about the development was interesting—but she was here to mend fences with Fraser.

"Thanks for telling me... But look, I wanted to say I'm sorry I lost my temper so badly," she began hesitantly. Fraser looked steadily at her and said nothing. "But you *did* provoke me with that bloody letter," she added, unable to stop herself.

Fraser's mouth twisted. "I'm not the touchy-feely sort," he said eventually, looking at the bubbles in his pint. "But what you said hurt me. I *am* ambitious, I *do* want to get into the Cabinet because it's there I feel I can do most good. I know you think I don't care about local issues, but you're wrong. I do. I intend to do things at national level which will certainly benefit my local constituents."

Sam kept quiet. Fraser was on a roll, and her comments would probably be unnecessary. *Oh, stop it!* she chided herself and concentrated on what he was saying.

"My views were based on the fact that local people *need* somewhere to live, Sam. They're not interested in the ecological debate, they want a home of their own."

"We weren't trying to stop anyone getting a home! We were just trying to get the building work moved somewhere else!"

"But you *did* want to keep your view, didn't you?" Fraser pressed. "Seen, I must add, by the more well-off members of Sherton. The low-income families live out of sight of our picture-perfect village."

"It wasn't like that. We wanted to save something beautiful for future generations—"

"*Which* future generations, Sam? Do you have any idea of the birth rate in Sherton? It's one of the lowest in the county. The average age of our villagers is forty-three—way past normal child-bearing age. If we're going to keep the village alive, we need new, young people and young families moving into the area."

Sam was silent, floored by his comments.

"*That* was the reason I wouldn't support you, Sam. Not because I'm anti-nature, or pro-developer, *or* because it was *you* involved in the campaign. It was because the village will die if we don't get new people in it, and they'll need somewhere to live."

Sam tried to say something, but nothing came out of her mouth. She felt slightly ashamed, as if she'd been caught cheating.

"The thing with you, Sam, is you *say* you're a socialist, but you're doing it from a very comfortable position of education and relative wealth. The people who need these houses are *real* working class—and they don't give a toss about the environment. Don't kid yourself you're very different from me, or Charlotte. You're not, you're just posturing."

Sam stared at him, struck dumb. *I keep being told this! Is it really like that? Am I posturing?*

"Charlotte mentioned you had some nasty threats. Has that stopped?"

"It's eased off since the broken window, although I had some dog shit posted through my door the other day," she said.

He stared.

"Yes, I've been in touch with the police and no, they haven't found anyone," she added. "I hope whoever it is will eventually find something else to be cross about, someone else to bully."

"I'm really sorry about that," Fraser said seriously. "You must let me know if it starts again. There are some idiots around."

"Thanks."

Sam paused. Some of Fraser's words had pricked her.

"I just wanted to do what I thought was best," she finally said in a low voice. "I'd do it all again, regardless of the crap. But I *am* sorry about the row."

Fraser sighed. "I know. I just wish you'd remember that we're *both* trying to do what we think is best. Neither of us give the other credit for it."

"No. But you're part of my family..." To her surprise, he put an arm round her shoulder and hugged her.

"It won't change, you know. We'll continue to disagree. Where we need to improve is limiting the fall-out zone," he said, and she nodded. There was an awkward pause.

"My time to get them in, I think," Sam said, and grabbing her bag, headed for the bar.

In Manchester, Jonas stretched to ease the crick in his neck. At least he'd managed to finish *one* important task, he thought with some satisfaction. He'd been avoiding calls from Connor all day, and he knew he'd need to talk to him at some stage. His best friend had been his usual blunt self when Jonas told him about how things were between himself and Sam.

"You look at her like you'd like to lick her all over!" Connor had said. "What the hell were you thinking of, not telling her the truth immediately? And as for the garden opening—God, you couldn't have messed up more, could you?"

Jonas winced now, thinking of the language Connor had used, and the names he'd called him—the very kindest of which had been 'eejit'. But it was too late. That bird had flown. He needed to get on with his life, without one petite, blonde gardener in it.

He looked next at the email from his public relations company and grimaced. The press coverage was fair, and they'd been lucky. The analysts were calm, finally. They would have to keep up the effort to rebuild their reputation, a fact that delighted the PR company, which was sharpening its pitch technique.

At least he should be home on time this evening. It felt like months since he'd last had dinner with Magda, but it was only a couple of weeks in reality.

There was a message from his PA that Dr Walters had called again. Jonas ignored it, he'd call him tomorrow. He didn't need anyone fussing over him at the moment.

Apart from Sam, the thought came into his mind.

"Wow, why the scowl?" Neil said, coming into the office.

"I'm knackered. I'm going to go home early today."

"Good idea. In fact, why don't you work from home for a few days?" Neil said, casually. "You've been working around the clock recently."

"I'm perfectly fine."

"That's not what Dr Walters told me when he bent my ear an hour ago."

"What?"

"Dr Walters, having called you five times in as many days, collared me instead. He didn't go into any details, obviously, but asked if you'd made the arrangements for your funeral already, and could he have the date, so he could put it in his diary. He was *very* cross."

Jonas was outraged. "The bloody nerve!"

"But he's right, isn't he Jonas?" persevered Neil, leaning on the edge of the desk with his arms folded. "You *shouldn't* be back at work yet."

"I'm fine."

"You're not, you look a wreck. Your temper's dreadful. Half the admin staff hide when they see you coming."

Jonas sat back and gave Neil a cold look. "Trying to step into my shoes, Neil?"

"Well, if you end up killing yourself, I suppose someone will have to," Neil returned without blinking. There was a silence.

Jonas sighed.

"Okay, okay. You're right. Maybe I do need to ease up. I haven't had the results from the last set of tests yet." Neil, sensibly, made no comment. "I'll get off before the traffic builds up."

"Excellent. Don't worry, I'll be on the phone if something comes up I can't handle."

Jonas looked at him. Neil grinned. "You know—as your right hand man?"

Jonas smiled faintly. "I'd better watch my back," was all he said.

"And ring your bloody doctor," Neil added as Jonas headed for the door.

Sam turned over the page of the calendar on her desk.

It was September next week. Business would pick up again as householders returned from holiday, inspired by beautiful gardens in hotter climates, and before you knew it, it would be Christmas.

With the end of August, so much seemed to be ending too. Her thoughts strayed to Jonas and she resolutely busied herself tidying her desk. She turned over the magazine page for the garden competition and a pang went through her. The closing date had gone.

Maybe next year...

She drew a breath and hitched her jeans up around her waist, as they sagged slightly. She ought to buy a smaller size, she supposed. She aimed the crumpled page at the bin and as usual, missed. She walked over to pick up the ball and drop it in, just as Steve popped his head into the office.

"Hello—all right?" he asked.

She forced a smile. "Fine, thanks. I'm glad I've seen you—come in." He looked wary, and Sam grinned this time in genuine amusement. "Don't be a wuss. If you'd screwed up, I would have *come* to find you."

He sat down rather gingerly, as if the seat was hot. She thanked him for his hard work and told him what the lecturers at the college had said. Then she offered him the job, and he gaped.

"Proper, like?"

"Yes, proper, but don't think you can skip college, because to get a pay increase, you're going to need to qualify. This is what I was thinking of offering you, when you do."

Sam passed the draft contract to him and he read it, going pink.

"Well?" Sam knew the offer was more than fair, it was even generous, but she'd had a good look at the figures and prospective business and she could afford it. If the calls they were getting translated into work, she'd have to take on another worker, too.

"I dunno what to say," Steve stuttered.

"Yes?"

"God, aye! Thank you! I'm really grateful..."

She patted him on the shoulder and he left, clutching the contract to show his mum. Sam continued to shift papers around her desk. She found the number of that blasted journalist who had called to quiz her about designing Jonas' garden. God knows how they'd found *that* out.

She'd ignored it and all subsequent calls. Jonas had gradually disappeared from the business news and the local press and she was strangely bereft.

And after that Sunday at Brook Lodge, she'd heard nothing from him.

She found her cheeks wet, tutted to herself and blew her nose. She drew her sketch pad towards her.

The pub was heaving for the late summer festival. Sam craned her neck and caught sight of Amanda and the Lovely Luke, guarding a table in the garden at the back of the Dog and Duck. She squeezed through the crowd at the bar and finally making it outside, dropped onto the seat with a whoosh.

"Blimey! It's bloody manic in there!"

"Been like this since two o'clock," said Amanda, taking the wine out of the ice bucket and looking in vain for something to pour it in. "Damn, we forgot to get you a glass. Bugger."

Luke made to uncurl his long legs from the bench and Sam waved him down.

"Don't worry, I'll get it, I need the loo anyway."

Sam weaved her way to the ladies and waited in line for five minutes. She felt her phone buzz and peered at the message from Amanda which said they'd need another bottle soon. Shaking her head, she squeezed and sidled her way to the bar.

With a less-than-cold bottle of rosé in her hand and a glass for herself, she smiled her thanks at the harried barmaid, and carefully turned around. She dropped her phone and cursing, she bent to pick it up. She hit her head on someone's elbow on the way up.

"Oof!" she said and came face to chest with Jonas. She drew in a deep breath and his smell, spicy and earthy, filled her nostrils.

"Sorry," he said. Sam was elbowed out of the way by someone getting to the packed bar, and she fell headlong into him. It was her turn to apologise.

"God, it's a madhouse!" he said, his arms automatically coming around her. Sam blinked, her brain short-circuited by the feel of his body against her. The noise in the bar seemed to be muffled as his eyes locked on her.

"I--" he fell silent.

They stood there for a second or two and then Jonas seemed to come to his senses.

"Let's move away from the bar," and his arms fell away from her. Getting a firmer grip on the bottle and her glass, Sam followed him to the side of the counter, where there seemed to be fewer bodies.

"Sorry about that," he said. "Did I hurt you?"

"Wha- oh no, I dropped my phone. Stupid of me."

There was a pause.

"How are you?" she asked, irritated that her voice sounded a bit thin and reedy.

"I'm good thanks. You?"

"Yes, fine." Pause.

Good god, could we be less scintillating? She thought.

"I read about the development of Lower Edge Fields—that's *really* good news!" she said, remembering. He smiled.

"Yes, I know the action group felt very strongly about that. It seemed a good opportunity to me."

But that wasn't because of us, was it? It was because it was an OPPORTUNITY.

She nodded and then couldn't think of anything to say. The air suddenly felt heavy around her and she found herself staring at his face, drawn to his green eyes. She looked down quickly.

"Sam--" Jonas stopped. "Sam, I'm *really* sorry about what happened. All of it."

Sam hung her head, her stomach churning.

"I know. So am I," she said in a low voice, which he dipped his head to hear.

"Dad! There you are—oh, hi Sam! It's like, *crazy* in here, isn't it?" Magda said, her voice ripping the atmosphere between them. Sam stood back and breathed as though she'd been underwater for a long time.

"Hi Magda. Still enjoying the garden?" she said brightly.

"Yeah, and my Nanna's coming to see it next week! She was really peeved she missed the opening—I know she'll love it!" Magda was looking at them both curiously. "But are you on your own? Do you want to join us?"

"No, no, I'm with friends," she said at once. She indicated the wine. "They'll be missing me..."

She smiled at Jonas, winked at Magda and walked away as fast as the crush would let her.

Magda peered at him, and Jonas plastered a smile on his face.

"Shall we try and find a seat outside?" he asked.

"Yeah, good idea. How was Sam?"

"Good, she said."

"Did you talk much?"

"No, it was a bit noisy."

They sat down on the grass and watched the parade of flowers, strange and wonderful shapes covered in thousands of flower heads. Magda rather sourly said she thought she'd prefer to see the flower heads attached to stalks, in the garden.

Jonas politely refused to be drawn into the rounders tournament, citing health grounds (and he *must* get in touch with Dr Walters, he thought guiltily, sipping his Guinness). Magda, laughing, pulled off her sweatshirt, called him an old man, and skipped off to make a brilliant catch and score a couple of rounders.

He watched absently as the crowds milled around him. He felt hollow, despite the laughter and good-natured atmosphere. His mind dwelt on every word of that short, stilted conversation with Sam. He'd been on the edge of asking if he could call her. He didn't know what had stopped him. Something.

He felt someone watching him and looked up to see Magda, her eyes narrowed.

"You look miles away!" she teased, coming to sit down.

"I was. Did you win?" he said.

"Of course. Are you feeling ok? You look a bit...down."
"I'm a bit tired. It's been a hell of a month."
"Shall I take you home, old man?"
"Cheeky brat. Yes, you can."
"Do I need a chair, or can you walk?"

He threw her sweatshirt at her and they went home. He wished he didn't feel quite as old as he did.

29

"So that's it?" Jonas said to Dr Walters.

"It is. We can't find any abnormalities in your blood, but I'd like you to come in for a white cell count in six months' time." Dr Walters looked disappointed that he was better, Jonas thought.

"So I can go back to work?"

"Officially, yes you can. Although we both know you've been back at work for at least a month."

Jonas smiled wryly, buttoning his shirt.

"You've obviously seen the news."

"Some," Dr Walters said. "I don't usually read the business pages, but yes, even I've been aware. How is it all going?"

"I think we've got it under control, but I think it'll be a while before we try and go into partnership again." Jonas tucked his shirt into his trousers.

Dr Walters was watching him closely. "Is everything else all right? I can see you're looking a bit frazzled, if you don't mind me saying."

"It's been a hectic few weeks."

Dr Walters looked steadily at him, but Jonas said nothing more. The doctor shrugged. "Right. Good to see you're back on form, you have my number if you need to get in touch."

Jonas thanked him, shook his hand and with a whisk of curtains, the doctor disappeared.

He was cursing the parking charges when a voice he knew hailed him.

"Hello stranger!" said Gerry Lord, wafting over in a cloud of perfume.

"Gerry! How lovely to see you!" Jonas said sincerely, kissing her on both cheeks.

"Are you better?"

"Apparently, yes."

"I must say, you look a teeny bit tired, darling. Are you *quite* well? And have you lost weight, too? Then again, you've been all over the media, haven't you? So I suppose that's understandable."

"Yes, it's been a bit busy. But what are you doing here?" Jonas asked, moving the conversation away from the bags under his eyes and the crisis in his company.

"I'm here to see Anthony—my new man. He broke his leg last week and I'm keeping him company when the tyrant nurses allow it."

Jonas looked at her properly for the first time. She looked radiant, confident, secure. "Your new man obviously suits you," he said.

She smiled like a cat and Jonas could almost imagine her purring.

"He's divine. I'd introduce you, but it could be a tiny bit awkward..."

Jonas laughed, for the first time, he thought, in a long while. "No, probably best."

There was a pause.

"Well, it's been lovely to see you, but I must go. I'm glad you're better!" She air kissed either side of his face and was gone before Jonas could do anything but wave. He watched her shapely behind in a very tight skirt climb the steps to the entrance and grinned as she checked to see if he was still watching. He raised a hand in salute and she disappeared inside.

He sat for a moment in the car, thinking of Sam.

With a grimace, he started the car for the drive home.

"Hopeless!" wailed Magda. The text from her father said he was 'cured' and would call into the office before coming home. "All our work..." she muttered crossly, showing her phone to Lisbeth who was leafing through a glossy magazine.

"How *is* your dad? Like, really?" Lisbeth asked after a moment, tossing away the magazine. Magda thought for a moment and then shrugged.

"I dunno. He looks a bit tired and his face is always *still* somehow—you know, like he's plastic or something. Why?"

"Aunty Sam came round for lunch last week—the first time she's been round to our house for ages. She's dead skinny and barely ate anything, and even Mum mentioned it."

"What did Sam say?"

"Oh, something totally unconvincing, like she had a lot of work on and kept forgetting to eat. But that's rubbish, I think..."

"D'you know, I could've sworn that something was happening when we bumped into Sam at the pub, before I arrived. But do you think Sam is attracted to Dad?" Magda asked.

"S'possible. But that's no use if they never meet again. How do we get them to talk to one another?"

"I haven't a clue. I've been trying to persuade Dad to go down to the pub, join a darts team, *anything* to get him out of the house, so they might bump into one another again, but he just comes in from work, slumps on the sofa and then goes to bed. He's barely been out to the village since the festival."

"Well, I daresay he has been working hard..."

Magda snorted in an unladylike way, and then raised her head as her grandmother's voice drifted up the stairs. Niamh had arrived a few days ago. Her grandfather would join her after his business trip in Europe.

"Magda! Is Lisbeth staying for dinner?"

"Are you?" Magda asked.

The Garden Plot

"No, I need to get home, Mum's expecting me. But we ought to get together soon to see what we can plan—"

"What are you two scheming about?" Niamh said, opening the door. She looked at them and laughed. "Oho! What have I stumbled on? No, don't tell me, I don't want to know, I'll only be horrified. Magda, this came by courier," she passed over a large white envelope.

Magda frowned, and then caught sight of the logo on the corner. "It's the garden competition!" She tore open the flap and wrenched out the contents.

"What's it say?" Lisbeth asked breathlessly.

"Omigod, omigod! Sam's made it into the final! This letter is asking when they can come and view the finished garden!"

"What?" Lisbeth suddenly looked aghast. "When do they want to come?"

Magda was scanning the letter, written on thick, heavy paper.

"'At your convenience, but within the next three weeks…'"

"The *next three weeks*? How are we going to manage that *without* your Dad knowing? We're back at school!"

"You entered the garden into a design competition without your father's permission?" Niamh asked, catching on very quickly.

Magda bit her lip. Niamh waited. "But Nanna, I *paid* for it! It's such a brilliant design, I just wanted for Sam to be recognised for it!"

"Do you not think your father should have been consulted? It *is* his property!"

"It's sort of complicated…"

"I'm all ears."

Niamh folded her arms and waited.

Stumbling a little, Magda told the tale of their attempts to get the adults together, with Lisbeth adding her comments.

"Did you tell Sam about this?" Niamh pointed to the letter.

"She *said* she didn't want to enter the garden, but she looked, like, *sooo* disappointed about it. So no, she doesn't know," Magda admitted.

"You entered the competition against the express wishes of your father *and* the designer?" Niamh stared and Magda went red. "Magda, what were you thinking?"

"I know, I know. But if you'd have seen her face when we talked about it! And then Dad got all arse-y when we were talking about it at the garden launch and the conversation just went downhill! It's not until October and everything will be better by then..."

Niamh shook her head in disbelief.

"Really, Magda, I'm lost for words. And surely the competition organisers will write to Sam about this?" Niamh frowned.

Lisbeth nodded, but added quickly that she'd taken Paul, the office manager into their confidence, and he was watching the mail. Niamh's eyebrows rose again slightly, but she simply asked, "So when will she know she's in the final? Presumably she needed to know at *some* stage?"

Magda exchanged a look with Lisbeth.

"I don't suppose we'd thought that far," admitted Magda. To her enormous relief, Niamh's face lost its severe look and she laughed. Magda almost sagged with relief.

"Oh Nanna! Dad's been so *miserable*! And when he was with Sam, he was *totally*, like, different! The air used to—like—oh, *hum* between them!"

"'Hum'? Goodness," said Niamh.

Magda looked beseechingly at her grandmother. "But now—I'm not sure what to do. I thought the garden opening would smooth things over, but it got all complicated somehow and I don't really understand why..."

Niamh thought for a moment. "Are you sure they're attracted to one another?" Magda looked at Lisbeth and then nodded vigorously.

"They just need to get in the same room, don't they Lisbeth?"

"Well... I think Aunty Sam is as miserable as Magda says her dad is. I haven't seen her look so...sad and lost before."

Niamh rose to her feet. "I think it would be best to double check before we do anything rash. I might pay her a visit."

Lisbeth looked alarmed.

"Don't worry dear, I'll just call to congratulate her on the garden. After all, I was away for the garden launch. I'll just be passing on the way to the village, or something."

"It's a bit out of the way to be just passing," Lisbeth murmured doubtfully. Niamh waved aside her concerns.

"I'll think of something." She swept out of the room. There was a silence.

"*Will* it be all right?" Lisbeth bit a nail.

Magda grinned, feeling suddenly much more positive. "Nanna will handle it—she's a wonder."

Sam was trying to get enthused about the designs for a very modern garden for a new client. It wasn't going well. She screwed up the paper she'd been doodling on, and threw it at the bin, which it predictably missed. There was a knock at the door, and Andy poked his head around.

"Sam, Magda's grandmother is here to see you about the garden. Are you available?"

Sam stared and then nodded. A minute later, a tall, elegant woman walked into the room. Sam offered her hand almost in defence. Mrs Keane's features reminded her strongly of Jonas and she drank in the sight of her.

"Niamh Keane—I'm very pleased to meet you, Samantha—or do you prefer Sam?" They shook hands, the slim fingers surprisingly strong and Sam instantly fell in love with the lilting voice tinged with a soft Irish accent.

"Sam—Samantha was what my father used to call me when I'd done something wrong." Niamh Keane laughed and the sound flowed round the room like soft toffee. Sam gestured her to a chair. After this promising start, an uncomfortable silence fell. Then Niamh spoke.

"I know it's awkward, given the wretched development and my son playing hide-and-seek, but I wanted to stop by to say how wonderful the garden is."

Sam didn't know what to say. What did Jonas' mother know? Did she know of the row they'd had? Or their 'nearly-fling'? Looking into the guileless grey-green eyes, Sam decided not.

"Thank you. I'm really pleased you like it," Sam said breezily. She thought she saw a twinkle in the eyes watching her.

"Magda invited me to her launch event, but I was in the middle of the Mediterranean at the time. The design is inspired—I wondered how you'd come up with the ideas. I'm an avid gardener myself and I'd love to know."

Sam pulled out the plans and explained to Niamh how the garden took shape. Niamh was a good listener—almost *too* good, Sam thought, trying to remember to curb her tongue. But the temptation to tell the story of the design was very strong and Sam swept through it, explaining motifs and historical references and planting. She was careful to keep well away from any comment on the owner of the house, however. Niamh nodded, smiling.

"Well, you've certainly delivered brilliantly. And now we're being blessed with this wonderful Indian summer, too! I have plenty of opportunities to use it! Is that a photo of your team?"

Sam turned to look at the bookcase behind her. There was the snapshot of her with Andy and Steve, which Magda had taken on her phone. They looked happy, she thought wistfully. She herself looked excited, almost misty-eyed.

"Yes—Andy showed you in, and Steve is at college today. It was a team effort and one of the best projects we've worked on."

"Why was it?"

Sam turned, taken aback by the swiftness of the question.

"Um... Well it was a good design and it turned out really well. It suits the house, and I think it will suit Magda. And her father, of course."

Niamh's eyes glinted and she smiled. "Of course. May I see the picture?"

Sam passed it to her and her visitor looked closely at it. "It's a lovely photo," she commented as she handed it back. Sam smiled, meaninglessly.

"We're delighted with the way it turned out." Her tone signalled a close of the discussion and glancing at the clock, she was surprised to see that more than an hour had passed. Her visitor rose and put out her hand in farewell.

"Well, I've taken up too much of your time, but it's been wonderful to hear from a fellow enthusiast—thank you! The garden is simply lovely."

Then she left.

~

Lisbeth watched Magda's grandmother return to the house, and they both met her in the hall.

"Well, Nanna? What did she say?"

"She's a passionate, talented garden designer who really knows her stuff," said Niamh thoughtfully. "She's got an almost instinctive feel for places and plants, and how they go together... Connor thought so, too."

"And Dad?" Magda prompted impatiently.

Niamh became practical. "Well, she was very careful to avoid almost all mention of your father, and she's definitely lost weight—I saw the photo you took when the garden was completed and she's certainly thinner now than she was—what?—more than a month ago?"

Lisbeth nodded.

"So I agree with you that she's unhappy. And I know your father's not his usual self."

"What can we do?" Lisbeth said.

"Something will present itself, I'm sure. You just have to be ready to take advantage."

30

"Magda! Are you in?" called Jonas as he set down his briefcase. Magda ran into the hall.

"Dad! What time do you call this? You're early!"

He kissed her on the top of her glossy head. "Cheeky brat. Is Nanna around?"

"Yes, she's in the garden, reading. Shall I bring you a gin and tonic?"

"That would be nice. What are you after?"

Magda looked aggrieved. "Consider me insulted."

He laughed and shrugged off his jacket. He felt bone tired and a seat in the garden with his mother and a G&T would be nice. Wouldn't it?

The problem was, when he looked at the garden, he could see the ghost of Sam walking around the flower beds, her hair glinting in the sunlight. Everywhere, he saw her skill and—he recognised it now—her love for what she did.

He walked slowly across the garden to his mother, sitting on the chequerboard patio with a glass and a book. Niamh waved a greeting at him.

"Hello ma," he swooped to kiss her cheek.

"Jonas! How lovely to have you home early!"

Smiling faintly, he took the seat next to her. "Anyone would think I never came home," he grumbled good naturedly.

Niamh looked at him steadily. "Well, even you must admit you don't, recently. How was your day?"

Jonas told her the brief details, portraying meetings as humorous when in actual fact, they hadn't been. At least the media had found another company to torment. If he was honest with himself, he couldn't remember his work feeling so...*grey* before. So lacking in sparkle. So dull.

He noticed Niamh was watching him closely and he straightened his shoulders instinctively.

"What are your plans for this evening?" she asked.

"Actually, I thought I'd relax a bit, check email and then go for a gentle run, when it gets a bit cooler. I could do with a bit of workout... I've missed it."

"Have you forgotten your father arrives tonight?" Niamh said, quirking an eyebrow.

"God, yes I had. What time does his flight land?"

"About eight. I'll go and pick him up from the airport."

Jonas frowned. "You will? Isn't there a driver to pick him up?"

"Jonas, I haven't seen your father for nearly two weeks. I'd quite *like* to meet him," Niamh said gently.

Jonas apologised, thinking he must be getting hard in his old age —or his mother was getting more sentimental.

"When will you set off?"

She glanced at her slim watch. "In about an hour, just to allow for traffic. About the same time as you go for your run, I imagine," she said. She glanced up as Magda came across the lawn with a tray of drinks.

"I'm going to meet Opa in a while," she said as Magda put down the tray carefully and presented her father with his gin and tonic with a flourish.

"Oh, yes, he arrives later, doesn't he? But you're going yourself?

281

Shall I save some supper for you? Mrs Brown left macaroni cheese and lamb cutlets."

"I don't think we'll want to eat late, but perhaps I could see what's in the freezer if your grandfather wants something. Coming?"

"Mmm...yes. Yeah, right. Back in a minute, Dad."

Jonas watched as they walked across the garden and sighing, took a deep drink, welcoming the hit of the gin on the back of his throat. He watched the ice bounce against the slide of the crystal and wondered where his va-va-voom had disappeared. Neil had practically ordered him out of the office today.

Jonas had packed his briefcase with papers he probably wouldn't read and left. Even the idiots driving on the motorways failed to spark any reaction from him on the way home. If he didn't know better, he'd have said he was depressed.

He took another drink and then stopped, holding the glass to the light. Perhaps he should lay off the booze if he felt like this...

Reluctantly, he placed the glass on the table and closing his eyes, he leaned back in his chair, feeling the early evening sun on his face. A run should help to sort him out. Hopefully.

Sam sighed with relief as she stepped out of the shower.

She'd been filthy, and even now, after twenty minutes in the shower, there was still dirt under her fingernails. She perched on the side of her bed, her towel tucked around her. When she'd sorted her fingernails, she dried her short hair—*in need of a trim soon*, she thought severely—and made an inventory of her aching muscles.

God, am I getting old? It never used to be like this—where I can barely move after doing a day's work....

Wandering into her garden in her dressing gown with a steaming cup of tea, she idly pinched off the spent heads from a couple of pansies and felt the warm sun on her face.

Sam sat on her bench, looking with pride at her space, her private heaven. She would need to do a bit of tidying this weekend, if she could face it. She needed to do a lot of deadheading and tie up that clematis. She carefully tucked a loose strand of honeysuckle around a fence post, inhaling the perfume. It would have soothed her, if it wasn't for the hard lump in her stomach.

The thought struck her that having a place of your own was important, a huge comfort when the world was unwelcoming.

She sat quietly, feeling the drink cool in her hands and watching the sun stroll through the blue evening sky. Sighing, she threw the remains of the tea on the garden, and went indoors to dress. The renewal letter for her Labour Party membership was on the kitchen counter. She wasn't sure whether she would bother renewing it. A ping from her phone announced a text message from Amanda, inviting her to dinner on Saturday night. She grimaced.

Not too sure about playing gooseberry at the moment, Amanda. She picked up her phone to send a polite refusal text and then paused. She'd send it later.

It was too hot to dress in anything tight, so she slipped a light linen shift over her knickers, and pushed her feet into flat sandals.

Food. Her stomach curled at the thought while grumbling at the same time.

"Oh, snap out of it!" Sam muttered to herself as she started to open and then close, the kitchen cupboards. The freezer yielded no more tempting options, and sighing, she reached for a takeaway pizza menu.

If Lisbeth discovers the amount of takeaway food I've been eating, I'll never hear the end of it she thought wryly. She picked up the phone to call in an order, decided it was too early, and put it down again.

Finally falling on to the sofa, she sat in silence for a moment. Then she picked up the television remote and started channel hopping.

Jonas waved his mother off in the car and turned to Magda.

"Right—I should be about half an hour, maybe a bit longer."

"OK," Magda said, brushing his cheek with her lips. "I may be over at Lisbeth's doing some reading when you get back, so have you got your keys? Right then, see you later. Love you."

Nice that someone does, thought Jonas as he started to jog gently. His muscles didn't hurt, but they felt weak.

The ground was stony along the lane, so he went steadily, getting a smooth rhythm and trying to keep his breathing even. He thought his chest felt a bit tight.

Lack of exercise, he puffed. He'd been a couch potato for way too long.

He knew where he'd be running. Jessop's Field had lovely views, and the paths went in and out of trees so he wouldn't get too hot...and Sam might be there. She'd said she went there in times of stress, and if *he* was stressed, wouldn't she be? And if she was stressed, she'd be walking, trying to get some peace. Like him.

He picked up the pace a little, trying to get there faster. Once through the gates, his senses seemed to sharpen, looking for her.

Jonas ran on, nodding to dog walkers and one or two other runners. But no Sam.

Almost reluctantly, he turned towards the pond, keeping up his gentle pace, taking in the glorious landscape, gently rolling curves and lush green, even this late in the summer. He grimaced. He'd done as much as he could with the plans, without costing the company a fortune, but even he was starting to think it would be a crime to build here.

The pond had attracted kids paddling and swimming, lovers, people with dogs—but no sign of Sam. He ran round it three times, but on the third lap, admitted to himself she wasn't there.

Suddenly, he felt a constriction in his chest. His legs grew heavy, and he felt his breath coming in harsher gasps than before. He slowed his pace abruptly, feeling a sharp pain in his side and his vision blurred.

Jonas put his hand on a tree to steady himself.

I must get home, he thought, as the trees swam around him...

Sam finished chewing a slice of pizza and looked askance at the remaining three-quarters of the meal. Perhaps Lisbeth would want it for lunch or a snack if she popped round this weekend.

She was part way through a weasel excuse to Amanda's dinner invitation when the phone in her hand rang, startling her so much she almost dropped it.

"Hello?" she said breathlessly when she finally got the phone under control and to her ear.

"Sam! Oh, thank God you're at home!" came Magda's panicked voice down the phone.

"Magda?"

"Oh Sam! It's Dad! He's ill, he's—he's—he's—"

"Wha—what's happened? Magda, slow down, I can barely tell what you're saying!"

"Dad's collapsed in his bedroom!"

"What? Where's your grandmother?"

"Gone to the airport to pick up Opa! And I can't reach her, she's forgotten to take her phone!"

Sam took a deep breath.

"Magda, I need you to calm down and call for an ambulance. Tell them what's happened as slowly and carefully as you can. Is he breathing?"

"I think so—he's just so still! He went for a run, I didn't think he should have... Oh, I'm so scared!"

"I'll be round as fast I can. Call the ambulance now!"

"Come quick!"

"I will—now *phone the ambulance!*"

Sam closed the call and grabbed her car keys. Her hands were shaking so badly, she fumbled with the lock on the cottage and swore roundly as she struggled to close the door.

She drove automatically, her mind racing with possibilities. Had Jonas had a heart attack? Had the virus returned? Oh God, was he *dying*?

She drove as fast as she dared through the country lanes, muttering to herself—"Let him be ok, let him be ok, let him be ok..."

Sam cornered the road to Brook Lodge almost on two wheels, tumbling out of the car and cursing as she saw that the ambulance hadn't arrived.

"What on earth—?!" she bit out under her breath. "Where the hell are they?" Strangely, the front door seemed to be wide open, and after hesitating briefly, she ran in.

"Hello?" she called. There was no answer. "Magda? *Magda*!" She peered up the stairs, heard nothing and started to climb the stairs, two at a time.

"Where are you, for God's sake!" she muttered as she ran along the corridor, opening doors to empty bedrooms until she found the room that was unmistakably Jonas' bedroom. She drew in a deep breath to her aching lungs, pushed the door and stumbled in.

Just as Jonas walked out of the shower room.

31

Sam stood rooted to the floor in shock, feeling the blood drain from her face. Jonas was rubbing his hair with a towel, his shoulders glistening with water.

He stopped abruptly.

"Sam! What in God's name are you doing here?"

Sam tried to speak but her throat seemed to close up and nothing happened. Jonas walked towards her and she took an instinctive step backwards as his lean figure towered over her.

"Sam! What's happened? Are you ill?" Jonas asked, taking her by the arms and shaking her gently. Sam sagged and finally found her voice.

"I—I—I thought *you* were ill. Magda called me and told me you'd collapsed."

Jonas narrowed his eyes at her.

"Magda? What has that little madam been playing at? Scaring the life out of you—out of us both!" He let her go to look down the hallway. "I thought she'd gone out. Magda! Are you in the house, you bloody nuisance?" he called.

Sam sank on to the blanket chest at the bottom of the bed in relief. *He's alive. He's alive,* was the thought going round and round her head. She felt close to tears and took a shuddering breath to get a hold of her emotions, and to try to slow her racing heartbeat. She watched as Jonas stormed around the bedroom, cursing his daughter, and out of sheer reaction, she giggled.

Jonas glared at her and Sam couldn't stop her giggle from turning into a laugh.

"What's so bloody funny?"

"It *is* funny, you're shouting, wearing only a towel..." she spluttered. "Please, put something on."

Jonas looked down at himself and huffed in exasperation. He swung around and strode into the bathroom. He emerged two minutes later wearing a white robe.

"That's better," Sam approved.

"This isn't anything to be amused by!" he snapped. "Magda's been playing some stupid game and you looked as white as a sheet when I saw you."

Sam tried to sober up. "Well, I'm very pleased you're OK," she said. "Magda sounded frantic when she called me about fifteen minutes ago."

"I'm fine," he declared grimly. "While I was running I did feel very strange and dizzy at one stage, and I got a really bad stitch—but I just waited and it all passed and I walked home. Slowly. What precisely did Magda say?"

"Just that you'd been for a run and you'd collapsed. I thought it was your illness, or that you'd had a heart attack."

The smile faded from Sam's face as she remembered her terrified thoughts as she drove to Brook Lodge, dreading what she might find, and nudging her into thinking what she might have lost.

Jonas watched her, and she saw his face soften. He took a deep breath and hesitantly held out his arms.

"Come here."

After a second's hesitation, she went into them silently, breathing in the clean scent of him as his embrace wrapped around her.

She felt his lips brush her hair and she sighed and mumbled into his chest.

"What?" he said.

"I'm sorry," she said, lifting her head.

"I'm pleased you cared enough to come."

"No—I meant sorry about everything..."

Jonas sighed.

"So am I. I should have told you who I was." He kissed the top of her head.

"Yes, you should."

"I was going to—I promise. I left it too long, I had planned to tell you on the Saturday you were coming to look at the garden. But it all blew up before that. I'm so sorry." He hugged her. "You've lost weight," he commented.

"So have you." Sam had been doing her own inventory, and thought his jaw looked sharper than she remembered.

Jonas sighed again and rested his chin on the top of her head.

"We need to talk," he said. Sam looked at him warily. She didn't want another row—but he was right.

"OK." She made to pull away, but he drew her over to the bed and she perched uneasily on it.

There was a silence.

"Damn, I don't know where to start," he said finally, pushing his hand through his damp hair.

"Perhaps I should tell you what I already know?" suggested Sam. "I know you're the boss of Halcyon, I know that you've changed some of the plans and that now you're building on the brownfield site. I know you've been ill. I'm not sure why you lied to me, and I'm not really clear how the boss of a sustainable development company comes to be building on Green Belt land..."

He winced at that.

"We were supposed to be silent partners—Anglo Homes do a lot more house building in the UK, we wanted to see how it was done. They wanted to learn about sustainability, they said. It seemed a good match."

Sam raised her eyebrows.

"Yeah, yeah," acknowledged Jonas. "We recognised things were not going as planned when we realised they only used our plans when the objections started coming in. They hadn't used any of our suppliers...oh, a thousand red signals, but we missed them. Or underestimated their importance."

"And now you're working alone?"

"Yes—I like Tyler's uncle, but not him. He's a bit of a..."

"Shyster?"

Jonas grinned and Sam felt a flame in her stomach as his face lit up.

"I couldn't possibly comment."

Sam thought for a moment.

"Are the houses going to be very expensive? I've seen a lot of comments in the local paper about how 'sustainable' means it costs more. Despite what you might think, Sherton's not a well-off village."

"No, we know that. I've started a new division in Halcyon which will concentrate on affordable and sustainable housing for new owners, young families and the like. I imagine we'll take a bit of a hit financially for the first few years, but it will form part of our CSR effort."

"What's CSR?"

"Corporate social responsibility," he translated for her. "My chairman's not keen, but I'll try to make him think it was his idea..."

"Mmm, I used to do that with my Dad. Smaller scale, obviously."

They smiled at one another. Sam had a sensation of falling and said hastily,

"OK, and you're building on Lower Edge Field."

To her surprise, she saw his skin tinge pink.

"Ah. Yes, we are. I thought it would be sensible to follow it up." He looked down.

"But there aren't many more houses being built, it seems to me," she said watching him closely.

"Not many, no."

Sam finally caught on. "You're reducing the number built on Jessop's Field?"

He nodded. She narrowed her eyes.

"Yes. Just good commercial sense."

I don't believe you.

"And about me—I'm a widower with one daughter. My wife drowned eight years ago. My mother's Irish and my father's German. I kept my mother's maiden name because no-one could pronounce my father's, and Mum wanted to keep her Irish heritage alive," Jonas continued, tracing circles on the duvet.

"Really? What's your dad's name?"

"Schipzelburgen."

Sam laughed. "Sounds a very feminist thing to do for a man who thinks that a woman shouldn't dig a garden!"

Jonas went pink again and deciding not to tease him further, Sam continued.

"I met your Mum—she came down to see me at the office."

Jonas looked surprised. "She did? What for?"

"Well, she *said* she just wanted to tell me how much she liked the garden," Sam said thoughtfully.

"Perhaps she wanted to meet the first woman I've employed since becoming head of the company."

Sam was surprised. And then cross.

"Me? *I'm* the first woman? I take back all I said! Jonas, that's bloody *medieval!*"

He held his hands up. "I know, I know. Magda agrees with you and so does my mother." He stopped.

"But how the hell did you manage to get to your advanced age—and to the position of CEO—without being prosecuted?" Sam said, aghast. "I thought you were just being a bit weird and mixing up my name with Dad's—but you weren't, were you? You really *are* that sexist, aren't you?"

He put up his hands in a weak protest. "You should know that when I discussed this with my deputy Neil, we agreed I was a dinosaur. I didn't like what I'd become, and I've been trying to rethink my attitude ever since the day we met here." he said. She gaped at him. Reluctantly, it seemed, he began to speak again.

"My wife Nicole was a successful businesswoman—she was

smart, elegant, beautiful and made money like no-one else I've ever known," he said. "She was all that, but she didn't want to be a wife. Or a mother, much. Nicole got pregnant by mistake far too early in our marriage. I don't think she wanted children—she was back at work within two weeks of Magda's being born, to my mother's horror. Nicole saw Magda as an obstacle to doing what she loved, an inconvenience. Magda would have gone through a series of nurses, governesses and boarding schools if I'd not put my foot down. I've stayed away from women like her ever since. Hence—"

"Your Neanderthal attitude towards women in business?"

He looked shamefaced. "Sounds a bit lame doesn't it? But yes, I suppose that's what prompted it and I've never dumped the habit," Jonas finished a little awkwardly. "I realise my attitude is an issue. Magda forced me into thinking about it and I'm trying to change, but it might take some time."

Sam didn't know what to say and she thought for a moment about it.

"Well, I'm sure Magda will be dragging you by your ears into the twenty-first century," she said eventually.

"Will *you*?"

Sam stared.

"I still would like to get to know you better, Sam," he said, looking steadily at her. "I know there's been a lot of crap but I'd really like to take you out. I'm not one of the bad guys—and I'm trying to become the kind of father that my daughter deserves," he mused.

His words struck her heart. How nice that would be—having a father who aspired to be good *for* you as well as good *to* you.

She took a breath.

"I'm sure you will be. I've seen what you've done to the development and I think you *are* one of the good guys," she said in a low voice. His green eyes zeroed in on her and he took her hand.

"Shall we start again?" he asked.

Sam's pulse started doing a drum solo. She could feel his body heat, smell his fresh, clean shower gel. She could feel her skin prickle with awareness. She hadn't felt like this for years. Well, since that moment on Jessop's Field. With Jonas.

"I think...I think I'd like that." He had to bend his head to hear her.

He raised her chin gently and kissed her. A sweet, tentative kiss. She swayed towards him. The atmosphere seemed to implode around her, and before she realised, she was leaning over him, pressing him into the bed cover. She could feel his heart thudding against her breast and his tongue stroking her lips. She groaned, pressing her suddenly rock-hard nipples against him. His robe fell open.

Gasping, she fell away. "God, I'm so sorry! Is this a good idea? I'm not sure it is! Oh God..." she gabbled.

He chuckled softly, his arm over his eyes.

"You're asking *me*? Frankly, I want to rip your clothes off you! So—do I think this is a good idea? If you intend for this to be a one-off, then no, it isn't. If you're happy to arrange dinner—*lots* of dinners—then yes, I think it's an *astoundingly* good idea." She tore her eyes from his green gaze. "Sam? I want you, you know that. But I also *like* you. And I want to be with you, a lot. I haven't felt like this for a long time. I thought you felt the same. Do you?"

She hesitated and felt him tense. Incurably honest, she sighed. "When I ran through that door I was terrified you might be seriously ill, and that I might have lost you. So, yes, I do feel the same. But..."

"You're not the sort of girl who puts out on a first date." He sighed. "No--" he put a finger against her lips as she made to speak. "I want whatever makes you happy. Relax. I'll wait as long as you like."

Sam shook her head. He'd misunderstood. Her body felt electrocuted, acutely aware. She could feel his breath in her hair. She felt the warmth between her thighs. She heard the wails of her libido and the ache in her crotch. She closed her eyes and took a deep breath.

"Well, if you want whatever makes me happy, you'd better be *damn* good," she said in a low voice, turning to him and kissed him, hard. The kiss went on and on. Sam realised he was waiting to see what she would do and she pressed her hips against him to send a clear message.

And then she was on her back, his hands around her face. He knelt beside her, his face intent on unbuttoning her dress. She watched his face as he undid the last one and the linen dress fell apart, revealing her white cotton knickers.

He drew the dress down her arms and threw it on a nearby chair before sinking alongside her and kissing her deeply. Her hands clenched in his hair, pressing him closer. His lips teased her, nibbling, sucking and tasting, while his hands stroked her sides, her hips and the underside of her breasts.

She pressed her knee between his legs and drew her thigh gently against him, feeling his erection against her skin. He raised his lips from her mouth to gasp, and she grazed her teeth against his neck. Sam couldn't get her hands to him, he was still wearing the robe, and she growled her frustration. They both reached for the tie of his robe.

"No," Sam pushed away his hand, and with deliberate slowness, she undid the knot of the robe. Sitting up, she pushed the towelling over his shoulders and stroked her hands down his chest and over his hips, finally able to touch his skin. He sucked in his breath.

"You are beautiful," she murmured, intent on tracing the contours of his muscles, down to his hips and his erect, satiny penis. He groaned, as if he was in pain.

"Sam..." Jonas leaned over her and kissed her breasts and flat stomach, trailing his tongue over her hip bones. "God, Sam. If we need to stop it needs to be *now*," he said tightly. "Are you really sure?"

"Really sure," she said.

He reached into a drawer, tore the foil and she helped smooth the sheath down his length. She wrapped her arms around his shoulders and nuzzled his neck, lifting her bottom as he slid off her underwear.

She felt his fingers stroke her clitoris and groaned, her eyes closing. He slipped his finger inside her and she lifted her hips to welcome him. A few moments of this torture and her breath was coming faster. He moved between her thighs and put his big hands on her hips. She felt his length slide along her. She gasped and shifted, urging him on.

"Look at me, Sam," he grated, and her eyes locked on to his. He pushed into her slowly. She gasped with pleasure as he moved surely, filling her.

Sam ran her hands over his shoulders, feeling the muscles move and clench. She scraped her nails over his smooth skin and felt his lips against her neck and breasts. She tensed her thighs and Jonas gasped. Sam smiled up at him, loving the firm thrusts and moaned as the tingle started between her thighs.

She clutched him as she orgasmed, digging her fingers into his muscles and crying out into the quiet of the house. It was only a second later he followed, rearing up, his arms rigid. He groaned as he sank down, and she hugged him close.

Sam looked at Jonas' face, relaxed and handsome. She stopped caring about the consequences, kissed him gently and closed her eyes in pleasure.

Down the hall, hiding in the linen closet with the door ajar an inch, Lisbeth and Magda heard the distant conversation and then, quiet. They looked at one another.

"Has it worked? Are they together?" whispered Lisbeth.

"Looks like it." Magda turned to her in the cramped cupboard and they high-fived one another.

"I think we could call that a success," breathed Magda smugly.

"I hope they're so happy together that they forget how Sam got to be here," Lisbeth warned. "Still, we'll split the blame— I could have stopped you and I didn't."

Magda beamed at her. "You're a mate. I'll get told off, but hey—I'm back to school next week. It'll be fine." She waved away any concerns, and they giggled.

They were still in the cupboard congratulating themselves when they heard a strange cry from the bedroom.

"Was that Sam?" Magda said after a second's silence.

Lisbeth flushed and looked very uncomfortable. "I think we need to leave," she said nervously.

"Yep, with you there. We can go down the back stairs."

They slid out of the cupboard and raced down the hallway, away from the noise in the bedroom and things they'd rather not think about. Yet.

Sam turned over and propping her head on her hand, looked at the big man at her side. She'd slept deeply for about ten minutes, awakening with a start and then relaxing as she caught sight of the clock. The fading sun laced through the drapes.

"Hi," she said softly, stroking her finger along his straight, strong nose.

Jonas smiled without opening his eyes. "Hi." He took her hand "OK?"

"Oh yes. You?"

He opened his eyes and they glinted like glass green at her. "I feel wonderful."

She blushed.

He chuckled, and nipped the fingers stroking his nose with his teeth. She lay back, feeling deeply content and relaxed. *See?* Said her libido smugly. *See what amazing sex can do for you?*

"Can I get you something?" Jonas said, watching her closely as he reached for his robe.

"I could murder a cup of tea."

"No problem. Incidentally, my parents will be coming back this evening and my bloody daughter is around somewhere. This doesn't mean I want you to go—it's so you have a choice."

Sam stretched and put her hands behind her head, watching with satisfaction as Jonas' eyes fell on her body. "I'm not sure I can cope with the start of a new relationship at seven o'clock and meeting the whole family at eight." She smiled at him to soften her words, and he nodded.

"Tea coming right up."

Jonas was humming as he waited for the kettle to boil. His phone buzzed. He read the message and laughed. He slipped the phone into the pocket of his robe, made the tea and went back to Sam.

Sam was sitting in his bed, the sheets tucked neatly under her arms. He paused at the door, rather liking the sight.

"Magda has confessed and begs both our pardons." He put the tea down and reached for the phone, and passed it to her.

Hi Dad. I know U'll B mad, & I'm sorry. But I knew there was something between U & Sam—right, wasn't I? That she came over says smg abt how she feels abt U, right? Tell her I'm sorry for scaring her. Magda XXXXXXX.

"She's a smooth-talker, that lass of yours," Sam said.

"It's a manipulative thing to do to you. Can you forgive her?"

Sam took a sip of tea. "I suppose so. She was very convincing on the phone, I was almost out of my mind with worry... But seeing where we are now, I suppose it would be churlish not to."

'Out of your mind with worry?' Excellent! noted Jonas, well satisfied.

They sat in companionable silence as they drank, until Sam said, regretfully, "I should be going."

Jonas sighed. "Yes, I suppose you had, if you're going to avoid my parents. But come to dinner tomorrow night, will you?"

Sam smiled shyly. "Of course. I'd love to."

Later, she texted Amanda. *Sorry, can't come to dinner* she wrote. *Got a hot date.*

32

"You've done *what?*" Sam gasped at the two teenage girls standing awkwardly in front of her the following day. When they'd turned up this morning, Sam had expected an awkward conversation about the phone call yesterday. She'd been ready to be grave and disappointed. But she hadn't expected this.

"I entered you into the competition. You'll have got a letter by now," said Magda, looking at the floor of the cottage.

"I've had no letter, I'm sure. I sorted my desk only yesterday..."

Just before that dreadful, and then wonderful afternoon her libido prompted slyly. Sam re-arranged her face.

"Well, no, *you* wouldn't have got a letter—I've had Paul watch your post. He's probably got it in a drawer somewhere," mumbled Lisbeth.

"What?"

Sam's head was spinning, wondering where her rather nervous, timid niece had gone. Dragging her mind back from that thought, she returned to her main concern.

"But what on earth will your father say? You might have paid for the garden, Magda, but it *is* his house! And I didn't want to enter the competition! I told him I didn't!"

Magda looked mutinous and Lisbeth intervened.

"*Really*? You didn't want to?" Sam had the grace to blush. "Look, we know the entry was a bit—unconventional--" Sam rolled her eyes, "--but you *did* want to enter, didn't you? And you're friends with Magda's Dad now, aren't you? So he might not be all that mad."

Sam ran her hands through her hair. "God, I don't know what to think!"

"I just wanted it to be a surprise..." muttered Magda, starting to look tearful. Sam sighed and pulled her into a hug.

"I know, sweetie. But after your exploits yesterday—" Magda ducked her head, and Sam went on, "—how are we going to tell your dad?"

"I know, I know... I'll just have to show him the letter I got." Magda seemed to stiffen her shoulders and Sam was momentarily very amused.

"Well, he can only send you off to summer camp," she said with a grin.

"I think you're both wrong," Lisbeth said firmly. "I reckon he'll be chilled."

"Before we talk to Jonas, I want to know about it all," Sam said, picking up her phone. "Paul? Hi, I'm sorry to call on a Saturday morning. I wondered if there's been any post for me that you put 'somewhere safe'? Yes, she's here with me, and Magda. Right. Where is it? Fine. I'll see you Monday."

She disconnected the call. Lisbeth looked worried. "He won't get into trouble, will he?"

"No, I imagine you twisted his arm big time." Sam looked at them, cross and reluctantly admiring for their scheming. "Come on, we're going into the office."

The correspondence was hidden beneath a tidy pile of invoices in Paul's pristine desk. Magda looked in awe at the immaculate organisation.

"Jeez, he even colour codes his paper clips!" she said to Lisbeth.

Sam frowned. "There are two letters," she said, puzzled. She opened the first, running her eyes down the elegant typeface, feeling her face flush with pleasure.

My garden! A garden I designed is in the final of a national competition!

"Yes, this is your entry," she said to Magda. "So what's this, then?" She opened the second envelope. Her eyes scanned the page and then stopped abruptly, focused on one part of the letter.

"Did you write on behalf of your father as well?" she asked Magda.

"No, I wrote from me," said Magda, looking over her shoulder. Sam pointed to a part of the letter and Magda's eyes widened.

"'We appear to have a double recommendation for your garden design at Brook Lodge. You indicated in your entry that our reference would be Ms Magda Keane, and we have written to her asking for access to the garden. However, the entry to which *this* letter refers has been submitted from Mr Jonas Keane, enclosing the plans and asking for the garden to be entered. We are investigating with Mr Keane, although your original entry will still stand,'" she read. Lisbeth gasped.

"No way!"

"So *Dad* entered you as well!" said Magda, a grin lighting up her face.

Sam steadied herself with one hand on the desk. *Jonas* had entered her design? What had changed his mind? And he'd done it while he was still rushing around talking to God-knows-who about his company? She blew out her cheeks.

"I think I need to have a quiet word with your Dad."

"You're coming to dinner tonight, aren't you?" Magda said knowingly. Sam felt her cheeks grow hot.

"Yes, but that's hardly going to be a good place to speak with him," she said. "I'll run you back and grab him for ten minutes."

Brook Lodge was basking serene and golden in the late summer sun. It gladdened Sam's heart as she drove up the drive.

Jonas was coming down the stairs when Magda threw open the front door, and his eyebrows rose as he saw all three of them.

"A delegation like this is rarely good news," he said drily, although his eyes seemed to caress Sam as she stood awkwardly in the hall.

"Hi—can I have a quick word?" Sam said, suddenly breathless at the sight of him.

"It's about the garden competition, Dad!" Madga obviously didn't want to be left out of the discussion.

"Ah."

"I thought you said we couldn't enter!" Magda said, accusingly.

"I wasn't the *only* one who didn't want the garden entered, if I recall!" Jonas snorted. "I changed my mind. And while we're on the subject, madam, what are you doing, taking decisions about my property without consulting me?"

His velvet voice suddenly cooled, and Lisbeth and Sam edged closer together, while Magda squared up to her father.

"Have they written to you?" she demanded.

"Yes, I had an email this morning."

"Well, if you remember Dad, it was my trust fund that paid for it. So as the *client*, I decided I had a right to enter the work I paid for!"

Jonas looked struck, and then rallied. "But I don't see your name on the mortgage Magda!"

"But you *will* see my name on the garden design contract!"

There was tense silence as they glared at one another. And then Jonas threw back his head and laughed. Magda's face turned smug.

"You ought to be a lawyer," he said, smiling. "So we *both* wanted to get Sam some kudos for the design. I'll call them on Monday to explain why Sam got two entries." He turned to Sam. "Are you ok with the garden being entered? Is that what you were here for?"

"Yes, I thought I'd better clear everything before I started speaking to the organisers. I'd hate to be disqualified because the owners of the house couldn't agree... But also, I've been really ungrateful to Magda—and you! I'm utterly thrilled to have been entered! And to have reached the finals!" she said, turning to Magda.

"And Lisbeth," said Magda. "It was Lisbeth who pointed out the contract was with me and not Dad."

Sam stared at Lisbeth in astonishment.

"Well spotted, Lisbeth," Jonas said while Lisbeth's fair skin flushed.

"I see everything's been sorted out," commented Niamh from the living room door, with a man Sam had never seen before. He was tall and bearded and was regarding her with twinkling pale grey eyes.

"You must be Magda's Opa—have I pronounced that right?" Sam said, putting out her hand. He shook it gravely.

"Excellent. And yes, I'm Friedrich. You must be Sam. Niamh has mentioned you."

Oh dear. I hope that was a good mention.

"All good things," he reassured her, without missing a beat.

God, I must try to create some sort of poker face! Sam thought.

"An open book, my sweet," murmured Jonas, putting a casual arm around her shoulders. Sam looked up at him, not knowing whether to laugh or be cross.

She became aware of Lisbeth and Magda's satisfied expressions. A horrified thought flicked across her brain—and then was dismissed.

Not possible, she thought. *It's not possible that they could have set **all** this up.*

Niamh suggested they go into the garden and ordered Jonas to get his diary, or phone device, or whatever infernal electronic thing he used to manage his time—so they could go back to the competition organisers with dates to visit.

They settled on a date and small talk followed. Sam was aware of being gently quizzed by Friedrich about her business and her family, but she didn't mind. She felt the warm sunshine on her face and looked at the garden with pride. It *was* lovely.

She became aware of Jonas watching her.

"Okay?" she asked him.

He smiled.

"I wondered if you were staying here until dinner."

"Oh, no! Am I in your way? I can go..." She made to scramble to her feet, but Jonas put his hand on her arm.

"You misunderstand. I didn't want you to be stuck here all afternoon if you had things to do. I'd love for you to stay."

"Actually, I would like to talk to you," Sam said in a rush.

"Sounds ominous."

"No, it's more of an apology..."

"Shall we walk through the garden?"

As they walked, Sam tried to think where to start.

"What's up?" Jonas prompted her.

Straight in, Sam.

"I've been a bit of a hypocrite, I think," she said. He frowned, but said nothing. "I think somewhere in all this I turned into a NIMBY--a 'not in my back yard' person? I talked a lot about saving the village, but really, I just wanted to protect the place I've known all my life. I didn't want anything to change. I didn't think that people might want what I've already got—a home of their own. All you do is give that to them."

"I make my living this way—I'm not a saint."

"I know—but I think I thought that *I* was!" she laughed, the breath catching in her throat. "I was so convinced I was right, that everyone else who disagreed with me was a destructive moron—when I think of it now, I'm so ashamed." She hung her head.

He put his hand on her arm and she stopped, turning to face him.

"It's just a different perspective," he said. "You were right that there are better places to build than Jessop's Field. Don't beat yourself up about it. Hopefully we've worked out a compromise and you can have both houses *and* a view."

"I should thank you—"

"Shut up Sam."

"But—"

He kissed her for a long time and a few minutes later he raised his head.

"I can think of a million ways you can thank me, Sam. When we're alone I'll go into detail about them."

"God, I hope they're not going to get, like, embarrassing!" muttered Magda, watching them walk away. She was wondering what she'd started, and feeling envious in a way she didn't quite understand.

Both Niamh and Fredrick laughed.

"But you want your father to be happy, yes?" asked Friedrich.

"Of course!"

"And it *was* your idea—yours and Lisbeth's—was it not?"

Both teenagers nodded.

"Then I think we can safely say that you have achieved your goal. Jonas looked a different man last night."

"I shouldn't worry about your father being embarrassing, you'll be back at school very soon, so they can get through the first few weeks more or less out of your view," Niamh consoled them.

Magda and Lisbeth perked up.

"God, yes—I'd forgotten about school! Wow, what a mega-relief!"

Their laughter drifted over the garden and may have reached Sam and Jonas, but they possibly didn't hear. They were busy.

SIX MONTHS LATER

Cursing under her breath, Sam struggled into the black dress and Charlie finally closed the zip.

"Well sis, you look amazeballs, as Lisbeth would say," she commented, looking over Sam's shoulder into the mirror.

Lisbeth, nursing a small glass of champagne, chuckled from the corner.

Sam stared. The dress softly clung to her breasts and thighs, leaving her shoulders bare. The diamond pendant Jonas had given her for her birthday nestled against her throat, and her mother's diamond studs twinkled in her ears. Her hair shone, and a tiny silver and diamanté flower, courtesy of Lisbeth, caught the light as she turned her head.

"Blimey," she said. Charlie and Lisbeth laughed.

"You ought to win just for the dress!" Lisbeth volunteered, taking another sip from her glass.

Charlie pursed her lips and grumbled about her only daughter getting half-cut.

Sam grinned. She didn't care about winning, actually. It would be nice to win, but business was booming, and she thought she might be in love.

"Ah well. It'll be a wonderful evening, regardless."

To her surprise, Charlie hugged her. "You deserve this, Sam. Dad would have been proud of you."

Taken aback, Sam had to blink away tears. She stood mute and Charlie took a deep breath. Thankfully, Lisbeth took charge.

"No snivelling, otherwise your mascara will run. C'mon mum, before this gets soppy! Enjoy your night, Aunty Sam—text us when you know the result."

They left with a great deal of noise and flapping, finally leaving Sam alone in the cottage, waiting for Jonas.

Less than a mile away, Magda, looking nearer to twenty-one than sixteen, was determinedly tying her father's bow tie. Jonas, who was quite capable of tying it himself, stood quietly and patiently while Magda fiddled.

"There! Now you look respectable!"

"Did I look disreputable before?"

She slapped him on the arm.

"Stop fishing! Do you know Dad, since you started going out with Sam, you've become very needy with the compliments. Like, *really* needy!"

Jonas looked pained.

"I need reassurance like everyone else, you know," he said and he was only half joking.

"But really—Sam, like—well, she *adores* you!"

"She does?"

"There you go again!"

"No, Magda—I'm not joking. *Does* she?"

Magda rolled her eyes.

"*Seriously* Dad? Have you seen the way she looks at you?"

Jonas was silent for a minute as he took that in.

"Are you ok with her?" he asked eventually.

"Are you kidding? She's awesome!"

"You like her more than Gerry?"

"*Much* more than Gerry."

Jonas shook his head.

"Sorry—I'm being an idiot." He smiled at her and saw her eyes soften.

"I can't believe you don't see it—everyone else does. Perhaps you should try and look a bit more objectively, rather than be dazzled by her."

Jonas shook his head again, unable to believe he was taking advice on his love life from his daughter. He hesitated, and Magda put her head on one side.

He took a breath. "I've never talked to you about my relationships...but if things ever turned out that way, would you be okay with having a stepmum?"

Magda's eyes widened, and Jonas wondered if he'd said too much, too soon. "Theoretically, of course," he added hastily. "Not immediately, obviously."

Magda grinned at him. "Obviously. But, *theoretically,* Dad, I think it would be a great idea, I want you to be happy."

As long as you get to vet the candidates? thought Jonas, with a smile of his own. "Thanks for tying my bow tie," he said and kissed her nose. She hugged him.

"We'd better go and pick up Sam or she'll think we've stood her up," he said into her freshly washed hair. She stood back, blinked her eyes, smoothed his jacket and smiled.

They left arm in arm.

∼

Both Sam and Jonas were silent for a moment as she stood in the open doorway. Sam thought he looked magnificent, his strong jaw perfectly framed by the snowy shirt and black tie.

"Wow."

"I could say the same," Jonas said a little hoarsely.

Sam gave a nervous laugh. "Shall we just send Magda, and stay in?" she joked. Well, half-joked.

"Actually, I wanted to ask you something before we went to the awards," Jonas said, stepping into the cottage. Sam paused as she reached for her bag.

"What?"

"I wondered if you would do some work for my company."

Sam blinked. "Me? I'm no property developer!"

"I want to make more of the garden space in our show homes and demonstrate what people could do with the gardens—rather than just lay everything to lawn with a few shrubs."

Sam considered. "Um... I will, *if* you increase the amount of space you allow for the gardens in your planning. At the moment, they're about as big as a pocket handkerchief. I can work with small gardens—we do it all the time—but I'd rather stand up for my principles that everyone should have a garden big enough to grow things, and for children to play in."

She looked at his expressionless face and her heart sank. "Are you okay with that?" Jonas frowned. "I know you've marked me down as just a softy liberal, but I want to do my bit as a businesswoman. Dad would want me to. So I want to try to use unemployed labour in the same way I do at WGD," she added.

"How will that work if we're building in Germany, or the Netherlands?"

"I don't know—you employ loads of people to find solutions to problems—have them work this out!"

Jonas blew out a breath. "I can see I'm going to have a fair old battle with the Board on this. More space means more cost, employing apprentices means more insurance, more people to train them, which means more cost too."

"But *your* company does business based on its principles—why can't mine?"

Jonas smiled wryly. "You're absolutely right of course. If I do this—will you work with me?"

"Do you want me to?"

"Absolutely. You've got a wonderful talent. I'd like you to work with Connor. I've known him for years—you'll work brilliantly together."

Sam stared.

"Will he want to work with a Billy no-name like me?"

Jonas smiled.

"He will. He does. He thought your design for Brook Lodge was genius."

"He did? Blimey…" She smiled as a buzz of excitement started to shiver along her veins. "Ok, then…since I'm in such exalted company."

"Shall we shake on it?"

Sam looked at him quizzically and then her brow cleared and she laughed. "I know what you're doing! You're getting me tied up before I've found out if I've won the competition!"

Jonas put out his hands and smiled charmingly. "Guilty as charged. Connor also mentioned that I might not be able to afford you after tonight. What do you say?"

"Have one of your people get in touch with one of mine," she said, and then grinned at him. He kissed her.

"You'll have to put more lipstick on," he said unrepentantly when he released her a couple of minutes later.

"And *you*, Dad, will need to wipe your mouth!" said an exasperated Magda from the door. "Are you two coming to this awards thing or not? *Honestly!*"

"We're coming," said Sam meekly, finally picking up her bag and heading to the car.

WANT TO KNOW WHAT HAPPENS NEXT?

The next book in the series, *Love-in-a-Mist*, follows Sam's fledgling relationship and introduces Jonas' best friend, garden designer bad boy Connor McPherson.

Love-In-A-Mist
Book 2 in the English Garden Romance series

When Lady Susan, owner of historic Ashton Manor asks Connor McPherson to design a garden to host a wedding ceremony, he can't refuse. The reason? His best friend Jonas Keane is getting married there! And now he's accepted the commission, he needs to get on with it to meet the summer wedding deadline. If only the rain would stop.

While owner Lady Susan shares Connor's vision of a garden for future generations, snooty estates manager Ella Sanderson couldn't be *less* enthusiastic.

Tall, aristocratic Ella who manages the farms and estate at Ashton Manor knows what she likes—and she *doesn't* like Connor's design. She's horrified at the ultra-modern plans and thinks a more tradi-

Want to know what happens next?

tional garden would complement the house better. To top it all, Connor is just the type of man she's learned to mistrust. Bright blue eyes and all that Irish charm may have captivated her employer Lady Susan—but not her! She wants to protect her employer, and while she can't go against Lady Susan's wishes, she *can* just... not help.

The stage is set for a stand-off between the hot-tempered Irishman and the cool, calm and collected Ella as the weather worsens and money begins to run short.

But when the problems force Connor and Ella to work together, Connor slowly begins to realise that beneath her buttoned-up exterior, the estates manager has a passion equal to his own. And a secret story she's hidden for years.

As she battles to get the garden she hates launched in time for the wedding, Ella finds herself increasingly drawn to the feisty designer. Who, she discovers, has his *own* secrets to protect...

Meet old friends from *The Garden Plot* in *Love in a Mist*, Book 2 of the English Garden Romance series.

Sign up for news of the release date at my website www.sarasartagne.com.

AFTERWORD

Thank you for reading my debut novel and thank you for supporting independent authors. Writing can often be a bit of an echo chamber...scribbling away, but no-one is reading! So—if you liked *The Garden Plot*, please leave me a review. It's an enormous help to authors just starting out! And if you'd like to know when I'm releasing the follow up book in the English Garden Romance Series, *Love in a Mist*, sign up to my mailing list on my website —sarasartagne.com.

I won't send endless emails, but enough to say hello, tell you news and offer some freebies. Talking of which, if you sign up to the mailing list, I'll send you a free novella called *A Bouquet of White Roses*, which tells how Sam's mum met her dad, and started the whole story.

You can get this, for free, by signing up to my mailing list. Alternatively, if you'd like to connect on Twitter, say hello to me at http://www.twitter.com/SSartagnewriter.

ACKNOWLEDGMENTS

Writing a book can be incredibly difficult. I'd like to thank the following people:

Jan Page, aka Jess Ryder, for her unstinting support and guidance, and for pointing out plot holes you could drive a bus through;

Jilly Woods, for calm common sense, insightful comments and wry good humour in the midst of her own self-publishing journey, and

J A Clement, whose enthusiasm got me started in the first place and without whose technical support, this would still be a sheaf of A4 pages.

And finally, I'd like to thank my wonderful Fiona, who has always believed in me.

ABOUT SARA SARTAGNE

Having wanted to be a journalist when she was a teenager, Sara actually ended up on the dark side, in PR. From there, it was a short skip to writing for pleasure, and from there to drafting her first book. The Garden Plot is the first novel in a trilogy based around gardens and having green fingers—passions which Sara has for real.

She recently moved from London to York and is loving the open skies and the green fields. And a HUGE garden!

Printed in Great Britain
by Amazon